Praise for *The Brotherhood o*

"In a book that is eerily atmospheric and remorselessly inventive, Belcher transforms the most mundane premises into something wondrous and marvelously complex. He blends reality and myth to create a new take on urban fantasy that moves out of the city and onto the lonely roads between them, creating a whole new world for readers to explore. His prose is infused with subtle humor and insight. His characters, with all their flaws, are wonderfully realistic, making their quest strangely believable, poignant, and utterly engrossing."   —*RT Book Reviews*

"*The Brotherhood of the Wheel* is a special kind of horror novel. It's the kind of book you spend all night reading, because it's so disturbing, you just have to keep going until the monster is dead—or at the very least, has exited the scene. Perhaps it's because the urban myths R. S. Belcher employs are so immediate to contemporary American culture, evoking disturbing images of haunted children and newly menacing big-rig trucks, or because the deep world-building brings a familiar setting to strange, dangerous life. Either way, this is a gripping, deeply twisted ride through the dark heart of America."

—*B&N Sci-Fi & Fantasy Blog*

"Urban legends and ancient folklore come together in Belcher's unusual series opener featuring long-haul trucker Jimmie Aussapile. . . . Jimmie is an affable everyman who only wants to help people and provide for his family. With characters impossible not to root for, this fun, non-stop tale (set throughout the Eastern half of the U.S.) has genuinely creepy moments, rendered vividly by Belcher's fertile imagination."

—*Publishers Weekly*

R. S. BELCHER

THE BROTHERHOOD OF THE WHEEL

A TOM DOHERTY ASSOCIATES BOOK **TOR** NEW YORK

THE BROTHERHOOD OF THE WHEEL

Copyright © 2016 by Rod Belcher

A Tor Book
Published by Tom Doherty Associates
175 Fifth Avenue
New York, NY 10010

www.tor-forge.com

Tor® is a registered trademark of Macmillan Publishing Group, LLC.

The Library of Congress has cataloged the hardcover edition as follows:

Belcher, R. S., author.
    The Brotherhood of the Wheel / R. S. Belcher. —First edition.
        p. cm.
    ISBN 978-0-7653-8028-9 (hardcover)
    ISBN 978-1-4668-7253-0 (e-book)
I. Title.
    PS3602.E429B76 2016
    813'.6—dc23

                                    2015032633

ISBN 978-0-7653-8029-6 (trade paperback)

Our books may be purchased in bulk for promotional, educational, or business use. Please contact your local bookseller or the Macmillan Corporate and Premium Sales Department at 1-800-221-7945, extension 5442, or by e-mail at MacmillanSpecialMarkets@macmillan.com.

First Edition: March 2016
First Trade Paperback Edition: March 2017

Printed in the United States of America

0   9   8   7   6   5   4   3   2   1

TO THE MEMORY OF MABEL T. BELCHER.
The greatest mother, father, friend, and supporter
a man could ever ask for. This one is for you, Mom.
They are all for, and because of, you.

The difference between a fairy tale and a truck driver's story is that the fairy tale starts with "Once upon a time," whereas the truck driver's story starts, "You ain't gonna believe this . . ."

—AN OLD TRUCKER SAYING

THE BROTHERHOOD OF THE WHEEL

ONE "10-31"

Jimmie Aussapile's Peterbilt tractor trailer thundered down dark I-70, relentless as an ugly truth. The big rig's engine was the booming voice of an angry octane god, demanding you lead, follow, or get the hell out of the way. Jimmie navigated the shifting maze of weaving cars. He blew past the shadowed towers of other 18-wheeler cabs, the faces within illuminated by the ghostly green light of instrument panels, speaking their tales to their brethren across the ether of Channel 19. Long-haulers wired on caffeine or meth or song or sweet baby Jesus. Whatever it takes to keep the gears jamming, the cargo flowing, and the rig between the lines.

Jimmie was a tall man, still in decent shape for his age. He had been lanky a long time ago, but now he cultivated a solid beer gut. His hair, what was left of it, was blond and had completely abandoned his head except for the fringes and the long ponytail that fell between his shoulder blades. His bare head was covered by a gray mesh baseball cap that had a hideous character from a cartoon called *Squidbillies* on it. The cap had been a Father's Day present from his little girl last year and Jimmie wore it whenever he was on a run, for good luck, regardless of how much shit he got for it. His eyes were a fierce green that seemed to glow brighter than the lights from his instruments. He wore a pale scrub of a "road beard," and he had a lump of chaw in his right cheek. His teeth were yellowed from the habit and a little crooked. He wore a black T-shirt that sported a faded Harley-Davidson logo on its pocket. Over that was an open denim work shirt, and over that was a black Air Force–style crew jacket with a patch of an American flag on the left arm. He wore a wallet on a chain, attached to his worn jeans, and a straight razor was tucked away in one of his steel-toed work boots.

Jimmie scanned the other big trucks on the road, looking for a specific one—a Mack, with a yellow cab and a yellow-and-white trailer, and a specific driver—a man he and the others had been hunting for a long time but had always been one step behind. I-70 was a primary artery through St. Louis, considered to be the nation's first interstate highway. Traffic was heavy tonight with 18-wheelers trying to keep to their schedule in spite of the bad weather.

Jimmie's rig was a Peterbilt 379. The cab was white, with a red Jerusalem cross pattern on the hood and the doors. The truck had chrome pipes and a custom grille carrying the mark of the Crusaders' cross as well. His handle, Paladin, was written on the driver's-side door, like a signature, in red paint.

The cab swayed rhythmically like a baby's cradle in time to the hum of the road. An amulet of Hermes, a small clay tablet depicting the Egyptian god Min, a Saint Christopher medallion, a gris-gris dedicated to Legba, Loa of the Crossroads, and dozens of other charms and talismans to gods and saints, patrons and protectors of travelers and roads, swung from the console above Jimmie's windshield. Aussapile downshifted to avoid a slow-moving car. His gearshift looked like a pistol-grip shotgun partially sheathed in the transmission well. The red Crusaders' cross was stamped on the pearl handle grip of the shotgun.

The CB radio squawked. A distorted voice called out through the shroud of static, a ghost from the electromagnetic spectrum speaking in the secret language of the road, a code only partly known to laymen and lawmen. Jimmie knew when you were on a long run those voices gave you comfort in the knowledge you were not alone in the wasteland of the Road, not alone driving throughout the heartland of America in the darkest of hours, the only soul awake in the lands of the dreaming dead.

"Breaker, breaker, Paladin, got your ears on? C'mon," the voice on the CB said. "This is Dallas Star, rolling a bobtail, southbound, headed home. I got nothing for you, brother. I don't see your lost bulldog. Over."

Jimmie tapped the mike button for the wireless headset he wore as he steered the 18-wheeler through the freezing rain he had fought since

Nashville. Technically, it was spring, but winter wasn't leaving without a fight. The highway was a black mirror, reflecting the sudden, stabbing planes of crimson brake lights and the baleful lances of high beams—celestial phenomena from some diffused void on the other side of ice-covered asphalt.

"Much obliged, Dallas Star," Jimmie said into the mike. "Have a good one today and a better one tomorrow; you're clear. Break 1-9, this is Paladin. Anyone got a 20 on that yellow-and-white bulldog? Headed out of Nashville, running west on I-70? We're on a clock here, brothers and sisters. Anybody got anything?"

The man in the yellow Mack truck had tortured, raped, and murdered six women in five states in the past year. He was a long-hauler, and a little over four hours ago he had abducted woman number seven, a "lot lizard," a truck-stop prostitute, from the Nashville TA truck stop. Her pimp and a few of her friends had seen her get into the yellow truck, and then the truck drove away with the woman screaming for help, struggling to get out of the cab, only to be forced back inside by the driver.

Several drivers, lot lizards, lumpers, and lot attendants had seen the whole thing play out, and word quickly and quietly spread across the radio frequencies to Jimmie, who was running a load of steel up to Illinois. Jimmie sent out a coded message on Channel 23 to make sure he wasn't stepping on the toes of any of the others. It was a courtesy, but Jimmie was glad when all he got back was "*You're point on this, Paladin; call the play.*" Jimmie had seen hardened gearjammers weep like children when they found the desecrated body of victim number three on the blacktop shoulder of I-55 near Sikeston about nine months ago. This son of a bitch had been like a ghost, but now . . . now Jimmie had him, could feel him close, feel his oily soul somewhere up ahead. He thought of the terror eating at that poor girl right now, and, as always, he thought, What if it was Layla or Peyton in that truck, waiting to die.

He accelerated. Somewhere up ahead was his man, and this was ending tonight.

The sociopath's thoughts were full of hooks piercing flesh, electricity blistering skin, and sour, stale smells that equated to associations not found in a human lexicon. He was behind the wheel of his own 18-wheeler. He owned it. He owned the whimpering, sobbing piece of trash cuffed and gagged behind him in the cab of his Mack, too. He could hear her trying to talk, trying to pray behind the cloth curtains that separated the driving area from the back of the cab, where he worked and played. Her voice was muffled by the tape over her mouth, but he could hear her sobbing, choking, snot-filled pleas. He thought she was praying to him. His rig was his universe and he was god here, master of life and death.

His birth name was Wayne Ray Rhodes, but that name had meant nothing to him since he read the book. His true name was the Marquis. That was what he called himself in the writhing snake pit of his mind; it was what he made the trash call him as he tortured them. It was the name they had to use as they begged for their lives. He didn't know what a marquis was. It sounded cool as shit, though, and real badass. Nobody fucked around with someone named "the Marquis."

Marquis was the name of the fella who wrote the stained, coverless paperback he found on the piss-covered floor of a rest-area bathroom. The name of the book was *The 120 Days of Sodom,* and while Wayne Ray didn't understand a lot of the fruity egghead talk in between the fucking, the descriptions of having control over a piece of trash, of degrading her, giving her pain, and being the god who decides her fate . . . now, that he understood, the way a carrion eater instinctively hungers for death. He had known what he was at sixteen when he tortured his first prostitute, burning her with cigarettes before he blew her head off with his .38.

He had been so inspired by the book that he had converted the sleeping compartment behind his cab into a torture chamber, complete with suspended chain restraints, a surgical table, and a horrific array of torture implements both medieval and modern. It was wired for video and sound, of course, and the Marquis had an extensive collection of recordings of him interrogating the trash, torturing them, and then, of course, disposing of them. In his mind, the Marquis wasn't murdering or even killing anyone; he was a trash man, and he was disposing of walking garbage. It would have made Jimmie Aussapile physically ill to see just how many DVD recordings, each in a specially labeled jewel case, the Marquis possessed in his rolling dungeon. It was far more than six.

On the filthy bunk on which the Marquis slept, on the semen-, shit-, and blood-covered sheets, dusted with Fritos chip crumbs, a nineteen-year-old girl struggled against the cuffs that pinned her arms behind her back. Like the Marquis, she, too, had a handle, a secret name. They called her Supergirl in the truck-stop parking lots because of the tattoo of the stylized "S" shield she had on her lower back. She had a real name from before. Before she left the foster home, before the hitting and the nightly visits by the thing that forced her to call him Dad. Her name was Marcia, Marcia Hughes.

At first Marcia figured this was going to be another rough trick, another rip-off, when the nasty, squint-eyed old man smacked her and started to drive away. Cuff her, rape her, and push her out of the cab at about ten miles an hour. It happened, usually a few times a month, less if she was lucky. Her worse concern had been that she wouldn't lose any more teeth in the transaction.

But as the truck bounced onto the on ramp of I-70 a Mason jar rolled across the floor. There was something floating in the cloudy fluid inside the jar. It was pale and spongy, with some dark hair, swaying like seaweed in the ocean, sloshing around. Then Marcia saw the harsh, fluorescent light above the steel table in the cab catch the gleam of the clitoral piercing and Marcia knew, she *knew*. It was the decaying remains of a woman's mutilated vagina. The fear was screaming, screaming like a fire alarm in her mind. This was no rip-off, this was one of the tricks that went past sickness; this was one of the monsters that rolled in off the highway to the lots, one of the things that gobbled you up and you were never seen again. Marcia screamed, her patchwork soul wanting to flee her body, but the duct tape held it in. She was gone. No one would ever find her, no one would ever know. No one would miss her. No one cared.

The Marquis's truck passed the I-70/I-44 interchange, headed south. On the left, the Gateway Arch rose, illuminated, out of the icy mist, a monument to America's expansion; the never-ending hunger to move farther out, the drive to move faster, and to move with unfettered freedom. The American dream was a race. The Mack truck's passage did not go unnoticed.

. . .

"Break 2-3, Paladin, Paladin, you got your ears on?" Jimmie's CB crackled. The voice held a distinctive New York accent. "Handle's Mr. Majestyk. I'm northbound on 70, just past the I-44 exchange, and I just had eyes on your yellow-and-white bulldog. He's headed southbound on 70, coming up on the 251C exit. You copy me?"

Jimmie stomped the accelerator pedal, a wolf grin spreading on his face. "Hot damn!" he said, and clicked the mike open on the radio. "10-4, Mr. M! I owe you big. Thank you kindly."

"Just go get that *stronzo,* Paladin. I'll be 10-10, give me a shout-out if you need any help. The wheel turns, brother. . . ."

Jimmie's truck skidded as he threaded between the traffic. The ice was starting to make the highway a lot more dangerous to traverse at the speeds he was moving. "Breaker 2-3, this is Paladin. Is there anyone out there in a position to get that truck off the road, c'mon?"

Blue lights strobed in Jimmie's side mirror. A Missouri state-police cruiser had slid up behind him. "Aw, damn it!" Jimmie said. He switched the CB channel over to 19, the one used by most trucker drivers and monitored by the police. "Break 1-9 to that bubble-gum machine riding my tail, I got a real good reason I'm speeding, Officer. I . . ."

"Boy, you got any idea how fast you going?" The trooper's voice came in clear over the CB speakers in Jimmie's cab and over his headset. "You doing in excess of twenty-three miles per hour, now aren't you, son?"

Jimmie's eyes widened and the smile returned. "Yes, sir, I reckon I am, Officer," he said, and switched back over to Channel 23. "Break to that county mountie back there. You one of us? C'mon?"

"Go get him," the trooper replied. "I'll clear the road for you if you slide on into the back door here. I'll put out a BOLO on his truck right now. Once you land him, I'll get you all the backup you need. Over." Jimmie could almost hear the grin in the trooper's voice. "Oh, and consider this a warning about that speeding, Paladin," the trooper said. "You slow your ass down, coming through my jurisdiction, cowboy. The wheel turns."

Jimmie laughed. Damn if the wheel didn't turn.

The state trooper's siren howled and the cruiser sped from behind Jimmie's rig to in front of it, going well over a hundred miles an hour. Cars and trucks began to clear the lane for the trooper, and Jimmie accelerated to follow his escort, yanking the cord for his air horn and letting loose with a rebel yell.

The Marquis slowed to a near-crawl. "What is this shit," he muttered. Traffic had thickened. Ahead, there looked to be some kind of road work going on. There had been no signs or notifications on the digital message boards that dotted the highway. A crew of orange-vest- and hard-hat-wearing Missouri Department of Transportation workers with flashlights were directing traffic to move slowly through the choke point, marked with crimson road flares and a flashing yellow arrow sign. They looked thrilled to be out in the freezing rain. Cars and trucks honked as they jockeyed to merge from three lanes down to one. A portable digital road sign built into a trailer announced, ALL MULTI-AXLE VEHICLES MUST DETOUR TO EXIT 209A GRATIOT STREET. FOLLOW SIGNS TO DETOUR ROUTE.

The Marquis's truck slowly merged into the single open lane and began to descend the exit ramp. One of the highway crew, a foreman, unclipped a handheld CB radio that was tuned to Channel 23 and spoke into it. "Paladin, this is Roadway Rembrandt. Your bulldog is off the highway and getting detoured right to where you said you wanted him. The wheel turns."

Almost a thousand miles away, outside Washington, DC, in the suburbs of the nexus of federal power, FBI Special Agent Cecil Dann was asleep in his recliner for the third time this week. A stack of case files sat next to the chair, beside his dinner plate and the remains of the meal his wife, Jenna, asleep upstairs, had left in the fridge for him. The Danns' dog, a coal-black pug named Oscar, eagerly finished off Dann's dinner. The flat-screen television droned on, showing the John Wayne version of *True Grit*. Oscar didn't seem very interested as he gnawed on the steak bone. Agent Dann even less so as he snored. Dann's cell phone rang; the ringtone was the theme to *Dragnet*. He sputtered and opened his eyes, sitting up, and spilling the files he had fallen asleep reading.

"Wha . . ." he muttered, wiping drool from the side of his mouth. The phone rang again. "That's not even my ringtone."

Dann's hair was salt-and-pepper, and it made him look more like a college professor than a federal agent. He had played CIAA baseball through school, had almost gone on to the major leagues before the FBI recruited him straight out of North Carolina A&T. He still had the build and the gait of a pitcher. Dann was the assistant special agent in charge of a division of the FBI's Violent Criminal Apprehension Program called the Highway Serial Killings Initiative. It was a program established by the FBI back in 2009 to track unsolved murders that occurred near interstate highways and to look for the patterns that might indicate the signature of a serial murderer. There was a map of the United States on Dann's office wall. Each red dot on the map was an unsolved murder on or near the highways. The map bled red—over five hundred cases reported, with more coming in every day. The rough estimate was that, at any given time, HSKI had about two hundred suspects committing serial murder across the roadways, a nightmarish circuit of pain, loss, and death. HSKI had cleared twenty-five cases during its first year in business, but, as the stack of files Dann brought home with him every night indicated, the FBI was bailing water with a teaspoon.

Dann blinked and looked down at the screen of his ringing smartphone. Where the number of the incoming call should be there was a line of text instead: *"Answer it Cecil."*

He answered the call with a swipe of his finger. "How the hell do you do that?" he said into the phone. "Do you have any idea what time it is you're calling? Because I don't, but it's late, I know that!"

"Listen carefully, Agent Dann. The I-70 Torturer is a long-haul truck driver named Wayne Ray Rhodes." The voice was automated, the kind you got when you received a spam phone call. "You have just received an email with DMV and GPS information on Rhodes's truck, a mug shot of Rhodes when he was arrested for assaulting a prostitute in 2010 in Illinois, and a link to his information in your suspect database."

Dann shook his head, "*Our* database? Really? I don't suppose you gift-wrapped him for us, too, did you?"

"Rhodes should be in the custody of the Missouri State Police shortly in St. Louis," the stilted electronic voice continued. "Jimmie Aussapile is pursuing him as we speak."

"Aussapile," Dann said. "Again. Busy fella." Dann climbed out of his recliner and knocked over his tower of files in the process. Oscar the dog, his meal disturbed, scampered away. Dann looked around for his shoes. Quietly, Jenna descended the stairs, pulling on a robe over her nightgown. She mouthed the word "Work?" to him, and Dunn nodded as he continued to look for his shoes while quickly trying to jot down notes on a pad of paper.

"Listen, I don't know who you people are," Dann said to the voice on the phone, "where you get your information or how the hell you do what you do, but you are interfering with multiple federal, state, and local investigations, and you can't just keep doing this. . . ."

Dann looked down at the floor, covered with his scattered files. Black-and-white crime-scene photos looked back at him. Women, girls, torn to shreds and worse, so much worse; many still had no names, so many unavenged. He tried to gather them up so that his wife wouldn't have to see.

"But thank you," he said, "for this one."

"Your shoes are under the coffee table," the automated voice said before it hung up. Dann looked at the screen of his phone. It now said, *"The wheel turns."* Beneath the words was a stylized circle with a central hub and three equidistant spokes radiating out from it. After a moment, the symbol and the words disappeared and were replaced by Dann's FBI seal wallpaper and the military time on the East Coast: 0145. Dann quickly began to dial the phone as he retrieved his shoes from under the table.

"This is Assistant Special Agent in Charge Dann," he said. "I need you to get me someone in the St. Louis field office right now, and scramble me a tactical team and a jet. I want wheels up in an hour or less. Thank you."

"Cecil," Jenna said, placing her hand on her husband's shoulder, "what was all that about?"

"Apparently," Dann said, wresting his shoe away from Oscar's teeth, "Triple A has some kind of black-ops division."

. . .

The Marquis's truck growled like a junkyard dog as it glided past the industrial wasteland of South Wharf Street. His headlights caught the frozen rain as it continued to spill from a dark and merciless sky. A single, swaying yellow caution light blinked as it was buffeted in the wind and the rain, no audience to heed its mute warning. Crumbling concrete walls on either side of the street were smeared in vibrant, tangled graffiti, the secret language of the city's soul. Above the painted walls, the gravel lots, and the chain-link fences were the silent black conveyor-belt towers of the rock quarry that covered several city blocks in every direction. The detour signs had led him here, and now the Marquis thought perhaps it was fate. This was the perfect place to pull over into a deep shadow, wait out the storm, and play with his newest toy. As he slowed to find a good spot, he didn't notice someone else already using the shadows.

Francisco Pena sat behind the wheel of his taxicab in the darkness, watching as the yellow-and-white semi rumbled by. The vibrations of the big truck made the Saint Fiacre medallion on Frank's rearview mirror sway slightly. Frank had driven a hack for fourteen years in St. Louis and owned his own cab for most of that time. When the call came in tonight about the killer on the road, he knew he had to do all he could to help stop this man, the way once, many years ago, the others had helped him, saved him. He raised his microphone to his lips and keyed the mike.

"He just passed me," Frank said. "He's in position. The wheel turns."

The Marquis slowed as he scanned the desolate street for the perfect spot where he could have some time with his newest acquisition. The darkness of the road ahead was pierced as high-beam headlights suddenly snapped on. Another semi straddled both lanes about a hundred yards ahead, idling in the icy rain and mist. Condensation trailed from its twin-towered exhaust pipes, like smoke from the curled lips of a crouching dragon. The Marquis lurched to a stop, his own engine idling now.

"What the fuck is this?" he snarled. As if to answer, his CB suddenly hissed with static. A voice broke the stale, evil silence of the Marquis's cab.

"Break 1-9 to that bulldog up ahead of me, you got your ears on son? C'mon?"

The Marquis picked up his mike and clicked it on, one of his eyes bugging out in anger, the other squinted up like Popeye. "10-4. You got the Marquis here." Wayne Ray pronounced his handle as "Mar-qiss."

"That fancy poor-boy rig you're driving there is blocking the road, asshole."

"Handle's Paladin," the voice replied. "Now don't you be a-cussin' on this here channel, Hoss. That's against the law. . . ."

Off in the distance, the Marquis heard them—sirens. Distant, but a chorus of them, growing slowly louder, closer.

"See," the voice on the CB said. "That's the FCC coming to get you right now. Nobody likes a potty mouth. Best pack it in, Marquis."

A cold sweat covered the nape of the Marquis's neck, a terrible awareness of what was happening to him. He glanced back at the trash lying on his bunk. Her wet eyes held a glimmer of hope. The Marquis had to fight the urge to vomit. He revved his engine, and the whole truck shook.

"Get out of my way, Paladin," he said.

"They know, Wayne Ray," Jimmie said into the mike, revving his own engine now. "They know what you did to those girls, and they're coming for you."

"Let me go, or I'll kill the whore," the Marquis said, sweating and blinking. "Move!"

"You'll kill her anyway," Jimmie said, "and quick is a damn sight more merciful than what you had planned for her. If you let the girl live, that will show them you can have compassion. It will help you, Wayne Ray, and right now you need all the help you can get."

"Fuck compassion," the Marquis screamed, spittle flying from his blued lips. He jammed the accelerator and shifted the large gearshift with a silver skull as the knob. The Mack lurched forward, accelerating. "And fuck you!"

Jimmie slammed his boot and the accelerator to the floor and jerked the shotgun gearshift as the Peterbilt blasted toward the charging Mack truck. "C'mon, you sick bastard," Jimmie said as the two trucks headed straight for each other. "Bring it!" Jimmie punched a button on the console above his head, and the cab was filled with staccato metal guitar—Metallica's "No Remorse."

Many large corporate fleet trucks came equipped with speed governors to keep them moving at a respectable but less legally actionable speed. Pretty much any semi could pull a full trailer load up an eight-degree incline at a hundred and twenty-five miles per hour. Independents like Jimmie and the Marquis liked to tinker with their engines, giving them thirteen- or eighteen-speed transmissions and making them capable of greater speeds, much greater speeds.

Both trucks were hurtling like rockets toward each other on the dark, icy road. Their speedometers creeping higher and higher . . . seventy mph . . . eighty mph . . . eighty-five . . . ninety . . . Less than ten yards separated them now.

Jimmie was sweating. His eyes locked on the windshield, on the brilliant lights and the massive grille that now encompassed his universe. His hand was steady on the wheel. This was it. He had faced this before—over there in Khafji, on the Road, when the cannibal sages of Metropolis-Utopia had almost gobbled him up, and the time with Ale and the others when they rode into the deep darkness to save Ale's old lady and her baby son. Jimmie knew the shape of death, the dry taste of dust and the bittersweet wine on her lips. The crazy sumbitch would blink, he'd swerve . . . hold . . . hold . . .

Saving Ale's baby. Jimmie suddenly flashed to his wife—to Layla, and the baby in her belly, his baby. Layla was home right now, waiting for him. Waiting with Peyton, his fourteen-year-old little girl. Their brights blinded both men as the trucks came closer and closer.

Who would keep them safe from things in this world like the Marquis, and worse? And Jimmie Aussapile knew there were things so much worse than the sick little madman barreling down on him. Who'd keep them safe? His family was waiting for him.

Jimmie's courage shivered. He began to jerk the large steering wheel to turn and try to avoid the crash. But the blinding lights of the Marquis's Mack suddenly swerved to the left. The maniac had turned, and the two cabs rushed past each other, like passing freight trains. Jimmie's driver's-side mirror exploded as the trucks passed, and sparks flew off the Marquis's trailer as they narrowly averted a crash. Jimmie downshifted and clutched the wheel tight as he applied the hissing air brakes. The wheels of the truck squealed in defiance. If he hit a patch of ice right now, he was dead.

Behind him, Jimmie heard a crash that sounded like a bomb blast, a heavy jarring boom; and he knew, even without his mirror, that the

Marquis had jackknifed his rig—sliding sideways, with his trailer going one way and the cab the other. Jimmie's truck groaned to a stop with a final hiss of the brakes. He shifted the gears and shut off the engine. The sirens were louder now and closer, a screaming flock of banshees coming for retribution and judgment. Jimmie found the hidden catch on the gearshift and slid the fully functional sawed-off shotgun free of the transmission well one-handed, as he struggled out of the cab and into the cold night.

The Marquis's truck was partway through one of the graffiti-covered barrier walls; the cab and the trailer were on their sides in the shape of a massive "L." The overturned trailer blocked both sides of Wharf Street. Jimmie spat out tobacco juice, pumped a round into the 12-gauge's chamber, and ran as quickly as his age, weight, and the slick road would allow toward the overturned cab. The sirens were very close now, blocks away. He saw a dark form drop off the top of the capsized cab and grunt in pain as he hit the frozen asphalt. It was Wayne Ray Rhodes. The gangly killer got to his feet and ran toward the now smashed chain-link fence, sliding through it and disappearing inside the quarry. Frank Pena, the gypsy cabbie, appeared around the side of the wrecked cab. The sirens were here now, all around them. State police and St. Louis PD cruisers were swarming both ends of the street.

"I smell gas," Frank shouted. "It could start burning any second!"

Jimmie had reached the shredded fence and was struggling to get his gut through the narrow passage. "Get the girl out," he said to Frank. "Make sure she's okay. Tell the cops where he went and that I'm back there, too!"

"Be careful, Paladin!" Frank shouted to the trucker over the sirens and the police radios.

Jimmie disappeared into the darkness. It was hard to hear anything above the sirens and his own labored breathing. The chaw in his cheek was like a ball of sour acid now, and for the millionth time he swore he was going to give the shit up. He slowed and looked around the narrow path between lines of conveyor belts, pulverizers, and storage sheds. He clicked on his heavy, baton-like Maglite flashlight and held it away from his body as he scanned.

There were dunes here. Massive mountains of sand and gravel. The backhoes and huge dump trucks were dark slumbering guardians as Jimmie moved as quietly as he could among the hills. There was the loud crack of a gunshot and the sound of something sizzling the air near him before it crashed into a conveyor ramp. Jimmie swung the light around and saw the Marquis, near the top of one of the ice-covered hills of cinder. The killer fired at Jimmie again with his snub-nosed revolver and Jimmie dived to the ground, dropping the flashlight, and quickly belly-crawled for cover behind a backhoe. Getting shot at—he hadn't done this shit in a spell. He still heard his old DI screaming at him to keep his fat ass down and out of the barbed wire. That was a million lifetimes, and at least eighty pounds, ago. Jimmie grunted as he crouched behind the massive front tires of the tractor and fired off two rounds in the direction of the Marquis. He couldn't see Wayne Ray, but he heard a satisfying crunch he assumed was the killer tumbling down the other side of the cinder pile, either hit or fell trying to avoid the gunfire. Jimmie was cool with either one.

Jimmie hustled, running, popping the hot cartridges out of the shotgun's breech, and fumbling to slide two more shells into the gun. He moved to the far side of the sand pile as the quarry's lights snapped on. Sweeping floodlights illuminated the machinery and the work roads between them. Jimmie was a silhouette against the halogen suns. He ran faster and snapped the breech shut on the gun. He rounded the sand dune and saw the back side of the cinder hill. Wayne Ray was getting to his feet, gun still in his hand. He saw Jimmie at the same time Jimmie spotted him. He squinted and fired from a kneeling position, cussing as he did. In his mind, Jimmie heard his dad's voice: *You charge a gun, son, and back off a knife. . . .*

"Stay the hell back!" the Marquis bellowed. "I got a gun!"

"Shit," Jimmie said, adding a few extra syllables to the word, as he ran full steam toward the killer and fired off a blast of the shotgun as he ran, the gun bouncing. The air around the Marquis was full of hot, angry bees. Wayne Ray flinched as several pellets stung his cheek and arm. Jimmie was on him, and the two men leveled their guns at each other from spitting distance. Jimmie was panting, his breath silver smoke in the cold, wet air. The Marquis was shaking more from fear than cold.

"I'm not going to fucking prison," Wayne Ray said, cocking the revolver.

"Should have thought about that before you butchered all those women, Wayne Ray," Jimmie said. "Whatever they do to you in there won't be a tenth of what you did to those poor souls."

"Shit!" the Marquis said. "I was jist killing whores. It ain't like they're some damned endangered fucking species!"

Jimmie took a deep breath. "Come on, now," he said to the killer, "drop the gun and let's walk on out. They'll buy you a big old cheeseburger and fries while your crazy ass confesses." Wayne Ray didn't move. One of his eyes kept scrunching up, as if it had a will of its own. His gun hand was trembling.

"I could shoot you," Wayne Ray said. "Kill you and then kill myself. Couldn't miss your fucking gut from here."

"You talk too damn much to do that," Jimmie said. "Now put that gun down and walk out with me, or, I swear to God, I'll empty enough shot into your fucking kneecap that you'll be begging me to kill you, and at this range I might end up taking your fucking pecker off with it. Last chance."

"It ain't fair," Wayne Ray said. "I was jist doing what everyone else does—killin' whores."

"It truly is an unfair world, Wayne Ray," Jimmie said. "Cowboy the fuck up. You did this—now face it like a man."

Jimmie lowered the shotgun slightly to aim at the killer's knee. The Marquis gently lay the revolver on the cold ground.

"Think they'll make a movie about me?" Wayne Ray asked, putting his hands on his head.

"Yeah," Jimmie said, sighing. "They probably will."

. . .

The girl was alive. She broke her collarbone in the crash, but she was crying tears of joy and thanking Jesus a whole lot as the paramedics wheeled her on a gurney to an ambulance and sped her off to the hospital. She never saw Jimmie, but he saw her, and it made him smile. Someone handed him a paper cup of really bad coffee, and he nursed it and checked his watch. He was late, really late. His cell phone had been blowing up from the dispatcher. He turned it off. Most of the cops, paramedics, and others on the scene just tried very hard to ignore him. Jimmie knew the routine. He needed to get going, but there was someone he had to talk with first. He just hoped that afterward he wasn't going to jail.

A few hours after Wayne Ray Rhodes had been put in the back of a police car and sped away, a tall black man with salt-and-pepper hair, dressed in an oxford shirt, slacks, and an FBI windbreaker, walked up to Jimmie. He nodded in the direction of the overturned Mack truck. It was still surrounded by cops, state troopers, forensic technicians, and, now, federal agents.

"Another low-profile operation," Agent Dann said. "Very subtle."

"We git 'er done, Cecil," Jimmie said, spitting some tobacco juice, from the new nest of chaw in his cheek, into the empty paper coffee cup. "Damn sight more than I can say for you fellas."

"And who, exactly, is 'we,' Aussapile?" Dann asked. "How do you people do what you do?"

"Rhodes is a solo," Jimmie said. "He's not part of the Finders or the Zodiac Lodge or one of the other serial-killer packs. Lone mad dog—no one was pointing him or giving him aid and comfort. He's got enough Polaroids and videos in there to clear pert near fifty cases for you, though. Thought you'd want to know."

"How the hell do you know about the . . ." Dann sputtered, but then collected himself. "The official bureau policy on those so-called child-abduction cults and serial-killer clubs is that they do not exist and don't use the highways as their private hunting grounds. It's all urban myth."

"Well," Jimmie said, "that's a comfort coming from the folks who said the same thing about the Mafia."

"Who *are* you people?" Dann asked.

"We're urban myths, too," Jimmie said. "I got a load of iron to get to Chicago. Am I free to go now?"

"What if I bust your ass until I get some real answers?" Dann said.

"The same thing that happened the first time we met and you tried that shit," Jimmie said. "Can I go?"

Dann nodded. "You saved her—that girl. Go. But I'm not giving up on this, on whoever you people are."

Jimmie climbed into the truck, groaning with the effort. His back and knee were acting up again in this cold. "And that is exactly why we contacted you tonight. Keep up the good work, Cecil. Thanks for coming out so quick, and for trusting us."

Jimmie's rig pulled away from the federal agent and headed back toward the interstate and his dwindling deadline.

"I never said I trusted you," Dann said to the retreating brake lights.

. . .

Jimmie got back on the highway, taking I-55 across the powerful, lazy Mississippi River into Illinois and onto I-64 headed for Chicago. With a little luck and a decent tailwind, he might not be too late. That was good, because this was his third load with this company, and the last two had been late because of business like tonight. He doubted they would contract him for a fourth one if he screwed this job up. With the baby on the way, and Layla not working at Walmart right now, they needed the money pretty bad.

The road drifted beneath him, white bullet lines flashing by, acceleration making them an endless thread. Green road signs with white lettering announced his progress, as did his GPS. He was making good time now, humming with the rhythm of the road. He switched the CD player back on and clicked to change the disc. "Far from Home," by Five Finger Death Punch, kept him company. Jimmie sighed. He was ready to go home for a spell. He missed his wife, missed his family. After tonight, he felt that he deserved a little break, a little peace. He needed home.

That was when he saw her. He slowed instinctively, even though part of his mind was screaming to ignore her, pass on by. The deadline, peace and quiet. Home. So far from home.

He drove past her. She was pale, almost washed out in the glare of his lights. She looked about fifteen, maybe younger, and was dressed in a dirty white lace sundress. A jean jacket, too big for her and covered with buttons declaring the logos of various bands, was her only protection from the cold and the rain. She wore simple leather flats over dirty feet. Her straight brown hair fell to her shoulders but didn't appear to be wet in the freezing drizzle; none of her looked wet, but she shivered all the same. Her face pleaded with him silently in his headlights.

"Damn . . . it," Jimmie muttered and slowed down more. He pulled over to the shoulder of the highway about fifty yards past her, putting on his emergency blinkers. He shut off the music.

His passenger-cab door clicked open almost immediately, far too quickly for the girl to have even sprinted up to meet him from where she had been standing. The hitchhiker climbed into the cab. She seemed to bring some of the bone-aching cold from outside with her. The cab suddenly got very cold, and Jimmy could see his breath swirl before him. He looked at the girl's emotionless face. He knew what she was going to say before the words formed on her pale, almost blue, lips.

"I'm trying to get home," she said. "Can you please give me a ride home?"

Jimmie knew what she was. He felt his blood freezing in his veins just looking at her. He wanted to run, to scream and jump out of the cab—a natural reaction, a survival instinct as old as the little lizard brain part of his mind. He thought how this little girl had been close to Peyton's age when she . . . He took the instinctual fear below, locked it back up in its antediluvian vault. He nodded slowly to the girl.

"Sure, darling,'" he said softly. "I'll get you home. Do you remember your address?"

She gave it to him. It was in Granite City, Illinois. In his head he calculated the detour. Not that far, but any delay could cost him the contract. They drove in silence, the girl staring straight ahead.

"What's your name?" Jimmie finally asked as the silence and the cold settled in the cab.

"Karen," she said. "Karen Collie."

"Nice to meet you," Jimmie said. "Jimmie Aussapile."

"I know," Karen said. "You have a reputation." Jimmie felt as if someone had stepped on his grave.

They drove in silence. Occasionally, the GPS would announce a course correction in a pleasant voice, but otherwise the cab was as still and cold as a tomb. They made their way back onto I-55, and eventually they came off the ramp in Granite City. It was a small industrial town, full of steel mills and small neat rows of working-class houses in blue-collar neighborhoods. Jimmie's rig glided down the empty street and came to a stop in front of a small, neatly trimmed lawn and a modest but well-kept whitewashed house. The mailbox in front had a wooden carving of a robin on it, and the name on the side of the box was Collie.

Jimmie had done this many times before, and it was always terrifying, always sad. He turned to the passenger seat. "Well," he said. "You're home now, darlin'."

The pale hitchhiker, dressed in white, looked at him with wide, sad eyes. For the first time since she entered the cab, he saw emotion cross her features. It was fear.

"It ate my friends," she said. "Gobbled them up—Mark, Steph, Aaron, Kristie—ate their souls. . . . It didn't get me. . . . I was lucky." She pulled back her hair and showed Jimmie her neck. A looping dark scar extended from behind her ear across her carotid. "I didn't give it a chance to eat the bright part. I escaped."

Jimmie had never had this happen before. "What . . . what are you talking about, Karen?"

"Sometimes your dreams are haunted houses," Karen said. "I dreamed this. Please stop it, Jimmie." Her voice was almost fading out, like a cold, dying breeze. "It's hunting now . . . growing stronger . . . *an fiach fiái* . . ." She fought for each audible word. "You can't escape it once you've seen it. It will devour everyone if you don't stop it. It's using him to get out. He's . . . terrible. He's like . . . crib death, like terminal cancer with a will. He's been killing for it for so long . . . feeding it for so long."

The pale little girl looked at Jimmie and her eyes were wet, but no tears came. "Is this a dream? When you die do you live in your dreams? Please, Jimmie the Trucker . . ." She wiped her eyes and tried to smile at Jimmie. It was a sweet smile, but the sadness remained like a shadow. "Please. Tell my parents I love them . . . and that I'm okay now. I'm okay."

In the span of a single blink, the hitchhiker was gone, vanished. Jimmie rubbed his face. He looked at the little white house, its windows all dark, but the porch light burning, still burning, for Karen. Jimmie climbed out of the truck and made his way, groaning a little, to the front door. He rang the bell. He only had to ring once; the lights in the living room snapped on quickly. The door opened. A man and a woman in hastily donned robes looked at him with eyes that were weary, weary from years of sleepless nights, years of jumping every time the phone or the doorbell rang. Years of guilt and fear, and unanswered questions had gnawed at their guts, their hearts. The couple looked old, older than they should.

"Mr. and Mrs. Collie," Jimmie began, taking off his baseball cap and holding it tight in his hands, "My name is James Aussapile, and I'm here about your daughter, Karen. . . ."

Hector Sinclair awoke on the cold concrete floor of the holding cell, his head stuffed thick with cotton balls soaked in pain. His face was about six inches from the filthy, seatless, stainless-steel toilet bowl in the cell, and his mouth tasted as if he had spent quite a bit of time last night bent over it. He blinked and rolled over onto his back. Looking up, he got a splendid view of another resident of the drunk tank, a four-hundred-pound bald black man who was using the toilet to take a piss.

"Good morning, Sunshine," the Pisser said, smiling. He was missing his two front teeth. "Did I wake you?" He chuckled, zipped up his pants, and navigated his way through the pile of still sleeping drunks back to the bunk he had claimed when the cops threw him in at three-thirty that morning.

Hector groaned and struggled to his feet. Several of the bodies around him moaned and cussed, having to move a bit on the floor to avoid being stepped on. There were only four bunks and about a dozen men in the cell. Most were curled up on the floor, as Hector had been, or propped in a corner of the cell, sleeping it off sitting up. Hector's face was numb, and his side and hands hurt from the dull ache of bruises.

He made his way to the small steel sink mounted on the wall beside the toilet. There was no hot water. He turned on the faucet and a feeble trickle of water drooled out. He gathered as much of the freezing water in the cup of his hands as he could and then bent over and splashed it in his face. He did it again and again, running his wet hands through his now dripping hair.

Hector had the face of a young man in his twenties with green fire burning in the eyes of an old man. He had tried hard not to look himself in the eyes since he had come back to the world from over there. His face, like his body, was angular and taut. He had a spiky mane of bright red hair that on its best days had been likened to something a Japanese anime superhero might sport, and he wore long mutton-chop sideburns. Hector's build was slender, slight but muscular. He splashed more water in his face and checked his teeth to make sure none were loose from the fight last night. The pain in his head was bright and sharp now, and his guts were churning bile.

"Hey, princess?" the Pisser said from his bunk, where he had been watching Hector. Without looking away from the sink, Hector flipped off the smiling man and went back to splashing water on his face and head and drinking big cold gulps of the water.

One of the drunks on the floor near the sink started. "Fuck, asshole!" the guy said. "Getting me fucking wet, mutherfucker! That shit's cold!"

Without missing a beat, Hector kicked the guy hard in the balls. They had taken his boots away, but the barefoot kick still had plenty of force behind it. The drunk on the floor made a sound like a golf ball getting stuck in a pool intake filter and curled and shuddered as he puked on himself.

"That warm you up, shithead?" Hector said, slicking back his now soaking-wet hair. His accent held a touch of North Carolina by way of Glasgow. He turned and looked at the Pisser sitting on his bunk like a gap-toothed Buddha, a broken smile on his broad face.

"Yeah?" Hector said. "What?"

"You one of them biker boys, right?" the Pisser said. "Took four of them to bring you in last night. I heard them talking about you when they dragged my ass in."

"How many it take to get you in here, cupcake?" Hector asked. His torn, bloody, green military T-shirt was soaked.

The Pisser laughed. "Six," he said, "but then I ain't no badass biker boy." The Pisser nodded to Hector. "Tru."

"That short for Truman, or is that your badass gangsta name?" Hector said. "I'm Heck."

"Truman," Tru said after a slight pause. "And Heck is—?"

"—short for raising all kinds of heck," Hector said. "You got a smoke, man?"

"Shit," Tru said, laughing. "I respect my mutherfucking body, man."

Heck looked the huge man up and down, and pulled his wet T-shirt off. "So did you eat a few of them deputies before they threw you in the drunk tank, 'cause it looks like they're kind of slow digesting."

Tru laughed. "You are one hi-larious mutherfucker," he said. "I'm serious, you are a card." Tru held up two hand-rolled cigarettes. Heck used the few dry spots on the T-shirt to dab off his face, hair, and chest, and then navigated shakily over to the bunk.

Tru grunted and slid over. "What," he said, pointing with one of the rolled joints at Heck's chest, "the fuck is that shit?"

Heck had a black-ink tattoo that covered most of his upper chest. It was two rows of letters with a single line of numbers beneath it, the words "yes" and "no" near each collarbone, and the words "good bye" on his flat stomach just above his navel.

"Ouija board." Heck plucked one of the blunts out of Tru's hand as he sat down. "It's for talking to the dead. Not that they have much to say that's very interesting."

"So you one of those satanic, 'bite the heads offa bats' biker boys?" Tru said, looking around and then striking a match. "Doing all that creepy, *Ghost Adventures* kinda shit? 'Cause I am all about the love of Black Jesus, my freaky friend, and Black Jesus, he rebukes that shit, hard."

"I guess I dabbled some when I was younger," Heck said. "My family was into that shit. I got this when I was sixteen, along with my MC ink. I've kinda grown out of it. Lot scarier shit in this world than some dead asshole playing with the light switch and the thermostat."

Tru held the match, and Heck lit his joint, puffing on it a few times until the tip was cherry. Then Tru lit his own.

"Thanks," Heck said, and took a long drag on the cigarette.

"So you been in a biker gang," Tru started.

"Club," Heck said. "Motorcycle club. MC."

"Whatever," Tru continued. "Since you were sixteen, man?"

Heck showed Tru the tattoo on his left biceps. It was a circle of Celtic knotwork with a large sword crossing it horizontally. On the blade of the sword was a slogan: "*Braithreachas.*" To the right of the circle and the sword were the letters "MC," and above it was a crescent bar that held the words "Blue Jocks" in highly stylized Gothic letters. Below the circle was another crescent, upturned, and bearing the words "North Carolina."

"All I've known was MC my whole life," Heck said. "Even as a baby. My grandfather founded the Jocks back in the early seventies. I was riding dirt bikes at ten, I was a prospect at fifteen, member at sixteen."

"The Blue Jocks," Tru said. "You're one of those bounty-hunter assholes outta Cape Fear, right? Scottish outlaw bikers? You guys ain't no better than the fuckers you turn out for bail money."

"One-percenters," Heck said. "'Outlaw bikers' sounds all Marlon Brando, man. Chasing bail jumpers pays the bills. Beats cooking crank."

"Well, you are one pale blue, *Braveheart*-looking Scottish mutherfucker," Tru said, laughing, a cloud of smoke preceding the chuckle. "So where were your boys when four cops were dragging your narrow ass to jail?"

Heck held the smoke tight in his lungs; the pain in his skull was diminishing. Finally, he exhaled. "Riding solo. I don't remember much. Been fucking up a lot lately. I'm an asshole. No need to get anyone else dragged into my shit."

Tru nodded. "Fair enough, man. I can respect that."

The heavy steel door at the end of the hall clanked open with a boom. Heck pinched out the burning tip of his joint and then did the same to Tru's. He dropped both cigarettes into Tru's palm, and they vanished as if he were a stage magician. There were footsteps and voices echoing down the cinder-block hall of cells. Several of the bodies on the floor of the cell began to stir at the sounds of activity approaching. A Harnett County sheriff's deputy, dressed in gray and blue, with a baseball cap on, escorted another man to the door of the cells. The man was in his twenties, short and skinny. His face was almost comic in its proportions, with a pronounced nose, big ears, and large deep-brown, almost black, eyes. His skin was riddled with acne scars, and he had long, oily brown hair that fell down to the collar of his flannel shirt. Under the flannel was a

T-shirt with the logo of the band Tool on it. He wore ripped-up jeans and heavy, steel-toed work boots.

Heck offered up a fist to Tru. "I think my ride is here," he said.

Tru returned the fist bump and nodded. "Later, easy rider. See you on the other side," Tru said.

"That's the man, Officer," the big-nosed man said, pointing at Heck, mock outrage on his face. "He's the one who stole my skin-care products!"

"Shut the hell up, Jethro," the deputy said to Big Nose. "Your stupid ass shouldn't even be back here. Is that pot I smell?"

"Is it?" Heck asked, stepping over the bodies slowly stirring on the floor to the door of the cell. "It's hard to smell anything over all the funk in here."

"Okay, Sinclair," the deputy said. "You're free to go. This here bounty hunter just paid your bail; I wouldn't recommend jumping it."

Heck looked at the big-nosed man and smiled. "You bailed me out, Roadkill? That's so sweet. . . . Um, where the hell were you about eight hours ago, when I was napping next to Lake Piss?"

"You're welcome," Roadkill said. "Your gratitude is touching, Heck." Roadkill nodded toward Tru, who was watching all this from his bunk, amused. "That the missus?" he asked.

The deputy unlocked the cell door. "C'mon, move it, Sinclair."

"I owe you a solid, Terry," Roadkill said to the deputy. "Thanks, Cuz."

"Yeah, yeah, just don't make it a habit, Jethro," the deputy replied.

Roadkill sniffed Heck, who was pulling his wet T-shirt back on. "Damn, son, you smell like you took a dip in Lake Piss. Let's get you cleaned up. We're riding for your old man today, and your mom will have my hide if you show up looking as sorry as you do now."

Outside the Harnett County Sheriff's Department detention center, it was late morning. It was bright. Birds chirped. The blue skies and the sunshine might fool you into thinking spring had arrived on schedule, but the wind was cold and cutting. Heck groaned a little as the sunlight flashed into his eyes. He fished his sunglasses, cigarettes, and Zippo out of the pockets of his leather jacket. He had recovered it from the property counter when he was released, along with his boots and his cut—the sleeveless black leather vest that bore the colors of the Blue Jocks. The patches on the back of the cut matched the markings of Heck's tattoo. Heck put on his shades, lit a Lucky Strike, and slipped the cut on over his leather riding jacket.

"Damn," he said, zipping up the jacket. "This wet shirt is killing me. It's cold as balls out here, man."

"Serves you fucking right, asshole," Roadkill said as he opened the door to his beat-up old Ford pickup. He pulled his own MC cut off the driver's seat and slid it on over his flannel. Cops frowned on sporting colors in their house. Above the right breast of Roadkill's cut was a patch that said SERGEANT AT ARMS. "Lucky they didn't throw your drunken ass into the Custer County stir. Fucking hellhole, that is."

"Hey," Heck said, climbing into the cab of the truck. He eyed a Sheriff's Department cruiser as it glided into the parking lot. "What is your problem, man? You that pissed off I got a little fucked up and got in a tussle? Shit, Jethro, we've been doing that since we were both thirteen."

Roadkill shook his head. He pulled his own sunglasses off the visor above the driver's seat. He slammed the door to the truck's cab and started the engine. "Gear is in the hospital," he said quietly as they drove out of the parking lot and started to drive down Bain Street.

"Wha . . . what happened?" Heck said.

"We had a hunt last night," Roadkill said. "That beastie that's been ripping people out of their cars on I-140 and leaving their intestines up on the Dan Cameron Bridge? We'd started calling the thing Meat Tinsel. Well, we got a lead on it, and we sent out every warm body we could get ahold of. That wasn't you, Heck. Your ass wasn't answering your phone. Again."

They turned in silence onto West Cornelius Harnett Boulevard. Heck smoked his cigarette and stared out the open window. They were passing suburbia: Dollar General stores, Food Lion grocery store, McDonald's, Advanced Auto, KF-fucking-C. He had ridden up and down streets like this most of his life. When he had been over there, all he could think about was how much he missed all this . . . bullshit. Bullshit, and stuff, and normalcy. Boring things that you took for granted until they weren't there anymore. No, that was wrong. They were there, far away, a mystical place called "back in the world." You were gone, on the moon.

For a moment, the thing in the Afghan desert was laughing in his mind, his memory. Its laugh was everywhere, and Heck was back there. He smelled the smoke—the greasy, charred pork smell of Abe's and Rich's and Javon's flesh burning; he heard them screaming. The smell of hot brass and the clatter of the M249 machine gun as the bullets passed harmlessly through the laughing, growling, living pyre. It cooked them, cooked his friends, his crew. The things the fire said to Heck in the ruins as the bodies burned . . . He closed his eyes behind the sunglasses. He saw his old friend Gear burning with his brothers, burning in the laughing, immortal fire. He swallowed hard.

"I was busy," Heck finally said through a dry throat. His palms were wet. He took a long drag on the cigarette.

"Jesus Christ, Heck!" Roadkill said. "Gear was the one that kept that asshole jumper in Newark from blowing a hole in you? Remember? He took that bullet for you? Seriously! What happened to you over there that has fucked you up so bad, man!"

"Nothing," Heck said. "I'm good. What the hell happened?"

"We were down three guys already," Roadkill said. "Muzz, Ed, and Billie were all down in Tallahassee on that five-hundred-thousand-dollar bail skip. And since Ale passed . . . well, everyone was expecting you to step up and take over as president. Gear shouldn't have been on point last night, man—it should have been you."

Heck exhaled a stream of thick smoke that was caught by the wind rushing past the car window and carried away. "Back the fuck off me, Jethro," he said, his voice low and gravelly.

"Gear lit the thing up with that old surplus M2 flamethrower we traded Mullet's old Panhead bike to the skinheads for," Roadkill continued. "The thing ashed pretty good, but Gear got too close, got caught by the claws—god, they were like damned hedge clippers—foot and a half long, at least. Then he was on fire, screaming. Third-degree burns over a quarter of his body, and a collapsed lung, man. So, no, fuck you—I will not back the fuck off. This MC, it's your and my family's legacy, Heck, and our future. A lot of people have bled for it, and keep on bleeding for it."

"What do you want from me, exactly?" Heck said, flicking the butt of his cigarette out the window. "Ale is gone. We're scattering his ashes today. I'm home, but I'm clearly not the guy who needs to be running the Jocks."

"That is bullshit," Roadkill said as they turned left onto Lillington's North Main Street. "You are. Everyone's known it since you were, like, twelve, Hector. Hell, even you."

"Well, everyone was wrong," Heck said. "Clearly."

"Since you got back you've blown off most of your friends, your family, and the club," Roadkill said. "You stay drunk and pick fights with any mouth-breather you can provoke. You've been in the pokey twice in the last month, Heck—"

"Three times now," Heck corrected with a grim smile.

"Look, if it's about losing Ale, I understand," Roadkill said. "And I'm here if you need me, man. Or is this some kind of post-stress psych thing?"

"Shut up and shut up some more," Heck said. "I'm okay."

"Hmm," Roadkill said. "Look, my friend, you keep that shit bottled up and it's going to blow sooner or later. You need to come to terms with it."

Heck looked over at Roadkill, shaking his head. "What, you're Dr. Phil now? Tell me why the hell I'm being lectured on how I should live my life by a fucking werepossum. . . . I mean, c'mon!"

"Now, that is just straight racist," Roadkill said. "And it's *half* werepossum on my mama's side, thank you very much, and you know that!"

"I know that you can turn yourself into a scuttling little garbage-eating vermin," Heck said.

"You know what?" Roadkill said, lurching the truck over to the side of the road. It stopped in a cloud of dust. "You *are* an asshole, and I'm done trying. Get the fuck out of my truck. Walk."

Heck threw the door open and climbed out. He slammed it behind him. "Okay," he said.

"Yeah, walk," Roadkill said again. "Run, you jerk. See if you can outrun yourself and everyone who wants to help your stubborn, stupid ass." His voice cracked a little as he said it. "I've been making excuses for you and apologizing for you for months, man, and I'm done."

Heck heard the hurt in Roadkill's voice. He recalled when they were both nine and he had made fun of Jethro accidentally shifting into a possum when they were playing by the creek in Heck's backyard. Heck had teased Jethro as he climbed up the hill, naked, a giant possum's tail still grown just above his butt, clutching his wet clothes like armor against the laughter. He fought against tears, claiming that his eyes got wet when he fell in the creek.

Suddenly, Ale had been there, all tall and strong with a mane of gray hair, a thick, long beard the same color, and those kind, strong, stern eyes. Odin, Zeus, the Lord Almighty, and Ale. Ale wrapped an old army blanket around Jethro and turned to Heck.

"What to do you think you're doing?" Ale said to the boy. The smile slid away from Heck's face. "You going make fun of your best friend because he's different? You need to rethink that, boy. One day it might be you who's the different one, Hector, and who's going to be there for you when everyone is pointing? We're all on the outside sometimes, Heck."

Heck put his hand on the open window of the passenger-side door of Roadkill's truck. "I'm sorry, man," he said. "Thanks for sticking up for me. I've been an asshole, and I'm sorry. I'll see you at the clubhouse for the ride." He started walking. The truck crunched gravel slowly as it pulled up to accompany him.

"Well, stop being an asshole and get in," Roadkill said. "I'll take you home to clean up. Your mom's been worried about you."

. . .

They rumbled down Market Street, the throaty growl of big V-twin engines announcing their presence to the pedestrians the way a lion's roar announces its arrival to the scavengers at the water hole. Gasoline-fueled thunder pealed down the street as the Blue Jocks cruised toward the Road to Nowhere. They were forty riders strong, headed out of the Jocks' Wilmington clubhouse. They crossed the Cape Fear River on Route 76. They picked up a half-dozen more members joining the pack by the time they were opening up and hauling down U.S. 74 toward Bryson City.

At the center of the procession, Heck was driving Ale's old 1941 Harley flathead with a sidecar. In the sidecar, Heck's mother and Ale's old lady, Elizabeth Sinclair, sat like a reigning queen in black leather. Her long white hair, pulled back and tied in a ponytail, fluttered in the wind. She wore aviator-style sunglasses but refused to wear a helmet. Clutched in her arms, to her chest, was a small wooden cask. The Blue Jocks' colors were burned into the cask. It held Ale's ashes.

Heck did not wear conventional headgear. He wore a matte-black, open-faced helmet with a polished, stainless-steel face mask that was sculpted to look like a grinning Japanese demon—an Oni—with a leering, tusked smile and short, blunt horns.

They crossed over into South Carolina and picked up another dozen riders when they passed through Florence, as that city's chapter of the MC joined the ride to honor one of its founders. Thirty more riders joined them as they rode through Columbia on U.S. 20. The procession also gained other followers, bikers from other MCs who were friends of the Blue Jocks, riding respectfully at the rear of the procession.

The cities and towns gave way to lush, cool forests of tall, proud trees as they rode through the southeastern tip of Sumter National Forest, a cathedral of green. They picked up a few dozen more riders as they moved through Spartanburg and Hendersonville. They were well over a hundred strong as they headed up I-26. The Asheville chapter, fifty strong, awaited them on the final ride into the Great Smoky Mountains National Park. Cool, green woods covered both sides of the road as the procession, swelled to close to two hundred riders, now approached the end of Nut Hill Road. A large sign, weatherworn and hand-painted, greeted the bikers as they approached. The sign said, WELCOME TO THE ROAD TO NOWHERE—A BROKEN PROMISE! 1943–?

During World War II, the Tennessee Valley Authority, under the auspices of the federal government, announced plans to construct a hydroelectric dam that would flood eleven thousand acres of land, much of it inhabited. In true bureaucratic fashion, the TVA purchased or seized almost sixty-eight thousand acres in Graham and Swain Counties, displacing more than thirteen hundred families in the name of the project, and progress. These families included women and children whose husbands, fathers, and sons were off fighting Fascists in distant lands. It also included elderly folk who had lived on their families' lands their entire lives. These families received no assistance from the government in relocating. Those who refused to sell their ancestral homesteads were forced off their land.

The government promised to repay the state for the loss of Highway 288, which would be flooded in the project, and to build a road and a bridge so that the families that had been driven from their lands could visit the more than twenty-eight cemeteries that would survive the flooding. Burial grounds where generations of their kin had been laid to rest were now isolated by the sweeping away of the land. Again, in true bureaucratic fashion, the promises were not entirely kept. The state received some funds to compensate for the lost highway, but the road to the grave sites was never completed. Six miles of road, a bridge, and a quarter mile of tunnel was all that came to fruition—a true road to nowhere. To the Blue Jocks, this place was hallowed ground.

A few miles down the unfinished road, the procession slowed and came to a stop at the yawning entrance to the massive tunnel. Everyone made a path, and the old Harley, with Heck and his mother riding, was allowed to move through. Heck shut off the engine and pulled off his demonic protective mask and helmet. He helped his mother out of the sidecar. He was wearing a kilt with the tartan of his and his mother's clan, the Sinclairs. Roadkill took a massive sword out of the sidecar after Elizabeth departed and slipped the strap of its sheath over his shoulder. The blade was a good two feet longer than him, so he had to angle the sheath.

Elizabeth pushed the few stray strands of white hair that had flowed free during the long ride out of her face and removed her sunglasses. She was an imposing woman. Age had given her features more character but had taken away none of her striking beauty. She shared the same color and intensity of eyes that Heck possessed—burning emeralds. A few inches shy of six feet, Elizabeth was taller than her son, and she knew how to use her height to add to her overall, regal presence. She turned to address the procession—an endless sea of chrome pipes and bars, black leather cuts and tartan kilts, beards and tattoos. The unruly crowd grew silent when Elizabeth raised an arm for attention.

"It would have meant a lot to Ale that you all came out for him," Elizabeth began. "He would have cussed you all like a sailor with a sore tooth, and then he would have teared up when he thought no one was looking. That was the kind of man Ailbert Mckee was. Strong, fierce, uncompromising. But with a good, kind, heart." Her voice faltered; the tears were close, but Elizabeth refused to let them take this moment from Ale. "He was a loving father to our son, Hector. He treated me as an equal, a wife, a friend, a counsel, and always, always like a lady." She laughed a little, using it to fight back the sadness. "Even a few times when I didn't deserve that." Laughter murmured through the crowd.

"Ale was always a gentleman. He was a wise president to the MC. He was unstoppable in battle, forgiving in peace. He lived by the code of the knight, of the samurai, of the outlaw. Ale always believed that if you lived outside the law, *especially* if you lived outside the law, you had to have honor." Elizabeth glanced briefly at Heck, who lowered his eyes.

"A very, very long time ago," Elizabeth said, "Ale and my father, Gordon, and the other founders—the originals of the Blue Jocks—came to this place, this Road to Nowhere. They dreamed their dreams here. For all the Blue Jocks, for all outlaw knights, this road is the beginning and the end. They swore the first initiation oaths of the MC here. Every prospect is made a member on the other side of that tunnel, every man who wears our cut passes through the underworld, endures the darkness, and comes out into the light."

Night was beginning to fall, and the sun was filtering through the dense foliage above and beyond the great dark tunnel, golden bursts of radiance through the green. At a slight nod from Elizabeth and a gesture from Roadkill, the two surviving original members of the Blue Jocks stepped forward. One of them was Glen Hume, Roadkill's father, and the other was Reggie Haney. The men were old, their faces carved thoroughly by life and experience, but they both looked as if they were made of fire-hardened hickory, worn but never worn out. Both still proudly wore their cuts and their clan kilts. The MC's piper, Jim Gilraine, a burly bear of a man with a beard that made him look like a dangerous Santa, also stepped forward and prepared his pipes to play. As sergeant at arms for the club, Roadkill moved to stand beside, and slightly behind, Heck. Roadkill could see the pain hiding behind Heck's lidded eyes. He nodded to his old friend, and Heck nodded back. Elizabeth continued, clutching the small wooden box to her breast.

"At the end of their time, each of our men comes here to rest," she said, her voice growing stronger, carried on the wind of the approaching night. "Today, we honor our fallen, we honor the best of us, what every man who calls himself a man should seek to emulate. Ale McKee was a standard, not just for the MC but for how we should conduct ourselves in this life. His like will never come this way again, and he will be missed—but never forgotten."

The tears were hot on Elizabeth's cheeks. She could hold them no longer. "Goodbye, my love," she whispered, clutching the cask tighter, her tears darkening the wood. "Goodbye, my heart."

Reggie and Glen stepped forward. Elizabeth kissed the cask and then handed it to the two men. As solemn as soldiers folding a flag, Glen and Reggie draped the box with the blue-and-black tartan of Ale's clan and then folded and placed his cut on top of that. Glen walked with the draped cask to Heck and offered it to him. Heck noticed that Glen's eyes were filled with tears, as he presented the box with his stepdad's ashes to him. Heck nodded and accepted the burden with open arms. Why did he feel nothing? No tears, no sadness . . . nothing. He had loved Ale, even if the past few years had tested that love. He should at least feel guilt . . . anything. There was nothing except a vague anxiety.

Heck turned to his mother, and they both walked solemnly toward the dark mouth of the tunnel. At the entrance, Roadkill met them; he wrestled to draw the massive sword, a Claymore that had belonged to Elizabeth's father and had been passed to Ale upon his death. Etched into the blade was the word *Bráithreachas*. It looked like the sword that was on Heck's tattoo and on every Blue Jock's colors.

"When you walk in darkness, you do not walk alone," Roadkill said, handing the massive blade to Heck, who cradled his stepfather's cask in one arm and held the Claymore in the other. He rested the seven-foot blade on his shoulder. The piper began the *urlar* of "Mackay's March" as Heck and Elizabeth entered into the blackness.

The first few yards in were muted by the fading light behind them. The walls of the tunnel were covered in a bizarre mosaic of graffiti art, name and date tags, slogans and symbols, all of it sliding and melting one into another, like a gigantic, winding, looping snake made of color and words. Heck remembered walking the tunnel years ago when he was initiated into the MC. He had heard all the stories about the tunnel and the markings on the walls since he was a kid.

"*They move*," Roadkill had said. "*The stuff on the wall . . . it's alive . . .*

I've heard stories about all the ghosts from those old family cemeteries; they're all in the tunnel. One guy walked in and never came out. . . ."

The strange part was that when Heck walked through the Tunnel to Nowhere six years ago, as a prospect, he had the strangest feeling he'd been here before, moved through these shadow-painted mazes, felt the images on either side of him shift and grow into almost blurry three-dimensional images of other places, lands governed by other laws, held back by a spray-painted fence of art and symbols.

The world fell into the void. Darkness swallowed Heck and Elizabeth as they continued to walk down the tunnel. The light behind them was a memory now, and the light ahead was a distant feeble splinter. The pipes had faded away, diluted by the heavy mantle of the tunnel, and, perhaps, by the darkness itself. The only sounds were their footsteps on the pavement and their breathing, echoing, muffled by the weight of the world pressing down on them.

"You're not scared, are you?" Elizabeth asked Heck, breaking the silence and making Heck jump just a bit. He couldn't see her face, but he knew she was smiling.

"No," he said, a little quicker and a bit more emphatically than he should have.

"Good," she said. "I guess there are advantages to being hungover, then."

"I'm not hungover," Heck said. "I'm still a little drunk."

"And driving a motorcycle in your condition?" Elizabeth said. "With your sainted mother on board? Hector Conall Sinclair!"

Heck laughed. "Didn't you use to tell me I was conceived while you were in the same condition on a bike going about a hundred miles an hour, 'sainted mother'?"

It was Elizabeth's turn to laugh. "And I stayed that way as much of your childhood as possible," she said. "Made for a better environment for all of us, don't you—"

A cold wind howled down the tunnel, swirling dead leaves, condom wrappers, and crushed red Solo cups. The wind carried voices on it—whispering, hissing, laughing, voices as dry as the dead leaves.

"*Sinnnnnnnnnnclaaaaaaiiiiirrrrrr*," they rasped.

Heck felt his mother's hand on his arm in the darkness; fumbling, he handed her the wooden cask with Ale's ashes. Both hands free, he hefted his grandfather and stepfather's blade from his shoulders. It occurred to him, suddenly, that it was his now. Ahead, two figures became visible, wreathed in a dirty, washed-out light. They were robed, like monks, their faces hidden in the darkness of their hoods. They came from either side of the dark tunnel and blocked Elizabeth and Heck's way.

"You see them?" Heck asked his mother, stepping between her and the figures.

"Yes," Elizabeth said. "I've seen them before. A long time ago, when you were a baby. They are not ghosts."

Heck dropped to stance, right foot behind his left foot, resting on the balls of his feet, as Ale and Granddad had taught him when he was only a boy. Heck had been a terror to teach swordplay to, because he was left-handed, and because he never quite got the gist of swinging at half speed.

"The boy's a blur of energy and destruction," Granddad had said, laughing as he nursed a nasty bruise on his arm from one of Heck's blows. "Once he gets some discipline in that skull of his, he'll be a damned terror with a blade."

He didn't have the room, with Elizabeth behind him, to safely build momentum with the monstrous sword by swinging it in an ever-faster figure-eight pattern, so he grabbed the dull, lower part of the blade between the smaller set of flaring quillons—a sort of secondary hilt—and rocked back to use the blade almost like a spear. He thrust at the figure on the left and shifted his stance to use his target as partial cover for the hooded form on the right. The blade passed through the chest of the hooded figure, as if Heck were stabbing smoke. As a child, he had heard the stories of Granddad using this same ancient blade to lay low a slavering, man-eating Windigo that had shrugged off gunfire and knives of mere steel. Fear tickled his stomach, and he was suddenly back in the desert with the laughing fire.

The figures advanced. The whispering voices seemed to be at Heck's ear, or maybe in his mind.

"Come back with us, Hector . . . come back . . . you belong . . ." they

hissed and advanced with clawed hands the color of dead fish. It felt as if someone were vomiting in Heck's skull. Scalding, putrid thoughts were filling up behind his eyes, trying to eat the light out of them.

A slender hand flashed out over Heck's shoulder, past his head. It was Elizabeth's. She brandished a palm-size stone; it looked like a river rock, smooth from wear. It was glowing with a clean, brilliant white light from within, which seemed to repel the filthy, wavering glow of the hooded apparitions. Heck's blade suddenly touched something solid as it thudded against the specter's chest.

"Piss off," she said. "You are not going to muck up the final ride of the finest man I ever knew, a man who kicked your sorry tails on more than one occasion, I might add. Now get."

The hooded figures withdrew from the now dangerous sword and the light of the rock. They stepped into the deepening shadows, their aura fading, extinguishing, as the daylight at the end of the tunnel became the color of pale ash.

"Bastards," Elizabeth said, and spat. The rock had stopped glowing, and she slipped it back into her jeans pocket. "Thank you for saving me, son," she said to Heck, and kissed him on the cheek. "Come along, we need to get through before the light's gone."

Elizabeth picked up her pace, striding, her man's ashes under her arm. Heck slung the Claymore back over his shoulder and hurried to catch up.

"What was that?" he asked.

"Cairn stone," she said. "Was your grandfather's. It's *Conair Cloch,* one of the Path Stones."

"Con-air, what?" Heck said.

"Never mind," Elizabeth said. "I'll explain when you're older."

"Yeah, yeah," Heck said. "I've heard that before. That's what you said about sex."

"Oh, you figured that one out," Elizabeth said. "Quit your bitchin'."

They stepped out of the far end of the tunnel into the final brilliant rays of day, shimmering across the dark waters of Fontana Lake. The choppy water split and refracted the sun's parting kiss to the earth, scattering the light.

"Beautiful," Elizabeth said. "Let's take him into the woods." Heck nodded. He leaned the Claymore against a low stone wall and followed his mother.

They moved deeper into the old forest. Ancient maples and birches, survivors of the TVA culling so long ago, surrounded them in the dimming light. The lake was ahead of them. Elizabeth lowered the cask to the damp, cool forest floor. She snapped the brass fasteners on the box and opened it. Within was a simple silver urn, held in place by a black velvet compartment. She lifted Ale's urn free of the cask and held it in her hands, held it close to her face. "You want to do it?" she asked, looking away from the urn and to her son. Heck stared at her for a moment too long.

"He'd want you to do it," Heck said. "Ale and me . . . not so much, not for a while."

"He loved you," Elizabeth said. "He'd do anything for you. You *were* his son, Hector, blood or no."

"Let's not do this," Heck said. "We're losing the light."

"That," Elizabeth said. "That right there . . . I swear, the two of you had so much in common. You're both the most stubborn, bullheaded men I've ever known. You and Ale put off saying 'I'm sorry' and saying 'I'm proud of you' for too damn long, and you both ended up regretting it."

"What do you want here?" Heck asked. "I know . . . I know . . . I missed him by twelve fucking hours, and I know nothing will ever give me those hours back. You want some big damn cathartic scene? Well, that ain't how either of you raised me. Ale would have told you and me both to cowboy the hell up and get on getting on. I'll make my peace with this, with him, in my own damn good time, Mom. Now drop it. Please."

Elizabeth opened her mouth to say something, then thought better of it and nodded. "Then walk with me while I send him along," she said. "We used to joke that we'd mix him up with some good pot and smoke him."

"Now, *that* sounds like Ale," Heck said with a chuckle. "That would be some bitter-ass smoke."

"Yes," Elizabeth said softly, as she offered a pinch of her lover's ashes to the night wind. The wind carried them toward the water. "But I think it might surprise you how sweet it would be, too."

The return trip through the dark tunnel was uneventful. The specters had all fled. When Elizabeth and Heck emerged back where the Jocks and the other MCs were waiting, cycle headlights burning to fill the edge of the tunnel with light, a raucous cheer went up, and Jim the piper began to play "The Warrior's Code," by the Dropkick Murphys.

"I think if Ale was here right now," Heck said, jumping up onto the sidecar of the Harley and shouting above the hoots, whistles, and music, "he'd say, 'Let's go get shit-faced!'" The crowd erupted in howls that would have made Viking raiders piss themselves. The wake was on.

. . .

The Ashville chapter of the Blue Jocks hosted Ale's wake at the home of the chapter president, an affable fellow named Muskrat, who had done fifteen years for manslaughter. The party spilled out of the hundred-year-old farmhouse that Muskrat, his wife, and kids called home and onto the twenty acres of land that had been in his family for well over a century. The number of attendees swelled as word of the party got around, to more than two hundred MC members, prospects, ol' ladies and sweetbutts, hang-arounds, and supporters.

Bonfires and campfires littered the huge yard. The night air was full of the revving of motorcycle engines, laughter, deep-bass bellows, the murmuring river of mass conversations and music—everything from Johnny Cash to Cage the Elephant. The Eagles' "Desperado" played, and couples danced close, hands on hips or in pockets, while Heck nursed his third Budweiser, standing on the porch of the farmhouse. The porch was illuminated by strings of plastic Halloween skulls of every color. Heck sat against the rail and took a draw off his bottle.

He watched a skinny prospect from the Spartanburg chapter spin and flip flaming devil sticks for a crowd, leaving glowing trails in the wake of the booze-doused sticks. Near one of the ubiquitous keg stations, a brother was on hands and knees puking while several Jocks and their ol' ladies laughed uproariously at the spectacle. That very cute redhead in the corset, tutu, and knee-high boots walked by for the third time, glancing not so shyly at Heck and giving him an inviting smile. Somewhere, a guy was calling out for the immediate attention of someone apparently named Juanetta.

Roadkill walked up the steps, weaving a bit, and leaned on the rail to steady himself. "Well, ain't you a mopey bastard," he said. "All this in front of you and you're gonna sit there . . . I don't know . . . having . . . thoughts, or something."

"Just enjoying the show," Heck said. "Had a few?" he asked, a smile tugging at the edges of his face.

Roadkill drained his blue plastic Solo cup and nodded. "Indeed, my good man," he said. "There are some of the Ashville club's mamas here. I intend to drink until I look good to them. There's plenty of sweetbutts to go around, man. Don't want the mother chapter's future president pissing off the troops 'cause he doesn't like their stock of clubhouse girls."

"Thanks, bro," Heck said. "Not tonight. Not feeling it. 'Sides, I am not going to be the prez of the MC."

"That remains to be seen," Elizabeth said, walking up to her son and Roadkill. Heck was surprised to see her. She had been holding court since they arrived, talking and drinking with the presidents of the seven other Jock chapters here, as well as reminiscing with Glen and Reggie. "Walk with me, Hector."

Roadkill slapped him on the back as he descended the porch stairs and fell in step beside his mother. The Eagles had been replaced with Led Zeppelin's "When the Levee Breaks."

Elizabeth led him away from the party toward a dark, relatively quiet section of field. "We have a new problem," she said.

"Who's 'we'?" Heck said.

"The club," Elizabeth said, "me, you—especially you."

"What?" Heck asked.

"Do you know who Cherokee Mike is?" Elizabeth asked. Heck thought a moment and then nodded.

"Yeah," Heck said. "Mike Locklear. He's a Nomad. Used to be with the Charlotte chapter. I seem to recall he was an asshole."

"He is," Elizabeth said. "The worst kind—a dangerous and smart asshole. It's not widely known, but he went Nomad to avoid getting kicked out of the MC entirely. He just got out of Central Prison, and he's looking to stake a claim to be president of the mother chapter. He wants Ale's job, Heck. He wants your job."

"It's not my damn job, Mom!" Heck said, throwing his hands up in the air. "Regardless of what you and Ale wanted. Maybe Mike will do good by the MC."

"He won't," Elizabeth said. "He'll destroy it, Hector. Cherokee Mike wants to take the Blue Jocks into the meth trade. He was opposed to the club doing bounty hunting to pay the bills. He's always wanted the club to get into drugs. He wanted to make deals with the creatures out there we hunt. Not stop them from hurting people, not destroy them, use them to advance our position—his position. It was Ale that kept him in check. Now Ale's gone, and Mike figures it's his time."

"Well, if he's such an asshole he won't get voted in," Heck said. "He'd have to be accepted back by the mother chapter, by Wilmington, then he'd have to get enough support to—"

"You don't understand," Elizabeth interrupted. "Mike is no outlaw; he's got no code, no honor. He doesn't care about traditions. He's a gangster, a thug, and he will wreck anything that gets between him and what he wants, and he wants the MC. You can stop him, but there's not much time."

Heck shook his head. "Are you kidding me, Mom! Is this just some new bullshit way to drag me into Ale's chair? You want me to go fuck up Cherokee Mike and tell him to leave Wilmington alone, I will. But don't pull some mind-fuck on me, trying to get what you want."

"He's already threatened Glen," Elizabeth said softly. "Said something might happen to the garage and to Jethro if he doesn't get patched back in. Reggie, too. He's making moves, buying or scaring people. He will burn down everything your grandfather and Ale built. You try to go after him now, you will wind up dead, or in prison, which is exactly what Cherokee Mike wants."

Heck looked up and let the air out of his lungs with a *whoosh*, running his hands through his tangled hair. The stars burned above with ancient, cold fire; each was a story already told and ended. He saw Ale's face, weathered and smiling—as much as Ale ever did smile. The memory, the mental snapshot, came from the moment he first knew this man was his father, sure and true—balls to bones. He had been three, and it was one of his first memories, one of his best. He turned back to his mother, his green eyes bright and cool. "Okay," he said. "I'll do it. I'll be president."

Elizabeth sighed. She hugged her son for as long as he would allow it. "Now," she said, "you need to be initiated."

"I am, Mom," Heck said. "At sixteen, remember?"

"No," she said. "This is different. A secret only the originals know. The Blue Jocks are part of something much older, much bigger than us. And it is an unspoken law that every president of the MC must be a member of both societies to lead."

"Are you serious?" Heck said. "What, are we hooked up with the fucking Shriners or something, Mom? In case you forgot, the Blue Jocks hunt monsters, Mom . . . *real* fucking monsters. It can't be more secret or weird than that. If this shit with Cherokee Mike is so serious, I don't have the time or the inclination to go learn a bunch of fucking secret handshakes and how to drive a clown car."

Heck felt his mother's full, angry regard. He stopped. Even as a grown man, having seen combat and worse, his mother's disapproving gaze held him and stilled him.

"I love you, Hector," she said. "But you really do need to learn when to shut the hell up and listen. Unless we do this the right way, the traditional way, we will be just as guilty of destroying the Blue Jocks as Cherokee Mike. We have to be better. You have to be better. I know you can do it. I know, and Ale knew. It fell to him, as your father, to make you his squire. That's why he didn't want you to go. That's why he was so angry and disappointed. He wanted you to stay and learn from him."

"Why didn't he say that, Mom? Jesus!" Heck said. "If he had only—"

"He tried," she said. "You were too angry to hear him, and the old pigheaded bastard was too prideful to admit how much your rejection hurt him. He tried the best a man like him can. This was a secret, Hector. More so than the things the MC hunt when they aren't bounty hunting. The biggest secret you will ever discover in your lifetime, and a huge responsibility. It can't just be blurted out."

Heck paced in a circle, shaking his head. He sighed and rubbed his hair. "What do I do?"

Elizabeth produced a sealed envelope from her jacket pocket. She handed it to Heck. "Do you remember Jimmie Aussapile?"

"The trucker?" Heck said. "Yeah. He used to come by when I was little. He and Ale were tight. I figured he'd be here today."

"You used to call him Uncle Jimmie," Elizabeth said. "Jimmie's on the road, otherwise he would have been. I need you to find him. Give him this. Offer yourself to him as a squire of the Brethren."

"The what of the what?" Heck said.

"It's all I can tell you," Elizabeth said. "Once you offer and he accepts you, then Jimmie can explain more."

"How long does this take?" Heck asked. "You're making it sound like we don't have a ton of time before Mike makes a move."

"Months, years sometimes," Elizabeth said. "As long as it takes."

"Years . . ." Heck repeated. "Great. What about—"

"I'll handle Mike," Elizabeth said. "I'll stall him, slow him down. Don't you worry."

"You told me this guy wants me dead," Heck said. "He can't think too much of you, either, Mom."

Elizabeth hugged her son again and kissed him on the cheek. "I'll be fine. I'm a cunning old bitch. Go. You got a long ride ahead of you. Reggie said he'll get me home."

Heck started to walk toward Ale's hog.

Elizabeth's voice stopped him. "He was so proud of you," she said. "Proud to bust. Proud you were a marine. Proud you were his son. Proud of the man you had become. I wanted you to hear it this time."

Heck didn't look back; he started walking again.

Lovina Marcou parked her car a block away from the crime scene. She unzipped her leather carry bag and checked to make sure she had what she needed: her picks and pry bar, the compact UV wand, fingerprint lift tape, various powders and sprays to draw out prints from different surfaces, the Canon EOS 5D Mark III digital forensic camera. She always got nervous using the camera. It cost more than a month's pay, and, given what she was doing tonight, it would be hard to explain if anything happened to it.

She also had notebooks, measuring tape, a ruler, a pen-size Maglite flashlight, a voice recorder, and a box of latex gloves. Finally, she pushed aside her leather jacket, pulled her duty sidearm—a Glock 22—out of her shoulder rig, pulled back the slide to chamber a .40 round into the pipe, and replaced it in her holster. She exited the car, hefted her bag onto her shoulder, and looked around. It was a quiet, blue-collar neighborhood on a late Monday morning; the place was practically deserted. She locked the car and headed east toward Dewey Rears's apartment.

It was a short walk down Askew Street. Lovina walked past neat, well-trimmed lawns with fishing boats on trailers and unhitched campers waiting in wide, two-car driveways. It had warmed up and birds were chirping. The sun was warm on her face and arms. She turned left onto Beech Street and saw the apartments ahead on the left, just past a small building that looked as if it had once been a market or maybe a laundromat but announced that it was presently a barbershop.

Dewey Rears's apartment complex was two single-story brick buildings subdivided into five apartments each. There was a small island of cement next to each front door, a larger pad at the back. Large, gray HVAC units crouched like squat, ugly gargoyles next to each rear screen door, humming as they spewed out heat. The five units faced each other across a grass courtyard with two concrete sidewalks, one for each building. The grass hadn't been cut in a while and swayed slightly in the weak, humid wind.

Lovina knew this kind of complex very well. She saw the plastic kiddie pools, the aluminum chairs with nylon webbing, and the covered grills. By six tonight, the courtyard would be alive with kids playing and adults gossiping and getting drunk after a long day of backbreaking, soul-crushing work. She had grown up somewhere very much like this.

She also knew that at least a few little old ladies and disability dukes and duchesses were peeking through shades all day long, snooping. She didn't have the police report, and the address she had from the hit on the prints didn't include an apartment number. There were ten mailboxes mounted in two rows of five on aluminum posts at the edge of the virtually empty parking lot, but walking up to them would invite the attention of the apartment's invisible sentinels. There really wasn't a good way to do this. She had chosen late morning because she'd have the least exposure. Now it was time to just put up or shut up.

She pulled her badge lanyard out of her blouse, letting her CID badge and ID hang out around her neck, walked briskly into the courtyard, and saw the door marked with yellow crime-scene tape with a warrant taped up, third on the left side of the courtyard. She walked up to the door and set her leather bag down. Calmly, and as professionally as possible, she took out her small leather case and selected the proper pick and bar that she needed to open the deadbolt above the doorknob. She worked quickly as she could, blocking as much of what she was doing from view. The bolt was old and a little sticky, but Lovina had it open in less than twenty seconds.

"What chu doin' there, hunny?" a voice behind her asked. Lovina looked over her shoulder. There was a skinny little black woman standing on the sidewalk behind her, dressed in a pair of turquoise capri pants and a T-shirt that said "Grandchildren Are Angels from Heaven" in bright red, blue, and yellow letters. The T-shirt fell to just above the old lady's knees. She had on tortoiseshell sunglasses.

Lovina turned fully so the old lady could see her badge. She palmed the pick and bar. "Morning, ma'am," she said as blandly as she could. "Just getting some more pictures."

"Well, you ass me," the old lady said, "dat boy had sumthin wrong wi' him. He always talkin' 'bout crazy shit."

"Did you call the police?" Lovina asked as she opened the door.

The old lady shook her head as she shuffled forward to try to peek inside the sealed apartment. "Naw, it was crazy old Miss-ess Chalfont down the way," she said. "She heard all the screaming and commotion and called y'all."

Lovina nodded and slipped inside the door. "Well, thank you, ma'am," she said.

The old lady shuffled forward. "Been goin' to hell round here for a spell," she said. "All those damn kids wandering around, most of them actin' like they trippin'. I think that boy in there be some kinda of pet-o-phile," she said. "All them kids beating on his door, day and night."

"He had kids coming by to see him?" Lovina said. She had ducked under the tape barrier across the frame and had been slowly pulling the door closed on the old lady, but this stopped her cold. "Like coming in and out? You think he was dealing?"

"If'n he was, he sucked at it," the old lady said. "Heard them knocking and calling for him to let them in all hours. He must'a lost customers like that. Did y'all find drugs in there? Never smelled like he was cookin'."

"I can't discuss an ongoing investigation, ma'am," Lovina said, almost automatically. It was standard copspeak for when you didn't want to give away how much or how little you had, especially to gossips or reporters. "Well, I best be getting to work, now—"

"Where your car at?" the old lady interrupted. Lovina smiled her best civil-servant smile and shut the door on the old biddy. This was not how she had wanted to enter the scene, but she was on a clock, and she didn't have the option of coming in with her mind clear and quiet.

Dewey Rears's apartment was dark and still relatively cool in the gathering heat of late morning. It looked like a college student's flop—stained Goodwill couch and a leather recliner that didn't match the couch, with bandages of duct tape on it where the upholstery had split.

A folding metal chair was on its side on the floor; a small numbered placard sat next to it, a photographic marker for the forensic photographer. An overturned Pabst Blue Ribbon beer can, next to the flipped chair, was marked with another numbered card.

Something was turning in Lovina's head as she opened her bag and slipped on a pair of latex gloves—that pinprick of recognition, like the first glowing embers of building a fire. She needed to feed it and attend to it. . . . There was something here that she had latched on to. Now she just needed to let it grow in her awareness without smothering it to death. Move on.

There was a huge wall-mounted flat screen, several game consoles, and stacks of video games, cables, and controllers on the floor between the recliner and the TV. Crushed cans of energy drink and Mc-food wrappers were like islands in the sea of worn, dirty carpet. A *Star Wars: Episode VII* poster was taped to the cracked plaster wall behind the couch with yellowed Scotch tape. Around it were faded newspaper clippings and stock photos of constellations and UFOs. The place smelled of stale tobacco, with a hint of incense and pot beneath the smell. She felt an immediate connection to Dewey Rears—this was like walking into her younger brother Romero's college apartment. She couldn't help smiling at the revelation. And then her mind turned to Delephine, as it always did when she thought of family, and the smile fell away. Clock was ticking, time to work the scene.

Besides the living room dominated by the TV and the video games, there was a kitchen and a bedroom and bath. Lovina began in the bedroom. It was a filthy, stinky mess. Soiled underwear was on the floor, along with dirty clothing and balled-up socks. A teetering mountain of paperbacks, mostly SF and Fantasy, rested on the bed table with his reading glasses and his e-reader tablet. Under the bed were sour-smelling towels crusty with dried semen and boxes of porno magazines and DVDs. Black plastic trash bags were taped to the windows to keep the sun out. Rears's suitcase was jammed in the corner of his closet. His clean socks and shorts were in their drawers.

In the bathroom, Rears's deodorant, toothbrush, and cologne were all where they should be. He had blood-pressure meds beside the sink. The bottle was mostly full. Lovina looked up at herself for a moment in the mirror. She was a dark-complected black woman with strong, angular cheekbones and a haughty, almost aristocratic nose. Her eyes were hazel, the green in them flecked with gold, and they stood out in bright, stark contrast to her skin. Her hair was long, straight, and black. She favored straight bangs, with her hair falling to her shoulders. Today, she had it in a ponytail under a New Orleans Saints baseball cap. She looked damned good for thirty-five.

Dewey hadn't planned on leaving, Lovina thought as she exited the bathroom. He had either been taken or had left his home fully expecting to come back. There were also no signs of any drug possession or manufacture. The pot smell was faint and old. Lovina doubted that he had run out to sell some dope and run into a rip-off, or that someone knew he was holding and came to get the stash. Far from it—nothing about the condition of either door indicated forced entry into the house. Dewey Rears had either allowed his assailants in and they took him or he had left his home willingly.

There were a few signs that there had been some kind of commotion. The overturned chair and the Pabst beer can . . . She wished she could get hold of the police report. Maybe she could try to scam the local PD, but, given the politics and the territorial pissing contests of Louisiana law enforcement, it wasn't likely.

In a corner of the kitchen, past the sink filled with dirty dishes and the overflowing trash can, was a small breakfast nook that Rears had converted into a computer station and office of sorts. There was a computer hutch, an old, battered gray file cabinet covered in small magnetic tags each possessing a word, and a swivel computer chair that was patched with more duct tape than the chair in the living room. The hutch and the small cork bulletin board on the wall of the small alcove opposite the computer were covered with news and magazine articles. Many of the articles had Rears's name as the byline. They were all paranormal magazines like *Fortean Times* and *UFO Magazine*. On the ledge of the nook's single window was a small fish bowl with a beautiful blue betta fish swimming about, its regal tail whipping, as it circled a small yellow plastic pineapple house at the bottom of the bowl. She picked up the yellow plastic container of food and sprinkled a few flakes into the bowl.

The computer tower was gone from the hutch desk, and there was another forensic number placard beside where it had sat. There was no external drive, no USB drives; only the keyboard and the mouse remained. Lovina sighed and then began to look at the piles of paper on the desk.

Suddenly, she stopped and walked over to the fridge. She opened it. There was no beer inside, no PBR cans like the one found spilled on the living-room floor by the overturned folding chair—not the big leather recliner but the folding metal chair. She searched the overflowing trash can as well. No beer-can empties. The fire caught in her mind: Dewey had company when his visitors came calling. So the local PD was looking for two missing people, or a material witness had managed to flee the crime scene, or maybe his guest was part of the abduction.

She went back to the office nook. The papers on the desktop were old receipts and illegible scribbled notes. One note was a series of numbers: *"39.8282° N, 98.5795° W."* Scribbled after it was *"door to the Four Houses. Wyandotte County location 'reflection'? but not accurate. Don't think GPS works there. U.S. 36 and 281—Conspiracy of the highway commission? Numerology? Any connection to Metropolis-Utopia??? Ask Ballard?"* Lovina shook her head and put the paper back on the desk. *Who the hell was Ballard?*

Another crumpled piece of paper was a printout of a photo from the computer. It was blurry, grainy. It looked as if it was taken inside a forest in bright daylight. There were dark smudges, silhouettes of people with no features, just dark outlines, and behind them loomed a towering blur of shadow—arms, maybe—with massive antlers fracturing out from what looked like the head. In the corner of the picture, in Dewey's spidery scrawl, was *"Patient zero? Did this one start the whole thing? Meme? Viral?"* She dropped the wrinkled picture back on the desk. You can take only so much crazy.

Lovina opened the top drawer of Dewey's file cabinet and froze. Shawn Ruth Thibodeaux was staring back at her—the subject of a photo lying on top of the stack of files in the drawer. Lovina's heart jumped in her chest. The picture was grainy, and there was a date and time stamp in the corner of it, most likely a capture from a handheld video camera. The girl in the picture had black hair and pale skin. She was looking down, and she seemed to be right on top of the person taking the picture, almost charging them. There was another person in the picture beside her, but all that was visible was part of a clawing hand and the corner of a hooded sweatshirt. She lifted the photo out of the cabinet. It was Shawn Ruth.

The front door of the apartment crashed open, and two uniformed cops from the Tallulah PD entered, sweeping the room. When the fatter one saw Lovina standing in the kitchen, he leveled his 9-mm pistol at her, as he panted and sweated.

"Hands on your head! Now!" he shouted. Lovina complied with a sigh. She held on to the photo as she put her hands on her head. "Police!" the other cop, who Lovina didn't think looked old enough to shave, let alone be a cop, shouted.

"Yes," Lovina said. "I am."

. . .

"I don't give a damn if you brought Huey-fucking-Long back from the dead, lady!" Detective Sergeant Louis Pendalton bellowed across the interrogation table from Lovina. "Or what fucking letters are on your fucking shield—CID? BFD!" Pendalton slammed his bony fist down on the tabletop, making the ashtray, packs of Marlboros, Styrofoam cups of coffee, and files and paperwork all jump and bounce from the force of his anger. Lovina didn't blink, didn't jump. She stared at Pendalton like a cobra eyeing up a mongoose. "You come up here from high—and mighty—falootin' Noo Awle eens, and you proceed to shit all over one of my crime scenes? Your narrow little ass is goin' in the tank, Foxy Brown!"

"Sergeant, like I've been trying to explain to you and the officers who brought me down here," Lovina said, "I'm investigating a disappearance related to Dewey Rears. One of the unknown latent prints you got off his front door ran through the state lab, and AFIS rang the bell on a missing-child case of mine." Lovina held up the photo of Shawn Ruth Thibodeaux that she had found in Rears's file cabinet.

Pendalton was a short man, wiry, with huge, hairy forearms, who seemed to exude menace and irritation. He shook his head. "And why didn't you report in to me, file a supplemental? Make a fucking phone call? Nah, this is some kinda bullsheet ya'll DCI bastards is playing at. Well, I ain't playing."

Lovina noticed the diamond pinkie ring and the Rolex on Pendalton, and she knew how to play this. "Very well," she said. Her voice was slate, her eyes locking with the sergeant's, unblinking, anger simmering in them, but controlled, disciplined anger. "Let's both stop playing. I am on a DCI investigation at the request of your Division of Internal Affairs. I don't have to tell you jack shit about it, you backwater cracker cop. You really want to start pissing on an investigation of departmental corruption and a missing snitch, well, then, that's just fine by me. Puts you at the top of everyone's list, Sarge."

"Now wait one goddamned minute," Pendalton said, snapping the switch that killed the recorders and the video camera in the surveillance room. "Nobody said nuthin' about gettin' up IAD's ass . . ."

Before Pendalton could start sweating too much, there was a knock at the door. Lovina was both relieved and distressed to see her boss, State Police Lieutenant Leo Roselle, walk through the door. Roselle looked the way he always did, always had since Lovina met him, back in 2003, when she started with the New Orleans PD. Roselle was about one generation out of the bayou, a hirsute man with a single bushy unibrow, an olive complexion, and thinning hair. He always wore white seersucker suits and neckties in colors and patterns as vivid as possible. Despite his flamboyant attire, Roselle always looked stern and a little sad. Lovina went to work for Roselle about two years ago, at the state police's Department of Criminal Investigation.

"There a reason you talking to my investigator like she's some skell, Sergeant?" Roselle said as he entered. Another man, black, in a blue PD windbreaker, with a broad face, a shaved head, and a massive build, followed him into the interrogation room. "Maybe you care to explain all this to your chief while you're explaining it to me?"

Pendalton opened his mouth and then closed it. He jumped to his feet, obviously ready to make one last stand. "Your invest-te-gator here done broke into a crime scene and contaminated it. Now she's talking about some kind of IAD-DCI investigation bullsheet!" Pendalton looked to his chief, and the chief turned to Roselle.

"That true, Leo?" the chief asked. "You and IAD running a game in my house?"

Roselle looked blandly at Lovina, who remained as unknowable as the Sphinx. He turned back to the chief. "Now, Jim," Roselle said, "you know the drill. I can't discuss an ongoing investigation with the principals. I wish I could. . . ."

. . .

Lovina and Roselle walked out of the Tallulah Police Station on Green Street into the cool darkness of an early spring night. Roselle opened the passenger door for Lovina without a word, and the investigator got in. Roselle shut the door and climbed behind the wheel of his dark blue, unmarked State Police Chevy Tahoe. He started the car up. "Seven Spanish Angels," by Willie Nelson, played softly behind the squawk of his police radio. They had driven out of the department parking lot before Roselle spoke.

"You want to tell me what the hell you're doing up here, Lovina?" he said. Softly. "And do not feed me a line of happy horseshit about some secret IAD probe, please."

"Pendalton is on the take," Lovina said. "I can smell it on him."

"And catching cops who contribute to the 'rainy day fund' is not your current job," Roselle said. "Hell, you bust all the cops on the take in this state, from parish sheriffs to state police, you wouldn't have any cops left. 'Cept me and you, of course," he added in his usual deadpan.

Lovina couldn't help smiling. The little envelope that you got from your ward captain once a month, the one no one ever talked about but everyone took. It was part of the job. You didn't take it you might be a rat, might find yourself breathless from running down a skell in a pitch-dark alleyway and know no backup was coming anytime soon. Who the hell was going to risk not coming home to their family for a fucking rat? That being said, in Louisiana law enforcement there was bent and then there was crooked. Lovina had worked as hard as she could to stay clean and still do her job. It was a dance, one Roselle had been doing when Lovina was just a child.

"Truth," Roselle said. "No *conneries, oui*? This is one of your cold cases, isn't it? One of your missing children?"

Lovina nodded. "Yes," she said. "Shawn Ruth Thibodeaux, Mary Nell Labarre, and Pierre Markham. Missing since 2011 from Tremé. The oldest, Pierre, was sixteen."

"Storyville," Roselle said as he turned the SUV onto North Ceader Street. There was a cluster of liquor stores, check-cashing fronts, and fast-food restaurants. "Lovina, a sixteen-year-old-boy and two girls going missing in the projects isn't exactly news. You know that."

"Yes," she said. "I grew up there. I know. These kids don't fit that profile. No gangs, no drugs, stayed in school. Good families. Someone gobbled those kids up, Leo."

"So what brings you across the state five years after the fact?" Roselle asked. "And has me lying to a very good and well-respected friend of mine who is chief of a whole police department?"

"These kids left a friend's house a little after nine," Lovina said. "They had been goofing around on the computer, posting stupid teenage nonsense on Myspace, Instagram . . . nothing dangerous, nothing sent to anyone we ever traced as dangerous. In the three blocks from their friend's house to Shawn Ruth's mother's house, they vanished off the face of the earth. No trace until a few days ago. A partial latent print found on the inside of Dewey Rears's front door hit for enough points of comparison to get a notification sent to me."

"And how wide a net did you set for your comparison parameters?" Roselle said. He sighed as he pulled into the parking lot of a Dunkin' Donuts.

"Wider than normal," Lovina said. "But close enough to warrant a follow-up—"

"In your opinion," Roselle interrupted.

Lovina nodded. "Yes," she said. "In my opinion."

Roselle watched two teenage boys wander into the brightly lit coffee shop. He scanned them the way street cops do—a preemptive assessment, looking for threat and weakness. Lovina noticed two more kids, younger, both wearing hooded sweatshirts, looking like urban monks. They stood side by side near the pay phone, apparently waiting for someone, looking out in her direction, their faces shrouded in shadow. "Lovina, I know we had an agreement when you took this job," Roselle said, "and I know that agreement was the only reason you came to CID. But your sister is dead. Your family buried her. You found the people responsible, and you . . . you saw justice done to them. You have got to come to an understanding that *that* has nothing to do with *this*. . . ."

"I know that," Lovina said, her voice rising slightly. "I've seen enough shrinks and priests, drank myself blind enough times. I know very, very well that *this* has nothing to do with *that*."

"You are chasing ghosts, and you're neglecting living victims to do it," Roselle said.

"Those kids are still out there," Lovina said. "Their families haven't had a decent night's sleep for five years, Leo. Don't they deserve to know?"

Roselle sighed again. Lovina knew it was as close as he ever got to angry or frustrated. The man was always calm, placid water, no matter what was going on around him, or beneath that water.

"You've been a cop a long time," he said. "You ought to know by now you cannot save the world. It's just not that kind of world, Lovina. As your boss, I'm telling you to pack it up. I want you back at work. You have a desk full of active cases. Take the next few days off and get your head screwed on tight. Be back at work Monday. I'll see what I can do to shake loose any forensic findings the state lab gets on this and get them to you. But no more freelancing. Are we clear?"

"Rears's computer?" Lovina asked. "Who at the lab's working it?"

"Are we clear?" Roselle repeated.

"Yes," she said. "We are clear. Thank you, Leo." Roselle took a photo out of a plain manila folder and handed it to Lovina. It was the video capture of Shawn Ruth Thibodeaux reaching out toward the camera, her eyes hooded, looking down as she clawed the air. Lovina took the photo. "Thank you," she said again, smiling.

"Don't thank me too much," Roselle said. "I'm writing up those days off as a disciplinary suspension without pay. It goes in your jacket. That makes me square with the chief for lying to him."

"Has anyone ever told you you're a very good man, Leo?" Lovina said, putting the photo away in her bag.

"I'm not," Roselle said, blandly. "Just a sight better than what else is out there."

Roselle dropped Lovina off at her car. "See you Monday," he said. He waited until she unlocked the car and started it before he nodded and drove into the night. Lovina slipped her phone out of her jacket and punched a number from the phone's memory. Russell Lime answered on the third ring.

"Hey Love-e-ly Lo-vina," the senior technical director at the Louisiana State Police Crime Laboratory said. "To what do I owe the pleasure, *chère*?"

"Russ, you could charm the scales off a snake," Lovina said with a smile. "I wish it was pleasure, but it's business. You have a sec?"

"Course, *chère*, what you need?"

"I'm helping the local PD with that missing persons up in Tallulah," Lovina said. "I need this Rears guy's LUDs from his phone and a complete copy of everything from his computer and drives."

"He does have some weird stuff on his drives," Lime said. "All encrypted. He's got some kind of map program linked with GPS to hyperlinks of disappearances all over the country and going back twenty-odd years. Got it hooked up to some kind of cell-phone tracking program, and social-media archives, too. Very weird. It looks like he's been going to the sites of the disappearances and GPS logging them, tracking the coordinates."

"Really?" Lovina said. She suddenly flashed to something back at Rears's apartment. "I need all of that, everything."

Lovina heard the *tack-tack* of a computer keyboard as Lime spoke. "Sure enough," he said. "May take a day or two to get together all the—"

"I'm sorry to rush you, Russ," Lovina said, interrupting Lime as she started her car. She saw movement off to her right. Two kids shuffled along the sidewalk on the other side of the street, walking side by side. They both stopped in unison and turned toward her car when her headlights popped on. Both had on skater hoodies like the kids at the coffee shop. For a second, Lovina thought they might be the same kids. She pulled away from the curb and headed toward Dewey Rears's apartment. "But I need it tomorrow. I'll meet you at the lab in the morning. Case just got hot, and I don't want it getting cold on us. I'll buy the coffee and doughnuts."

The computer keyboard kept tapping over the phone. "Okay," Lime said, sounding slightly distracted. The tapping paused. "Uh, your name isn't listed as the investigator anywhere on here, *chère*."

"I know," Lovina said. "Like I said, everything is moving fast. I just spoke with Roselle a few minutes ago." She let the implication hang. She turned into the now mostly full parking lot in front of the row apartments. Her tires crunched under the loose gravel as she parked in an empty spot, killed her lights, and turned off the engine. "That's why I'm calling, Russ; I'm kind of already behind the eight ball on this one."

"No worries, *chère*," Lime said, the keyboard clacking away again. "I'll hold you to those doughnuts. See you about ten?"

"Sounds good. Thanks. Good night," Lovina said, and hung up. She put the phone in her pocket, grabbed her flashlight and her lock picks, and headed up the dark walk as quietly as she could. Half the apartments didn't have porch lights on, so she walked between bridges of light and wells of darkness until she came to Rears's apartment door once again.

She heard the sound of TVs through open windows, babies crying, and, under it all, the hum of cicadas. As she worked the lock in the darkness, by feel alone, Lovina remembered that her pops told her when she was little that the cicadas stopped their song before midnight, because that time was the height of the nocturnal predators' hunting hours, and they stilled to avoid the hunters devouring them. She thought she heard a shuffling sound in the darkness.

The lock popped open, again, and Lovina entered, keeping the lights off. She shut the door and snapped on her flashlight. The circle of light from the beam caught the overturned chair and the beer-stained carpet, the empty can. The apartment air was stale and warm in the darkness, almost claustrophobic.

She swung the beam in the direction of the kitchen and the office nook. She moved toward the desk, still cluttered with papers. She searched through the scraps, pushing aside the shadow-smudged photo she had seen earlier, until she found the note with the cryptic reference to Four Houses and the map coordinates. She thought for a moment about disturbing the scene and how angry Roselle would be at what she was doing. Even his calm must have limits. She did the equation in her mind, instantly, debating taking a photo of the scrap of paper with her cellphone camera versus just taking the scrap of paper. Every second she was here increased her chances of getting caught again. She tucked the note in her pocket.

There was a knock at the door. Lovina froze. If it were cops, they would be kicking the door in, as they did earlier. No, this was someone else. For a second, she thought maybe Roselle had tailed her. She'd rather get busted again. Maybe the guest who had been in the overturned chair had come back? The digital clock on the microwave said it was 9:36, too late for a casual visit for most folks. Lovina walked to the door, unlocked it, and opened it.

Two children were standing on the stoop, both boys. It took Lovina a second to realize that they were the two boys who had been loitering outside the Dunkin' Donuts. Both looked to be twelve or thirteen years old. Skinny, very pale, and both had on oversized pullover sweatshirts with hoods. Both boys had their hoods up, obscuring most of their faces in cloth and shadow. One had a black hoodie with the Misfits' skull logo on its chest; the other kid's was gray, with the Ron Jon Surf Shop logo over the breast. They both wore baggy jeans and Converse sneakers.

"Let us in," Misfit Hoodie said. "Please."

Lovina was speechless. The old lady had said kids had been coming around to see Rears, and these two may have been just neighborhood kids looking to score a nickel bag, but Lovina was having trouble thinking. The moment she saw the two boys, she had been filled with a horrible dread, a fear worse than anything she could imagine. It stunned her with its fierce, sudden intensity.

"Let us in," Gray Hoodie said. "Please, we need to come in."

The fear in her was worse than the most terrifying moments in the war—the first time she was fired on and had to return fire—worse than her years on the streets as a cop, sprinting breathless through dark alleys waiting for a shadow to pop out in front of her with a gun or a knife, worse than the fear of searching the ruins of New Orleans for Delphine after the storm. Worse than finding her, finally. Lovina felt drunk on fear, numb from it. Her instincts screamed like a scalded cat to pull her gun and fire or run. But her legs, her arms, were stone.

"What do you want?" she managed to say. Even her voice was trembling. What the hell was wrong with her?

"We want to come inside," Misfits Hoodie said again. "Let us in." The voice was monotone, like someone too drugged to feel anything or too insane to register emotion. Lovina had heard the tone many times before, in the back of squad cars, in emergency rooms and psychiatric wards.

"Let us in," the boys said in fluid, perfect unison. This time there was a little emotion, a little anger behind the words, but only a little. Lovina felt herself starting to move to one side to allow the boys to enter; she felt that this was some horrible nightmare she needed to wake up from. Her heart was a fluttering, terrified bird struggling to escape its bone cage. She tasted fear, bitter, sharp, and metallic, like tinfoil, in her mouth. If they came in, if they shut the door and she was alone in this dark place with them . . . no . . . no . . . Gun, get the gun. . . . Her fingers refused to work. She suddenly realized the cicadas had grown silent, long before midnight.

"No," Lovina heard herself say as if at from a great distance. Terror was like cotton stuffed throughout her mind and body, muffling everything, diffusing it. She moved back to block the doorway, and she felt the haze in her mind clear just a little, the fear lessen. "No," she said again. "Who are you?"

The boys looked up, and she saw their full faces for the first time. One was light-skinned black, the other white. They both had pimples, and their mouths were tight slits of contained rage. But it was their eyes—their eyes—that set off the alarm in Lovina's ancient, primal, reptile brain. Their eyes were completely black, filled with the deepest, darkest ink, devoid of any light, any detail, any soul.

"Let . . . us . . . in," the boys said in unison, the acid of anger dripping in their voices now.

"Shit!" Lovina said, and slammed the door hard in the kids' faces. She locked it, dropping her flashlight in the process. The half-moon of the beam's light rolled on the floor, then stilled. There was pounding on the front door now, louder, insistent. Lovina raced through the house. There was a back porch, a back door with a small mud room. She stumbled through the darkness, fumbling with her car keys. She threw open the door and sprinted for her car in the parking lot. Her feet slipped in the loose gravel that crunched under her feet. The thrill of panic, of your mind knowing what your senses can't tell you—knowing eyes are on you, behind you in the darkness, coming closer. She unlocked the car door and jumped in, slamming and locking it. She jammed the keys into the ignition, almost dropping them. She couldn't catch a breath; her heart was a fist, punching to be free of her chest. The car revved to life. She snapped on the headlights.

The two black-eyed children stood before her car, silent, their eyes empty mirrors of oil.

"No!" Lovina shouted and jammed the car into reverse. Gravel flew everywhere as the car fishtailed. The children stood bathed in the red light of her taillights for a moment, standing side by side, and then were lost to the darkness as she sped out of the parking lot and onto Beech Street. She didn't slow down, didn't catch her breath again, until she was on the highway and headed back to New Orleans, to home.

FOUR   "10-47"

The sky was on fire, golds, oranges, and reds burning at the razor edge of heaven and earth. The dark green Honda CR-V glided down U.S. 36 into the setting sun, into the furnace of light. The Honda passed farm fields stretching to the horizon in either direction. Occasionally, the endless looping monotony of farmland would be punctuated with weathered grain silos reaching to the bruised sky, or with a field of jade grass or a stand of trees. The Kansas tags on the SUV said KEROUAC, and the mellow, joyous music drifting out the open windows was Neutral Milk Hotel's "In the Aeroplane Over the Sea." The music for this leg of the journey was chosen by the driver, a lean, late twentysomething with a close-cropped fringe of a beard already turning gray and hair of the same color poking out from under his driver's cap. He wore a checked collared shirt, an unbuttoned tweed vest, and a stifling air of smug superiority.

"Look at that sunset," the driver said to his companions. "That, *that* is why I write poetry."

"You write poetry in a never-ending quest to sleep with every woman with a pulse, Gerry," said a dour slender girl in her early twenties, with long, straight, ink-black, dyed hair and thick black eye makeup. She wore a black minidress, torn fishnets, and Doc Marten boots and was sitting in the coveted shotgun passenger seat. "This music makes me want to cut someone besides myself."

The three passengers in the backseat laughed. One was a handsome, muscular young man with fashionably cut black hair. The boy was in his early twenties and was dressed in a blue-and-yellow Abercrombie &

Fitch polo shirt and jeans. He had his arm around the girl sitting in the middle of the backseat. She was a little younger than the boy but carried herself with a practiced maturity. She had long, silky blond hair with straight bangs across her forehead. Her eyes were a brilliant blue and held a wicked intelligence and sheen of cruelty to them behind thick-framed nerd-style glasses. She was attractive, with an athletic body, and wore a blue-and-white University of Kansas T-shirt and cutoff Daisy Duke–style jean shorts.

"If you kill Gerry, Lexi," the blonde said, "who's gonna buy us beer and weed?"

The girl sitting next to the blonde by the passenger-side rear door nodded in agreement. She was brunette, her long hair pulled away from her face and into a ponytail. She wore a dark-blue-and-black striped top and old, torn Levi's, as well as a pair of old Converse high-tops. She was slender and had less of a figure than the blonde, but her features were much more delicate and beautiful.

"Ava's got a point, Gerry," the brunette said. "Not to mention your death would probably cause the Rohypnol market to crash." Everyone laughed again except Gerry.

"Fuck you, Alana," Gerry said, and flipped the brunette off. "And fuck you, too, Ava! Last time I invite any of you assholes to a field party."

Alana fished her headphones out of her pocket and connected them to her phone. She was already wishing she had stayed home and binged on *Sherlock* on Netflix, as she'd planned. The only reason she was here was that Ava was her friend as well as her roommate. Lexi was her roommate, too, but, to be honest, she hated the whiny, self-absorbed little bitch. She saw how Lexi and Cole looked at each other and she hated it for Ava. She had talked to Ava about it several times, and Ava had laughed, saying that she didn't intend to stay with Cole past college, anyway, if that long. *What was the fucking point then, to be with someone you didn't even like or really want?* He was a means to an end, and that was Ava's first and governing principle. He kept her warm, he was pretty, and he fucked good. *What else could there possibly be, right?*

"Hey, Cole," Lexi, the goth girl, said. "You gonna let this ratchet old hipster talk that way to your girl?"

Cole pulled his arm out from around Ava and fished a cold bottle of

Heineken out of the cooler at his feet. "Shit," he said, grinning as he popped the cap off the beer with the church key on his key chain. "I'm staying out of this. I open my mouth, I either lose my girl or I lose my beer and I'm suddenly bankrupt. This is a definite fourth-down scenario, baby."

"My fucking hero." Ava smacked Cole's arm and claimed his beer as her own. "I skipped on coding for my midterm programming exam in Python this weekend to go watch Cole get drunk and piss on a cornfield, then pass out."

"Baby, anything you want to know about the python," Cole said, pulling Ava and his beer close to him, "ole Cole here can teach you with some hands-on experience."

"I know we're doing, like, sixty," Alana said, grimacing at Ava and Cole as the couple began to kiss. "But I think I'll take my chances with the asphalt; I'm bailing."

"Me, too," Lexi said, but her eyes were fixed on Cole and, for an instant Cole's eyes flicked to hers and they locked, holding the look a second too long. Lexi looked away quickly, and a thin smile came to Cole's lips. He kissed Ava deeply and took a furtive glance at Alana's chest as he did it. "How much longer till we're at your buddy's place, he of the shitty indie music?" Lexi said a little too quickly to Gerry.

"I can't get the damn GPS to work out here," Gerry said. "Like being on the moon. Look, Evan told me his folks' place was on thirty-six, about forty miles after you get off eighty-one. He said look for a bunch of mailboxes—one of them with a little windmill on it—"

"Fabulous," Lexi said.

"—and then a dark green grain silo on the left," Gerry continued, undaunted. "The gate for the access road is about five miles past the silo on the same side of the road."

"We are going to end up eating each other," Ava said, taking a long draw on Cole's beer. "I've seen this movie."

"That don't sound so bad," Cole said, giving Lexi a quick glance. Ava, not noticing the exchange, smacked him on principle. They both laughed and resumed kissing.

"No worries." Gerry fished a plastic baggie of pot out from under his seat. "Don't need technology to do everything for you."

"This coming from the man who once had a nervous breakdown because his Keurig machine broke," Alana said. "Don't be trying to roll and drive, Gerry."

Gerry tossed the baggie to Lexi. "Okay, co-pilot, do the honors," he said to her.

There was the hollow rattle of an empty bottle on the floor, and Cole was pulling another beer out of the cooler. He belched as he spoke. "It's going to be dark soon, man. How we going to see a fucking dark green silo in the dark, Gerr?" Ava checked her cell phone and frowned.

"No fucking signal!" she said. "I swear to God, Gerry, you get us lost out here . . ."

"Will everyone chill the hell out," Gerry said. "We'll pass this blunt, and by the time it's dead we'll be there. Be cool."

▪ ▪ ▪

Alana slipped in her earbuds and music swallowed up the world, Shawn Mullins's "The Ghost of Johnny Cash." She looked away from Cole and Ava and all the bullshit and looked out the window at the beautiful emptiness, the farmland, the swaying grass, the endless sky, painfully blue, now turning to ash. The world would be a really beautiful place if it wasn't for all the fucking people, she sometimes mused. That was a terrible way for a person who was studying to become a doctor to think, but she couldn't help it. She had chosen to come to the University of Kansas School of Medicine because she wanted to be somewhere where she could drive a little ways and be alone for miles in every direction. She hated cities, hated the mass mind that seemed to take over human beings when you stuffed enough of them together in a glass steel-and-concrete rat cage. She enjoyed and liked, and even loved, individual human beings very much. But the human race as a mob she had no love for.

She looked away from the increasingly mauve sky to Gerry. He was yapping away about something. He and Lexi were arguing, hands gesturing, heads shaking. Before the night was over, they would most likely be fucking. Gerry had already slept with Ava and Lexi; he wanted very much to sleep with Alana now. Not because he cared for her at all—she actually thought he disliked her quite a bit—but because she was a new conquest; he wanted the trifecta.

Gerry was a pig. He owned a little bistro back in Salina, called Kerouac's, which had become a haven for people who enjoyed paying too much for coffee and listening to open-mike poetry about how some fine-arts major's menstrual flow was a metaphor for getting over her breakup with her emo ex-boyfriend. Alana hung at Kerouac's because it was Ava's preferred hangout joint. Gerry had tried several times to move on Alana, and each time he got a very cutting critique of Kerouac's, his taste in clothing, and his general creepiness. Still, like any true horndog, Gerry was undaunted. In Alana's mind, Gerry figured he was one too many gin and tonics away from getting into her pants. She looked back out the window, listening to her music—now it was ACDC's "Back in Black." She wished silently for a world all to herself.

"What the hell?" Gerry said. On the road ahead, a dark shape had appeared at the edge of vision, straddling both lanes. It was a motorcycle with a lone rider barreling down on the Honda at dangerous speed.

"Is this guy out of his fucking mind?" Cole said, leaning forward. "He's playing chicken with us?"

"Slow down, Gerry!" Lexi shouted, covering her eyes and drawing her knees up to her chest.

"Shit!" was all Gerry had time to say. The rider was upon them. Gerry jerked the steering wheel hard to the right and jammed the screeching brakes to the floor. The SUV lurched off the road. Bags, coolers, everything loose in the car, was suddenly in midair in one horrifying, frozen instant of stretched time. Alana grabbed the passenger handle above the door. The image of her cat, Mr. Pointy, flashed into her mind, and she wondered who would feed him, take care of him? There was the sound—the sound of all the things in the world breaking, smashing at once. Then it was over.

The moment after a crash is surreal. As elongated and static as the instant before impact, the moment after is oddly peaceful and silent, like space. Alana looked around. She touched herself gingerly, ran a hand softly through her hair. She was okay. Cole had been thrown back into the rear of the SUV. He touched a jagged cut along his scalp. His palm was dark with fresh blood. Ava looked around as if she was coming out of a trance. Her glasses had been knocked off her face from the impact, and she bent forward and retrieved them. Gerry's and Lexi's airbags engulfed them, and both seemed okay. It was Gerry who finally broke the spell and spoke.

"Everyone . . . everybody okay?" he asked.

A general murmur of confirmation, then Cole's voice—angry, almost incredulous. "You have got to be shitting me! Motherrrrfucker!" There was a click as Cole opened the rear door of the SUV and began to climb out.

"Cole, no!" Alana shouted. "I need to look at that scalp wound! You're losing blood!"

"Cole, damn it!" Ava said, turning to try to stop him, but he was already out.

The others all struggled out of the Honda. The SUV's nose was buried in a deep irrigation ditch on the side of the highway. The front axle was bent, and one of the wheels was twisted at an angle that would barely allow the tire to touch the road even if they did get it out of the trench. It was darker now. Everything was covered in a dusty haze. The sky had lost most of its color, except for the brilliant crimson wound in the west. No stars had dared to venture out yet.

Cole was standing in the middle of the two-lane road. His breathing was shallow, almost panting. His hair and face were black with his own blood. His fists clenched and unclenched. About twenty feet away, the motorcycle rider stood, straddling his all-black antique motorcycle, which was idling, growling like a hungry hound. Alana thought it looked like one of those bikes that army couriers rode in World War II.

"Hey, you fucking asshole!" Cole shouted at the rider. "What the hell is your problem, man! You nearly fucking killed us, you psycho!"

The rider was tall, well over six feet, and gaunt. He was dressed head to toe in heavy black riding leathers. His full-face helmet and visor were black as well; so were his heavy leather gloves and thick, steel-toed boots. He regarded Cole silently, unmoving.

"Hey, dickhead!" Cole said, moving toward the rider. "I'm talking to you! See what you did to me? Did to our fucking car?"

"Cole," Ava said, running to his side. "Baby, please don't! He looks crazy."

Gerry, Lexi, and Alana joined the couple. The rider's helmeted head turned to regard each of the five silently. When the dark visor turned to

Alana, it felt as if ice water were filling her intestines. She looked down. The rider held Cole's gaze the longest. Cole glared back.

"Come on!" Cole shouted, Ava grabbing at his arm, trying to pull him back. "Fucking puss!"

"Someone call the PoPo," Lexi said softly.

"Can't," Gerry said, looking at his smartphone. "No service."

Alana quickly looked to see if she could spot some kind of identification on the rider's antique bike. She didn't see a license plate, no stickers or adornments.

The rider turned his gaze from the group, twisted the throttle on the handlebar, and the bike's engine went from a low growl to a thunderous snarl. The rear tire squealed as it bit into the highway. The stench of burning rubber was everywhere as the rider aimed the bike in the direction he had been riding and lifted his foot off the road. The bike lifted him and he tore off down U.S. 36 into the deepening night. In seconds, his diminishing silhouette merged with the darkness and was gone from sight.

"Well . . . shit," Lexi said. "I didn't know Charles Manson rode a bike."

"Fucking wimp," Cole said, still staring off into the growing night. "Kick his ass."

"You're lucky that psycho didn't shoot you," Alana said, moving Cole's hair aside and looking at the scalp wound. "Be still."

"Anybody got service?" Gerry asked, tapping his phone and shaking his head, "because we are going nowhere in my car. We are currently a three-wheeler. Shit, my parents are going to freak! This will make their insurance go up. They will fucking kill me!"

"Your parents?" Ava said, frowning, "Seriously, Gerr?"

"Okay," Alana said to Cole. "It's ugly, but it's not deep. Maybe a stitch or two. Get a shirt or something to hold over it until the bleeding eases up. When we get to a hospital, they may want to check to make sure you don't have a concussion. You're going to be fine, Cole."

"Thanks, Doc," Cole said. "Okay, anyone's phone working?"

"No," Lexi said. "This sucks."

It was almost dark. Everyone went back to the SUV. Cole used a bottle of water to clean his wound and wash his face and hair. He removed and wrapped his T-shirt around his head to stanch the blood. Lexi watched him covertly as he pulled his shirt over his head. He was beautiful, perfect. His muscles rippled under his tattooed skin.

"Do we have any road flares?" Alana asked Gerry, who was sitting behind the wheel, the driver's-side door open, busy drinking another of the rapidly dwindling supply of beers. He shrugged.

"Don't know," he muttered. "All I know is this whole day has sucked and I'm out of smokes."

"And," Alana added, as she headed to the rear compartment of the Honda, "you're getting drunk and being useless. Stick to your strengths, Gerr." Alana lifted up the compartment that held the spare tire. There was a canvas bag with a funnel, some oily tools, and a couple of flares. Alana wrapped the greasy flares in part of a roll of paper towels and dropped them into her tote bag. She also snagged a small plastic case that was a simple first-aid kit, hoping to find something to dress Cole's head wound.

Cole and Lexi passed a joint back and forth in the backseat and drank beer. Ava sat in front, next to Gerry, and played some game on her phone. The radio had produced nothing but static, so the CD player was softly playing "Interstate Love Song," by Stone Temple Pilots. Alana walked out onto the road where the rider had stood and looked down U.S. 36 in both directions. Nothing. Night had come, and this was the deep country. No lights, no sounds save the hum of the nocturnal insects arising with the death of the sun. Alana sighed. She took one of the flares out and read the instructions by the light of her cell-phone screen. She twisted the plastic cap on the flare and removed it, then struck the end of the flare to the coarse side of the cap, like a huge match. The flare hissed to brilliant life. She gingerly placed it squarely in the middle of the highway. Anyone who came by this godforsaken stretch of highway would have to stop now, she thought. They might be pissed, but at least they wouldn't just drive on without helping.

"Hey," Gerry said. "Did you know we aren't too far from the center of the lower forty-eight?"

"What?" Ava asked, looking up from her phone.

"Yeah, up the road is Lebanon," Gerry said, slurring slightly. He paused to drain his PBR and then crush the can. "It's the geographical center of the contig . . . con-tig-uous United States . . . kinda like ground zero. They got a little pyramid shrine with a plaque there and every-thing."

"Great," Lexi said, taking the joint, now a roach, from Cole. "So we really are in the middle of nowhere."

From the west, the direction the motorcycle had come, a pair of high beams stabbed out of the night. "Guys!" Alana shouted. "Car!" Every-one climbed out of the SUV, crowding near the white line at the edge of the road. Alana stood by the flare, watching the headlights get closer.

"Alana, get over here!" Ava said. "You could get hit!"

"They're going to stop, damn it," Alana said and held her ground. They could hear the engine now, a wheezing, coughing clatter. It was al-most comical. The vehicle came into view, a hulking shadow behind the bright lights. It slowed, the brakes making a horrid metallic scraping sound. It stopped a few feet from the crimson, hissing road flare with a shudder and a gasp. It was an old Ford pickup from the fifties, maybe even older than that, with a tow winch mounted in the bed. On the side of the doors, in faded and scraped paint, it said SCODE'S GARAGE, EST. 1932 FOUR HOUSES, KS; beneath that was JEREMIAH 12:14. Two men climbed out of the truck. One looked late thirties and was broad and muscular, dressed in a greasy undershirt and a torn flannel button-down. His jeans were covered in rips and grease stains, and his work boots were dirty. He had an unruly mop of curly black hair and about a week's growth of beard. His eyes were dark and sullen. One of his eyelids drooped. He had a buck knife sheathed on his belt. The other one, who exited the passenger door, was younger, maybe in his twenties, skinny and shorter. His dark hair was greasy and slicked back from his face. His ears and nose were prominent, and he wore a dirty blue mechanic's shirt with a white oval patch over the left breast that said TOBY in red embroidery. A tire-pressure gauge poked out of his shirt pocket, and his jeans were baggy, held up by a fiercely tightened belt, and as dirty as the driver's.

"Your car," the driver said. His voice was harsh, almost snarling. "We can tow you to the garage. Fix it up."

"Really? Gerry said, smiling. "Aw that's great, man! Great!" The tow-truck driver looked at him as if he were an insect from another planet.

Gerry's smile began to fall from his face. "Um . . . How far is the garage? I can't afford a lot for the tow. Sorry."

"Four Houses," the skinny one said. His voice was higher in pitch but equally aggressive. "We'll tow you. No charge as long as we do the work on the car? Sound square to you?"

"I . . . I guess." Gerry looked over at the others for guidance.

"Yes or no," the large driver grunted. "It's got to be a yes or a no. So what is it?"

"Y . . . yes," Gerry said. "Sure, man. Thanks!"

"Hey, isn't Four Houses, like, that old historical place?" Ava said. "Over in Wyandotte County, near Kansas City? It used to be an outpost or something a long time ago."

"Nowhere near here," Alana said.

"Nah," Toby, the skinny tow-truck mechanic said. "That's just an old story. The real Four—"

"Shut the fuck up, Toby," the burly driver rumbled.

"Sorry, Wald," Toby muttered, looking down.

"Let's get them hooked up," Wald said. He turned to the group. "Girls can ride in the cab, boys in the bed. Grab your shit out of the car."

Everyone grabbed the bags from the back of the SUV while Wald and Toby hooked the Honda up and hoisted it out of the ditch.

"Yeah," Gerry said, standing next to Wald as he worked the winch levers, "some asshole on a bike ran us off the road, man." Wald looked at him with his one hooded eye, twitching slightly, but said nothing.

Alana checked Cole's wound. She applied a thick square gauze bandage to the cut. "These guys are creeping me out," she said softly as he put his bloody shirt back on. "I don't think we should go, Cole."

"Gerry may be scared of the *Deliverance* boys, but I'm not," Cole said. "I'll keep you guys safe, no worries, Doc. I got a gun. It's in my bag."

"What the hell, Cole?" she whispered. "Are you really that drunk, or did you crack your skull harder than I thought, you idiot?"

"Relax," Cole said, picking up his gym bag. "It's a little .380. I always carry a piece on trips, in case shit like this happens. My dad hunts; I know my way around a gun."

"Great." Alana sighed, putting the first-aid kit back in her tote. "Come on, Ted Nugent."

The girls huddled together, cramped in the small bench seat in the back of the tow truck's cab. Cole and Gerry sat on either side of the winch arm, their backs to the rear window of the truck cab. The truck groaned as it pulled onto U.S. 36 and headed west. The engine made a hollow, choking *pock-pock* sound as it struggled to drag the weight of the SUV. Wald jerked the long gearshift, wrestling with it for a moment; then the truck lurched into gear, and the engine began to hum with renewed strength. The stars were out now, brilliant and endless. The fields and the patches of woods, the silos and the windmills and the barns were dark, featureless shadows. The only light came from the piercing brights of the old Ford. Toby snapped on the radio in the cab, and to the girls' surprise a radio signal came through. It was scratchy AM, but it was music—Patty Loveless's "Nothin' but the Wheel" sounding lost and tinny in the bottom of a well—but it was better than the silence of the road.

"We couldn't get any signal out here at all on our radio," Lexi said.

Toby nodded and looked back at her. His eyes drifted from her face to her short skirt and legs. "It's the only station we can get out here," he said. "The signal even comes in sometimes in Four Houses."

"Mind your hole, Toby," Wald said, keeping his eyes on the road. Toby was silent and kept his eyes forward. "Everyone just shut up. We'll be there soon."

The tow truck turned right onto Route 281. It was getting colder. Gerry and Cole both huddled as close to the back of the cab as they could and slid lower to avoid more of the biting wind. Inside the truck, the girls were leaning on one another for warmth and as pillows. The rhythmic hum of the engine and the gentle sway of the truck combined with the long day, the beer, the pot, and the stress to lull everyone to sleep.

There was soft music hissing from the radio, playing some big-band music from the thirties, maybe Tommy Dorsey, Alana thought, her eyes fighting to stay open. She looked over and saw Ava and Lexi both asleep. Out the back window, she saw the boys huddled and still. A peaceful memory of childhood—asleep in the backseat, safe, headed home—wrapped itself around her. Alana looked out the window at the dark countryside drifting by. For a moment she thought it was raining, that raindrops were running down the glass, smearing and distorting her view of outside, but it wasn't raining. The dark fields were blurring and warping, as if she were looking at them through a curtain of rain. There was a huge dark mountain off to the left. In her half-awake state the in-congruity of the mountain, which seemed closer now, seemed irrelevant, and, anyway, a few moments later, when she opened her eyes again it was gone. She felt a thrill of panic struggle to come to the surface, to wake her, but it was too little, too late, to keep her eyes open or her mind from slipping away. Alana slept, and the old truck hummed down the road, her rusted cradle.

"Get up." Wald's harsh voice broke the spell. "We're here."

Alana blinked, forced her eyes to open wide—a trick she had learned during long nights at the ER, to chase sleep away. She was cold, shivering. It was deep night, and the truck was shuddering down an empty two-lane. There were buildings on either side of the main road, mostly squat and dark. To her right, past a few slumbering houses and trailers, she saw a low, long one-story building with a sign in the window that proclaimed it BUDDY'S ROADHOUSE in red neon. A smaller sign in blue glowed OPEN.

A little farther up the blacktop and on the left was a once grand old house on a low hill that appeared to have been burned down to its rotted skeletal remains. The shadows of a deep forest were already be-ginning to encroach on the ruins. Alana felt a wave of sadness and loss pass over her as she looked at the dying old mansion. She didn't under-stand why.

"Where are we, exactly?" Lexi said, yawning and rubbing her eyes, smearing her mascara wings. The tow truck passed abandoned houses, mobile homes, and antique cars, squatting on cinder blocks in weed-covered fields. Under the buttery light of a sodium-light streetlamp—the only apparent one on the road—Alana saw a group of hoodie-wearing kids huddling, their faces dipped in shadow.

"Almost to the garage," Toby said to Lexi. "Then we can get you all fixed up proper. Find you a place to sleep." They passed another once beautiful, now ruined home on the right. It sat back off the highway by way of a winding gravel drive. A waist-high, chain-link fence circled the front yard and disappeared behind the half-collapsing house. A No

TRESPASSING sign was posted at the end of the driveway and was faintly illuminated with the tow truck's passing.

Alana thought she saw dark shapes moving in the yard behind the fence—guard dogs, perhaps. "What happened to these old houses?" she asked. "They look like they were burned."

"They were," Toby replied. "In the war."

"The Civil War?" Alana said.

"No," Toby said. "What's that?"

Wald gave him a withering scowl. Toby shut up.

"It's a shame," Alana said. "That's beautiful architecture. Don't you guys have a historical- preservation society around here?" Wald's laughter was one of the most horrifying things Alana had ever heard. It was as if the dried husk of a soul that resided inside him was being scraped out with a rusty rake—a bass moan and a sharp hissing.

"Preservation society," he muttered. "Funny."

About a quarter of a mile down the highway from the ruined house on the opposite side of the two-lane was a series of weathered, squat one-story bungalows clustered around what appeared to be a cement inground swimming pool and a tiny brick building. The building had a lighted sign hanging above the door that said OFFICE. A palsied, old neon sign in pinks, blues, and yellows shaped like an elongated eight-point star-burst was mounted on a crumbling cement base by the edge of the road in front. Many of the bulbs of the star were blackened and dead. It made Alana suddenly recall every cheap fifties no-tell motel she had ever passed on the highway. The sign said STAG'S REST MOTEL. Beneath it was a small white neon sign that declared simply VACANCY. The "N" in the sign fluttered on and off.

"God, I hope there's somewhere else to sleep in this hole," Ava muttered to Alana.

"I don't think so," Alana said.

After another mile of passing more dilapidated cars and vans, choked by rusty vines, and then a few more trailers, another fine old house appeared on the left. It was most likely built near the turn of the nineteenth century. This one, unlike its ruined cousins, looked in good repair and there were lights on inside, peeking out behind the thick drapes in the windows.

"What is that?" Lexi said, pointing out the window to the house.

"*Damn an Crone d'aois. Bealtaine an Horned amháin a chosaint dúinn,*" Wald said, almost spitting the words out like a curse. He raised his hand, extending his index and little fingers while folding his middle and ring fingers down, covering them with his thumb. Alana thought he performed the gesture the way a Catholic might cross himself. "That's the old witch's house," he said.

"Uh, rock on, dude," Lexi said with a grin. She made the same "finger horns" gesture with both hands and flexed her wrists. Wald snapped his head back to glower at the girl; his face darkened and his eyes were bright with sudden anger. Lexi's grin faded, and she retreated farther into the back of the truck.

"You need to be careful," Wald growled. "Folks here honor the old ways and don't take kindly to them being made light of. Hold your damned tongue, girly."

Lexi started to respond, but Alana tugged her arm gently and shook her head. "Not now," Alana said softly. Lexi flipped off Wald's back and crossed her arms, mouthing the word "asshole." The truck picked up speed as Wald hurried past the old house. They seemed to travel a little over a mile, passing a graveyard of cars, trucks, and campers, and more houses in various stages of decay, some occupied, others long abandoned, a few RVs, and more trailer homes. They finally pulled into the gravel lot of a dirty two-bay garage with a pair of old bubbleheaded Esso gas pumps out front that still seemed to be in service. The grimy, rusting sheet-metal sign hung on the roof said SCODE'S GARAGE.

"All right, we're here," Wald said. "Get out."

"Gladly," Lexi said. The girls climbed out of the cramped backseat once Wald and Toby had cleared space. They stretched. Cole and Gerry, yawning and shivering, climbed down from the back of the truck. Gerry looked around at the rows of dark, shabby homes and the deep, immense forest that yawned behind them.

"Where are we, man?" he asked.

"Apparently, this is Four Houses," Ava said. "You didn't miss anything. It's a real shithole."

Cole laughed a little. "At least they can fix up the car. Any hotels?"

"Oh, yeah," Lexi said. "You're gonna love it."

Wald started to climb back into the truck to back the Honda into the garage bay. Gerry caught him before he closed the door. "Hey, man, how long do you think it will take to fix this up?"

"Check back tomorrow," Wald said, and slammed the truck's door.

"They'll have rooms for you up at the Rest," Toby said to Lexi. "Be careful walking up there, you hear? Stay to the light."

"Toby!" Wald shouted through the partly lowered truck window. "Move your worthless ass!"

"Ah . . . thanks," Lexi said, hoisting her backpack while the others also gathered their gear. The group walked away from the garage. Their breath streamed from their faces as they regarded the side of the two-lane.

"Okay, anyone got any signal at all?" Ava asked, looking at her phone.

"Nope," Cole said, slipping his iPhone back into his pocket. The others nodded in agreement.

"Come on," Alana said. "The motel is this way. It's not too far."

"I get the feeling nothing is very far from anything in this town," Lexi said.

The side of the highway had a fringe of high grass littered with broken bottles, crushed and sun-faded beer and soda cans, gravel, and damp paper bags. They made their way carefully in the faint light the town provided. In between the few storefronts and occupied houses were long stretches of pitch-blackness.

"How much longer?" Gerry asked, already trailing behind. "My dogs are barking, man."

"Another mile, mile and a half," Alana said, looking back. "C'mon, Gerr, man up."

"We wouldn't even be out here, hoofin' it, if you hadn't talked us into this stupid party, Gerry," Ava added.

Gerry started to say something when there was a swishing noise off to the right, in the deep darkness. It sounded like someone moving quickly through the tall grass. It stopped an instant after they stopped talking and moving.

"What was that?" Lexi asked.

"Probably just an animal," Cole said. "Raccoon, or a rabbit. No big—"

"I really fucking hate this," Lexi said as they began to walk again.

"We're going to get jumped by dogs or wolves or some weird redneck mutants. Anyone got a flashlight?"

"I got an app on my phone," Ava said. "Hang on."

The darkness was split by a bright white beam from Ava's phone screen. She moved to the front of the group, beside Alana, and swept the ragged circle of light before the group.

"What time is it," Cole asked. "My phone died."

"A little after nine," Gerry said. "They sure as hell roll up the sidewalks here, don't they?"

They trudged on and moved a little farther off the awkward terrain of the shoulder of the road and toward the edge of a wide field that stretched between clusters of dark, empty houses.

"So about sleeping arrangements," Cole said, grinning. Ava stopped and swung the bright light of the flashlight around to catch Cole in the face.

"One room boys, one room girls. If you seriously think anything other than sleeping is happening tonight, then you do have a concussion." Everyone laughed. The rustling sound returned closer and ahead of them. The laughter stopped.

"What *is* that?" Alana said. Ava turned and spun the light in front of them again. Standing in the beam were four figures directly ahead of them. They were man-shaped but had no features, no details to them at all, as if the darkest corner of the night had torn itself free and been given arms and legs, and a vacant face. Lexi screamed.

"Shit!" Alana said. The shadows moved toward them, grass bending as they pushed through it, as if they had mass, substance. "Run!" she shouted. "Everybody run!" There were more shouts now; it was Gerry, bellowing with fear.

"They're back here, too. Oh fuck, oh fu . . . Ahhhhhhh! No! No!"

Ava swung the light around to see Gerry being grabbed by two of the shadows. He was screaming. His skin was growing almost translucent, and black veins were running across his face and arms. A stain was growing in the crotch of his jeans as he pissed himself. The things dragged him out of the circle of light. He screamed again and then made a choking, gurgling sound and was silent. Cole had a gun in his hands now and was shooting at the things. He grabbed Ava's arm.

"Come on!" he shouted. Ava turned the light back to where Alana was standing to call for her to follow. She was sitting on the ground, her arms held by two of the shadow things. Alana's eyes were rolling up into her head, as if she were in shock. She managed to focus for a second and looked at Ava.

"My bag . . . flare . . ." she whispered. The two shadows' fingers slipped through Alana's shoulders, her skin, as if they were nothing more than smoke. Alana became pale, almost blue. Black veins began to spread across her skin, especially her face. The shadow men raised their arms violently, and Alana's arms tore off at the shoulders in a spray of blood. Alana's expressionless face animated into a shriek of pain and fear, as her arms flew off into the darkness of the field. She slumped in the grass, twitching, and then was silent and still.

Ava felt her world spin, tumble, and start to shatter. There was a strong hand on her arm. She screamed, in anticipation of the icy black fingers slipping under her skin.

"No! No!" Ava screamed and pulled away. She staggered toward Alana's body and grabbed the canvas straps of the bag. The hand grabbed her again. It was pulling her up, pulling her forward. A gun was barking again and again. It was Cole pulling her forward. He had Alana's blood all over him. Ava kept screaming, but she was running now, running ahead, the light from her phone bouncing and jumping across the grass in front of her. She heard the rustling behind her, getting closer, but no breath, no panting of a living pursuer. She knew those things were gaining on her. She ran faster and looked over her shoulder with the flashlight. The shadow was almost on her but, as the circle of light caught it, it steamed like smoke and slipped back into the night, falling farther behind.

"Run! Run! Fucking run! Jesus!" Lexi was screaming ahead. She was approaching a house near the road. Ava saw her jump up on the porch and start beating on the door. "Let us in, Let us fucking in please! God! They're going to kill us!" The porch light snapped on as Cole and Ava reached it. Ava looked out into the yard. The shadows were all around them. She counted eight, empty darkness with a thin blur at the edges of them to separate them from the night. No eyes, no mouth, no indication of pity, or any emotion. They moved the way humans move, but with an almost jerky quality, like a film missing a few frames; as if they weren't quite in sync with the rest of the world. They stopped just at the edge of the porch light, spread out, and waited.

"Please," Lexi was sobbing. "I just want to call my mom and go home, please let us in!" She struck the door with a sudden frantic anger. "Let us in, you motherfuckers! They are going to kill us!" She slid down to the base of the door and cried, her whole body heaving. Ava looked at Cole. He was sweeping the pistol in his shaking hand, back and forth, covering the shadows. He looked like a scared little boy playing guns. Ava realized that he was fighting so hard to be brave, for her, for Lexi. She felt very sorry for him in this moment. He was scared as shitless as they were, but he felt he had to be something else, had been taught to be something else. He hadn't cracked yet, but he would.

"What are they?" Cole said. "They look like a special effect, like something from a movie."

"They can't be real, they can't be real," Lexi muttered, her face against the door. "I'm back in the hospital, I'm in the hospital. . . ."

Ava beat on the door. She looked down at her cell phone; the charge bar was in the red. The flashlight drew an enormous amount of power from the small phone's battery. "Please," she called out. "Let us in, we need help!"

"Go away!" a muffled voice on the other side of the door said. It sounded like a woman. "You brought them right to our door. Go on! Get the hell out of here! You trying to get my kids killed, or worse! Go!"

"Please, ma'am," Ava said, leaning close to the door. "Our car broke down on thirty-six. We just came into town to get it fixed. These things came out of nowhere. Please, help us!"

There was a pause. Then the voice on the other side of the door said, "You poor children. I can't help you. No one can help any of us. Head for the Crone's house. Just up the road a spell. She'll protect you, if you can make it. *Dia duit.*"

"What?" Ava said. The porch light went out, and darkness devoured them.

Lexi screamed. She pounded on the door with her feet and her hands. "Goddamnit! No! Let us in, let us in! You're killing us, you crazy bitch!"

Ava acted—there was no time for thinking. She reached into Alana's tote and pulled out one of the road flares. She remembered watching Alana pull off the plastic cap and strike the flare to it like a match. She did it as Cole fired off the last few rounds of the pistol. She heard the shadow people moving toward them in the dark, heard the rustle of the grass as they swarmed in. She stuck the flare once, nothing. Lexi was making gurgling sounds. She could feel something filling the darkness ahead of her, rushing at her. She struck the flare to the cap, and the world erupted in ruby red fire and light. The shadow directly in front of her caught the flare's blast where its face would be if it had one. It staggered backward, collapsing, losing its sharp outline as it fell, like ink diluting in water. Ava jumped off the pouch and swung the flare around. A star of searing pain bit her hand, but she held on. She didn't look back at Cole or at Lexi. As she ran, she shouted, "Head for the old house up ahead, run!"

She sprinted, her lungs greedily demanding air. She heard Cole shout something and heard Lexi scream again. She didn't look back. Ahead, she could see the mansion with the warm light spilling out from the heavy drapes in the windows. She could feel the things behind her moving closer and closer. She refused to look back. She refused to think of the others. Run, run! As she got closer, she began to scream as much as her burning lungs would let her.

"Help! Please help!" she shouted, panting.

More gunfire. A rapid staccato of shots somewhere behind her and off to the left. The porch lights came on in the house. It was the most wonderful thing Ava had ever seen. The front door was opening. Ava's feet were thudding on the wooden stairs leading up to the porch. An old woman stepped out on the porch. She was broomstick-slender and very old—in her eighties or nineties, easily. Her iron-gray hair was pinned up in a very proper bun, and she had sharp features, a wickedly pointed nose and chin but very kind blue eyes, almost blazing out of her wrinkled face.

"Down, dear," the old lady said as she leveled a wicked-looking pistol in the general direction of Ava's head. Ava gasped and dived for cover, hitting the porch as the old woman's gun barked again and again. There was a hissing sound, and brilliant light everywhere. Streamers of fire trailed from the gun to the shadows as the old woman's bullets struck three of them. The shadows fell soundlessly, dissolving into the ocean of the night, gone.

The old lady knelt, quite properly considering the narrow, ankle-length skirt she was wearing, and picked up the flare as she shot another shadow with the fire-streaming bullets. She tossed the spurting, hissing flare on the gravel drive and offered the now free hand to Ava.

"There we are," she said. Ava now recognized a very pronounced and proper English accent. "Be a good girl and get up and inside, if you please." Ava scrambled to her feet. She looked around for Cole or Lexi but saw neither of them in the yard or on the road. There were dozens of the shadow things now standing mutely at the edges of the stairs, out in the yard, and even down to the road. They were everywhere. A cold realization settled in her that her friends and her lover were gone. She was alone in this. She stepped inside the old house.

The old lady backed herself into the doorway after Ava, the still smoking gun in one hand. With her other hand, she presented the reversed peace sign to the assembled shadow people—the symbol in the U.K. that was used for flipping someone off. She shut the door and busied herself securing the numerous locks, bolts, chains, and bars that fortified the door. Completing her task, she turned to Ava, who was panting and sobbing on the floor of the foyer. The old woman nodded. "You're safe, my dear," she said. "You survived your first night. That makes you a citizen now. Welcome to Four Houses."

FIVE   "10-7"

The afternoon was warm in Lenoir, warm enough to open a window, turn on ceiling fans, and think about where you stored the air conditioners for the winter. The achingly blue sky was clear and the sun bright as Jimmie's rig, minus the trailer, rolled up Stonewall Street. It was damn good to be home. Jimmie had traveled to many places in this world, and a few other worlds he cared not to dwell on. He had seen breathtaking wonders and beauty traveling the Road, but no place ever filled him with as much joy as this little patch of two-lane that led to his front door.

He slowed and signaled as he turned left on to Resaca Street. His house was at the corner of the two streets, a barn-red, two-story farmhouse, built in the early twenties, with a wraparound porch. The weathered cement foundation and few basement windows peeked out under the porch. Wide cement steps ran from the porch to the yard, and Jimmie noted that he needed to run the lawn tractor; the grass had gotten tall since he'd been gone. He saw Layla's little stone circles in the yard, filled with blooming purple and yellow wildflowers, and he smiled.

Jimmie tugged on the cord near the ceiling of his cab twice, two short bursts on the air horn. He always did that just as he pulled onto his street. And, as always, Layla was rushing out the door to greet him, as fast as her eight-months-along belly would allow. She was prettier than her flowers, Jimmie thought, prettier than anything he'd ever seen.

Layla Aussapile was a slender woman with long legs and arms. She was toned, not from hours at the gym but through the work of her days. Likewise, her skin held a healthy golden tan, somewhat wan now from the winter months, but Layla browned not by a conscious effort of lying in a tanning bed. She grew up fishing on the banks of the Yadkin River, working in the yard with her dad, and wrestling and playing tackle football with her three brothers, often getting the best of them. Layla was tanned because her life had been lived in the sun. Her blond hair was straight, and fell about halfway down her back. Silver was beginning to replace some of the blond, but Layla had no intention of surrendering to hair dye, telling Jimmie she had earned the gray, like medals on the battlefield. She had large brown eyes that could look like molten chocolate or the darkest storm, depending on her mood. Some might say her nose was a little too narrow, too sharp, her teeth not perfect in their alignment, but Jimmie would have punched them out for it. And, yes, she was named after that Eric Clapton song. Layla was wearing a pair of cutoff jean shorts and one of Jimmie's old sleeveless white T-shirts as she raced out the front door and across the yard. The shirt would normally have fallen to her thighs, but now it barely managed to stretch to cover her round, swollen baby belly. She waved frantically with one hand, laughing, and held her belly with the other.

Jimmie pulled onto the grass beside the driveway that was in front of the detached garage. He avoided his pickup, Layla's car, the trailer, and his Harley, which was covered with a tarp. The engine of the semi idled for a moment and then rumbled to silence with a hiss. Layla was running across the yard toward the truck, holding her belly. Jimmie climbed down out of the cab. Layla threw her arms around him, hugging him as tight as she could. Both of them were laughing. Jimmie lifted her and held her in his arms, her hands clasped behind his neck. They kissed, deep and long, and squeezed each other tight. Finally, the kiss reluctantly ended. She rested her head on his shoulder as he carried her toward the screen door at the rear of the house. Jimmie groaned a little, quietly, at the exertion.

"You say one word, Jesse James Aussapile, about my weight and no wild pregnancy sex for you tonight!" Layla said. "On second thought . . . yes, wild pregnancy sex tonight . . . maybe now."

Jimmie approached the back door; Layla untangled enough to open it for him, and he carried her into the kitchen. There was a boy sitting at the kitchen table, eating Froot Loops. He was maybe sixteen and had a constellation of acne across his pasty face. His shaggy, dyed, ink-black hair fell across one of his eyes. He wore a black T-shirt with the logo of the band Sleeping with Sirens on it. Jimmie stopped and looked at the kid. The kid looked at him blandly with his one visible eye and slurped some milk out of his spoon.

"S'up," the boy said in a monotone. Jimmie looked at Layla, who had a smirk on her face.

"Christian, this is Jimmie, Peyton's dad," Layla said to the boy. "Jimmie, this is Christian, Peyton's . . . friend." Jimmie slowly lowered Layla to the kitchen floor, and she headed out of the kitchen. "I'll let you two boys get acquainted, and I'll see if Peyton is ready yet, Christian."

"Ready?" Jimmie asked, sitting across from Christian. "Ready for what? What, exactly, is my baby girl ready for?"

Christian seemed immune to the menace in Jimmie's voice. "Uh, we're going to this, uh, thing, y'know."

"No, no, I don't know. Explain it to me, English scholar," Jimmie said, leaning forward across the table. "What grade are you in anyway?"

"Uh, I'm a junior."

"You understand Peyton is only fourteen, right?" Jimmie said. "And you're what? Sixteen?"

"Umm . . . I'm, uh, fifteen," Christian said. "It's cool, man, we're just hanging out."

Jimmie felt the blood thudding in his ears. "Cool? It's cool that you're hanging out with my little girl? Christian, do you know how many guns I own? More than I'm pretty damn sure you can count. What, exactly, are you planning to do with yourself after high school?"

"Uh, y'know . . . college and stuff," Christian said. He lifted the bowl and drained the remains of the Froot Loops milk out of it. He stared at Jimmie like a coma patient. Jimmie had started to open his mouth when Layla and Peyton entered the kitchen. Jimmie was always amazed when he saw his wife and daughter side by side. Peyton had the long blond hair of her mother, except hers was almost platinum, flashing in the sun like sunlight reflecting off water. She had Jimmie's green eyes, but brighter, and a hint of his nose, but the rest of her was all Layla. Peyton was wearing cutoff jean shorts that were way too short, in Jimmie's estimation, and a yellow T-shirt with a Pokémon creature on it. His daughter squealed with joy when she saw him and rushed to Jimmie's side.

Jimmie stood and hugged her back. "Hi, baby," he said. "How's my girl?"

Peyton turned to Christian. "Dad, this is Chris," she said. "We're going over to Jen's house and then go see a movie, okay?"

Jimmie began to speak, but Layla was already on it. "It's fine, Peyton," she said. "Home by eight, like we discussed. And answer your cell phone if you want to keep it!"

"Okay, Mom, I will!" Peyton said. She hugged Jimmie again and kissed his cheek. "Bye, Daddy! I'm glad you're home! See you tonight!"

"Wait a sec . . ." Jimmie began as Peyton and Christian started to walk out the kitchen door.

"Hush," Layla said, taking his arm. She waved to the kids, and the kitchen door crashed shut. The kitchen was silent except for the *whoosh* of the ceiling fan.

"What . . . was that?" Jimmie said, looking at his wife.

"That," Layla said as she closed the box of cereal on the table and put it away in the cabinet above the microwave, "is 'y'know,' Christian, and he'll be gone in a week unless you make a big deal about him." She took the cereal bowl and spoon off the table and put them in the sink.

Jimmie sat down at the table. "Where does she find these guys?" he asked.

"He's actually one of the better options out there right now," Layla said. "You missed the gangsta' wannabe who kept taking her to the mall food court to get frozen yogurt and talk about 'thug life.'" Layla laughed, and it plucked a chord in Jimmie's soul. This kitchen, the smell of her shampoo, and her pure laughter. He was home.

"Besides," Layla said, pulling off his cap, wrapping her arms around his neck, and kissing his bald head, "I had ulterior motives—we got the house to ourselves till eight."

They both laughed, they kissed, and slowly, hungrily, lovingly, they rediscovered each other.

. . .

That night, after dinner, after watching TV with Peyton, Jimmie and Layla held each other in their bed. The house was dark and quiet. The clock radio was playing "Remember When," by Alan Jackson, softly.

"I missed this," Jimmie said, kissing her head.

"You say that every time you come back," Layla said.

"Yep," Jimmie said. "Every time."

"Well, enjoy it while you can, cowboy," she said. "Remember feedings at 3 A.M.? Poopy diaper smell? No sex that lasts longer than three minutes—"

"Three minutes? Thank God," Jimmie said, grinning. "I'm safe!" Layla tweaked his nipple. Jimmie responded with a grunt of pain, and they both wrestled and tussled and laughed. Eventually, it died down, and they were still, once again, tangled in each other.

"Bully," Jimmie said.

"Hush or you'll get another purple nurple," Layla said.

"I missed Ale's send-off," Jimmie said.

"I know, baby," Layla said. "But he would have understood, you know that. Besides, you did such a nice job at his service. Lizzie understands, I'm sure. I did expect you'd make it, though. Was there a problem on the run?"

Jimmie was silent.

"Did something go bad?" she asked. She felt him tense. "What happened, Jimmie?"

"I . . . I was late on the run," he said. "I had to wait an extra day to get access to the loading dock because I missed the schedule. So that made it almost two days late. They paid me, but they said don't expect another contract. I was expecting to have at least six more with them over the next few months. We needed that money."

"What happened, baby?"

"Work," Jimmie said. "The other work."

"Oh," Layla said. They were quiet for a little while. Then Layla spoke. "Can't they leave you be for a while, Jimmie? They got other people they can—"

"That's not how it works. I can't talk about that," Jimmie said. "You know I'm not allowed to."

"Yeah, I know," she said, untangling herself and sitting up in the bed. "Secret society, oath of silence, blah, blah, bullshit . . ."

"Shhhhh," Jimmie said, sitting up as well. "Will you keep it down!"

"Who's listening to us in our bedroom, Jimmie?" Layla said. "The

NSA? S.H.I.E.L.D? Cobra Commander? Besides, you said that FBI guy already knew who you were."

"He's different," Jimmie said. "They're up to something with him, and he's okay."

"So you can tell some stranger, some FBI agent, what's going on but not your wife? Really, Jimmie?"

"It's not just me, baby!" Jimmie said. "If you're not a Brother or a Squire, you can't—"

"You honestly think that the men in your little club don't tell their wives, their girlfriends?" Layla said. "Let me tell you something, Jesse James Aussapile, women are the first and most dangerous secret society. Do not cross us. We know, Jimmie. We know what our men are doing, and we don't like it when you do stupid, dangerous stuff and try to keep it from us."

"You think what I do is stupid?" Jimmie said, his face reddening.

"No, baby, I know you do good out there. I just hate when you clam up and won't tell me what's going on. You know you can trust me, right? You do trust me?"

"I trust you with my life," Jimmie said. "Of course I trust you, Layla. I . . . I just . . . I made a promise. I swore a vow, like the one I swore to you, and if I break that, then what kind of man am I? What kind of husband? What kind of father?"

They looked at each other for a while. Layla rubbed her belly. Finally, she asked, "Did you get him, Jimmie? The dragon? The bad guy? The monster? The whatever-it-was this time? Did you stop him?"

"Yes," he said, looking down, not meeting her eyes. "I did, and it cost you and Peyton, and the baby, some peace of mind, cost us a contract."

She lifted his chin gently until they were looking at each other, eye to eye. "I'm proud of you," she said. "You save lives. You help people who have no one else to help them. You stand by your friends and your family no matter what, and you keep your word. That's rare in this world. Money's gonna come and it's gonna go, baby. We'll eat PB and J and drink Kool-Aid if we have to. We've done it before, we'll do it again. I'm proud of you, James. I'm proud of what you do. I love you."

"I love you, too," he said. They kissed and held each other. The kiss deepened, and there was no world outside of it, and in time the words didn't matter anymore; the secret between them was lost to a lifetime of knowing. Eventually, they slept, and even in the depths of slumber they touched and held each other.

. . .

"Did you ever tell Mom?" Jimmie asked. "About the Brotherhood? What you did, what you saw out on the Road?"

"Hell, yes," Don Aussapile said to his son. "Of course I did. You think I'm stupid or something? Hand me a three-eighths torque."

They were in Don's gas station—Don's Wreck and Repair, located on Jennings Street in Lenoir, right at the corner of Morganton Boulevard. Jimmie's father was a slight man in his mid-seventies. He wore his thin gray hair short, with little regard for its appearance. Don was dressed in a light blue work shirt with his name in a white oval above the pocket and a pair of dark blue Dickies work pants. His face was weathered, lined with the ruts of life, but there were smile lines there, too. Don, while about a good foot shorter than his son, and a little frail-looking from age, had arms tight and rippling with compact muscles, covered with faded tattoo ink. Jimmie had no doubt that his father could still whup a man if he needed to and give his son a run for his money in arm wrestling. The USMC anchor was still visible on Don's forearm. Jimmie had the same tattoo in brighter, sharper contrast on his arm.

"You actually mean to tell me you haven't told Layla about what goes on out there? On the Road?" Don said, accepting the wrench from Jimmie. "You're damn lucky you're not divorced, son. I always told you she was a damn good woman."

"But what about the oath?" Jimmie said. Don laughed and shook his head as he carefully tightened nuts on the section of the old Chevy Malibu's engine he had been working on when Jimmie arrived.

"The oath"—Don grunted a little from the effort of the tightening— "is all well and good. A man puts a gun to my head, ties me to a chair and says he's gonna slice me ear to ear if I don't tell him about the Brotherhood, I'm ready, willing, and able to die to keep that secret. We all are." He stood from his exertions under the hood and looked at

Jimmie. "But, son, there are fates worse than death, and keeping se-crets from your mama is one of them. I told her everything, every time I came home."

"Everything, Dad?" Jimmie said. "Some of the stuff out there . . . the things that crawl in off the Road . . ."

"Oh, shit, son, of course I didn't tell her about that stuff," Don said. He walked into the small office off the garage bays. Jimmie followed. "No one should ever have that stuff in their head," Don said. "You know that, especially people you care about." He opened the drink cooler and removed two sweating brown glass bottles of Budweiser. He handed one to Jimmie. They opened their beers and sat, Don behind the desk and Jimmie on the edge of it. Don took a sip from his bottle and then contin-ued, "But the day to day . . . the work . . . tell 'em. It kept me off the couch for the last fifty-three years. Well, more or less. So tell me what happened with this Vanishing Hitchhiker you picked up."

Jimmie took a long draw off the beer and wiped his mouth. "It was different from any Vanisher I've run into before, Pop. She knew me, knew my name. She was talking crazy stuff, too, about someone killing her friends. She told me I needed to stop it—whatever 'it' is, exactly."

"And what are you planning to do about that?" Don said.

"Look into it," Jimmie said. "I talked to her parents—nice folks—they've been sick not knowing, but at least I hope they get some peace, knowing she passed."

"If they believed you," Don said. "Might have thought you were nuts. You're lucky they didn't call the cops on you, son."

"Oh, they believed me," Jimmie said. "They said they'd been waiting for me for years."

"What?" Don said.

"I told you, Dad, this one is weird," Jimmie said. He pulled a cassette tape out of his shirt pocket and walked over to the grimy, duct-tape-covered old jam box that his dad had kept on top of the file cabinet in his office since Jimmie was a kid. He pushed a button, and the cassette door silently yawned open. Jimmie slid the tape inside and closed the door. He pushed the play button. There was a hollow hiss as magnetic memory resurrected sound from the long-dead past. A radio was play-ing softly in the background of the recording—"Call Me Maybe," by

Carly Rae Jepsen. A young girl's voice suddenly eclipsed the background noise.

"Heeey," the girl's voice said. "It's me!" Her voice was slightly distorted and hummed a little on the tape. She was too close to the mike. "Dream-journal stuff today. It was weird . . . very weird. No, creepy, old British lady, or the girl dressed in green leaves, or the man with the deer horns this time. No, this time it was some old trucker guy." She laughed. "He had gross teeth and a big gut—"

"Sounds like she's got your number, son," Don said. Jimmie hushed him.

"—and a baseball cap with the Squidbillies on it," she said, laughing. "I need to stop watching Adult Swim at bedtime. But, you know, he did have really kind eyes. He said his name was Jimmie, and I realized that the old lady and the leaf girl both mentioned him to me. They said he was a knight of some kind or other, and that he would help me. . . ."

Don leaned forward in his chair and rested his chin on his fist, listening intently. The tape played on. "Part of it was like the other dreams . . . like being in the woods with the deer-man chasing me. I could hear it crashing behind me. . . . I could smell the blood from the people it had killed. It stank of blood, reeked of it. I heard dogs barking . . . they were chasing me, too . . . I didn't fall, but I almost did a few times.

"Then I saw them just as I got to the edge of the trees, and this part scared me really bad. There was Mark's car sitting on the side of the highway, cars and trucks rushing by behind it, but they were moving slower than everything else. Then I saw Mark and Aaron and Stephanie and even Kristie. They rose up out of the field between me and the car, and the highway. They . . . they weren't my friends anymore. Something was wrong with them . . . inside. The wrong was leaking out their eyes . . . I heard the dogs close behind me, heard them growl, felt their breath on me. And then I woke up. . . ."

Jimmie looked at his dad. Don was still silently listening, but Jimmie could see the dark clouds drifting behind his father's blue eyes. The tape went on: "I know something is going to happen to me, to them. The deer-man is waiting for me. I'm not sure what he's waiting for, but I know the dogs will come for me, for all of us. It's got something to do with . . .

Four Horses? I think Four Horses was what the old British lady said to me, anyway. I just hope that Jimmie the Trucker is real, and that he can help. I'm saving this tape, just in case. . . . Okay, enough weird stuff . . . I got to get to breakfast before Dad eats all the bacon. . . ."

There was a moment of only the background radio music, the faint shudder of wind against the microphone, then the clunk of the stop button as the recording ended. Jimmie pushed the stop key on the player and ejected the tape. He put it back in his pocket. He took a slip of folded paper out of the same pocket and handed it to his dad. "That was Karen Collie at age thirteen, my Vanishing Hitchhiker," Jimmie said. "She taped that two years ago and kept the tape and this in an envelope with instructions for her parents to give it to 'Jimmie the Trucker' when he finally came.

"Karen and the kids she mentions on the tape, her four friends, all went missing in October of 2014. Mark Baz, one of the missing kids, had his car found with all four doors open, keys still in the ignition. Purses, backpacks all in the car. They just vanished off the face of the earth."

Don unfolded the paper. It was a pencil drawing of Jimmie, and the detail was good. "Little girl had herself some talent," he said.

"Yeah, her folks said she loved to do art," Jimmie said.

"Not just art," Don said, handing the picture back to Jimmie. "I think the girl was a road witch, son."

"A viamancer?" Jimmie asked. Don nodded.

"Or, at least, maybe she had the potential. That makes it even more our turf to look into this. You said this happened in Illinois?"

"Yeah."

"I know a guy, used to be an Illinois state trooper. He's retired now, but he's a Brother. I'll give him a call and see if he can give you some help on this."

"Thanks, Dad," Jimmie said.

"So when you leaving, son?" Don asked.

"I'm headed out tomorrow. I got a contract to pick up a load in Arizona. I figure I'll head out early enough to take a few days to look into this." Jimmie hesitated for a moment, taking a swig of his beer and looking out at the lazy early-afternoon traffic on Morganton.

"What?" Don asked. "Spit it out, son, what's wrong?"

"Dad, I . . . I screwed up and lost a long-haul contract. It was Brotherhood business and I don't regret it, but . . ." Don nodded.

"I understand," he said. "You're a little short." Jimmie said nothing, but his eyes told Don all he needed to know. "You didn't screw up. You made a choice. Hell, I had to do that all the time when I was out on the Road. You balance a paycheck to a life—shit, son, that ain't no choice at all. When you were a kid, we were so damn broke I couldn't pay attention."

Jimmie smiled. "Thanks. I'm sorry to ask."

"You didn't," Don said. "I offered. I think your mom and I can lend a hand for a spell, son. You got my second grandbaby on the way, and what kind of Pop-Pop would I be if I didn't help out? I got your back, son."

They hugged.

"Thanks, Dad."

"Don't ever be sorry to ask for help," Don said as he embraced his son. "And don't ever regret doing the right thing. Ever. And, son?"

"Yeah?"

"Whatever it is that you're diving into out there, you make damn sure you come back from it. Y'hear?"

"Okay, Dad," Jimmie said. "Will do."

"Come on," Don said. "I'll get Edgar to watch the place. Let's go surprise your mama. She'll be happy to see you."

■ ■ ■

The next morning, Jimmie got up at five, well before daylight. He was careful not to wake Layla as he padded down the carpeted hallway to the shower. He dressed quietly and headed downstairs to make coffee. He smelled the rich aroma on the landing. The lights were on in the kitchen and, as he walked, he saw Layla, in one of his old flannels, pouring him a fresh cup of coffee.

"Fifteen years and I still can't sneak past you," Jimmie said, taking the mug she offered.

"Baby was using my bladder for a punching bag," Layla said. "I'm getting to the place where it's hard to find any way to lay and sleep that's even remotely comfy. Besides, you know I hate to wake up and you're gone."

"I just didn't want to disturb you," Jimmie said.

"You've been disturbing me for a long time before now," she said, and touched his cheek. "Kiss me."

He did, as he always tried to, kissing her as if it might be the last time. Because it might be. Nothing was certain but this moment.

"I wanted to tell you," Jimmie said. "I'm headed out on some of the other business before I head to Arizona." Layla frowned, looking up into his eyes.

"Why are you telling me? Is it dangerous? Is something wrong?"

"No, no, baby. I just . . . I wanted you to know what's going on out there," Jimmie said, brushing the strands of her golden and silver hair out of her wide, dark eyes. "I don't want you to ever feel shut out from me, you understand?" She nodded. "I couldn't do what I do without you, without Peyton, and without the baby. You are the most important part of my life, and I never want to make you feel like you ain't."

"Be careful," Layla said, and kissed him again. He held her tight, holding the memory to sustain him. "Go fight the dragon. I've got it covered here, baby. Now git. Coffee's getting cold."

Jimmie closed the kitchen door, his breath swirling around him. He climbed into his truck and tossed his duffel bag in the seat beside him. The truck started with a grumpy rumble, then surged to life. He made the notations on his log, checked all his instruments, and finally grabbed the pistol grip of the shift and began to pull out of the yard and down the road.

As he turned onto Stonewall Street, he saw Layla's silhouette in the open front door. Her shadow, arms crossed over her belly, a hand slowly raised to wave goodbye, was the last sight of home Jimmie saw before the Road took it away.

Stepping into the offices of the Louisiana State Crime Lab was, at first glance, like stepping into any other cubicle farm—work spaces with three partition walls, desks, computers, pictures drawn by tiny hands with large crayons pinned to cube walls, stress balls, and family photos.

Lovina, now dressed for work in a dark navy Brooks Brothers pantsuit and gray sleeveless top, looked around for Russell Lime. She had her badge lanyard out, hanging around her neck, since she had to show her ID at the lobby to gain access to this part of the building. She walked between the cubes, and the differences between the lab and any other office became apparent just by the fragments of conversation that drifted past her:

"The assailant's blood tested positive for HIV, and type is the same as the other three victims. We're still waiting on DNA results. I know . . . I know! Well, look, it's going to take two to five days . . . yes, I know . . . I'll see if I can rush it, but don't . . ."

"The spatter pattern at the crime scene would be consistent with blunt-force trauma from a sledgehammer, yes. . . . You've got a possible weapon? Good! I need you to . . ."

"The brand of bleach he forced his daughter to ingest is consistent with the brand that was found in his trunk. The chemical burns in her throat . . ."

Lovina took a left at a wall of file cabinets full of horror, death, and petty inhumanities and saw that they had moved Russell to a larger, private office with a window on the edge of the floor. She walked past the doors to laboratories, conference rooms, and other offices. It always made her smile to flip on the television and see the spate of crime dramas with forensic labs. She tried to imagine the lab techs and criminalists she knew zipping around in designer clothing, driving Hummers to respond to crime scenes. And any forensic scientist or cop would trade his soul for a magic computer that got you DNA results or hits off partial prints in a few seconds, along with a photo of the suspect, an address, and a list of his hobbies. Those shows fell into the realm of science fiction.

The title on the glass of Russell's door said RUSSELL LIME, SENIOR TECHNICAL DIRECTOR. Lovina rapped on the open door and waved when Russ looked up and broke into a wide smile. "Love-e-ly Lo-vina!" he said. "How are you, *chère*?" Russell Lime was in his early seventies. He was still dangerously charming, and every woman who spent more than five minutes with him knew that. Lovina also knew that the dirty-old-man routine was all show. Lime's heart belonged to his wife of forty-eight years, Treasure. Russ was a tad over five feet and rawboned. He had a full head of snow-white hair that he combed back from his face. He had prominent ears and an animated face with expressive hazel eyes that actually twinkled sometimes. His nose was a little bulbous and red. He looked like one of the elves at the North Pole crossed with an elderly Tom Waits.

"I'm good, Russ, how are you?" Lovina said, holding up a plastic bag and a large cup of coffee. "Good as my word—coffee and doughnuts from Blue Dot."

"Ah!" Russell exclaimed. "*Vous êtes aussi doux que vous êtes belle, chère!*" He stood and pulled a chair by the door over to his desk. He gestured for her to sit.

"*Merci monsieur. Tu es très gentil,*" Lovina replied, and sat. As Russell began to dig into the doughnuts, he handed her a small USB flash drive. She nodded and slipped it into her pocket. "This Rears's computer data?" Lovina asked.

Russell nodded, talking around the doughnut in his mouth. "Everything I could decrypt," he said. "This fella is into some very weird stuff, darlin'. UFOs, Bigfoot, Mothman, ghosts, demons. Looks like he's been some kind of paranormal investigator and writer for years now."

Lovina sipped her hot tea and nodded. "I got that impression from his apartment. Russ, you find anything that would make you like this guy for the abductions you said he was tracking?"

"I wish I could say yes, beautiful, but I'm sorry. He was visiting the scenes of the abductions, but he was keeping track of those visits like they were business expenses. If he was involved in them, it seems foolish to keep records of them on his computer."

"Wouldn't be the first foolish criminal we've met," Lovina said. "Russ, you think you could help me with some technological hoodoo?"

Russell laughed and leaned back in his chair. "*Chère*, if it hums, buzzes, clicks or whirrs, I am your man."

Lovina grinned. "I'll bet you are." She slipped a piece of paper from the pocket of her leather jacket. It was the folded computer printout of the photograph of Shawn Ruth Thibodeaux, charging toward the person taking the picture, her head lowered and a look of savagery on her face, as if she were fighting for her life. She handed it to Russell. "I need to know everything you can tell me about this picture," she said.

Russell took the photo, looked at it, and then looked at Lovina a bit longer than he should have.

"What?" she asked.

"Nothing, dear," he said. "Okay, well, for starters, this photo is one of several located on Rears's computer hard drive. Come over here, let me show you."

Russell stood and insisted on wrestling her chair over to his side of the desk, facing his large flat-screen monitor. Lovina entertained his gallant nature as much as possible; considering the chair weighed almost as much as he did, she provided a little help to the old man.

"Rears has that photo here," he said, clicking on a file-folder icon titled "BEK Confirmed" on his computer screen. The file expanded, and columns of photos appeared. The majority of them were of kids who looked like the two boys in hoodies Lovina had confronted at Rears's apartment last night, right down to the inhuman, ink-black eyes. There were dozens of photos of children or teens with the same dead eyes.

"What is it?" Russell said, looking at her. "You all right, *chère*?" Lovina nodded.

"Fine, Russ. What is all this?"

"One of the newer versions of the Boogeyman brought to you by the Internet," Russell said. "These, my dear, are Black-Eyed Kids, or BEKs, if you're into that whole LOL, SMH, OMG nonsense that passes for language these days."

"What are they supposed be?" she asked.

"It's the latest iteration of the stolen-away-by-fairies myth," Russell said, clicking on the picture with Shawn Ruth in it. The photo filled the screen. "Back in the olden days, people believed the fay folk would sneak into your house at night and steal your baby away, replace it with a changeling—a fairy baby. It was one of the early explanations for mental-health issues and missing persons, or just weird behavior.

"As our technology became more sophisticated and science began to understand the universe a bit more, the myth changed to alien visitations and abductions to fit the times. Now, in our age of callousness being considered cool, impersonal sexting, and social-media posts passing for relationships, where our children are so connected to the world and so alone, so alienated from it, we have cyber-urban myths; we get BEKs. These kids are putting their own twists on the old scary story by the campfire. I'd wager most of them have never seen a real campfire. They're reflecting their own culture, their own fears, in these stories, these creatures."

"But this, this isn't real, right?" Lovina said, leaning forward. "These kids are wearing cosmetic contact lenses, or these pictures have been Photoshopped? Right?"

Russell narrowed his eyes at her and then broke into a smile. "You have a run-in with something, Lovina?" he said. "You seem a little . . . unnerved?"

"It's nothing," she said. "I just hate weird."

"You picked the wrong city and the wrong career, then," Russell said with a laugh. "There was a case a few years back, in Wisconsin, where two teenage girls lured a third out into the woods to sacrifice her to some urban myth called Slender Man. It's madness, chère. Give me bank robbers and forgers any old day of the week."

"Yeah, ain't that the truth," she replied. "What can you tell me about my picture, Russ?" He minimized the photo on the screen and opened another program.

"Of course, dear," he said. "I'm using FairPlay and a few other programs to give this one a good going-over. This might take a spell. You want to use my laptop to review the other stuff on Rears's drive while you're waiting?"

"Thanks," she said.

Russell set her up at a small desk in the corner of his office and opened the drive for her on his computer. She casually scanned the contents, looking for anything that might jump out at her. Once she was sure Russell was deep into his work, she clicked open Rears's files on Black-Eyed Kids.

She noticed that beside the photos in the file Rears also had notes and detailed interviews with parents and friends of missing children in more than thirty states. Shawn Ruth's family was among those interviewed. There was also a map of the U.S., with each abduction he had investigated pinpointed on it, along with hyperlinks to news articles about missing children, abductions, and the sex-slave trade. Another layer of links connected the map to some of the photos in the file, which, in turn, were linked to the interviews and any media coverage about the missing children. Another layer of links bizarrely connected all his data to a map of the U.S. highway system, showing, for each disappearance, the relative proximity to highways and major routes.

"Russ," Lovina said, turning in her chair, "did Rears try to access the FBI database at any point on his computer? Especially the Highway Serial Killings Initiative?"

Russell looked up from his screen, his white eyebrows raised. "As a matter of fact, in between frequenting numerous porn websites, 4chan, and 9GAG, he made several inquiries to the bureau's site, and that section in particular. He even incorporated the map they have on there of the national unsub cases into that interactive database you've been perusing. Guess what turned up?"

"A highway serial case near every abduction point," Lovina said, nodding, as she clicked between the layers of the database. "At least one, most more than one. Looks like Rears was onto something."

"Or involved in something," Russell said. "This may have been his way of keeping trophies of his victims. And going back and interviewing the victims' families, making them relive all the horror he caused. That's powerful stuff to these monsters."

"Anything that would tie him to a crime in here?" Lovina asked. "A photo of a victim or a crime-scene photo he shouldn't have? Anything past theory?"

"Nope," Russell said. "Like I said, clean as an investigative-reporting whistle. You don't like him for this, *chère*?"

"I don't," she said. "Just doesn't feel right. "Of course, my gut has been known to be wrong."

"Well, darlin'," Russell said. "It wasn't wrong on your prize photo here." He gestured for Lovina to come look at his monitor. "This photo shows up on a few Black-Eyed Kid and paranormal websites. Its point of origin is an IP address that goes back to a cell-phone service in Granite City, Illinois. Any current cell activity to that phone number has been flagged by the FBI and the Illinois State Police—"

"—due to it belonging to a missing kid," Lovina said.

Russell nodded. "Exactly," he said. "They found the phone at the crime scene, but no kid. I'm requesting access to the Illinois State Police case-management system. Give me a second." A page with the Illinois State Police seal at the top and columns of case file numbers filled the screen. He selected the case number and, after a moment, a police report appeared. A picture of a smiling young girl with long brown hair was in a box in the upper left-hand corner of the report. "Here we are. Cell phone belongs to Karen Collie, age fifteen at the time of her disappearance. She went missing along with friends: Stephanie Bottner, Aaron Kline, Kristie Plunkett, and Mark Baz. All of them teens, all good kids with no record of any trouble. They were going to the mall, and when none of them showed up back at home that night Mark's parents filed a report. They found Mark's car in the mall's parking lot, but all five kids were gone without a trace."

"Sounds familiar," Lovina said. "Group of kids, no history of trouble. All just up and disappear. So Shawn Ruth and her friends go missing five years ago. Then they show up on a cell-phone photo from this

Collie girl several states away, who also goes missing with her friends two years ago. Russ, what are these Black-Eyed Children supposed to do, exactly?"

"They approach people," Russell said as he read from a website. "Usually in pairs. They are teens in apparent age, and they ask to be let in to wherever the witness is—their house, their car. They keep asking."

Lovina felt her breath catch in her chest, a cold, tight hand clutching the air in her lungs. "So what happens?" she asked. "What happens to you if you let them in?"

Russell grinned and wiggled his eyebrows. "No one knows . . . because if you let them in you're never heard from again. Muwhaha-haha!" he laughed, doing his best mad-scientist impersonation.

The spell broken, Lovina shook her head. "Hilarious."

Russell grabbed another doughnut. "Well, that's part of the myth, anyway," he said. "They're always saying they were sent to gather you. But they never say why or to where. Are you holding out on me? Did something happen?"

"Russ," Lovina said, leaning forward in her chair, "Do you . . . do you believe . . . in any of this? Have you ever seen something you couldn't explain away?"

Lime leaned back in his chair. "Yes, of course I have," he said. "Any cop, any EMT, nurse, lab rat, fire and rescue—we've all had those unexplained things that happen when you're on the job. We see the world with the curtains pulled back—we see horror that other human beings can't even begin to comprehend. Then, every once in a while, you get something that goes so far beyond even that—beyond the street, beyond reason, sanity, logic. Back in 1972, I had a corpse, on the table, dead for over forty-eight hours, Y incision and all, open his eyes and speak to me—without lungs attached in his chest anymore, mind you."

"What did he say?" Lovina asked.

"'Fuck Nixon,'" Russell said.

"I'm serious," she said.

Russell nodded. "So am I, *chère*. I swear it. What has you so jumpy? You know you can tell me—what is it?"

"I think I ran into a pair of these . . . kids at Rears's apartment last night," she said. "They had the eyes, the voice, everything. And, Russ, I was terrified of them, and now I couldn't tell you why. You think I'm crazy?"

"No," Russell said. "Not even a smidge. I take it you refused to let them in the apartment? Were you alone, was Roselle with you? Local PD? Anyone?" Lovina shook her head. Russell frowned. "I see."

Lovina saw the wheels turning in the old scientist's mind. She pointed to another photo that had been in the computer file with Shawn Ruth's photo. She recalled seeing a crumpled printout of it in Rears's apartment office. It was a blurry photo depicting shadowy outlines of people, a forest in daylight. There was a central figure, dark and featureless against the sunlight and blur, with branches, perhaps, behind the looming figure—they looked like massive antlers growing from the shadow's head. "This one," she said. "Russ, what can you tell me about this one? Rears had some note on it about 'patient zero,' or something."

Russell frowned slightly and went back to work on his computer. He pulled up the photo and began to examine it with both his eyes and an array of forensic computer programs.

"That's interesting," he said, furrowing his thick white eyebrows. "You do have a knack for picking them, *chère*."

"What?" she said, looking over his shoulder. The photo was a blur of pixels on his screen. He clicked a control, and it zoomed back a few magnifications but was still blurry. In the right corner of the photo, Lovina could now see a symbol superimposed over the photo. "What the hell is that, Russ?"

The symbol came into focus a bit more. It was a circle, and above it was a crescent turned on its side, so that it touched the top of the circle and the two points at the end of the crescent pointed upward.

"I don't know," he said, "but I aim to find out. I'm running it through Forensic Image Analysis and a few other databases, including what the Feds have access to—the SST and BCOE over at the Department of Justice. It may take a spell to cook, but we'll get something. It looks like this photo has had a history online since the late nineties. It's a tangled mess, but I'll see what I can get for you, darlin'. It may take a day or two to hear back. You, uh, need me to let Roselle know it will be a bit, keep him off your back about the delay? I know you said the case is hot right now."

They looked at each other. Russell had an odd look on his face. Lovina had seen it before. Russell's inner bloodhound was close to chasing down a hidden scrap of truth. She shook her head.

"Okay," she said. "Roselle has no idea I'm here. I'm on the beach. I'm mucking around in a case that's not mine, and it's far from hot. But I am onto something, Russell. Shawn Ruth, those other kids, this Karen Collie girl . . . they're gone like they were swallowed up whole. Rears was onto it, too—"

"Or part of it," Russell interrupted. Lovina held up a hand.

"Maybe, maybe he is . . . was," she said, "but I think he stumbled onto something and that something came for him. How many missing-children cases are there in Rears's database?"

"'Something'?" Russell said, narrowing his eyes. "You think Black-Eyed Children snatched Dewey Rears because he knew too much? Lovina, darlin', knowing the world is odd and having any kind of walk-into-court proof of that strangeness is a whole 'nother animal. You have a solid career here, *chère*. You start talking this cooyon and—"

"How many, Russ?" Lovina asked. "How many missing children?"

"About eight hundred kids," Russell said. "But, Lovina, and please forgive me for bringing this up, but no matter how many of them you go hunting for, no matter how many you find, it don't change what happened to Delphine."

Russell felt the name strike Lovina like a slap, and he regretted having to invoke her dead sister, but they both knew why she had latched on to this case, why she always chased them. They were quiet for a moment. The murmur of the lab's usual chaos filled the empty space.

"I know, Russ," she said finally. "You have always been a good friend to me and to my family. Mama always appreciated all you did for us when Pops was in the hospital, at the end. And all the help you've given me over the years when I started on the job. I appreciate all of it, more than I can ever say. I don't want to cause you any trouble. I understand you can't—"

"The hell, I *can't*!" Russell said. "Pardon my language, Lovina."

"Russ, you got a good thing going here. I don't want to get you mixed up in my crazy," she said.

"Then don't," he said. "If Roselle gets wind of this, I will tell him everything looked in order on this end. He don't ask, I don't tell."

Lovina leaned over and hugged him. "Thank you," she said. "You're a good friend, Russ."

"A good friend would tell you to stop this damn fool nonsense before you do lose your job over it. You have a lot of people who care about you—Roselle, me—and none of us want to see you suffer for this obsession of yours."

"Russ, if it had been your sister those animals . . . did that to—"

"I'd do the same damn thing," he said. "I know, darlin'. But you can't find all of them, you can't save all of them."

"Eight hundred kids, Russ. All connected to one missing man. Isn't that worth at least a little inquiry?"

Russell sighed and took the last doughnut. "I'll tell you what I get on the history of your blurry-antler 'patient zero' picture and that symbol on it."

"Thank you, Russ," she said, and handed him the crumpled paper she had taken from Rears's place. "I found this in Rears's apartment. It's some GPS coordinates and a bunch of babbling about Four Houses or something. Can you try to make some sense of it for me, please?" Russell nodded.

"And there was someone in that apartment with Rears," Lovina said. "I'm betting a print is going to come through the system off that overturned beer can or something else in there."

"If they've been printed," Russell added. "You want me to run it down for you?"

"I want to find whoever it is," Lovina said, "before someone else does."

"I'll call you," he said. "I'll keep all this on the DL, *chère*."

"On the DL?" Lovina said, and laughed.

Russell chuckled. "Always good to see a smile on that pretty face," he said. "My love to your mama, as always."

"Love to Treasure as well," Lovina said. "How is she, Russ?" The twinkle left Lime's eye at the mention of his wife's name, but the smile remained, set on his face. "Oh, Russ . . . is she—"

"Back to the hospital for a spell," Russell said. "Been there about two weeks. They say it's the cancer again, but I think she bribes the doctors to tell me that so she can get a little break from me." He chuckled; it was a dry sound in his throat. Lovina hugged him again, tight. He patted her back gently. "It will all be fine, *chère*," he said. "Just fine."

Lovina lived in the Contesta Apartments, third floor, overlooking Decatur Street. She had lived there since she started with the NOPD, back in 2004. Even when the Quarter was trashed by Hurricane Katrina a year later, Lovina had stayed, along with the other die-hards who refused to let the most deadly force of nature in U.S. history drive them from their city. She remembered sitting in her dark, hot living room, only a stale humid breeze from the open balcony doors to cool her; dressed in her sweat-stained police uniform, drinking water in plastic bottles provided by the Red Cross and the National Guard. This place, this city, was home. She had fought for it, cried for it when it fell, reveled in it when it arose, and shed her most precious blood here, in New Orleans. Some places marked you, made you theirs.

She unlocked the front door, and as she did she heard the click of the lock on the door across the hall, Lake's door. She turned to see her neighbor open his door and step out.

"It's about damn time you showed your narrow little ass up in here, sugar!" Tyson Lake said, hugging Lovina. "That four-legged little misanthrope you call a pet was about ready to maul me!"

Lake was a slender, six-foot-four black man with delicate features, large expressive eyes, and a body that had been sculpted to perfection by long hours of worship at the temple of iron and sweat. She was a drag queen, working a burlesque show down in the Quarter at the Golden Lantern, over on Royal Street. Miss Lake, her stage name, had been named for Mike Tyson by the father and mother who no longer talked to Ty. Tyson had actually played a few years in the Erie BayHawks, a D-League NBA team that was a feeder for talent for the Orlando Magic. Ty had been pretty good, but he fell in love and decided to quit living a life that belonged more to his dad than to him. Lovina was Lake's only family now.

Lovina hugged her neighbor back. "You mean to tell me you afraid of a trifling little pussy hissing at you, girl?" They both laughed.

"Mmmhmm," Lake said. "Them nasty things scary."

"Sorry about last night. I expected to be back yesterday afternoon. The case got hot," Lovina said, opening her door. "I'm actually just home to tell Wafflez to leave you be and to grab some clothes. Do you mind feeding her, Ty? I hate to ask."

"It's no trouble, Love," Lake said. "You know I got you, boo. Something . . . odd happened last night, though. I thought I should let you know."

"What?" Lovina asked, flipping through the mail that Ty had left on the small table by the door, just inside her apartment.

"There was a pounding on your door last night," Ty said. "Round three or so. I had just got home from work, and it was so loud it scared me. I looked through the peephole, and there were two kids beating on your door—boom, boom, boom, not stopping. No pattern, y'know, like, knock, knock knock, then stop. . . . They just kept on pounding."

Lovina felt a sick fear twist in her gut, like rats gnawing on her intestines. "Boys?" she said. "Hoodies? Ty, did you see their eyes? Did they look at you? Did they see you?"

Lake shook her head, frowning. "No," she said. "Only through the peephole. That was the weird part. By the time I unlocked the door and opened it, they were gone. Not by your door, not in the hall, no sound of them headed down the stairs, just . . . gone. Love, what's wrong? You look sick, honey, what's happening? Let me help."

Lovina walked into her apartment, gesturing for Lake to follow. "Listen to me, Ty, please listen. I mean this. Do not approach those kids if they show up again. If they knock on your door, do not answer it. Do you hear me?"

"Yeah, but—"

"Just don't," Lovina said. "They keep knocking, you call the cops, y'hear me? But you *do not* answer that door! They are dangerous, and I'm . . . I'm not sure what they are, exactly."

"Okay," Lake said, placing her hand on Lovina's shoulder. "Okay, Love, I will. I promise. This some kind of work thing?"

"I guess," Lovina said. "They must have tracked me somehow. This can't be real, can it? This is stupid. Things like this don't really happen . . . do they?"

"Talk to me," Lake said. "I sure as hell ain't gonna judge you, boo. You tell me."

"I'll tell you when I'm back from this," Lovina said. "I promise. Right now, just please do what I say, Ty. Okay?"

Lake raised her hands as if she was surrendering. "Okay, okay," she said, turning back toward her apartment. "I'll feed the little creep while you're gone. Do you need me to turn over the engine on the Charger while you're—"

"No," Lovina said. "I'm taking Dad's car."

"Not a cop car," Lake said. "You sure this is about work, boo?"

"Jesus!" Lovina said, stepping into her kitchen and opening the fridge. She fished out a cold bottle of Dixie beer and opened it. "I must be the worst damn liar in town." Lake hurried toward the door and began to pull it shut.

"Too damn earnest for your own good! Love you, Love," she said, and blew Lovina a kiss. "Be careful, baby, and I'll stay clear of weird little skate punks. You be safe, boo!" Lake shut the door and the apartment was quiet. Lovina sat at her kitchen table, pulled her pistol from its shoulder holster, and placed the .40-caliber Glock 22 on the Formica tabletop. She was scared, no getting around it. Those kids had found her, had made their way to her door hours before she was even in back in New Orleans. So it was either the same night-eyed kids she had faced at Rears's apartment and they had managed to cross space in an impossible amount of time or it was different kids, sent from the same unknowable source on the same cryptic mission. *"They're always saying they were sent to gather you,"* Russ had said, *"but they never say why or to where. . . ."*

Lovina took a long draw on the beer, let it slide down her throat, and felt calmness settle over her in the act. Dixie had been Pops's brand. They didn't make it in town anymore, but it was part of the mythology of her dad and it always gave her some comfort. She remembered the first time he let her have a swig. She had been twelve, helping him work on the Charger. The first taste of beer was horrible, gross, and strange. Pops had laughed at the face she made. "Good," he had said. "Now you won't be all-fired curious to try it again, will you, Smiley?"

The thought brought the grin back to her face, the same grin that had made Pops give her the nickname. He called her that up till his last breath. She tipped the bottle to empty air.

"Look at me now, Pops," she said. "Look at me now." She took another drag on the Dixie. Her cell phone buzzed. She pulled it out of her pocket and looked at the screen. It was Russell.

"Hello, Investigator Marcou," he said with mock formality. "I'm calling about that weirdo case you're not really supposed to be working on."

Lovina stood from the table, leaving her beer and her gun, and walked into the bedroom. She found her gym bag on a shelf in the closet, unzipped it, and opened it on the bed. "You got something already, Russ? Damn, you're good."

"Indeed," Russell said. "But don't let the missus know. The file on that Karen Collie girl—you remember I said it was inactive for over a year?"

"Yeah," she said as she sniffed a T-shirt, decided it was clean enough, and tossed it into the bag.

"Well, it just became active again, today. Someone with Illinois State Police access opened it up and gave it a good going-over."

"Hot damn!" she said, and crammed a pair of jeans into the rapidly filling bag. "Can you get me a name, Russ?"

"I will by the time you get to Illinois," he said. "Still digging on that photo, too."

Lovina heard a sound in the living room, some movement near the door. Her heart became stone, crushing the air out of her lungs. "I got to go, Russ," she said softly. "Thanks."

She heard it again, maybe someone very slowly opening the front door. Someone small, trying to be quiet. Her mind flashed to her service piece, sitting all the way in the kitchen next to a sweating beer. She opened the night-table drawer and pulled out her backup, an oddly elongated-looking revolver with a wide, squat barrel. She checked the load on the Taurus Judge Magnum—the pistol fired three-inch 000 shotgun shells—five-ball buckshot. She clasped the ugly-looking gun with both hands in a Weaver stance, her finger off the trigger as she moved slowly, quietly into the living room, where the noise was coming from, by the door. Lovina held her breath and stepped out, leveling the revolver in the direction of her front door, ready to the take the shot.

Wafflez, the tortoiseshell cat, looked up from wrestling with the TV remote on the floor by the door, where she had dragged it. The remote thudded softly against the door. Wafflez looked slightly annoyed at Lovina, but then she always looked that way. Wafflez meowed.

"Shit," Lovina said, and lowered the hand cannon. "Good to see you, too, you little asshole." Wafflez padded over, purring, and rubbed against Lovina's leg. Lovina knelt and rubbed Wafflez's head and neck. The cat purred like a tiny motorboat and nipped gently at Lovina's fingers. "Let's get you fed and the litter box cleaned up and get me on the road before I end up killing some Girl Scouts selling cookies door-to-door."

. . .

There was street parking for the apartments and a small lot in the back, but Lovina paid extra to use a garage down the block to house her dad's car, now her car. She pulled the cover off the 1968 Dodge Charger. The car was matte-black, with a 440 V-8 RB engine and six-pack carbs, a four-speed manual tranny, and a Dana 60 rear axle.

Pops had won the car in 1970, in a very illegal and dangerous race on I-20. He risked his life for the car because of Steve McQueen. *Bullitt* came out in 1968, and Pops fell in love with Chargers and Mustangs. When he saw the car growling like a tiger ready to pounce on the start line, he had to go after her. Lovina was pretty sure that if the Charger had been a woman her parents' marriage would have crashed and burned long before she was ever conceived. She had loved the car because Pops loved it. She had spent long afternoons—Saturdays and Sundays—working on it with him. There was never any doubt in anyone's mind that Lovina would get the Charger. Sometimes, when she missed her father, wanted his advice or just to feel him close, she would work on the car, or take it out on the highway and open it up.

She opened the trunk and tossed in her gym bag. She also set a small canvas bag in the trunk. The bag held the Taurus revolver, a very illegal 12-gauge double-barreled shotgun sawed down to a snout and modified with a pistol grip. There were also handcuffs, a stun gun, boxes of ammo, and shotgun shells for all the guns, a few flash-bang grenades she had "acquired" from a buddy of hers in NOPD SWAT, and a chopped-down, full auto AR-15 with a folding stock, a scope, and extended banana clips. She closed the trunk and climbed into the bucket seat. She turned the ignition, and the Charger purred to life with a throaty snarl. The sound always made her grin. It had made Pops grin, too.

"Okay, Smiley," she said to herself. "Let's go find some kids and kick some boogieman ass."

The Charger's tires squealed as she pulled out of the space, turned, and drove out of the darkness of the cool garage and into bright afternoon. Lovina shifted, and felt the car respond like an extension of her own body, perfect humming union; breath and fuel, flowing. She snapped on the radio, and Bayou 95.7 greeted her with Robert Plant's song "Big Log." The highway beckoned, and she was as ready as she would ever be. Russ would call soon and give her a name in Illinois, whoever had reopened Karen Collie's case file, and she would start there. The music, the purr of the engine, of her heartbeat, all fluid and perfect and right. Lovina drove; Pops rode shotgun.

Part of Jimmie's mind wished he hadn't seen the sign, its stuttering fluorescent glow against the summoning of the darkness, as night began to slowly devour the day at the ragged edges of U.S. 150. Only one in a thousand, in ten thousand travelers, would have felt the fear, the nausea, swell in them at the sign the way Jimmie did. That was the whole point, wasn't it?

"Oh, damn it," Jimmie muttered. He slowed and pulled into the gravel lot to the side of the restaurant. There were other 18-wheelers parked here as well, most with trailers, all empty and still. There was a paved parking area in front of the restaurant, with about a dozen cars filling the painted spaces. There were dingy, unwashed old sedans, a classic VW bug, and a couple of vans and work trucks. At least two of them looked like old police cars that had been purchased at auctions. Even from across the lot, Jimmie could see that most of the cars were stuffed with trash, clothes, books, old newspapers, and magazines. A few had large plastic storage tubs stacked in the seats. A minivan stood out, though. It was clean, new, and had the little white family stickers in the rearview window. A family of five was presented in vinyl pictogram: Mommy, Daddy, Brother, Sister, and Baby Girl. A sun with a smiley face beamed above them.

"Aw, no, no!" Jimmie said, turning off the ignition and tapping on his CB-radio headset. "Break 2-3, break 2-3, anyone got their ears on, c'mon?" Dead, dirty static was the only reply. Jimmie switched on the special scrambler that only other members had, the scrambler that allowed quantum encrypted and decrypted transmissions on Channel 23.

It worked off principles like theoretical physics, numerology, and sacred geometry. Jimmie didn't get all the quantum *Star Trek*, big-bang-theory stuff; that was the province of the Builders, who thought the things up, but he knew that if there were any Brethren in range their radios would be receiving a call tone right now, a call to answer. "Break 2-3," he repeated. "Break 2-3, c'mon, somebody? Anybody, this is Paladin. I got a situation here, c'mon?" No answer. There were so few of them left, and so much highway.

Jimmie sat in the cab for about ten minutes. He wasn't a praying man; he hadn't been since Sunday school as a kid. He'd seen too many prayers, too much begging, pleading through tears and pain, go unanswered to put much faith in, well, faith. But he sat and a tiny part of him, the part that hadn't fully given up on faith, on happy endings, prayed to God Almighty that the family would walk out the door, get into their clean little minivan, and drive away. That the roadside restaurant with the twitchy fluorescent sign declaring it the COMPASS POINT GRILL would be no more than a ripple in the family's memory as they drove on to Aunt Sophie's, or wherever the hell they were going; that they would never know the meaning of the symbol that was behind the words on the sign, glowing like a beacon on the side of the highway—a circle intersected by a cross, with the lines of the cross stretching beyond the edges of the circle.

He waited. No one came out. He unlatched the shotgun from the transmission well, checked its load, and then grabbed a box of spare shells, stuffing them into a canvas gym bag along with the 12-gauge. He took a small .380 Colt pistol out of the glove box, jacked a round into the pipe, lowered the hammer, and clicked the safety back on. He slid the small automatic into his jacket pocket and zipped the bag with the shotgun partly up and climbed out of the truck, carrying it. The gravel crunched as he walked. He touched the hood of the minivan and found it still warm. Jimmie closed his eyes, took a deep breath, and pushed through the glass door of the Compass Point. The door had a small placard that announced the hours of operation, a cardboard sign that said OPEN, and a smaller red sign in spidery freehand print: "*IN GOD WE TRUST . . . EVERYONE ELSE PAYS CASH $.*"

The interior of the Compass Point was fluorescent, counterfeit day. The tiled floor was dirty and scuffed. The fake wood tables, orange plastic chairs, and upholstered booths had all been new in 1972. A plastic plant in a heavy, pebbled planter squatted by the register counter and the door. Old tumors of gum, gnawed-on lollipop sticks, toothpicks, and crushed cigarette butts were scattered in the gravel that filled the planter. Jimmie could smell the warm grease of French fries and onion rings drowning as they fried, the hiss of hamburgers and hash browns—smothered and covered—on a grill that hadn't been cleaned well enough. A jukebox near the restrooms was playing "Dire Wolf," by the Grateful Dead. Jimmie felt eyes fall on him from every direction, analyzing him, dissecting him, sizing him up, and he knew, he knew his odds in this place. For a second, he wanted to bolt back out the door, but then he heard the children and he knew he couldn't.

. . .

Paul Waclaw was trying to keep his ten-year-old son, Ira, from launching the straw paper like a blow-gun dart at his twelve-year-old daughter, Gabby, who had her face buried in her smartphone screen. Baby Jennie cooed as daddy Paul patted her back gently, resting the baby on his chest and shoulder. His wife, Stacy, returned from the restroom and sat down in the booth next to him.

"That bathroom," Stacy said in a hushed voice. "So clean! I'm surprised this place isn't on any of the travel sites. If the food is decent, I'll give them a really good review."

"Ira, don't shoot that at your sister," Paul said, gesturing toward the boy as best he could while balancing Jennie. "Don't shoot that at anyone!"

"Daaaad," Gabby said, not looking up from her phone. "Ugh, I can't get *annnny* bars in here—this place sucks. Why couldn't we stop at McDoooooonald's instead?"

"Gabby," Stacy said, "we're trying to support small businesses, remember? McDonald's doesn't need our money, and little mom-and-pop places like this do, dear. Now, put your phone away and look at the menu."

"I want nuggets!" Ira announced loudly. "And fries!"

"Okay, okay," Paul said, lowering his voice. "Ira, keep it down. Other people are trying to enjoy their food."

"Oh," Stacy said, smiling, "they have little names for their specials; I guess they're named after locals or something. The Albert Fish and Chips sounds good. I'll think I'll have that."

"This Richard Chase Tomato Soup and Grilled Cheese sounds good, huh, Ira? You want that, pal?"

"I guess," Ira said. "If they don't got nuggets."

"Okay," Paul said. "Gabby?"

"Uh," Gabby said, scanning the laminated menu. "Can I just get this Dean Corll Cheesecake?"

Stacy sighed. "No, young lady, you can't. You need to eat something else." She looked over the menu at her daughter. "How about this Ed Gein Bar-B-Que? That sounds good!"

"That name's familiar," Paul said. "I think he was a governor or something."

The waitress, a tall, gray, gaunt woman in a stained apron and pink polyester pantsuit uniform that might have been stylish around the same time as the furniture, walked over to them, her order pad in hand. She reeked of cigarette smoke and something organic and spoiled.

"Y'all ready to order, hon?" she said, addressing Paul. Her name tag read MYRTLE.

"Almost there," he said, slightly apologetic. "You know how it is with kids, right? Like herding cats." He laughed, and so did Stacy. Myrtle said nothing, but nodded.

"Right. I'll be back with some water for ya'll," she said and walked away, her stiletto heels clicking on the tile.

"She's sketch," Gabby said in a whisper. Ira laughed and nodded in agreement. Myrtle looked back at the booth when the boy laughed. She gave them a look that bordered on raw hatred, then went back behind the lunch counter and busied herself filling glasses with water.

"You two stop that!" Paul whispered. Baby Jennie was starting to make fussy sounds, and he handed her off to Stacy without even a thought. "You don't judge people by how they look," he said. "Even if they are a little creepy . . . and she is."

"Paul!" Stacy said as she pulled open her blouse and draped a blanket from the baby bag over her shoulder. "That is an awful thing to tell the children. The poor woman can't help how she looks or comes off." She looked into her baby's eyes. "Can she, Jennie? No, she can't. You hungry, baby? Come here, sweetheart." Stacy slipped her breast free of her bra cup under the blanket and then pulled the blanket aside long enough for her daughter to begin suckling, then she slipped the blanket back into place. Paul noticed a change in the diner's clientele. They all froze; many stared at the Waclaws' booth like hungry dogs. Paul felt a palpable energy build in the room. He didn't like it, but he couldn't name it with words or even cogent thoughts. The trucker, with his baseball cap, ponytail, and potbelly, seemed to be the only other one to notice it. He sat at a table near them, and he, too, was scanning the patrons now, his hand slipping into his jacket pocket.

"*Eww* gross, Mom!" Gabby said, making a finger-down-her-throat motion. "Do you have to do that?"

"It's perfectly natural," Stacy said, and then grinned. "I did it for both of you." Ira and Gabby laughed and groaned at the same time.

"Gag me!" Ira said, laughing. "Mom-boob, yuck!"

Paul wasn't laughing. He and the trucker made eye contact. Paul pulled his eyes away and looked at his family. "Uh, guys, maybe we should go eat somewhere else. It's not that much farther to Frankfort, and we can eat dinner with Maw-maw and Gran-Poppa if we make good time."

"Paul?" Stacy said, frowning. "What's gotten into you? Everyone's hungry, sweetheart."

"I just . . ." Paul began, and then his parental software kicked in, overriding his instincts, in this case. No reason to express these fears or concerns, to worry his family. He had no good reason to explain that he wanted to grab Stacy by the arm and shout for her and the kids to get to the minivan as quickly as they could and lock the doors . . . no rational explanation. No, it was nothing. Nothing. "Never mind," he said. "You're right. Let's eat and get back on the road."

"Y'all might want to reconsider that, folks." It was the trucker; he was carrying a chair from his table and setting it down at the edge of their booth. He had an oblong canvas bag in his other hand. He sat in the chair, putting himself between the Waclaws and the rest of the restaurant. The bag disappeared under the table. He looked at Paul and Stacy. "You need to get your kids out of this place right now, folks. It ain't safe, and you don't got much time. Please."

Paul looked over the trucker's shoulder and noticed an agitation among the other patrons and the staff at the trucker's actions. Whispering, furtive movements. He looked back into the truck driver's face and saw green eyes full of concern, with a hint of urgency and fear. Stacy was saying something to the man.

"Sir, you need to go back to your table before we have to get someone over here. You're scaring our children."

"Ma'am, they should be scared," Jimmie said. "Y'all need to get up and get out of here right now."

Stacy looked at Paul and nodded toward Jimmie. "Paul?" she said.

Paul took the cue. "Look, I don't know what your problem is," he said, "but you—"

"You ever hear of the Zodiac?" Jimmie interrupted him.

"Like the horoscope?" Paul asked

"Like the killer," Jimmie said. "There was a serial killer in San Francisco in the sixties and seventies called the Zodiac. He killed a lot of people, claimed to have killed even more. He was never caught. There have been copycats, too, lots of them."

"Dad?" Ira said, starting to look a little scared.

Jimmie kept going. Myrtle, the waitress, was headed back to the table now with a tray of water glasses. "The reason Zodiac was never caught," Jimmie said, looking from one frightened, confused face to another, "was because Zodiac wasn't a 'he.' Zodiac was a group of people, a club of murderers. They use the highways as their hunting grounds, their bone yard. They are very well organized, and they are not the only club like that out on the Road."

"Sir." Paul locked eyes with Jimmie. "That's enough. I need you to go, right now, or I'm having someone call 911."

"I wish you could," Jimmie said. "They have cell-phone jammers going in here. That symbol on the sign out front—the circle with the cross overlapping it—it's not for a compass, it's crosshairs, it's the Zodiac's symbol. This place is a hunting lodge for serial killers, and you, your family, and me are up the creek without a paddle if we don't get out of here right now."

Stacy was silent, holding the baby. Both the kids were silent, too. They all looked at Paul.

"If I'm a nut, then you walk out that door right now," Jimmie said, looking from one member of the Waclaw family to the next. He was starting to sweat a little. "No harm done to anyone, right? But if I'm telling you the truth . . . and I am . . ." Jimmie looked into Paul's eyes. "You saw how they looked at your wife, your baby? What's your gut telling you right now?"

"This fella bothering you folks, hon?" Myrtle drawled, looking at Paul. " 'Cause I can get a few of the cooks and busboys to get him out of here if he is."

Paul looked at Myrtle, with her dead, red eyes—like a rat's eyes. Then he looked back at Jimmie. The realization came to Paul that, besides his wife and kids, this trucker was the only person in the whole restaurant with eyes that had anything resembling human life behind them.

Jimmie nodded slightly to Paul. "Let me get y'all out of here," he said softly. "Please."

"No, that's okay," Paul said, looking up at Myrtle and forcing a polite smile. "This nice fella just told us about a little antiques place up the road, and we're going to head up there now. The kids weren't hungry, anyway. Thanks, though. I'll drop you a tip for your trouble."

There was silence. Every other patron in the Compass Point had stopped talking, as if their conversations had only been window dressing. Every single one of them heard what Paul had said, softly, to the waitress.

"Well sheeeeee-it," Myrtle said, her eyes slitting like a reptile's. "We were gonna give you a decent last meal with a little something extra in it to make you and the bitch and rug rats easier to handle, but noooo— have to go the hard way." She let the tray of glasses hit the floor without batting an eye. Paul, Stacy, and the kids jumped at the clatter. "Bunch of fuckin' snobs with your fancy-ass clothes and your laughing like you're better'n regular folks." Myrtle glared at Stacy and the kids. "I'm gonna flay your fucking little ankle-biters, you stuck-up bitch, you hear me? Skin 'em alive!"

In her hand, which had been holding the tray, Myrtle gripped a small, silver-plated pistol. She pointed it at the baby in Stacy's arms, and her eyes came to life. Jimmie was on his feet, between the family and the waitress and the patrons, his pistol in one hand and the 12-gauge, pointed toward the ceiling, in the other. He aimed the pistol at Myrtle's head and cocked the trigger.

"You point that gun away from that little girl, or I swear to God I'll blow a hole in that evil head of yours," Jimmie said through gritted teeth. "Back off!"

Myrtle sneered at Jimmie, and then her rat eyes flicked to his raised shotgun, and she saw the Crusaders' cross on the grip. Her eyes widened. She stepped back toward the center of the room. The gun moved from the baby to Jimmie. "Templar!" she hissed, "Templar! He's a fucking Templar!"

Paul had no idea what a Templar was, but the waitress's call galvanized the other patrons and the staff of the Compass Point to action. "Templar . . ." the patrons hissed. "Temmmmplaaaaarrrr . . ."

Weapons appeared, almost out of thin air—knives, retractable metal batons, guns. Two men who looked as if they were some type of utility workers, in coveralls, took out a hand ax and what looked like a battery-powered, circular surgical saw from their toolboxes, respectively. A couple—a normal-looking man and woman a moment ago, holding hands and snuggling—now brandished a terrifying hypodermic needle full of an unknown substance and a chemical-soaked cloth that the man retrieved from a plastic baggie. Rough-looking men in dirty white shirts and aprons, hairnets covering their heads, exited from the kitchen. Some of them brandished baseball bats; others had shotguns of their own. One busboy had a samurai sword, the kind you might buy at a pawnshop or on the Home Shopping Network at three in the morning. He also wore a belt adorned with small, mummified human heads. The other waitress on duty—a slightly younger, stockier blond iteration of Myrtle—had a large butcher knife that she brandished as she cracked her gum and blew a pink bubble. The blonde moved to the door of the restaurant, flipped the Open sign to Closed with her free hand, locked the door, and lowered the blinds, covering the glass door's view of outside.

The patrons and the staff began to form a circle around the Waclaws and Jimmie. Jimmie took a step forward, bringing the shotgun down to cover the killers to his left—between them and the door—and kept his pistol centered on Myrtle.

"Everyone up," Jimmie said to the family. "Stay behind me. Stay together. We're getting out of here."

"The hell you are, Templar!" Myrtle spat. "You're all alone, fat man, and you're sweating. You scared? You could still run. Give us the sweet meat and you can go on your way."

Jimmie risked a look back at Paul and his family. They were up, out of the booth, huddled behind him. They all took a step to the left, toward the door. The pack of killers slid left with them and moved forward a step in the process.

"Oh, yeah," Jimmie said, evenly. "I'm scared. I'm pissing my pants at you jackals. I'm swooning so much, my hand might twitch a little when I shoot you and only blow a hole through your throat instead of your head, lady, so keep talking. We're all walking out that door, all of us."

"No," a deep, muffled voice said above the thud of heavy boots. The pack of killers parted as a final figure appeared out of the kitchen. "You're not." The voice came from behind a thick black hood, almost square in shape, like a grocery bag. The hood had large eye slits, and behind them were polarized sunglasses. The man in the hood was huge, well over six feet, and he moved with a fluid, confident power. He was wearing dirty jeans and black combat boots. His muscled arms were bare save for black leather gloves and the full-sleeve tattoos of neo-Nazi symbols and slogans. His massive gut and barrel chest were covered with a black T-shirt, and a black tabard—a sleeveless jerkin, like the ones knights of old wore over their armor. The tabard fell below his knees. It was banded by a belt that held a military-style pistol holster, a sheathed hunting knife, and a coil of what looked to be clothesline. On the chest of the tabard, the Black Knight bore his grisly coat of arms in red—the crosshair circle that was on the Compass Point's sign—the Zodiac's mark.

Jimmie's nostrils flared at the bitter stench of hot urine. One of the Waclaws had peed himself, probably the kids. He didn't blame them. The idea crossed his mind for a bit, too. He swallowed and moved the pistol to aim at the Black Knight's chest. He tried to muster a dry chuckle.

"What are you dolled up for? You the restaurant's mascot? Like the guy in the rat costume?"

"You can't kill all of us, Templar," the Black Knight rumbled. "You will get off a few shots, if you're lucky, and you know that. You knew that coming in here. Then we will devour you, crush you, break you. You will die on this floor alone and for nothing, and then we will play with your charges for a long, long time."

Some of the killers laughed. Others clapped with glee or whistled and hooted as if their driver had just won at Indy. One of the cooks punched the jukebox buttons. The box hummed and clicked.

"I swear, on all that's holy, you will go down first," Jimmie said to the Black Knight. His palm was wet on the grip of the .380. Sweat burned his eyes. To his left, he saw the pack moving forward. He fanned the sawed-off shotgun back and forth, and they stopped.

"Of course you do," the Black Knight said, his voice even and calm behind the hood. "I am a Lodge Master, my victims are legion, Templar. In the afterlife, each one of them will be my slave in paradise. I have no fear of death. Can you say the same?"

Jimmie thought of Layla, Peyton, and the baby and he was dizzy with fear for a moment, just a moment. He thought of running; any sane person would run, beg, plead for his life right now. But he knew these things that hid behind people masks would never, ever let him go. Then he heard the sniffle of one of the Waclaw children, making the same sound Peyton made when she was sick or scared, and the fear was put away, far away. He felt a flush of anger settle over him like a mantle of fever. The jukebox began to play "The Old Man Down the Road," by John Fogerty.

Jimmie glanced over his shoulder at the Waclaws, then back at the Black Knight. "Here's what's going to happen," he said, his voice strong and unafraid. "I'm going to shoot up that door with the shotgun. If we're lucky, those dumbasses will keep standing between it and this twelve-gauge. You and your family run like hell and don't look back, y'hear me?" Paul nodded, but the trucker these maniacs called Templar couldn't see it. "And, you, asshole," Jimmie said to the Black Knight as he began to squeeze the trigger, "git your ass ready for paradise."

The door to the Compass Point exploded. Parts of the wall on either side of the door evaporated as well in the explosion. Glass and debris flew everywhere. Jimmie was as shocked as everyone else. He hadn't fired the shotgun yet. Was that a grenade? The killers in front of the door were tossed everywhere, screaming, bleeding, some expiring. There was the gravel-throated roar of an engine, a motorcycle, and through the smoke and the heady gasoline-oil smell, through explosive residue and the dying screams of evil men, a rider drove his bike, a T5 Blackie, into the Compass Point. The rider was dressed in jeans and boots, with a black leather riding jacket and an MC cut over it. He wore an open-faced helmet and a steel mask that bore the grinning face of a Japanese demon. The rider stopped a few feet in, resting his foot on the glass-and-blood-soaked floor. He released the left handlebar and fanned the assembled killers with a clattering MP9 machine gun. The squat little gun was slung over his shoulder and close to his chest. Jimmie swore he heard laughter behind the steel demon's face above the bark of the MP, the music, and the shouting.

Jimmie pumped a few rounds from the pistol into the Black Knight, who was going for his own gun. The hulking nightmare jerked backward and fell. Jimmie was almost a hundred percent sure the Lodge Master had on Kevlar, but he was down for a second.

"Go, go, go!" Jimmie shouted to Paul and his family. The Waclaws stayed low and ran for the demolished front of the Compass Point. Jimmie moved with them, covering them as best he could. One of the cooks was aiming a shotgun at the kid on the bike. Jimmie fired his shotgun first, and the cook and several other killers went down, bellowing in pain from the buckshot. A bullet whined past Jimmie and hit the cash register on the shredded counter by the nonexistent door.

The biker, who Jimmie could now see was with the Blue Jocks, Ale's club, had emptied the MP and was replacing the magazine when the Lodge Master rose and fired at him with his pistol at nearly point-blank range. Without missing a beat, the kid let go of the MP, which slapped against his chest, and revved the bike. He drove a kick into the Black Knight's balls and then swerved the bike to avoid hitting the lunch counter, as he stopped again. The Black Knight made a very satisfying gurgle and fell to his knees, dropping his gun in the process. A swarm of killers moved like a wave of rage to crash against the rider. Jimmie chambered a fresh shell and fired the shotgun again at the front of the mob. Buckshot ripped through the killers and many fell, while others dived for cover, shouting. The rider produced another grenade and lobbed it toward the back of the restaurant. A stray round sparked off the rider's handlebar, ricocheting and howling as it passed.

"Are you kidding me?" Jimmie shouted, and tried to hide behind the wrecked counter by the door. The grenade went off, and there were more screams and cries of pain. Part of the building groaned to stay standing from the shuddering blast, and gray dust and debris rained down. Several twisted and warped HVAC ducts jutted through the ragged remains of the grid ceiling, like a compound fracture puncturing skin.

Jimmie stepped out of the demolished front and saw the Waclaws in their clean little minivan, headlights on. Paul was behind the wheel. He nodded to Jimmie, mouthed the words "Thank you," and then tore out of the lot, gravel flying, as they got back on U.S.150. The family sped away into the darkness.

More gunfire, almost a conversation of sporadic pops from pistols, responded with burps of automatic fire from the MP. Jimmie figured they had ten minutes, tops, before cops and state troopers responded to this little war. He put the .380 back in his jacket and chambered another shell into the shotgun and carefully peeked inside.

The few surviving killers were hiding behind overturned tables or under the tables in booths. Bodies were everywhere. The rider was scanning the room with the MP9. He nodded toward Jimmie. "You ready to go?" he said through his steel demon face.

"The Lodge Master," Jimmie shouted back from the cover of the side of the ragged hole where the door to the Compass Point had been not so long ago. "You get him?"

"He scuttled into the kitchen," Demon Mask said. "No worries, I'll get him." He pulled out another grenade.

"Hold it! No!" Jimmie shouted, but it was too late. The rider pulled the pin and tossed it into the kitchen through the serving window behind the lunch counter. A plate of gravy fries, an order someone never got the chance to eat, still sat on the windowsill. The grenade flew by and bounced around the kitchen floor and then settled by the stainless-steel base of the grill and the ovens. The rider revved his T5 and shot toward the open hole he'd made in the front. Jimmie was running, diving behind one of the parked cars, as the rider cleared the interior of the Compass Point an instant before the grenade went off.

The whole back of the building erupted into a fireball as the gas lines in the kitchen caught. The roof flew skyward, then tumbled down, devoured by the flames. A second explosion, then a third, and the Compass Point was lost in ravenous fire and thick plumes of black smoke that poured skyward. Jimmie waited by the hole where the door had been, leaning against a filthy sedan, shotgun ready. The rider shut off his bike, climbed off, and stood beside Jimmie, MP9 leveled. No one else came through the hole, only thick smoke, as if the killers' rotted souls were trying to flee into the cold night.

"Thanks," Jimmie said to the Demon Mask. "I was a goner—that family, too. I wish we could have done this with a little less"—there was a series of small pops, and then a rumble from another explosion in the ruins of the restaurant—"of that," Jimmie said as hot debris thudded down on several of the nearby cars. "But you saved my skin, regardless."

"No worries, man," the rider said. He pulled off his helmet, revealing a mane of bright red hair, and balanced it on the handlebar of his bike. He began to worry at the straps of his face mask. "Uh, who were those guys, anyway?"

Jimmie's face conveyed his shock and some of the horror that hit him at the rider's remark. "You . . . you didn't know they were Zodiac Lodge? You . . . just . . . rode in and started killing people?"

"Yeah," the rider said, a slight Scottish accent in his voice as he pulled the mask up over his face. "I knew they were bad guys when I heard them threatening you and the tots. Like I said, no worries, man." The rider was a boy—well, a young man, to be more specific, in his twenties— with bright green eyes, wild, red hair, sideburns, and sharp features: almost pointed ears, nose, and chin. He had a grin on his face that Jimmie suspected seldom went away, even when he was machine-gunning a diner full of people.

Somewhere off in the distance there were sirens, still far off but coming closer and from several directions. Jimmie was weary of that sound. "That," Jimmie said, as the rider heard the sirens, too, "is a worry . . . *man*. Come on, let's get the hell out of here."

"Wait," the rider said, grabbing Jimmie's arm, "I've been looking all over for you, and I need your help."

"Looking for me?" Jimmie said.

"Yeah, the redhead said." I missed you at your house, and Layla said you—"

Jimmie felt something twist in him when he heard his wife's name spoken in this unholy place, by this strange kid who seemed to embody innocence and violence in equal measure. He lost it for a second—all that adrenaline he had been pumping surged back again. He grabbed the boy by the MC cut and slammed him back against the dirty car.

"You went to my house!" he bellowed, slamming the kid again. "You talked to my wife?" Again, smashing him against the car. "You brought this crazy shit to my door?" To his credit, the rider took the abuse for as long as he could. He drove a knee into Jimmie's gut, and the trucker groaned as the air whooshed out of him. Jimmie staggered back and let go of him, then surged forward with a powerful cross to the kid's face, sending the rider flying across the hood of the car. Jimmie leaned over to grab the fallen shotgun. When he popped back up, leveling the 12-gauge, the rider was up on the other side of the car and facing him down with the MP9. The sirens were getting louder, closer. The fire was a storm of smoke and unbearable heat. From behind the Compass Point came the rumble of a car engine. The Lodge Master, still in his hood, pealed out of the parking lot and sped away in the opposite direction the Waclaws had. He was driving an old Pontiac Safari station wagon with fake wooden paneling on the sides.

"Figures," the redhead said to Jimmie, watching the car's lights vanish over the horizon. "Maybe we should stop trying to fuck each other up and go get his poser ass?"

"His lodge has been destroyed," Jimmie said. "He messed up. His fellow Lodge Masters will do worse to him than we ever could." He lowered the shotgun. "We need to get out of here, too."

The rider lowered his gun.

"Sorry, man. I understand you wanting to keep Layla and the kids safe. My bad. You know it was a hell of a lot more fun wrestling with you when I was a kid."

Jimmie stopped mid-walk to the rig. He turned around, the lights coming on behind his eyes.

"Hector?" Jimmie asked. "Hector Sinclair?"

Heck laughed and nodded.

"Yeah. Hi, Jimmie. You didn't recognize me, didya? No wonder."

"I thought you were still in Afghanistan?" Jimmie said, walking toward Heck.

"Haven't been home long," Heck said. Jimmie offered his hand, and Heck shook it. "Look, you're right. We have got to go. I need to talk to you. Want to catch up down the road? I'll follow you."

"Hell, yeah," Jimmie said. "Let's hit it."

Jimmie's rig rolled out of the gravel lot of the Compass Point, Heck's T5 trailing it down U.S. 150. In his newly repaired rearview mirror, Jimmie saw, far behind them, the swarm of red and blue emergency-vehicle lights converge on the inferno. The Compass Point's road sign flickered for a moment and then went dark forever.

. . .

They pulled up at a truck stop near Bardstown at about one in the morning. The place was called the Rooster's Run, and it had a restaurant connected to a convenience store. The Muzak speakers in the ceiling were playing Elvis and Conway Twitty songs quietly under the murmur of conversations. The noise was punctuated by the banter of weary travelers—civilians and truckers who had stopped for gas, Slim Jims, Slush Puppies, a burger, or to grab a hot shower or some shut-eye in the TRUCKER ONLY lounges upstairs. Others had stopped just to stretch their legs a bit, shake off the hypnosis of the highway, or to experience some kind of real human interaction, even as mundane as talking to the clerk behind the counter for a spell, before returning to the road.

Jimmie ordered coffee, black, and Heck ordered a plate of pancakes, two servings of bacon, and a carafe of orange juice to go with his large milk and his glass of Mountain Dew. Jimmie watched Heck wolf down his food. His hands no longer shook as he held his coffee mug. Heck seemed to have no lasting effects of the firefight at the Compass Point, other than the munchies. Jimmie recalled Ale and himself being that way once. Though this boy wasn't Ale's biological son, he sure acted a lot like him at that age. Had they really ever been that young? Now Ale was gone, the latest in an ever-expanding roll of good friends, brothers, who had lived and laughed, and raised hell in his green days, and had now passed on into the hall of memory. Jimmie felt the years creep into his bones and his muscles more and more every year—a war of attrition.

"Sorry about the misunderstanding back there," Heck said, between shoveling food into his mouth. "I thought you knew who I was. You throw a mean hook for a seasoned citizen."

"I've been throwing it since before you were born," Jimmie said. "I was still picturing you from that photo your mom shared on Facebook a few years back—all clean cut from basic. I don't think I've seen you in person since you were . . . nine?"

"Yeah."

"I'm sorry I couldn't make Ale's send-off," Jimmie said, sipping his coffee. "I was on the road, on a job."

Heck nodded, his cheek wadded full of food. He swallowed and then chased the food with a swig of his milk. "Mom understood," he said, reaching for the dwindling pile of bacon. "I think her and Layla talked on the phone. Hell, man, I almost missed it myself. It's okay. I'm pretty sure Ale would have called bullshit on the whole thing, anyway."

They both laughed. The waitress drifted by and poured more coffee for Jimmie.

Heck ordered a half-dozen scrambled eggs with hot sauce and toast. "'Sides," he said. "From what everyone told me, you did a real good job at the funeral, Jimmie. My mom appreciated that a lot. Thanks."

"Ale was a hell of a guy," Jimmie said. "Good man, good friend. Saved my ass more times than I recall in the Gulf and again when we got back home and I rode with the Jocks."

"You were a Blue Jock?" Heck said. "No shit?"

"Not exactly. They offered to patch me in, but I had a few other things going on. I rode with them on a few of the early hunts—the bail-jumping stuff and the *other* hunts, you know . . . and another thing that was . . . well, it was a long time ago. You were still shitting in your diapers at the time, as I recall. I changed a few of them. You're welcome, by the way."

Heck chuckled and nodded as he scooped up another bite. "I'm sure I can repay the favor in a few years," he said. He kept looking at his plate of food as he asked the next question. "So, that far back, you must have known my old man, yeah? My real dad?"

Jimmie stiffened, paused before he took a sip of coffee to give him a second to think. "Yeah, I guess I did," he said over the rim of the mug. "What did Elizabeth and Ale tell you about him?"

"Not a lot. They froze up, like you just did, every time I'd ask. I know Mom met him when she was pretty young," Heck said. "He had the baddest-ass bike she had ever seen. I know he was a serious dick—abusive, cruel to her, and possessive. I'm pretty sure he did some real bad shit to her and dragged her into worse. He split before Mom knew she was pregnant. Ale came along and picked up all the pieces and raised me like I was his." Heck looked up from this food. He leaned back in the booth and stretched. He yawned a little. "Just wondered if you could fill in a few of the details. I figured if he rode back then, and you did, too, you must know—"

"Look, Heck," Jimmie said, "that was a long time ago, and, like I said, nobody knew your father very well, except by . . . reputation. He was bad news—the worst, actually. And I understand you wanting to know. I know it must eat you up to only have these vague scraps of him, but trust me, you're better off not knowing. Much, much better off, son."

"I'm not your fucking son, mate," Heck said, his voice raised and his eyes bright with sudden anger. "And you have no clue what's best for me." He slipped a silver flask out of his leather jacket and unscrewed it.

"You ain't going to start drinking and then ride that bike, now, are you?" Jimmie said, setting down his mug.

"Nah," Heck said. "I'm not starting. Been at it for a spell. You don't think I drove into that greasy spoon to save your ass without a little tip first, do you?" He raised the flask and took a long draw on it. Jimmie reached across the table and pulled it away from him. "What the hell, man?" Heck shouted.

Jimmie screwed the cap back on the flask and handed it back to him. "Put that shit away," he said. "You're going to get yourself or someone else killed doing that. You know that! Ale would've—"

"Yeah, yeah, fucking, yeah!" Heck said, standing. He slid the plates and the glasses off the table and they shattered on the floor. The restaurant was silent. "Ale would've been pissed as hell that his fucking son wasn't a goddamned knight of the fucking round table! Well, fuck your precious Saint Ale. He's fucking dead, man—died a dried-up old man in a hospital bed! He got fed from a bag, and shit and pissed into a bag, too. I saved your fucking ass back there, and I don't need to explain myself to you, to fucking dead Ale, or any-goddamned-one else!"

Heck peeled a couple of hundreds off from a wad of bills in his pocket and dropped them on the table before he strode out.

Jimmie looked at the money, looked at the mess, and took another drink of his coffee. "Ale would have done something exactly like that a long time ago," he said to no one in particular. He found Heck outside smoking a cigarette, leaning against the wall of the convenience store. Jimmie stuffed his hands into his jacket pockets and leaned back next to him. The headlights of departing semitrucks washed over them. The lot smelled of diesel and greasy fast food.

"How long you been back in the world?" Jimmie asked.

"Long enough to fucking know better," Heck said, blowing the smoke out his nostrils.

"Don't always work like that," Jimmie said.

"Don't give me any of that PTSD, VA Hospital bullshit," Heck said. "I'm just a fuck-up with a very bad temper. Adds to my charm." He offered Jimmie a Lucky Strike.

"No thanks," Jimmie said. "More of a cigar man these days. You sound like you've been down this road before. The VA tell you it was PTSD?"

"Something like that," Heck said. "It was a tidy label to hang my substance abuse, alcoholism, and violence issues off, don't you think? I didn't stick around to tell them I disagreed with the diagnosis. Look, I'm okay. I've always been this way. Over there just . . . framed it for me . . . explained it in simple terms. It . . . showed me."

They were silent for a moment. Heck dropped his cigarette and crushed it out with his boot. He reached into his jacket. "And that," Heck said, "makes as perfect a segue as I can imagine for this." He handed Jimmie a sealed envelope, slightly crushed and folded. "For you. Enjoy."

"What's this?" Jimmie said, smoothing out the envelope and tearing it open. He pulled the single sheet of paper out of it and began to read it in the glow of a neon sign advertising Coors beer.

"Oh, yeah," Heck said, snapping his fingers. "I'm supposed to present myself to you as your squire, or some shit, of the Brethren—whatever that is. What is that, exactly?"

Jimmie's frown slid lower and lower as he read. *Oh, Elizabeth, no!* He lowered the paper and looked at Heck.

"I'm not going to get down on my knee or nothing," Heck said.

"Thanks for that," Jimmie said. He looked at the young biker, who raised and lowered his eyebrows like Groucho Marx and grinned. Jimmie sighed, spit some tobacco juice on the greasy pavement, and then said, "I accept you as my squire." He sounded as if he was repeating a prepared response—a traditional reply. "I'll do my best to teach you the ways of the Brethren, to put your feet upon the Road and stand with you against all enemies, and to prepare you to stand alone when my time is at an end. I will armor you with honor and arm you with truth. I will teach you until my dying breath. This I swear."

There was an awkward silence for a moment as Jimmie slipped the letter into his pocket. Another semi, a tanker truck, hissed and rumbled as it pulled out of the lot and headed back onto the road.

"So what is it?" Heck asked. "This Brethren . . . thing?"

"That," Jimmie said with a sigh, "is a long story."

The first thing that registered in her slowly awakening mind was the sensation of crisp, clean sheets and the smell of baby powder. Ava opened her eyes slowly, blinking at the bright sunlight spilling into the bedroom she was in. She was alive. It took a moment to process what had come before blissful oblivion—the shadow people, the screams of her friends, running in the dizzying dark—it had all been real. Her whole body ached as she sat up in the bed. It was an antique four-poster made of dark cherry. Next to the bed was a night table with a glass of water, a King James Bible, and Ava's wallet, phone, and keys. Across the room, draped over a rocking chair, were her clothes and the bloody tote bag she had taken from Alana. Seeing the blood brought the memory of her best friend being torn apart to the front of her mind, eclipsing her thoughts. It made her wince, made her brain and stomach clench.

The bedroom door opened, and the old British woman who had saved her last night entered the room. "Good, we're up," the lady said. "How are you feeling, dear?"

"Okay," Ava said. "What time is it? How long was I asleep?"

"About two days," the old woman said. "I'm sure you're famished. Would you like me to prepare you some food?"

"Two days?" Ava asked. "Have the police been out? Have any of my friends shown up?"

The old woman pulled a chair next to the bed. She patted Ava's hand. "No," she said. "No police, and, I am sorry to tell you, no friends have come to my door. I am sorry, dear."

Ava felt the panic swell in her chest, clench her throat. "How can . . . how can people get murdered and the police don't even . . . What were those things, those shadow things?"

The old woman nodded. "I know, dear. Very little in this place makes much sense at first. I will try to help you as best I can. First, I'd caution you against trying to take too much in too quickly. You've already had so many terrible shocks for a person your age. To answer your question, there are no police here in town. We try to handle any such problems that pop up ourselves."

"'We,'" Ava said. "Who is 'we,' and who are you?"

"It was a bit too busy the other night for formal introductions," the old lady said. She offered her hand to Ava. "My name is Agnes, Agnes Dee Cottington, formerly of London and now a resident of Four Houses. It is a pleasure to make your acquaintance."

"I'm Ava James. Thank you again for saving me last night," Ava said, shaking Agnes's hand. Nice to meet you."

Agnes handed Ava the glass of water and leaned back in her chair. "The 'we' I was referring to are the other citizens of Four Houses. We tend to look out for one another and deal with our problems together."

"But those things wandering around your town—the police or the state troopers have to do something about that! My friends and I are going to be noticed missing in a few days, at the latest."

"Yes," Agnes said, an odd sadness in her voice. "You will, assuredly."

Ava groaned and pulled herself up out of the bed. She was wearing a very old-lady-looking nightgown. She felt as if she had strained or pulled a few muscles in the frantic running a few nights ago. "If it's been two days, I'm sure they're looking for us by now. May I please use your phone? My cell doesn't get reception out here. My folks must be out of their minds."

"I know, dear," Agnes said. Again the sadness, almost regret, like discussing a recently deceased loved one. Weird. Then again, older folks tended to dwell on the morbid, in Ava's experience.

"May I use your phone, to call them, call the police?" Ava asked again as she examined her clothes—grass and oil stains and the stale odor of fear sweat mingled with a whisper of her body spray. Gross.

"I would be happy to allow you to," Agnes said, "if we had one. I'm afraid there is no phone service here in town. I truly wish there were, dear."

"No cops, no phone?" Ava said, sniffing her T-shirt. She wrinkled her nose and tossed it back in the chair. I don't suppose you have any clothes I might be able to wear? Mine are kind of ick."

Agnes smiled. "Of course, dear. I think some of Julia's clothes will fit you. You look about the same size. I'll see what I can find. We do have hot and cold running water and an indoor bathroom, if you were concerned about our lack of amenities. Please, freshen up, and I'll find you some clothing."

The shower was heaven. The hot water eased some of her aches and dismissed others entirely. She washed her blond hair and brushed it out with a beautiful antique silver hairbrush that was on a table next to the basin sink. She wrapped a thick, clean towel about herself, wadded up her nasty underwear, and carried it in her hand as she padded back across the hall to the bedroom. Agnes was looking out one of the turret windows in the corner, the bright sunlight washing across her face. She seemed lost in thought. At the foot of the bed was an oak blanket chest, and on top of it was a cardboard box with the name Julia written on it in thick black marker. On top of the box were Ava's nerd glasses.

"You found them!" Ava said, picking up her glasses and putting them on. "Great! Thank you. Is everything okay, Agnes?"

The old woman's smile reappeared as she turned from the light.

"Yes, dear. As well as it can be, given the circumstances. Your glasses were on the front porch. You must have lost them in the scuffle. Look through the box and see if you can find anything to wear."

Ava opened the box and retrieved a purple pair of high-top Converse athletic shoes. They looked about her size. "So, um, who's Julia? Daughter, granddaughter?" Agnes sat on the edge of the bed, and Ava noticed that the bed had been made while she was in the shower.

"Julia stayed with us for a time. I always thought of her as a daughter," Agnes said.

"'Us'?" Ava asked as she lifted a thin white summer dress out of the box, clutching her towel to her with the other hand.

"My husband, Dennis, and I," Agnes said as she walked to the door.

"Dennis is downstairs having tea. I'll introduce you once we get you dressed, dear."

"Where is Julia now?" Ava asked.

"She died, dear," Agnes said, closing the door behind her.

▪ ▪ ▪

Ava stepped out of the bedroom wearing the dress. She had found a large guy's jean jacket to wear over it and she had put on the purple Chucks, since she had no idea what had happened to her flats. There had been a green army-style courier bag in the box that had a few tampons in the ubiquitous white plastic wrapper with trails of ghostly blue print on it, about eighty cents of loose change, a few wadded, mummified tissues, and a credit-card receipt dated 2001. She had transferred her own stuff and most of the contents of the bloody tote bag to the satchel and slung it over her shoulder. She descended the staircase to the first floor of the mansion and found Agnes sitting at a dining table beside an elderly man. She was preparing his tea. The man had a sunken face with kind brown eyes behind thick glasses, a mop of snow-white hair, and large ears. He wore a blue-and-green plaid shirt with a tan sweater vest over it. Ava noticed a cane leaning against his chair. As she entered, the old man attempted to rise, but he couldn't.

"Julia?" the old man said. He had an English accent as well. Agnes helped him settle back into his chair. "No," he said. "Forgive me, young lady."

"Dennis," Agnes said, "this is Ava, the girl I was telling you about who arrived in town the other night. She's going to be staying with us for a while. Ava, this is my husband, Dennis Cottington."

"Hi," Ava said. "Nice to meet you. Your wife is . . ."

"Brilliant," Dennis said. His smile was almost infectious. "That she is, young lady, that she is."

"A spot of tea?" Agnes asked, gesturing toward an empty chair beside Dennis. Ava sat, and Agnes began to pour her tea. "Those clothes look lovely on you, dear."

"Thanks," Ava said. She reached across the table and took a sugar cookie. "So how long have you guys been together?" she asked Dennis.

Agnes and Dennis looked at each other and almost burst into laughter. They settled for snickering a bit. "How old are you, Ava?" Dennis asked.

"Nineteen," Ava said. "I'll be twenty in a few months."

Dennis whistled and shook his head. "So young . . . This lovely woman here was the best thing I recall about being twenty. She agreed to be my bride over sixty-five years ago."

"Wow!" Ava said around a mouthful of cookie. "That's really cool you two have been together so long."

"I know I'm such a burden these days," Dennis said, taking Agnes's hand. Agnes squeezed his hand and kissed him. "That's quite enough of that," she said to him, her lips against his cheek. "We are a team, and nobody splits us up. Remember?"

"There was that one bloke," Dennis said, chuckling. "That junior minister when we were with the Circus, who had it in for me because he was keen to take a run at your nickers? Remember him, love?"

"Keeley," Agnes said, laughing at the name.

"Bloody Keeley," Dennis said.

Ava didn't understand, but she was laughing with them.

"With his pinched little fist-face," Agnes said, wiping away tears of laughter, "like a constipated bulldog. Oh, he was so awful to you, Denny! Didn't you push him off a ferry or something?"

"Punched him off one, actually," Dennis said, leaning back in his chair and gushing masculine pride.

"So you guys worked at the circus?" Ava said, sipping her tea. "Like the Shriners or something?"

"Not that kind of circus, dear," Agnes said. "Dennis and I worked for British intelligence for a time after the war. A division called MI6. Its nickname was the Circus, you see."

"You guys were spies?" Ava said, her face lighting up. "Like James Bond?"

"Why do they always say that?" Dennis asked Agnes. "Always! You know, I had a chance once to sock Ian Fleming square in his besotted jaw. I should have done it, Aggie, I should have."

"There, there," Agnes said to her husband. She offered the teapot to

Ava, who nodded. "It was nothing so . . . theatrical, dear," she said while pouring. "It was a job, one Dennis and I enjoyed a great deal."

"That's still really cool," Ava said. "Is that where you learned to shoot, like the other night?"

Dennis looked at Agnes. "Shooting? You didn't say anything about shooting!"

"It was nothing, dear," Agnes said. "Please don't get overwrought."

Ava noticed Dennis's color getting a little red, almost purple, and Agnes was obviously upset by the change. "It really wasn't a big deal," Ava said. "Agnes wasn't in any danger, sir."

Dennis squeezed his wife's hand. He started to say something, but Agnes silenced him with a single glance. "I see," he finally said.

Ava sipped her tea, then said, "I want to go out and look for my friends. Is it safe to do that with those . . . things around?"

Agnes nodded. "The shadow people come out at night," she said. "Light, any intense illumination, will drive them off. A sufficient amount or intensity, like my tracer bullets, will destroy them, as will direct daylight. You are safe enough in the day from them, dear."

"But not the bloody Scodes," Dennis said, dabbing his lips with a napkin. "It isn't right, but those bastards can walk in daylight just fine."

"The tow-truck guys?" Ava said. "Yeah, they were pretty creepy."

"Stay clear of them, Ava," Dennis said. "They're his dogs as much as those bloody curs in the junkyard and the woods. Bloody Scodes, the other bad ones, like the Scodes who grovel to him, bloody worship him."

"'Him,'" Ava asked. "Who is 'him'?"

"I think you've had your fill for the day," Agnes said. "You go look about for your friends. A good start would be Buddy's Place, the roadhouse."

"Could you . . . come with me?" Ava asked, looking down at her teacup. "If you . . . y'know, don't mind?"

"Oh dear, I couldn't," Agnes said, petting Ava's hand. "You'll be fine, though. The Scodes will keep to themselves unless they have backup: the others like them, or the creatures—the shadow people, the hounds . . . and the children. They all fear the daylight to one degree or another. I wouldn't let you go out if I thought it was dangerous, dear."

"This is crazy," Ava said, feeling as if the inertia of reason and reality had been switched off for a moment, like the sensation of those rides at the fair where the ground is dropped away from you. She felt a dizzy sensation of raw fear, a realization that she was awake and this was real, all of it, real. Gerry was dead. Alana was dead. Shadows walked here, killed here, without their owners.

"Are you all right, dear?" Agnes said, rising to go to her. She put her bony but strong and warm hands on the girl's shoulders. "I know. It's a lot to try to process, to accept and adapt to. That's why we don't need it all at once. There, there, it will be all right."

Ava swallowed hard. It felt as if she were swallowing her stomach back into her belly. She pushed her glasses aside and wiped away the dampness at her eyes that had begun to form as the fear ate at her. She smiled and nodded. "Yeah, I'm okay. Sorry. I just . . . I just lost it for a sec. I'm okay."

Dennis looked at the young girl. His color was back to normal. He watched Agnes give her a gentle hug about the neck. He cleared his throat—such a simple thing, really, yet it got harder each year, it seemed. "Aggie, go with her. Show her about the town, proper."

Ava felt Agnes tense at these words, and she suddenly understood Agnes's reluctance to go. It wasn't fear of anything out there; it was fear of leaving Dennis alone. The two women looked at each other for a moment, and that understanding passed between them, and something . . . deeper? Older? Ava didn't understand the connection, but it was there— steady, powerful, but slumbering. Whatever it was, it gave her comfort and a sliver of hope. Agnes had felt whatever passed between them, too, and smiled, a twinkle in her eyes.

"Oh, that's okay," Ava said, standing. "I'll find my way. I'm sure Agnes has more stuff to do than drag me around this Podunk town." She walked around the table and leaned forward to give Dennis a quick hug. "It's really nice to meet you. Thank you for taking me in."

Dennis patted her on the back. "You're quite welcome, my dear," he said. "Be sure you're back well before sundown—and stay away from those damned Scode brothers."

"Yes, sir," Ava said.

"Let me show you to the door," Agnes said. She led Ava out to the hallway, and Ava had a vague memory of lying on this floor, panting, hysterical, and exhausted from running for her life. The sound of gunfire and of Agnes bolting the stout front door, a smoking pistol still in her steady hand.

"Thank you," Agnes said to the girl quietly. "He constantly wants me to go out. He worries about me being cooped up in here with him, but I love this old house. I actually used to dream about it when I was a young girl. And I love him. I'll never leave him, never let him feel alone. He's the best man I've ever known in all my life. He deserves someone to watch over him and take care of him."

"He's lucky to have you," Ava said. "I'll be back before night. Don't worry, I don't want to get caught out there with those things. You said try the roadhouse?"

Agnes nodded. "Buddy's, yes. Here, take this, dear." Agnes opened the drawer of an antique end table in the hallway. Inside was her odd gun from the other night and a small revolver with a stub of a barrel. Agnes took out the small revolver, opened the cylinder, and checked the load and snapped it shut. She handed it to Ava, who took it as if she were being offered a poisonous snake. "It's a .38—very simple and safe. Pull the trigger and it goes off. You have five shots—the last three are tracers."

"What is that?" Ava asked, nodding toward Agnes's gun as she gingerly put the pistol into her messenger bag. "That gun looks like something from an old World War Two movie, or *Indiana Jones.*"

"It is," Agnes said. "It's a German Broomhandle Mauser. I learned to shoot with a gun like this."

"In MI6?" Ava asked. Agnes shook her head and laughed. It was a beautiful sound.

"Oh, no, I learned to shoot at my old charm school," she said. "It was called the OSS. My headmaster was a Mr. Donovan, and he was very insistent that all his young ladies and gentlemen be proficient shots. It's a skill that has served me very well, and still does."

Agnes unbolted the door. Outside, it was a genuine bright spring day. Spring proper was still a few days off, but the chill was off the land, at least for now. Tonight might be a different matter. A few butterflies were flitting about, seeming to chase one another in the high grass that surrounded the house.

"Be careful," Agnes said. "You should be fine, just use good judgment. I'll have dinner waiting for you tonight, dear."

Ava walked out onto the porch. "Agnes," she said.

"Yes, dear?"

"If this place is so terrible, so dangerous," Ava asked, "why are you and Dennis still here?"

The same forlorn look that Ava had seen as Agnes looked out the bedroom window returned. "That is a very good question," Agnes said. "One we can discuss over dinner. Go explore. Be careful. I truly hope you find your friends."

Ava set off across the field in front of the mansion. She noticed a cobblestoned driveway to her right that was overgrown and choked with high grass and weeds. The drive led to a roundabout in front of the house. She walked toward the drive and followed it down to the main road, the only road, which seemed to run like a black artery through Four Houses. She didn't see any postings for what the road's name or number was. She noticed that power lines and poles ran alongside the blacktop road, with lines running off to the various homes along the way, including Agnes and Dennis's home and a trailer that squatted in the high grass on the opposite side of the road.

A woman, her hair in curlers, was hanging up laundry to dry on a clothesline beside the trailer. She was wearing tattered blue jeans and a brown halter top. She looked to be in her forties. Two children, about eight or nine years old, were playing with broken toys near the cement base of an old water pump. The woman and her children all stopped when they saw Ava across the road. Ava waved to them and summoned up a smile. They looked at her as if she had an extra head. Ava stopped waving and proceeded to walk up the road in the direction in which she had seen the roadhouse the other night, when the tow truck brought them into Four Houses.

About a mile up, on her side of the road, Ava approached the blackened ruin of another fine mansion. She recalled the feelings, a strange sense of sadness and loss, that had washed over her when she drove past the old, burned house in the Scodes' truck. She still didn't understand it, but it echoed the strange connection she and Agnes felt earlier today—a kind of understanding without knowledge, without words or definitions.

The remains of the house squatted on a low hill, surrounded by tall grass. The grounds of the mansion were beginning to be swallowed by a heavy grove of trees, the harbinger of an encroaching forest.

Ava's foot fell upon the overgrown flat stones of the driveway to the house. She paused, a strange sense of déjà vu settling over her. She began to walk up the drive to the ruins. She wasn't entirely sure why.

She could see the house as it had been before the fire devoured it, see the beautiful, intricate gardens behind it. The fountains, the sounds of music and laughter in the halls. All the ghosts danced in her memory, but they weren't her memories. She reached the front lawn and stopped as if a wall stood before her instead of thin air. There was something . . . something in that stand of trees, in that dark forest, something. A dark shape stood at the terminator of the canopy's shade and the daylight. "Hello," she said. "Cole, is that you?"

She began to step closer to the forest to try to see. Was it Cole? One of the Scodes? Some other resident of the town? She could feel eyes that she couldn't see boring into her, like a drill. Panic rose in Ava, accelerating, tumbling panic, and she stopped her advance toward the woods. It wasn't Cole. She sensed that something didn't want her going any closer to the house, and for an instant she almost bolted toward the crumbling remains of the front doorway. While the arch gave no physical safety, Ava felt, *knew*, she would be safe in there. *That's why you burned it down, isn't it?* she thought, but it wasn't truly her thought . . . yet it was, too, like something remembered.

It took great effort to turn her back on the trees and begin walking back down the drive to the main road. She kept waiting for whatever was in the woods to spring out of the shadows and chase after her, but it didn't. Soon she was back by the main road and walking, not running, walking, toward the roadhouse, and any friendly, human contact. She looked back at the ruined mansion on the hill and the realization struck her, the reason the place had seemed like a safe haven. The old house—it felt like home.

The walk to Buddy's was about two miles, all told, Ava thought. The sun was still high in the painfully blue sky. A chilly wind had picked up, but it didn't ruin anything. It would be good kite-flying weather, Ava thought. There was a beat-up old red Toyota pickup parked in front of the roadhouse, the sides spattered with dried mud. A couple of bicycles leaned, unlocked, against one of the posts on the open porch. A huge Winnebago Chieftain motor home peeked out from behind the roadhouse. The neon signs were still on, and there was the sound of music inside. Ava pushed her glasses up on her nose and stepped inside.

Buddy's looked like every honky-tonk and roadhouse Ava had ever stepped into. Half the place was a bar, with tables dotting the sawdust-and-peanut-shell-covered floor. There was a TV mounted in the corner above the bar. It was turned off. The other half of the place was a restaurant and a performance venue, with long rows of picnic tables covered with red-and-white checkered plastic tablecloths and a small, dark stage at one end. There was a screen of chicken wire between the stage and the audience—presumably to protect the performers from the occasional free-flying beer bottle or shot glass. A table of men sat on the restaurant and stage side. They looked like lumberjacks—all heavy beards, flannel, and work boots. A man and a woman sat at one of the round tables on the bar side. They were sharing a pitcher of beer and a basket of hot wings. The couple wore leather riding jackets, and both had a wind-chafed look to them, as if they'd been on a long motorcycle ride. Ava didn't recall seeing any motorcycles out front, though. Everyone stopped talking and stared at her for a long, hard moment. Ava tried to ignore it, then stared back at the couple. That seemed to do the trick. They all went back to minding their own business. There was a jukebox by the door—an old seventies-looking affair still playing 45-rpm records with faded pictures of Pat Benatar, Kenny Rogers, and ELO album covers on its case. Ava remembered the old Pizza Den her dad used to take her to when she was very young. The restaurant had the same jukebox. A hissing, scratchy rendition of "I Want You to Want Me," by Cheap Trick, was playing as Ava walked in and made her way to the bar.

The lady behind the bar had sandy brown hair, cut to about neck length, and wore glasses. She had on a T-shirt for something called RavenCon, and was smiling. It was an infectious smile, genuine and warm—as if you were the center of her universe in the time she was looking at you. It made Ava feel safe and important. Ava smiled back; she couldn't help but.

"Afternoon," the woman said. "You're new to town, welcome! I'm Barb, Barb Kesner. What can I get for you?"

"Is it too early to start drinking?" Ava asked. "This place . . ." Barb nodded and reached for a glass under the bar. Ava heard the crunch of ice as Barb filled the glass.

"Not for a lot of folks around here," Barb said. She held the glass of ice in front of a bar gun and filled it with cola. She set it down in front of Ava. "But you're a little too young to be drinking the hard stuff, kiddo. Sorry."

Ava nodded and took the cold drink. "Thanks," she said, a little sullenly. While she could have told this woman that she had two joints, her remaining two, in her wallet and had been drinking since she was twelve, lost her virginity at thirteen, and had watched two of her friends die brutal deaths only a few nights ago, there was no reason to do all that. It was kind of nice, kind of normal, to think that she could get carded even in a weird little place like this. It gave her a feeling of connection to the rest of the world. She sipped her drink and relaxed a little inside.

"So, where's Buddy?" Ava asked after a few moments.

Barb laughed. "You'd be surprised how often that's the first question people ask when they walk in here," she said. "I'm the owner of Buddy's— me and my husband, Carl. The original Buddy, um, passed in 2010, and he had made it pretty clear that Carl and I should keep the place going."

"Passed, huh?" Ava looked into her glass like a fortune-teller scouring tea leaves for portents. "Lot of that going on around here, it seems."

"Too much," Barb said, softly. She lost her smile for a moment, but it quickly returned. "Hey, you hungry? We can fix you up something to eat?"

Ava suddenly realized that it had been almost three days since she'd eaten, and for the first time since hearing the name Four Houses she was hungry—starving, actually. "Yes, please," she said. "Anything is good. I don't have much cash, but I got my debit card and I—"

"First meal is always on the house," Barb said. "We don't have any ATMs here, and no phone lines for credit cards, so it's mostly a barter system with us, but we keep the menu cheap, just like Buddy did."

A man appeared in the doorway behind the bar. Ava assumed it led to the kitchen. He was burly, with a barrel chest and wide shoulders. He wore a black turtleneck and a gray driver's cap on his shaved head. He had intense dark eyes and a kind smile. The man kissed Barb on the cheek and leaned against the bar, beside her. "And the food is at least as good as when Buddy ran the joint," the man said. "Hi, I'm Carl Kesner—welcome to town. How about I get you a burger and fries?"

Ava smiled and nodded. "That sounds great. Thank you!" Carl disappeared back into the kitchen, and soon Ava smelled the burger cooking. She finished her Coke, and Barb poured her another.

"You haven't seen any other new people come by in the last few days, have you?" Ava asked. "Lexi, Cole?"

Barb shook her head.

"I'm sorry, Ava, but no," she said.

Ava was quiet for a time, nursing her drink. The man at the table with the woman kept stealing glances at her, and Ava tried not to notice. He had long, stringy gray hair that fell below his shoulders and an acne-scarred face that resembled the lunar surface. His gray handlebar mustache failed to hide his cruel, scowling mouth. The woman looked as if she was Native American, with long black hair, eyes like slate, a slender build, and a hawklike nose. She didn't seem to mind her companion looking Ava over.

Barb leaned across the bar to speak softly to Ava. "Don't mind Ricky," she said. "He's kind of a creep, but we'll make sure he leaves you alone."

Ava shook her head. "*You'll* make sure?" she said. "Why don't you guys have cops around here? My friends and I have been missing for over two days, and there are no state police, no searches, nothing on the TV or radio—do you guys even have TV and radio here?" Her voice was starting to rise, but Barb remained calm, placid, nodding slightly. "No ATMs, no phones, no cell service . . . those shadow things! Please, Barb, tell me what's going on here, and why do I seem to be the only person who thinks everything here is—"

"Insane?" Barb said. The wide smile was back. "Because you're new, sweetie, and you haven't gotten used to the madness yet."

Carl came out with a platter of fries and a huge cheeseburger. He set them down in front of Ava. "Let me guess," he said to Ava. "'What the hell is wrong with this place and these people,' right?"

Ava couldn't help laughing. She plucked a hot fry off the plate and nibbled it. "Yeah," she said. "Exactly."

"Barb and I came here in 1999," Carl said. "That big old Winnebago out back was ours. We were caravanners, out exploring the open road. We never expected to end up running a restaurant at the end of the world. And we were just as scared and confused when we found our-selves in Four Houses as you are now, Ava. We were lucky. Buddy had been here for a long time before us and he knew the score. He protected us, mentored us, and gave us . . . well, hope."

"We'll try to answer your questions as best we can," Barb said, refill-ing Ava's drink. "Sometimes the answers in this place don't make much sense when you hear them. You have to live them yourself. If we had told you about the shadow people before the other night, you would have thought we were crazy. Now you've seen, and you believe."

"What are they?" Ava asked.

"Everything bad in us," Carl said quietly, the gentle demeanor of his face giving way to his stern eyes. Ava knew that he was reliving his own horrible night of running and screaming, of darkness and death. "The Egyptians thought that when you died the soul split into its component parts and wandered, lost, angry, confused, and often hungry. The shadow was called the Sheut, and it was said to carry part of the person it had belonged to with it—the bestial, amoral, animal side. It was also supposed to serve the jackal god—the lord of the dead."

"The shadow people are . . . born," Barb said, "out of a transforma-tion, a horrible transformation. There is nothing good in them anymore, nothing that can ever be redeemed. Light kills them, hurts them. But in darkness, Ava, you do exactly what you did to survive the other night— you run. You run and don't look back."

A hand fell on Ava's shoulder, and she jumped on her stool. The sneering gray-haired man, Ricky, was leaning over her shoulder to whis-per in her ear. He smelled of sour beer and stale tobacco smoke.

"Heard you talk, darlin'," Ricky said with a voice like oil, pouring. "Those shadows, they serve him, do his fucking bidding. Pretty little piece of ass like you, you're gonna need someone to look after you here, keep you warm and safe—"

"Give it a rest, Ricky," Carl said. "Time to call it a day. You can only cram so much asshole into twenty-four hours. Take a break."

Ricky ignored him and kept whispering into Ava's ear. "The Scodes know the score," he said. "A few others, too. They serve him, bring sacrifices to the town, like you and your friends the other night. Sometimes he lets poor fuckers just drive on into town, like fucking tourists, bringing in fresh meat, new blood, trucks with food, supplies. It keeps things—" He reached over and took her burger, ripping a big bite off with his teeth and replacing it on her plate. "Juicy," he said.

Carl reached for something under the bar and began to move around the counter toward Ricky. His face was red and his eyes were stormy.

"Agnes," Ava said. "Agnes protects me."

Ricky snorted. "Well, shit," he said. "If that crazy old witch opened her door for you, then you're already fucked, angel tits. You think she opened up for you out of the goodness of her heart. You got something she wants; she schemes just as fucking much as he does. The two of them been fighting a war for this town for as long as anyone can remember, baby."

Ricky stepped away as Carl, brandishing a short aluminum baseball bat, moved between him and Ava. "Time to go," Carl said curtly. "Get out, Ricky. See you again soon. You can even up for the beer and food next time."

Ricky's companion, the Indian woman, took him by the arm and began to tug him in the direction of the door. Ricky raised his arms and backed away from Carl, still talking to Ava as he went. "You just remember, you need protection, you can always call on old Ricky!" he said. "I'll take good care of you, like I do all my girls." The door was open and sunlight was spilling in. Ricky looked even worse in direct sunlight. "Don't you forget, now, darlin'," he said. The door slammed behind him and his woman. The jukebox was playing another old scratchy single—the Hollies' "Long Cool Woman in a Black Dress."

"I'm sorry," Carl said to Ava. The men at the back table had risen to come to Carl and Ava's aid. Carl waved them back to their table. "Show's over, guys," he said. "Just Ricky being his usual sensitive self." Carl walked back to their table to talk to them.

Ava looked at Barb and ripped a piece of the burger off on the side opposite Ricky's bite. She chewed it with no expression on her face. "Juicy," she said. She looked up at Barb. "Do you trust Agnes? Does Carl?"

Barb was silent for a moment, looking at her reflection in the polished wood of the bar. "I do," she said. "We do. I don't know what she's up to sometimes, and she does have her own, I don't know, agenda, but I've seen her save lives many, many times. Yes, I trust her, and I think you should, too."

"That's assuming I trust you, too," Ava said with a smile, and took another bite of burger.

"Oh, absolutely," Barb said, the grin returning, full strength. "I'd trust me!"

. . .

Over the next few hours, Ava sat on her barstool at Buddy's and tried to learn the way this strange place worked by observation. Her professors would have described this process in regard to programming as "binding"—making an abstraction more concrete by associating it with other properties, building a model. So Ava tried to build a model in her head of how the program called Four Houses actually ran and what the hell its function was. She saw locals drift in and out. Most were like the lumberjack guys at the back table. They eventually left, and they all welcomed her to town as they headed out the door.

A few townies were more like Ricky—creepy assholes. Actually, that wasn't completely fair, Ava thought. Some were creepy, and assholes, but others were . . . damaged, maybe mentally ill. They reminded her a little of Lexi when she forgot to take her meds. She really didn't care much for Lexi and never really had, but she hoped now, prayed, even—in that vague way you can pray when you haven't done it since you were a kid—that Lexi was out there and alive, and, hell, she even hoped she was fucking Cole's brains out, as Ava knew she had always wanted to do. She didn't care, she just wanted them alive and okay.

She looked at one of the locals, a woman with frizzy red hair and bulging wide eyes, who Barb said was named Lacy. Ava wondered if it was living here long enough that made Lacy scratch uncontrollably and mutter to herself at her lonely table near the bathrooms. If it was, Ava was getting the hell out of here, now.

Carl and Barb told Ava to stay clear of the southern end of the town—the junkyard, Scode's Garage, and, especially, the deep woods.

"Why don't you guys just pack up and leave? Why doesn't Agnes get Dennis the hell out of here?" Ava asked as she placed a crumpled wad of money on the bar. "Why stay? And who the hell is 'he,' or 'him' or what-the-hell-ever it is that everyone is so afraid of?"

"You know, we've been here seventeen years," Barb said, "and I don't know if either of us could explain what 'he' is."

"The reason we stay is because . . . we have to, Ava," Carl said, as he handed her back the money, "and so do you. I'm sorry. All you can do, all that any of us can do, is try to make the best of this damn place, try to keep from going nuts, and help one another."

"Thank you, guys," Ava said with a wave as she headed out the door.

"Where you headed, hon?" Barb asked.

"Taking a hike," Ava said. "I'm going to get help—cops, troopers, an ambulance, something." Both Carl and Barb looked so . . . sad, as if what she said was the most awful thing either of them had ever heard.

"Keep your cool," Carl said. "Keep your head about you."

"Good luck, sweetie," Barb said. Ava stepped out into the warm bright afternoon and started walking north up the main road.

. . .

Once she was gone, Carl sighed and ran his hand over his smooth head. "Damn it," he said. "I hope she can handle what she finds out there. Remember that one kid? He couldn't stop running. He ran until something literally burst in his head. They found him dead on the road."

Barb nodded. "She's strong," she said. "I don't think she'll lose it too much, no more than you or I did."

"I hope you're right," Carl said. "We could sure use the help. Whatever he's up to, it's making that thing in the woods stronger. There are more of the children showing up in town, more hounds howling every night, more shadows. I don't think we have much time, sweetheart. Should we have told her about her friends, where they are?"

"No," Barb said, sadly. "She'd have gone after them, and then she'd be dead, or worse than dead. Her mind needs to ease into this place. She's strong, Carl, I can feel it. Whatever Agnes is about to counter him, that girl plays a part in it. Until then, we do what we've been doing—hold the line, try to keep hope and order alive. Wait for backup."

"The wheel turns," Carl said, hugging his wife and kissing her.

Barb laughed. "You haven't said that in a long time," she said.

"Feeling hopeful," Carl said. "At least, right this second I am."

Barb hugged him tight and rested her head against his chest. "The wheel turns," she said.

. . .

Ava walked briskly past another mile or so of homes in Four Houses, made up of rusted old campers, motor homes, and house trailers splayed like corpses in a sea of overgrown weeds and grass.

"No cops, no hospital, no phones, and, apparently, no damn lawn mowers," Ava muttered. She dug out her phone and her earbuds to listen to music, but the phone was dead. She tried to focus on the nature sounds—birdsong, the blustery wind. Out past the fringes of the town was low-growing grass, what looked like Kansas farmland. It was unattended, as far as she could tell, but it seemed more what she had seen on the ride out to the party: farmland, field for crops. No scary, thick, dark woods. It hadn't occurred to her until then, but Four Houses didn't even seem to belong in northern Kansas. The botany seemed wrong for the surroundings. Of course, that could just be her being paranoid.

She didn't have a clock or a pedometer, since her phone was dead, but it seemed the sun had sunk a bit in the sky before she saw the last of the dense forest off to her right, what she assumed from the position of the sun was east. Her guess was that she had walked about three or four miles at this point. There were still no mile markers and no signposts. She was thirsty and wished for another cold soda from Barb's bar.

Ava had walked long enough to sing all the Katy Perry songs she knew when she heard the engine. She stepped to the side of the road, uncertain of exactly where it was coming from. The echo of the engine got louder, and Ava suddenly knew. She knew it was from behind her, from Four Houses, and she knew that it was a motorcycle. Before she could try to find a place to hide, the black bike rolled into view, banking into the curve, then straightening to run down the center of the road. It was the same old World War II–looking bike that had driven Gerry off the road, the same rider, clad in black, head to toe, who had stopped after the wreck and looked at them as if they were insects. The rider slowed as he saw Ava on the side of the road and came to a stop, seemingly with no care for oncoming traffic. He looked at Ava through his mirrored black helmet visor.

"You!" Ava shouted, suddenly more angry than fearful. "You caused all this! Are you from Four Houses? Why did you run us off the road? Who are you?"

The rider said nothing. Off in the distance, Ava heard a dog howl as if it was in pain. Another dog took up the cry, then another, and another. There was a crunching sound, like dry sticks snapping. From the biker's black helmet, antlers began to sprout on either side of the visor, thick, heavy, and intricate. The antlers branched and grew faster, stretching out like the branches of a bone tree. When they stopped, they extended a good three feet out and up from the driver's head, made of dark bone, as if they were stained with old blood.

Ava felt a slight warm trickle as she began to lose control of her bladder at the sight of the rider, but she controlled herself and held the fear at bay, barely. Her legs were shaking—her whole body was. The rider looked at her and began to rev his motorcycle. Dogs were screaming, howling, above the sound of the angry engine. He pointed a leather gloved finger at her. Ava felt as if her heart were being gripped, stilled, by a leather glove full of ice. The rider knew her, had marked her.

The rider accelerated, and the rear tire screeched as it spun against the asphalt. The rider raised his leg to the peg and aimed the bike down the road south—back the way he had come, swerving, straightening. He rode away, his grisly crown steady, as he topped the next hill on the road, and then disappeared from view. The dogs' howling faded away. The sound of the bike's engine diminished and then was gone.

Ava ran. She ran for all she had in her, as if the Devil was behind her, as if he was going to come back and devour her. Running north, in the opposite direction he had sped off toward, into the unknown frightened her, but not finding help, staying in Four Houses with whatever that . . . thing was—that frightened her more.

She ran, her satchel slapping against her hip, the purple high-tops rising and falling, their rubber soles slapping against the warm pavement of the road. Her arms flew back and forth as she sprinted; tears burned her eyes. She knew she was running for her life. She knew he, it, whatever it was, would come back for her, claim her, and end her. She had no choice now—she had to run, to escape, or die. Ava thought she had run as fast as she was capable of running the other night, with the shadow people chasing her. She was wrong.

She finally stopped when her body refused to run anymore. Her lungs were full of acid, and she gasped at ragged mouthfuls of air. Her legs twitched with cramps and strained muscles; she staggered and doubled over, losing her glasses and finally clutching them in her hand as she staggered forward. She vomited—the cheeseburger, the fries, the Cokes. She cried and screamed, hugging herself, as she stumbled forward. This wasn't real, none of this was real. She couldn't be here, no. There were no monsters. Her mind found no haven in her desperate clutching at reason; she trusted her senses too much. The disconnection of her mind and body, divorced by numbing fear, didn't keep her legs from moving forward, toward help, some kind of help. She was a robot now, walking, because it was all she could do.

Ahead she saw dark, heavy forests appear on either side of the road, but far off, half a mile or more away, easy. The sun dimmed. She guessed it was about four; the sun was starting to crawl lower, and a panic returned to her exhausted body. *Be home before dark. . . .*

Time passed, miles. She was beginning to calm down again. Ahead, on the left, was a gravel road, a private drive. She began to walk toward the road to find the house, the farm it joined to. To beg to use their phone to call the police, to call her mom and dad. She noticed that there was no mailbox, and then she saw it and she stopped. Beside the beginning of the gravel road was a tree, and nailed to it were a set of large deer antlers. At the base of the antler tree were baskets of bread and fruit, butcher-paper packages dark-stained with blood, and small, lit candles, guttering in the cold wind. If she could have vomited again, she would have. Instead, she began to limp-walk faster as the sun began to drown at the terminator of the forest's canopy.

Walking, trying not to think. One foot in front of the other. About a mile up from the gravel road, she saw the beginnings of a small town. There were house trailers, and a few small shacks and cabins, some RVs parked among the wild, overgrown grass. She figured it was still a good hour or so before twilight, and she could find someplace to hole up. She slowed and a silent, shrill tone began in her mind. The garage she was approaching on the right had a sign, a grimy, rusting, sheet-metal sign hung on the roof. It read SCODE'S GARAGE.

No, no, this wasn't possible.

A tiny sound escaped Ava's lips. For a moment, she wanted to fall down in the road, but she didn't. She looked across the street from the garage and saw the same trailers, same RVs, same trash on the side of the two-lane she had seen a few nights ago. She was on the south end of Four Houses, after walking north all afternoon. She heard the wheeze and grumble of the Scodes' tow truck and watched as the truck pulled out of the garage parking lot headed north up the road. Scowling, Wald was at the wheel, and Toby sat beside him. In the rear of the truck were two people, sitting against the back window of the cab; both had old feed-grain bags over their heads. Ava recognized the goth clothing on the girl and the preppie shirt on the boy—it was Lexi and Cole. The truck was accelerating as best it could, and Ava summoned enough strength to try to keep it in sight as it headed north. All thoughts of falling down, of screaming until her mind fluttered free of her body, were thrown in the backseat. They were alive, and they were in trouble.

Ava caught a break. The Scodes' truck stopped a little ways up the road at the high, chain-link fence to the junkyard on the left. Ava recalled Carl's and Barb's warnings about the place as she watched Wald unlock the gate and then drive the truck onto the grounds. He then went back and closed and locked the gate. Several large, dark shapes moved about the grounds and barked at Wald as he went about his work. Black dogs, huge ones.

The sun was dimming. Ava thought for a moment about how to get in there and help Cole and Lexi, and then she realized that she had to help herself first. She felt guilt again, just as she had the other night, when she ran and didn't look back. She was a selfish bitch. She had known that about herself for a long time. But if she went in there now—no plan, no backup—she'd end up like them. No, she had to do this right. She walked past the junkyard, on the opposite side of the road, just as they had all done the other night. Ava saw the Scodes leading Lexi and Cole into one of the large corrugated-tin buildings that squatted between the teetering mountains of dead cars. She noted it and headed for Agnes's house.

On the way, she made a final stop. She visited the field where the shadows had first come on them. She searched the side of the road for Gerry's body, but it was gone. She found his cap, dirty and wet. In the field, she found Alana. The bugs had gotten on her, and some bigger predators had visited the body as well. Ava knelt next to her and cried for a while.

Agnes was waiting for her on the porch as she walked up the lawn. The old woman had the same expression she had this morning as she looked out the window—sadness, an inevitable knowledge that couldn't be expressed, only experienced, shared.

"I'm so sorry, dear," Agnes said. "I'm so terribly sorry."

"Tomorrow," Ava said, "I want to go get Alana. I want to bury her, if that's okay."

"Of course it is, dear," Agnes said, "We'll bury her next to Julia."

NINE  **"10-43"**

"So this girl, this ghost—" Heck said into his microphone headset.

"Vanishing Hitchhiker," Jimmie interrupted, on his mike.

"Why do you keep doing that?" Heck asked. "You keep interrupting me. It's pissing me off, man."

They were driving up to Aurora, a city just outside Chicago, to meet a retired state cop who was a member of the Brethren. Jimmie's semi was in the lead, with Heck's motorcycle following a short distance behind. They had pulled up at one of the town-sized truck stops on I-57 and picked up a Bluetooth CB radio headset for Heck. They linked it to a portable base unit that looked like a thick brick of a walkie-talkie with a stubby rubber-covered antenna. Jimmie explained that the unit had a special chip in it that would allow them to communicate securely with each other and with other members of the Brotherhood. The base unit was now clipped to Heck's belt and tuned to Channel 23.

"I'm trying to teach you," Jimmie said with a sigh. It was like talking to his own teenage daughter. "There are all kinds of ghosts, but this was a particular kind—a Vanishing Hitchhiker."

"What difference does it make?" Heck said.

"Vanishers are an urban myth," Jimmie said. "One of the ones that's real. You pick up some poor woman or girl on the side of the road. She's usually dressed in white. She asks you to take her somewhere, and you do, and then she vanishes right out of your car or truck. Sometimes she may say a few words about her death or the loved ones she misses. It's the ghost trying to get closure, to get home. As one of the Brethren, it's our duty to help shepherd them home. You need to know what they are, recognize them, and know how you can help them. That's what I'm trying to teach you, Heck. This Vanisher, this girl, Karen, she was different from the usual Vanishing Hitchhiker, though. She gave me a warning about something hunting kids. She knew me, by name, and she had known this was coming a long time before she disappeared, before she died."

"Sorry," Heck said. "Look, man, most of the creepy-crawlies I've hunted with the Jocks didn't want to talk; they just wanted to rip your head off and lay eggs down your neck hole."

"You're not hunting anymore," Jimmie said. "You're one of the Brotherhood. It's different. We protect, not hunt, not unless we have to."

"So Ale was a member of this Brotherhood, and my grandfather, too?" Heck said. They were starting to hit the tail end of the Chicago morning rush hour. The truck and the bike slowed and drifted into the lines of sluggish traffic creeping through the suburbs.

"Yep," Jimmie said. "Like I said, I used to ride with the Blue Jocks back in the early days. It was about the same time I was squiring to my dad. There are lots of secret clubs, societies, orders out there that eventually lead back to the Brethren. The Jocks is one of them, and the roots between the two run pretty deep."

"So what, exactly, did I join up with?" Heck said. "Like I asked before, what is this Brotherhood, Jimmie?"

"You're impatient as hell, boy," Jimmie said. "Like I just said, we protect people on the highways, on the roads. We guard the pathways of civilization. *A cultu vivit, nec moritur a viis suis salutem.*" His accent was pure Mason-Dixon, but his pronunciation was flawless.

"Where the hell did you learn Latin?" Heck asked. "And what does that mean?"

"The same place you're gonna learn it, boy," Jimmie said. "Your first homework is to work out what what I just said means. Now, get your head back in the game. We're almost there."

Aurora was miles of strip malls, movie Googleplexes, fast-food chains, and subdivisions—grids of neat little suburban life. Looming over it all was the big bad wolf of Chicago—close enough to entice but far enough away from the gunshots to feel safe. Gil Turla, the retired Illinois state trooper, opened the door to his modest Cape Cod on Bangs

Street when Jimmie and Heck knocked. Heck was impressed by the ex-cop's taste in cars—there was a cherry '57 Chevy Bel Air ragtop, powder blue, in pristine condition, parked in the driveway.

Turla still looked like a trooper—tall, broad shoulders, and in pretty good shape for his age. He kept his gray, thinning hair in a tight military cut, and he still sported the cop "micro 'stache"—the only facial hair regs allowed. Turla was wearing a wrinkled button-down oxford and equally rumpled chinos.

"Mr. Turla?" Jimmie asked. Turla nodded, giving Heck a quick threat assessment of a glance. It was the look every cop had given him since he was sixteen; he was used to it. Old habits died hard, Heck figured.

"Yeah," Turla said.

"The wheel turns," Jimmie said.

"The wheel turns," Turla replied, with a wary smile, and offered his hand to Jimmie. They shook. "You Don Aussapile's kid? Pleasure to meet you. You got a hell of an old man. Who's your, uh, friend?"

Jimmie smiled and nodded. "This is Heck Sinclair; he's my squire."

Turla's smile dimmed. He offered Heck his hand.

"I got all my shots," Heck said, shaking the ex-trooper's hand, "and I'm mostly housebroken."

"Mostly," Jimmie said. "You mind if we come in? We're here about the missing-persons report—those kids. Karen Collie? I was told you could help us."

"Come in, please," Turla said, stepping inside. "Get you fellas a cup o' mud? It's awful, but it's free."

Jimmie and Heck looked at each other warily.

"I don't like getting the stink eye from cops," Heck said.

"Try to act like you ain't scooter trash for ten minutes," Jimmie said before he walked in.

"Can't count that high," Heck said, stepping in front of Jimmie and entering the house first.

▪ ▪ ▪

About a half block down, on the other side of the street from Turla's house, Lovina Marcou sat in her Charger, sipped coffee, and took notes. She scribbled down the tag on the semi that had hissed to a halt in front of the ex-trooper's home, and the motorcycle. Both were North Carolina plates.

Russell had given her Turla's name and address as the person who had accessed the Collie girl's missing-persons file. Now he had an odd pair of guests from out of town showing up. She was glad she had decided to hang back and get a read on Turla before knocking on his front door. She'd wait, watch, and see where Bubba the Trucker and Goku the Ginger Biker led her. She picked up the phone to ask Russell to use his access to run the strangers' plates.

. . .

The living room and the kitchen were divided by a wall of open shelves, most of them filled with porcelain chickens of various sizes, shapes, styles, and colors. The room was dark, with only a table lamp on next to a large brown leather recliner. The room smelled of mellow pipe tobacco. The kitchen was well lit, well enough to see a sink of dirty dishes next to a dishwasher. Above the arch dividing the kitchen and the living room was a small wooden plaque, handmade with a wood-burner tool, which said, "Welcome to our kitchen: it may be cluttered but that's because it's filled with LOVE." There was a Formica-topped kitchen table with four chairs in the center of the kitchen. A thick brown folder sat in front of one of the chairs, next to a cell phone in a cloudy, sealed plastic evidence bag. Turla busied himself at a coffeemaker and gestured toward the kitchen table.

"Have a seat," he said. "There's the file. I got to get it back to my old partner in the next day or so. I looked up as much stuff online as I could; they never rescinded my access."

Jimmie and Heck sat. "Much obliged," Jimmie said. He pulled the thick folder in front of him and opened it. Heck reached for the plastic evidence bag; Jimmie grabbed at the bag and stopped him. "What are you doing?"

"Checking it out," Heck said. "Look, you want me to graduate from being your fucking squire, or whatever, then you got to let me do my thing, too, man. Let me see the cell." Jimmie reluctantly released the bag, and Heck began to open it.

"Don't break the seal," Jimmie said. "Chain of custody."

"Yeah, right," Heck said, slipping out his buck knife and slitting the adhesive tag that sealed the baggie. "Like that doesn't get fucked with all the time, anyway."

Jimmie looked back to Turla. The ex-cop nodded and shrugged, then went back to making the coffee and trying to find clean mugs. "We never recovered the Collie girl's cell," Turla said, "but these belong to the other kids. We found them in the car along with all their purses, car keys, backpacks. Weird. Tell me one teenager that ups and goes off without their damn cell phone. Things are practically glued to them."

Heck slipped the phone out and tried to turn it on. "Hey," he said to Turla. "You, uh, you got a charger I could use?"

Turla nodded. "Yeah, there's one hooked up on the night table in the bedroom down the hall," he said, gesturing toward the hallway past the den. "On the left."

Heck stood and headed down the hall.

"You sure he's okay?" Turla said softly to Jimmie after the biker was out of sight. "My skell sense is going off."

"Hey!" Jimmie said, turning to Turla. "He's my squire; you watch your mouth. He's the son of a good friend of mine—a Brother. Kid saved my life down the road, so yeah, he's okay."

"No disrespect," Turla said. "I just heard, you, know, how tough it's been for us to find new blood. Most of these kids out there aren't worth a damn. My son, I wouldn't even consider him for a squire."

"Sorry to hear that," Jimmie said. Turla was silent. The ex-trooper set a mug of hot coffee on the table next to Jimmie. He placed another where Heck had been sitting. "There aren't as many of us as there needs to be, for sure," Jimmie said. "We're still active in a lot of countries all over the world; we ain't dead yet, but you're right—we sure could use more warm bodies worth a damn."

"My daughter," Turla said, "now she could hack it. She's her mother's daughter, bless her soul. Every so often I think I should tell her all this, give her the option, then I think about my little granddaughter and I . . . I just can't imagine . . ."

Jimmie nodded and raised the mug. "I hear you. Got a little girl of my own, another on the way. Hard to imagine putting them in harm's way."

"Well, I hope this boy you got with you will make the cut," Turla said, raising his own mug. "Seems pretty tough. Hopefully, he's like his father."

"Stepfather," Jimmie said. "Here's praying he's nothing like his real old man."

. . .

Heck found the charger in the bedroom, next to a full hospital-style bed complete with oxygen tent, IV pole, and vital-signs monitors. The bed had a handmade pink-and-white comforter on it, neatly made. It hadn't had an occupant for some time, but there was a wooden chair next to it, and a folded paperback, a pack of Marlboros, and a half-full ashtray of butts joining the charger on the night table. The room smelled of stale smoke. Heck took the charger and waited to give the two old guys a few moments to talk him out; he knew they would. He suddenly imagined Ale in a bed like this, and saw his mom in the chair, next to him. The anger rose, flush in him, melting the ice he worked so hard to maintain. He should have been there. He could have been there. He made his pact with the anger, as he had been doing since he came home—it would get its hour to run free, to devour, and consume, and destroy. And it stilled in him—humming, waiting.

They'd had enough fucking time to critique him. With the charger in hand, he left this memorial to old pain as quickly as he could.

. . .

Lovina's cell buzzed, and she answered it. "What you got, Russ?"

"The bike is registered to a Hector Conall Sinclair. He's got a minor sheet—mostly assault, drunk and disorderly, possession of concealed weapon. Most of those charges came in the last few months," Russell said. "He's a member of an outlaw biker gang called the Blue Jocks—a Scottish-American club out of Wilmington. I talked to a Wilmington cop; he said that the Jocks are pretty clean as MCs go. They bounty-hunt to pay the bills. Some minor drug and weapons charges, the usual biker nonsense, but no organized-crime stuff."

"And the semi?" Lovina asked, as she flipped to a clean sheet of paper in her notebook.

"Registered to a Jesse James Aussapile," Russell said. "He's an independent truck driver, lives in Lenoir, North Carolina. Not much of a record, but it's the absence of one that's actually kind of interesting, given the circumstances."

"What do you mean?" Lovina asked. She noticed a movement out of the corner of her eye. A kid, a teen, walked slowly down the sidewalk on the opposite side of the street from her. The kid's hood was up, and the face was obscured. Lovina felt her hand leave the notebook and slide under her jacket for her gun. It stayed there.

"Well, Mr. Aussapile has been arrested and questioned literally dozens of times over the past two decades," Russell said. "He's been charged with interfering with police investigations, tampering with crime scenes, trespassing, possession of concealed weapons. Get this, mind you—once it was wooden stakes and a hammer, and the second time it was an aluminum baseball bat covered in weird symbols drawn on it by a Sharpie. Oh, grave desecration, robbery, arson, and attempted arson. Every single charge was dropped, every time. But that's not the best part. His file is flagged by the Feds, Lovina."

"What?" Lovina said, still tracing the hooded kid's laconic gait down the street. The kid looked up, as if sensing the intensity of Lovina's stare. He looked around—pimply face and normal eyes. Lovina felt her whole body relax. Her hand moved away from her gun. She was angry at herself for being so damned jumpy.

"Yep," Russell continued in her ear. "It logged me looking at his file, as a matter of fact. He's been pulled in by the FBI several times in the last year for questioning in regard to murder investigations and missing-persons cases. Would you like to guess which task force it was that pinched him every time?"

"The Highway Serial Killings Initiative," Lovina said, circling Aussapile's name in her notebook.

"Give the lady a Kewpie doll," Russell said. "This fella has been associated with all kinds of bad stuff all over the lower forty-eight for years, *chère*. No one's been able to pin anything on him, though."

"And now he's all interested in Karen Collie's disappearance," Lovina said. "Thanks, Russ. Can you see if he and this ex-trooper, Turla, have a history?"

"It's lucky for you my girlfriend is washing her hair tonight," Russell said. "Already on that. But, first, I saved the best for last."

"Spill," Lovina said.

"We got a hit off a print on the can at Dewy Rears's place," Russell said. "He did have company, and the guy had been printed for a security-guard job about four years ago. His name is Mark Stolar, twenty-nine. No record. Last address is his parents' home. DMV has nothing on a vehicle for him, either. I have a supplemental in to get his bank info and see if we can track any activity in the last few weeks. You have this before the Tallulah PD, *chère,* but they will have it in the next twenty-four hours. I'll try to stall it, but no promises."

"I understand, Russ," she said as she wrote. "Don't stick your neck out for me, you hear? It's far enough on the block already."

"Ah, Love-e-ly Lov-ina," Russ said. "You should know by now—I am a man who loves to live dangerously! You be careful! This Aussapile and Sinclair sound like bad news."

"It's cool, Russ," Lovina said. "I am, too."

. . .

"According to this report," Jimmie said, flipping back and forth between the pages of the file, "these kids all knew each other, attended the same school, same clique. They hung out at each other's houses. No indications of any drug use, no records. Hell, not even a speeding ticket or caught smoking dope. Nothing. They went to the mall, to celebrate this . . . Mark Baz," Jimmie said, looking back at another set of papers, "getting his license and a new car. Karen's parents told me she was sweet on Mark but she hadn't even told him."

"Could it have been a carjacking that went bad?" Turla asked, sitting down at the table and sipping his coffee. "Or a robbery?"

"Doubtful," Jimmie said. "The new car was found in the parking lot of the mall, like you said—keys in the ignition, the kids' purses, backpacks, tablets, and phones on the floor of the car. If it was a robbery, they kind of stunk at it. The only thing they stole was the kids."

"What else did the ghost girl say to you, exactly?" Heck asked as he fiddled with one of the kids' phones.

"Vanishing Hitchhiker," Jimmie said, looking up from the file.

"Whatever." Heck swiped the screen of the phone with his finger. "What did she say about her and her friends?"

"She said . . . it ate her friends," Jimmie said. "Ate their souls."

"What ate them?" Heck asked.

"Damn if I know," Jimmie said, closing the file. "She said it was hunting. Called it something in some language—'Fi-ach flyin'—or something like that . . . I don't know what it was. She said she escaped it."

"How?" Turla asked.

"A scar," Jimmie said. "She showed me a scar, like she had cut her own throat. She said it didn't get her."

"Her soul got free," Heck said.

"So where's her body, then?" Turla asked.

"This is the last picture she took on her phone," Heck said. "Sent it to a small list of her friends, including all the missing kids and a few others." He held up the phone for both men to see. It was a picture of a young girl in a hoodie, a savage snarl on her downturned face. She seemed to be right on top of Karen as the picture was snapped. Another figure was beside the hooded girl, but only a flailing arm could be seen. "It looks like she ID'd her attacker," Heck said. "So they were on her and the others pretty damn quick."

Jimmie flipped through the report. "Looks like they asked her friends if they knew the girl in the photo. No one did. They eventually chalked it up to them goofing around on their phones at the mall."

"Bull-fucking-shit," Heck said. "Those are some lazy-ass cops, man."

"Watch your mouth, boy," Turla said. "It's damn easy to Monday-morning-quarterback, after the fact. Those investigators did the best they could."

"That," Heck said, showing the picture to Turla again, "look like goofing around to you? That girl is out for fucking blood."

"All right, enough," Jimmie said. "So we got multiple attackers. Teenagers who apparently jumped them as they were getting in the car. We have no smashed windows, no phone or purse on the ground. No signs of a struggle at all."

Heck frowned and looked at the picture. He tapped the phone's screen.

"No blood, no prints, no witnesses, nothing," Jimmie said, flipping through the pages of the file. "Was there any video of them from security cameras, do you know?"

"It was an older mall, and it was in a pretty decent area," Turla said. "I understand they had some interior footage of them wandering, shopping at the food court, but nothing that led anywhere. They did a canvass of the mall and put the footage on the news. No leads from it, though."

"Did the cops know they were into weird shit?" Heck said, his eyes fixed on the phone screen. "All kinds of texts about occult shit, and the browser history is full of weird-ass websites. What the fuck are BEKs?"

Jimmie and Turla looked at each other and shrugged.

"Beats the hell out of me," Turla said. "A gang, maybe?"

"These kids were all over it, whatever it is—especially Karen, here," Heck said. "She was researching it. There's a text conversation between her, Mark, and one of the other missing kids, Stephanie, about some YouTube videos they had seen about BEKs. Here's another message where Karen is telling the other missing kids she thinks she saw BEKs across the street from her house. This was dated two days before they disappeared."

"There's nothing in the report about any of that," Jimmie said. "Some notes about checking her phone and messages, but nothing about BEKs, whatever the hell that is, or her being stalked."

"Yeah, more first-rate police work," Heck said, reading the texts and ignoring Turla's sour look. "Her friends pretty much talk her down. Let me see if I can get Internet on this."

Jimmie flipped to the photos of the car and the mall lot. "They search the area around the mall?" he asked. "From the sounds of this report, it was two detectives and about six uniforms and the CSI boys."

Turla nodded. He rose to get more coffee, and refilled Jimmie's and Heck's cups after his own. "They did a search the following day, when the car was found—it's mostly malls and more shops all around there—pretty built-up over there. They searched the lots, the surrounding alleys, and the mall dumpsters. Nothing."

"Well, shit," Heck said, scanning the cell phone's screen. "No wonder the cops didn't give this BEK stuff a second glance. It's about Black-Eyed Kids. Real Bloody Mary, scary-sleep-over-story bullshit. Urban myth." Heck looked to Jimmie. Aussapile lowered the file.

"Just like Vanishing Hitchhikers," Jimmie said.

The bag came off Lexi's head. She blinked at the feeble light straining through the filthy windows far above her. She was in a large corrugated-tin building, like a garage. The air was greasy with the smell of engine oil. She looked to her left and saw Cole, an ugly bruise on his forehead, and his lip swollen and split. Cole was blinking as well, having just had his feedbag hood removed after hers by one of the Scode brothers, Toby, the younger one. Toby's eyes wandered over Lexi's body, lingering on her legs and breasts before he finally arrived at her face. He smiled at her.

Lexi's black goth eye makeup was smeared from tears of fear and panic. She wanted to cover herself, but her hands were firmly bound behind her back at the wrists and upper arms by coarse rope. She could see that Cole was bound as well. He looked exhausted and frightened. Lexi had already screamed herself hoarse in the past few days. Was it just days? Time had already become slippery and hard to judge. Some cold, mercenary survival instinct came to her, and she knew in her bones, with every cell of her being, that she might die here soon, on the dirt floor of this metal shell. She heard dogs barking, snarling outside, and she looked up into Toby's bland face and smiled back as brightly as she could. *Pretend you don't want to throw up on him. Pretend he's a fucking rock star. It might help you and Cole get the hell out of here. He wants you, use it to survive.*

"You're gonna get to meet him," Toby said to her, his eyes dropping back to her chest. Lexi wanted to kick his rotten, yellow teeth in, but she needed any edge she had to live through this, and right now if looking at her boobs distracted him from noticing that she was trying to loosen her ropes, then keep looking, you hillbilly perv.

"Who?" Cole asked. "Who are we meeting? Your boss?" The answer came in the form of a steel-toed work boot driven into his side by Wald.

"Shut up," Wald said almost absently. "You don't understand a damn thing. Shut your hole, boy." Wald slapped his younger brother hard in the face and then jammed a thick, dirty finger at Toby as well. "And, you, stop gobbin' at the mouthy bitch's tits. You want him to find you derelict in your duties?"

Toby paled visibly. "No . . . no, Wald. I've been good. I do what he says, what you say. I say my prayers and do the sacrifices and everything."

"Come on," Wald said. "Let's get the others down."

Lexi looked at Cole as the Scodes walked away. "Are you okay?" she whispered.

Cole nodded, still wincing from Wald's kick. "Yeah," he said as he tested his ropes. "That hurt like hell, but I'm getting used to it. Evil old bastard. You okay?"

"This can't be real," she said. "Those shadow things? What . . . what happened to Alana and Gerry? Could they have dosed us with something when were asleep in the truck? Acid? Molly? I mean, this can't be real, can it?"

Cole was beyond tired. He heard the ragged desperation in Lexi's voice. He knew from Alana and Ava that Lexi had spent time in a mental hospital for cutting and depression. He knew she was hanging on to her self-control by her fingernails. He tried to summon up his father, his dad's relentless strength that had long ago become his avatar for what a man should be, how he should be. He tried to be brave and strong one more time.

"Maybe," he said softly, watching the Scodes as they wrestled with a series of heavy rusted chains anchored to the wall of the building on hooks. It was the kind of rig you'd use to hoist a car engine. "It's possible. Could be we were tripping, and that was just guys in dark clothing murdering our friends and trying to kill us."

"Maybe they didn't kill them," Lexi said. "Maybe that was a hallucination. Maybe we got to the party and someone gave us really, really bad shit and we're still tripping."

"Lexi," Cole said. He saw the tears forming in her dark eyes.

The Scodes grunted as they lowered a weight on the chains to the dirt floor. Two men—one fat and tall, the other toothpick-skinny and short—thudded to the ground. Both were covered in filth, smelling of blood, piss, and shit. They had feedbags over their heads as well. Their wrists were handcuffed, and they had been hung on winch hooks up near the rusted girders at the roof of the building. They both groaned as they hit the floor, but neither moved. Wald kicked them the way he had kicked Cole—first the fat one, then the skinny one.

"Get your worthless asses up," Wald rumbled.

"My legs," the muffled voice of the big guy said from under the hood. "They're numb, man. You've had us hanging up there for days . . . please."

Wald kicked him again. The hooded man screamed in pain and fear and managed to get on all fours. His smaller companion was equally unbalanced. Toby pulled the skinny man to his feet. Cole looked at Lexi. She shook her head. When both men were standing, Toby tore off their hoods. The big guy had dark curly hair that fell to his shoulders. He wore a RUSH concert T-shirt and had a goatee and a mustache; he squinted as if he needed glasses to see. The little guy had straight, greasy blond hair that fell to the base of his neck. He had a few days of scraggly growth on his face and wore a faded Slipknot T-shirt.

"Look, man, whatever you think we did, I swear we didn't—" The small guy was interrupted by Wald's punch to his jaw. The skinny guy spit blood and staggered backward but stayed on his feet. "Fuck, man!" he said, rubbing his jaw.

The big guy staggered over to his companion and helped steady him. He jabbed a finger at Wald. "Leave him the fuck alone," the big guy said. "He has no clue why he's here, asshole. Your fucking little monsters just grabbed him, too, because he was hanging out at my place."

"And you think you know so much," Wald said. "The only reason either of you is breathing is because he wills it. He has need of you, you bloated, whiny tick. He doesn't need your chum. Mind your tongue or I'll hang him back up and use the blowtorch on the soles of his feet."

Wald gestured for the two men to move over to where Lexi and Cole were sitting. "Sit down and shut up," he said. "He'll be here soon."

The prisoners looked at one another. The large man nodded. "I'm

Dewy," he said, nodding to Cole and Lexi. "Dewey Rears. This is my friend Mark Stolar."

"Hey," Mark said.

"Cole Wagner," Cole said. "This is Lexi Froller. We're students at the University of Kansas, Salina."

"Salina? Kansas?" Mark said, his voice cracking. "Holy shit, Dewey, how the hell did they get us all the way to Kansas in just a few minutes?"

"Teleportation is the most reasonable solution," Rears said. "They possess all kinds of paranormal abilities. How do you think they appear and disappear the way they do in so many of the eyewitness accounts? I'm just glad we're still in the solar system."

"Shit, Dewey," Mark said, fighting to keep his voice down, "these inbred motherfuckers are going to kill us, man! This isn't fucking *Scooby-Doo!* We have got to get out of here."

"What are you talking about?" Lexi said to Dewey. "Where did you think you were?"

"We're from Tallulah, Louisiana," Rears said. "We were abducted from our apartment by creatures, things that looked like children. I've been researching them for a book I was writing."

"Creatures?" Cole said, lowering his voice. The Scodes were standing near the closed large twin doors, smoking. Occasionally, Wald would cast a hate-filled glance in the direction of the prisoners. "You mean those shadow people? They killed some of our friends."

"Shadow people? No," Dewey said. "BEKs—I think the Black-Eyed Kids are some larval form of the shadow people. Allows them more access to the physical world or something. . . ."

"Jesus," Mark said. "We need to figure out how to get out of here, not discuss this bullshit."

"Kids?" Cole said. "Like, children?"

"He's right," Lexi said, the terror beginning to slip back into her voice. "We can talk about what the fuck these things are after we're safe! Please, Cole!"

"Black-Eyed Children," Dewey said. "They're agents, conduits. It works through them, somehow. Whatever it is, it's something far, far more terrible."

There was the growl of a powerful engine approaching and the hiss of shifting gravel outside, then pounding at the double doors.

"Shit!" Mark said.

Wald and Toby dropped their hand-rolled cigarettes and scrambled to unbar and open the large doors. The day was overcast, but the light still made the prisoners squint and turn their heads. The Scode brothers bowed their heads. Cole and Lexi recognized the figure at once from the day of the wreck, the day this nightmare began. It was the motorcycle rider, clad in black leather, straddling his rumbling antique bike, his features hidden behind the black mirror of his helmet visor.

"Lord," Wald said. It was the first time Cole or Lexi had heard any tone in the old bastard's voice but hatred and anger. Now he sounded respectful and afraid. "The prisoners, as you commanded. Thy will be done."

The rider advanced the bike into the building slowly, and once he was in Wald and Toby closed the doors and secured them again. The rider flipped down his stand and rested the motorcycle on it, then shut off the engine. He climbed off the bike, pulling his helmet off as he did.

"Yes," the biker said, his voice frost on slate. "You have served me well, Walden and Tobias, sons of Scode, as you always have." The biker's face was plain—not handsome, or unpleasant, the kind of features that are instantly forgettable. His short dark hair was slicked back from his forehead, oiled, and parted neatly down the center. His eyes were the most striking—brown, with an intensity, a terrible will, behind them. The rider's stare made Lexi feel that he was looking into her mind, her soul, X-raying every part of her. He did not blink. He was tall, average in build. It was hard to get a fix on his age. His physique and skin said that he was in his early thirties, his burning eyes contained a force far, far older.

The rider handed his helmet to Toby, who took it, still averting his eyes, and moved to stand before the prisoners. His burning eyes locked on Lexi, and she felt her mind shiver and grow still. It was hard to think, to see anything past the dark wells of his regard. Tiny black threads of vein radiated from the edges of his iris, across the milky sclera. His gaze shifted to the big man, Dewey Rears, and Lexi was free from the spell.

"Mr. Rears," the rider said. "You will perform a service for me. Rise." Dewey struggled to his feet. He looked at the rider but seemed able to shake off his cobra-like gaze.

"Who are you?" Dewey said. "You were outside my apartment when the Black-Eyed Children grabbed us in Louisiana." Wald began to strike Dewey, but the rider stilled him with a raised hand. The rider stepped closer to Dewey, and the journalist began to glisten with sweat, despite the chill of the air.

"The name I was born with was Emile Chasseur," the rider said. "I was born in a shack not far from here, in Four Houses, long before you or even your whore mother was born."

"Hey!" Dewey said, his face reddening. "Fuck you! Talking shit about my—" The rider nodded, and Wald drove a hard fist into Dewey's gut. The man gasped in pain and staggered backward but stayed on his feet. The rider grabbed him by the hair and pulled his face up, close to his own.

"That is no longer my true name," he continued. "I was given another name, a greater name, by him whom I serve, him who dwells within me. A title. If you interrupt me again, I will rip your tongue out and feed it to my dogs."

Dewey nodded and painfully straightened himself as the rider released his mane. The rider moved to Mark, looking at the frightened man, who would not meet his gaze, as he addressed Wald.

"They had mobile phones on them, correct?" the rider asked. "Even the most common of human trash possess them in this era, yes?"

Wald nodded. "Yes, sir. They all did. Shall I fetch them? We charged them, as you requested."

"Just this one's." The rider pointed to Mark and then turned back to Dewey. "Mister Rears will be making a call for us to an old friend," he said. "Then we will all be making a trip to the woods to . . . commune."

Dewey's fear-glazed eyes were fixed on the rider. "You're . . . you serve it, don't you?" Dewey said. "The thing inside the children, the thing the shadows are made of . . . You're its human face, aren't you?"

"All will be understood in the woods, Mr. Rears," the rider said. Now, I need you to make a phone call for me."

"The phones . . . they don't work here," Cole said. "No signal."

"They will work," the rider said, "because I will them to." He motioned to Wald and Toby, and they took Dewey by the arms and led him away from the others. The rider took an object from his jacket, a compact disc in a hard plastic case, and showed it to Dewey.

"You will call your old friend and boss, George Norse."

"The paranormal radio-show guy?" Mark blurted out.

"I've heard of him," Cole said. "He's on all over the country. He's got that TV show now, too!"

The rider's face was still as stone. He looked at Wald and Toby. "If any of you speak out again, I will have these men beat you to death with crowbars."

"Norse," Dewey said, nodding. "Yeah, yeah . . . me and George go way back."

"Yes," the rider said. "Exactly. You will tell him that you have been investigating an occult serial murderer and you have uncovered a shocking revelation that links him to paranormal forces."

"What?" Dewey said. "What serial murderer?"

"Me," the rider said, "of course."

"Oh God," Lexi muttered.

"Tell Mr. Norse you have video that will reveal the identity of the killer the media call the Pagan," the rider said. "Tell him you want ten thousand dollars for the video, and that your friend, Mark, will deliver it to him in his studios in Atlanta."

Dewey was shaking his head. "This is some kind of bullshit," he said. "The Pagan has been killing people since the fifties. There's no way that's you, man."

The rider slid a big hunting knife from a gravity sheath under his riding jacket. The heavy, flat blade flashed against the weak light from the dirty windows. Dewey saw the odd maker's mark on the base of the wide blade—a circle with a half-moon crescent on its side above it, the curve of the crescent barely touching the top of the circle; the points of the crescent, like horns, were ascendant.

"I've been killing people for much, much longer than that," the rider said. "Now make the call—do it exactly as I told you. Convince Mr. Norse that he needs this video for his television broadcast. Tell him if he shows it on his April 30th broadcast, then the killer has promised to call in to the show that night. Tell him the Pagan will kill someone that night if the video isn't shown. That should do the trick. Make him believe, Mr. Rears, or I will kill one of them." He gestured toward the prisoners with the knife. "And I will do it slowly. Very, very slowly, and make you watch."

Dewey felt his balls shrinking and retreating up into his stomach. He wanted to piss himself. He wanted to puke, and cry, and run. But there was no running. "Why me, man?" he whispered, tears and snot beginning to form at the borders of his eyes and nose. "Why us?"

"Consider it your penance for investigating his children," the rider said. "You wanted so badly to see them, to understand them, and now you're getting your chance, Mr. Rears. Sometimes it's better not to understand." The rider handed Dewey Mark's cell phone. "Now, make the call."

Dewey walked away, dialing. He talked to someone for a while, very animated, his voice rising.

"Uh, sir?" Cole said. "What are you going to do with us? We just came here to get our car fixed. Our parents are probably really worried about us. My dad's pretty loaded, he owns a couple of big farms. He can pay you and your guys here if you just get us—"

"You called me a 'fucking asshole,' a 'psycho,'" the rider said, moving to stand over Cole. "On the road, do you remember?"

"Oh God, no," Lexi said. "Please, don't."

The knife was cold on Cole's skin. The edge nestled behind his left ear. The rider was down on his haunches between Cole and Lexi. "You want him, don't you?" the rider said to Lexi. "I can see it in your eyes. Hell, I can smell it on you—the stink of lust. Tell me the truth, girl. Would you want him if I hacked off his ears, his nose? Maybe a few fingers? His eyelids? Would you still desire this boy? Tell me true; I'll know if you're lying."

"No," Lexi said. "No, I wouldn't want him like that. Please don't, mister. He's a good person."

Cole felt the blade trace a line down the back of his neck, behind his ear. He felt the silver sting of the razor-sharp edge of the knife, a cool shiver of pain. He closed his eyes. His heart was thunder in his chest. He was dizzy with fear; he wanted his dad there to make it all right, to shoot all these assholes and keep them from hurting him, hurting all these people. He wanted it all to go away. Then the blade was gone. The rider's mouth was inches from his ear. He could smell the man's breath—the stench of decay and the heady smell of wet moss.

"You must be intact for what is to come, or else he will be displeased and not accept you," the rider hissed. "So for now, boy, you get to live with your miserable fear and your pretty, pretty face. Enjoy it."

The rider was up and walking away from the prisoners, back to Dewey, who was off the phone and flanked on either side by the Scodes. Wald plucked the phone from his hand.

"You got it," Dewey said. "George is waiting for the video. He wants it for the TV show, this Saturday, the thirtieth, and he will start talking it up on the radio. Ten grand."

The rider smiled. He had small, white, even teeth. "Good," he said, and then walked to his motorcycle without another word.

Wald and Toby began to roust the prisoners even as the rider kicked his bike to life again. "Now it's off to the forest with the lot of you," Wald said. "He's eager to meet you."

. . .

The prisoners were loaded into the back of the tow truck again. Dewey and Mark in the bed, Lexi and Cole in the backseat of the cab. No hoods this time. The Scodes turned right out of the junkyard lot and headed south on the two-lane. The rider, on his motorcycle once again, led them. After about two miles, the rider pulled onto a gravel road. Lexi noticed a large tree beside the road. Antlers were nailed to it, and a roadside altar rested below the horns. She leaned over and tried to bury herself in Cole's chest. The forest—mostly black walnuts and shingle oaks—deepened on either side of the narrow road. The shadows grew longer, and the afternoon sun vanished under the dark canopy. Occasionally, you could see animal bones and feathers tied to strings, gently spinning, hanging from the branches of trees.

"We're going to die," Lexi whispered. "It's some kind of cult. They're going to kill us out here, Cole."

Cole wanted to cry himself, but he held it together. He wished he could think of something brave or hopeful to say to her, but she was right. "I won't let them hurt you," he muttered. They both knew how hollow the words were, but both tried to summon the dregs of belief in them. The road veered to the left, and now Cole and Lexi could see a very old house, more like a cabin, squatting among the tall trees. The rider came to a stop in the bare dirt patch in front of the house, as did the tow truck. Dusk was near, and the brilliant light at the terminator between day and night was swallowed by the darkness of the deep woods all around the house.

"Out," Wald said. Lexi had an odd moment of déjà vu. His voice was just as cold and uncaring as it had been when he woke them all the night he towed Gerry's car to this hellish town. Wald truly had nothing but cold hate in him, except for his cowering fear of Chasseur. Wald would wring their necks like a chicken's and give it not a second thought. She suddenly flashed to those terrorist-beheading videos on YouTube, those poor frightened people, their eyes dumb with fear, as they spent their last moments in this world—this amazing world full of music, words, art, laughter, sunsets, babies, chocolate, changing seasons, the sweet ache in your chest when you fall into or out of love, ice cream, the taste of ocean foam on your lips and up your nose, making love, fucking, dancing, dogs, cats, silence, noise, love, joy. To leave this world surrounded by nothing but bitterness, simmering anger, and cool madness seemed the saddest thing in the world. The realization of how far she was from kindness, from decent human beings, cracked something deep in Lexi—something she had worked so hard to glue back together. Churning emotions—thoughts she had locked away with the help of all the doctors, all the medicine, all the will to get better, to really live— it was all seeping out again in these, her last moments. Lexi hummed inside like a box full of stinging bees. She and Cole exited the truck while Toby wrangled Dewey and Mark out of the bed. Chasseur regarded the yawning, infinite woods, then turned toward the prisoners and the Scodes. He gestured toward the house.

"I was born near here," he said almost absently. "At the outpost." Chasseur kept glancing into the woods. It was the first movement he had made that did not seem choreographed and practiced to perfection. He was looking for something, at something, in the darkness of the woods. "What year was that, Wald? Do you recall? Your great-great-grandfather was alive then. He was a tinker—worked for the Chouteau Brothers, if memory serves."

"1827, Lord," Wald said. Lexi noted the shift in Wald's voice—fear, deference, like a mean junkyard dog that had been beaten into docility. "That was the year."

"Bullshit," Cole said, not sure exactly where the strength in his voice came from. Maybe it was anger. He was pissed at the sheer stupidity of being led off into the woods to die at the hands of a bunch of moron redneck cultists. "No fucking way you were born in the 1800s. Where did you get your fucking bike, man? Whittle it?" Chasseur turned from the woods and his thoughts to focus his neon stare on the boy. A slit of a smile formed on his cruel mouth.

"I cannot wait for you to meet him," the rider said, "in the woods."

"Look, man," Dewey said, "I swear I was researching all those kids going missing, the links to the Black-Eyed Kids. . . . I don't know shit about you, or your boys here, and I don't want to. I couldn't tell anyone where we really are, so you guys don't have to do anything harsh here. "Let us go and we'll—"

Chasseur removed his leather glove and placed a cold hand on Dewey's chest. The journalist gasped at the slight touch and was silent. "Places of power reflect, they echo," the rider said. "I felt the power in these woods as a boy. Here was where I first hunted. I would catch small animals— squirrels, mice, rabbits—and I would take them apart, see how they worked. I enjoyed the sounds they made as I did so."

"Jesus!" Mark said.

"Not quite. They said I was possessed," Chasseur said. "I suppose in a way they were correct. They drove me out of the settlement, outcast me. They chased me into these woods and hunted me. It was laughable. I could navigate this wilderness blindfolded. I killed three of them before they called off the hunt. I was nine."

The rider gestured for the Scodes to rally the prisoners and follow. Chasseur headed toward the back of the house. It was getting darker by the second as they passed a functioning water pump mounted in cement, several piles of firewood, and a wide low stump being used as a chopping block. The rider continued on toward the woods, and Wald and Toby pushed the prisoners forward.

"I lived in these woods for the next nine years," Chasseur said. "He came to me first in dreams, then speaking to me in the wind slicing between the branches. I began to see his design in the entrails of the things I killed. Slowly, I began to understand what he wanted, what he needed from me, and why he chose me for this great work."

Chasseur stepped into the tree line. Within a few steps, he was lost in darkness. The Scode brothers paused for a moment and then shoved the prisoners forward. The forest was thick around them, smothering in its closeness. It was getting darker, but that didn't seem to deter Chasseur. He moved silently, precisely, as he found the openings between the maze of green and shadow.

Dewey fell, stumbling and crashing down.

Wald growled and kicked him. "Get your fat ass up!" he snarled as his work boot knocked the air out of Dewey.

Cole was suddenly on the old mechanic, grabbing Wald's shoulder and spinning him around. "Leave him alone, asshole!" Cole said as he drew back a fist to strike Wald's scowling face. Cole suddenly felt the cold sting of a very sharp blade at his throat and heard the rider's cool, even voice behind him.

"Lower your fist," Chasseur said, and applied a tiny bit of extra pressure to the fat pulsing artery in Cole's neck. Cole complied. The knife stayed at his throat as Chasseur turned his gaze to Wald. Even in the quickly dwindling light, the rider's eyes were burning. "Did I give you leave to harm him, Walden?" Wald looked terrified—all the bitterness and angry joy he had from laying into Dewey evaporated at the rider's soft monotone question.

"No, no, Lord," Wald said. "I'm sorry, Lord."

"No harm must come to Mr. Rears," Chasseur said. "He must remain in good health. Do you understand, Walden?"

"Yes, Lord."

The blade was no longer at his throat, and Cole exhaled in relief, rubbing his neck. Wald helped Dewey to his feet.

"You okay, man?" Mark asked. Dewey nodded and rubbed his stomach, glaring at Wald.

Scode's stonelike scowl had returned, and he gestured toward the rapidly diminishing back of the rider as he continued deeper into the woods. "Move," he said.

As they began to trudge again through the narrow passages between the trees, Dewey nodded at Cole. "Thanks, man," he said.

Cole smiled and nodded.

It was completely dark by the time Chasseur's trek led them to the clearing. Cole wondered how they would find their way back. None of their captors seemed to have a flashlight or even a lighter. The clearing was about fifty yards in diameter, ringed by large, uneven, rough-hewn stones. The light came from the brilliant luster of the bloated, rising moon. At the center of the clearing was a huge ancient tree, rising up like a gnarled fist to heaven. It was a banyan tree, its network of vines and branches growing out of the crevices of the host tree, wrapping about them, melding with them, to make a vast web of branches, and transforming the long-ago devoured host into a vast gestalt. At the massive base of the dark tree was a series of low, relatively flat stones. Chasseur was headed toward them, and the Scodes made sure the captives all followed. The knee-high wild-rye grass hissed as the party moved through it. The rider sat on one of the low rocks, painted in dark shadows in the gleam of the moon. The Scode brothers forced the others to sit on the rocks as well. Everyone welcomed the rest, but the cold trickle of fear ran down into their stomachs. This was obviously the journey's end.

"He finally showed me the way to this place when I was a man," Chasseur said. "This is the heart of his woods, the heart of him. After so many years of offerings to him, he finally showed himself to me and gave me my true name and purpose."

There was a rustling in the grass all around them. Lexi and Cole froze at the memory of that sound, of the shadow people chasing them through the darkness. Large dark forms began to appear all around the stones they sat on, dozens of them.

"Oh shit, man," Mark whispered. "Fuck me. Fuck us."

They were in the shape of dogs—massive hounds, about four feet tall, two and a half feet at the shoulder, and looking as if they weighed over two hundred pounds. They were jet, not black, in the color of their fur but made of ink-black shadow itself, like the shadow people. Their eyes were the baleful light of the moon. Wald and Toby looked down, averted their gaze. Dewey stood, his legs quivering, as the hounds closed the circle and gathered all around and behind Chasseur. The rider petted one of the shadow hounds; it made no sound.

"Tell me," Dewey said. It was a request, it was a command. His voice quavered in fear; his whole body shook, but he kept looking, looking at the hounds, at the dark rider. "Tell me your name, tell me your master. I deserve to know—we all do, don't we?"

"You know what's coming next, don't you?" Chasseur said, standing. The spiderweb branches of the ancient tree spread out from behind his head like huge antlers. The pack moved as a unit, as a single organism, in response to the rider's movement. They all stood poised, ready to pounce. "You are a wise man. In another time you would have been revered and heeded. This is not an age of wisdom, unfortunately. It is an age of suffering and blindness. Soon it will be an age of blood, chaos, and unforgiving death."

Cole wanted to stand, to join Dewey, to fight, but the hounds froze him in fear, held his heart and stilled his legs. Chasseur stepped forward; the hunting knife shimmered with the ghost light of the cowering sun. The handle was old bone, yellowed with age. He grabbed Dewey by the hair and effortlessly threw the big man onto the flat stone before the tree. Dewey landed on his back, with a *whoosh* of air escaping his lungs.

"You do deserve to know," Chasseur said, raising the knife. "*Tá mé an Máistir na Hunt, tá mé bás ag siúl ar an Domhan. Agus mé éilíonn tú, as mo thighearna agus Máistir.*"

"No!" Dewey screamed. Mark struggled to get to his feet, but the Scodes held him down. Lexi covered her eyes, her reason scampering away from her.

"I am the Master of the Wild Hunt," Chasseur said. "You have looked upon the hunt and are marked and summoned. Your lifeblood feeds the Horned Man now."

Dewey looked up, past the madman now sprouting real horns out of his head, to the infinite stars, the cathedral of light in the cold, eternal vault of space. Then he saw what stood in place of the ancient tree now, the towering being whose antlers cradled the very stars within them. It turned its gaze—burning, pitiless, emerald fire—upon him and licked black, leathery lips capable of devouring worlds.

Dewey Rears's last thought as the knife pierced his heart was that the stars were a graveyard of dead, ancient light. Chasseur, the Master of the Hunt, tore the still hot, gushing heart out of the journalist's chest and held it aloft to the looming Horned Man. The heart burst into blue flames as it was devoured in Chasseur's hand. The shadow hounds fell upon the body, ripping and tearing, annihilating it, leaving no trace of skin, bone, or blood. They shifted as they fought over Dewey's remains, melting and flowing between the forms of shadow people and the shadow hounds. The hounds bayed—a sound that frayed nerve endings. It was the sound of soul-deep despair, the sound all human beings make at their moment of greatest loss. The howls curdled the very air, raking the night with talons made of razor-pain.

Cole, Lexi, and Mark all beheld the being that stood where the vast tree had been. It was impossible for their minds to process where the Horned Man began and the earth and the sky ended. Mark fell to his knees and tried to claw at his eyes and cover his ears, but the Scodes kept him from harming himself. Lexi screamed, accompanying the baying hounds. Cole held her tight as she screamed, but the light of reason had drained out of her eyes, replaced by a darkness that made the absence among the stars seem welcoming by comparison.

"So what is supposed to happen if you do let one of these black-eyed punks in?" Turla asked. They were searching the areas around the shopping-mall parking lots off Nameoki Road in Granite City. The ex-trooper had caught a ride with Jimmie, but Heck had insisted on taking his bike. They parked in the rear of the mall, where Jimmie's rig wouldn't get a second glace next to all the other 18-wheelers picking up or dropping off merchandise to the mall stores, snoozing in the their cabs waiting for the stores to open in the morning.

"That's the gotcha," Heck said, sweeping his head from side to side as he lit a Lucky Strike and snapped his Zippo shut. This was stupid. The whole area was urbanized as hell. There was no way a girl's body could be hidden here for two fucking years and not be noticed. "Nobody knows what happens, because no one ever sees or hears from you again. You go, 'Boo,' and all the Cub Scouts around the campfire crap themselves. It's all bullshit."

"Don't be so damned sure of all that," Jimmie said. He was walking a few steps behind Tula, and scanning the area opposite Heck. "That dog-man over in McHenry, not too far from here, the Hatchet Man in Bloomington, Aunty Greenleaf—the white-deer witch in Brookhaven, New York . . . I've seen plenty of things that were supposed to be bullshit, right up until they weren't."

"I've seen my share of crazy shit, too," Heck said, exhaling smoke. "But creepy little kids with solid black eyes that talk you into oblivion by whining to be let in? That sounds like Grade-A Creepypasta shit."

Turla looked at Jimmie. "What the fuck is Creepypasta?"

Jimmie shrugged. "Beats the hell out of me," the trucker said. He paused and looked around. "This is about as far as the original search grid went, right?" Turla nodded. "Okay, let's go wider and keep going in this direction."

"Why this way?" Heck asked.

"If she ran the other way, she was headed for the front of the mall and all the traffic on Route 203. Since not a single soul reported seeing her, with all that traffic and lights and stores, and they were parked back here, in the rear lot, I'm assuming she ran this way."

"Sounds legit," Heck said.

They kept heading west. Off in the distance, a train's horn bleated. They started across a wide, vacant field nestled between the various large industrial buildings. The sounds of the train got louder. They each clicked on flashlights as the island of light from the mall's lot diminished behind them. It was cold, and the winter wind, perhaps angry because spring was, literally, only a few days away, bit into the three men as they searched, the beams of their lights sweeping the dark field.

Heck paused and knelt. He shut off his flashlight and closed his eyes for a moment. Something was making the back of his brain itch.

"What?" Jimmie said to the biker.

"Shut up a sec," Heck muttered. There was an old pain here, smeared on the air, on the dirt of this place. Fear, regret, despair. Heck could almost taste it in the back of his throat, like black bile and molasses—thick, acrid, but sweet. Heck opened his eyes. "You're right," he said as he stood. "She ran this way, fell here, then got up and kept running when she saw them coming across the field for her." He pointed northwest, in the direction of another industrial building and parking lot past the field. "That way."

Jimmie looked at Heck for a long moment. "That's some damn good tracking, if you're right."

"I can't explain it, either," Heck said, "but I know I'm right about this."

"Okay," Jimmie said. "Good enough for me, I reckon. Let's keep moving."

Heck felt the deflection in Jimmie's words. No questioning about this weird feeling? No skepticism? Heck filed it away for another time. The trucker wasn't being a hundred percent with him, and sooner or later they would have words about that.

Past the concrete pad of a parking lot was a low hill, a grassy rise. Beyond that the searchers could see the slowly drifting colossus of a moving freight train. Its horn wailed mournfully again. They climbed the rise and looked down into a triangular quarter acre of sparse woods and scrub huddled near the train tracks. Off to the right loomed a white water tower, farther back from the tracks and slightly behind the woods.

"Okay," Turla said. "Like I explained to you guys, we're breaking it down into grids. You search your grid, make sure if there's gnat shit in it, you know it. Once it's secured, move on to the next grid space. We do this nice and organized, by the book. You read me, Red?"

Heck shrugged and then nodded. "Yeah, CSI: Granite City, I gotcha."

They began. The train passed after a few minutes, and the sounds of the city all around them became distant and muted. Their breath streamed out into the growing cold, silent banners of silver. The lights that ran along the train tracks at distant intervals fed deep, long shadows among the trees. There was trash everywhere in the woods—used condoms and condom wrappers, crushed soda and beer cans, broken brown and green beer-bottle glass, crumpled wet paper and plastic bags from nearby stores, and what appeared to be several piles of decaying human feces.

"Well, this must be the reading room for Granite City's homeless folks," Jimmie said, kicking some dirt over one of the piles. "What do we do if some cops wander by to roust the locals or we run into a rail-road dick?"

"You shut up and let me do the talking, *capisce*?" Turla said. "It's still too cold for the street folk to be outside yet. We should be okay."

It was getting late. The cold was settling into everyone's bones. Jimmie had needed to take a piss for about an hour, but he hadn't yet hit the point of ducking behind a bush. They kept looking, searching for anything that might lead back to Karen Collie. Jimmie moved to the next grid and paused. There was a slight dip downward, like a bowl, and at the bottom of it was a concrete square; at the center of the square was a heavy, flat metal grate. The grate was covered with trash and long-dead leaves. It was locked down with a padlock that looked much newer and shinier than it should. Jimmie began to sweep aside the trash. Broken glass tinkled as it was shoved away. Jimmie knelt and picked up a wide, sharp jagged piece of brown bottle.

"Hey," Jimmie said. "I think I got something." Turla and Heck joined him. Jimmie was examining the padlock. "This lock is pretty new. Maybe before it got put on, she . . ."

"This is a storm drain," Turla said. "All these parking lots and flat, nonporous surfaces around here, this is to catch and redirect rainwater runoff."

"Can we get this open?" Jimmie asked, tugging on the padlock. He and Turla looked at Heck.

"What?" the biker said. "You two fine, upstanding citizens just naturally expect the scooter trash to be able to pop a lock? That's insulting."

Both men continued to look at him. Heck sighed and knelt. He reached for the case file folder Jimmie had set on the ground and slid a large, thick paperclip off a bundle of papers in the file. He spent a few minutes bending and straightening the clip's wire and then snapped it in two. He bent one part into an L shape and then straightened the other end as best he could.

"Give me some light, you assholes," he muttered as he began to slide the wires into the keyway of the padlock. "I hope you know this is disrupting my crank-cooking schedule." In a few moments, the padlock popped open and Heck slid it off and tossed it aside. He helped Jimmie and Turla lift the steel grate and flip it back on its hinges. Turla swept his flashlight beam down into the dark concrete well.

"Gonna be tight in there," the former trooper said. "She could have crawled in and pulled the grate shut behind her, but there's maybe two and a half, three feet of clearance in that pipe."

Heck shined his flashlight on Aussapile's gut and then up and down over Turla's imposing frame. "Well, I guess we all know who's going down in there, don't we? You're welcome." Without another word, he dropped down into the shadows of the drain and vanished from sight.

Jimmie self-consciously patted his gut and shook his head. He knelt by the opening. He could hear Heck grunting as he struggled into the narrow drainpipe.

"You see anything?" Jimmie called out to his squire.

"Yeah . . . rats . . . fucking rats, Jimmie, and lots of rat shit and . . . wait." Heck's tone lost all its attitude in a second. "Guys . . . I think I found her. I see shoes, pants . . . Jesus, she's so small."

There was more scuffling and grunts as Heck tried to get closer to the body. Turla knelt as well and strained to listen. "Get the fuck off her, you fucking bastards," Heck shouted. There were hollow banging sounds and audible squeals. "Jimmie, man, there's not much left of her. The little bastards have been chewing on her. You were right about her cutting her throat. There's a piece of beer bottle in her hand laying across her chest. She cut herself and just laid here to die. Why would she . . . I mean . . . how? Shit, man. Fuck. She's just a little girl, Jimmie." Heck's voice was cracking, and Jimmie wished it were him down there in the hole with the little dead girl instead of the boy.

"You're doing fine, Heck," Jimmie said. "Hold it together, soldier. You see her phone?"

"Yeah . . . yeah," Heck said after a moment. "Beside her. Looks pretty trashed, though . . ."

Before Heck could continue, a bright beam from a powerful flashlight pinned Jimmie and Turla.

"Police," a woman's voice said. "Put down the flashlights and put your hands on top of your heads. Stay kneeling. You make a move and I'll blow you sick fuckers out of your shorts. Y'hear me?"

Her voice had a strong southern accent. Turla noted that she was standing with her flashlight away from her body, the same way he had been trained. "I'm a cop," Turla said, starting to rise. "My name is Gil Turla and I can—"

"You can get your ass shot if you keep standing up," Lovina said. "I know who you are, and I know you're up to your eyebrows in this shit, Trooper Turla. Stay where you are." Both men dropped the flashlights and remained still.

"Officer, my name is Jimmie Aussapile," Jimmie said. "I can try to explain all this to you, if you can try to keep an open mind about—"

Lovina was moving down the hill, slowly, sweeping the beam of her Maglite back and forth between the two men's faces. "Yeah, I know about you, too," she said. "You want me to keep an open mind about you and your buddies here abducting, raping, and killing children, asshole?"

"Bullshit," Jimmie said. "I've never hurt a kid in my life." The anger was welling up in his voice. "We're out, freezing our asses off a long fucking way from home, trying to find this little girl so we can get her home to her family and stop the sunabitches that put her here from doing this to any other kid. Who the fuck are you, exactly, lady? That accent is bayou, not Windy City. I don't see no uniforms, no badge, no backup."

"Yeah, who are you with?" Turla asked. He remained kneeling, but his eyes, squinting against the light, were accusatory.

Lovina was impressed. He might look like a redneck trucker, but Jimmie Aussapile was nobody's fool. No wonder he had skated without being charged so many times—the sick child-killing fucker was smart. Lovina was within a few yards of them now. She decided she needed to double-down. She held the Maglite with her gun hand, keeping the kill circle on Turla, since he looked a bit more fit to jump and make a sudden lunge. She slipped two pairs of cuffs out of her leather-jacket pocket and tossed them on the dirt before the two men.

"I'm the cop who will put fucking holes in you both and write it up as pretty as you please on the paperwork," she said. "Now, Aussapile, you cuff him behind his back."

"Look, you really don't want to do this," Jimmie said. "We're not who you think we are. We're the good guys. Swear."

"Cuff him," Lovina said.

Jimmie sighed and picked up both pairs of cuffs. He tossed them into the open drain. "Oops," he said.

Lovina shook her head. She was close enough now for both men to see her behind the light—athletic, but still a little curvy, dark brown skin, and shoulder-length straight black hair, with straight bangs that looked kind of like Bettie Page's. Her eyes were maybe hazel behind the glare of the light, but they were, for sure, one hundred percent no bullshit. Cop's eyes, soldier's eyes.

"Get down on your bellies, both of you," Lovina said. "And one more 'Oops,' Aussapile, and I will put a bullet in your kneecap. Down, now." Both men complied.

Turla looked over at Jimmie. "Well, that was a great idea," he said to the trucker. "You really turned the tables on her."

"Better'n being cuffed," Jimmie muttered.

"You, down in the hole—Sinclair," Lovina shouted, keeping her gun on the other two men and sweeping her flashlight toward the drain. "Climb up here nice and slow now." There was only silence. "Come on, Sinclair. You really want to be dragged kicking and screaming out of there by the uniforms, like a little bitch? I thought you were a badass biker?"

Moving to the edge of the drain, Lovina aimed her gun down in a Weaver stance, with both arms locked in a triangle, both hands steadying her .40-caliber Glock and the Maglite, together, as she took a quick look over the ledge of the drain and down into the dark. It was a good five-foot drop to the drainpipe below. The light caught Heck Sinclair's eyes, red, like a rat's, in the beam as he hurtled up toward her. The biker launched himself out of the well, springing up with a snarl. He cleared the drain with a good three feet to spare and tackled Lovina, who managed to snap off two quick, barking rounds at the almost flying biker. They crumpled together in the cold, trash-strewn dirt of the small basin by the drain, struggling.

"I am a badass biker," Heck growled as he tried to wrestle the gun out of Lovina's hand. "And I'd like to add that I feel the term 'little bitch' is hurtful and demeaning." She drove the Maglite, like a club, into the side of his face, accompanied by a metallic crunch. Heck rolled to one side from the impact, and Lovina scrambled to capitalize on his momentary discomfort and disorientation. She began to get to her feet. Heck swept his leg out and knocked her back down. As she fell, she twisted toward Heck and planted an elbow in his stomach. Heck groaned and rolled away from the cop, struggling to his feet. Lovina was half crouched, trying to do the same thing. She had heard Aussapile and Turla getting up during the struggle, and the panic of being piled on from different directions filled her with the numb momentum of pumping adrenaline. She fired another round, and this time it blew a hole in the shoulder of Heck's leather jacket, missing his skin by fractions of an inch. Heck paused, thinking for a second that he had actually been hit.

"I am not fucking around here, Hector," Lovina said.

"Do not fucking call me Hector," he snarled, rubbing his shoulder.

"Uh, excuse me, kids," Jimmie called out. "I'm sorry to interrupt, but

I'm going to take a shot in the dark and assume they're not with you, Officer."

Both Lovina and Heck turned their heads to look toward the top of the hill, where the trucker was pointing. There were six of them, children, all hooded by their jackets. They were silhouetted by the light pollution of the city, all still as statues. Jimmie's flashlight moved over them. Their faces were impassive, their eyes a cold, black void.

"Shit!" Lovina said. She lowered the gun and renewed her Weaver stance and grip, catching her breath. She recognized the two in the middle as the same ones she had encountered outside Dewey Rears's apartment, and who had pursued her. "You three get out of here. I'll deal with you later, I promise you that. Go on, run!"

The two children who knew Lovina each raised an arm. They did it in a fluid, perfectly coordinated motion. They both pointed at Lovina.

"You," all six said as one. "You need to come with us, you have been summoned. You have seen."

"Seen what?" Lovina asked. She looked at the three men, who were all looking at the kids and then at one another. "I told you to get the hell out of here, right now! Now go!"

"Come," the pack of children all said. "You must come with us." They began to move down the hill as one, slowly fanning out in groups of two.

"No," Lovina said, the same mind-numbing fear slipping into her again. She fought to shake it off, as she had before. The gun, raise the gun. Shoot. "No" was all she could muster. Suddenly, Jimmie was stepping between her and the approaching pack; he slapped his aluminum flashlight against his palm like a fighting baton.

"No," Jimmie said. "Lady's not going anywhere with you, whatever the hell you are. She's under my protection. You want her, you got to get through me. Now, come on!"

Heck threw up his arms. It was obvious from the shudder going through the old man's legs that Aussapile was scared shitless, but he was getting ready to tumble with whatever the fuck these things were— Black-Eyed Kids . . . yeah, right. He could rabbit. No, he couldn't. He wasn't some chicken shit who left anyone behind. He hadn't left his crew in the desert. He had fought that thing to the bitter end.

Heck was suddenly back in the drainpipe with the shrunken, skeletal face of Karen Collie near his own. She had such a sad look on what was left of her face. He could feel her fear, her regret, her pain. She was just a kid, with a million, million amazing things still to do with her life. These were the bastards who stole it. Heck felt the anger swell in him, the same anger that carried him through a dozen firefights, the same anger that allowed him to laugh as he took on a bar full of angry rednecks. The anger made him invincible. The anger felt like home. Heck slid the large combat knife out of his belt sheath and twirled it in his hand as the squire stepped up beside his knight.

"Yeah," Heck said. He hardly recognized his own voice when he got like this. "Like the man said. Come and get some."

Lovina blinked. The fear was falling away again. Behind her, she heard the oiled snick of a gun slide. She glanced over to see that Turla had pulled a .380 pistol out of a small holster hidden under his shirt. The former trooper moved beside her, his arms and hands also in a Weaver stance. "You ready?" Turla said softly. "Back-to-back."

The children were starting to move faster, almost blurring as they built up speed. The impassive look on their faces was now replaced by something primal, something that knew nothing of reason, only blood. At first Lovina thought it was her imagination, the fear, but now she could see that it was really happening. The Black-Eyed Children's mouths had widened; their teeth were now an impossible mass of slender, razor-sharp bone needles—hundreds of them in their mouths. With their dead eyes, it made them look like sharks.

"Why . . . why are you doing this?" Lovina asked as she moved to cover Turla's back as he was covering hers, both of them positioned to keep any of the pack from flanking Jimmie and Heck.

"Because," Jimmie said as he raised his makeshift club, "this is what we do, what we've always done. Fight the monsters."

Jimmie had one second to glance at his squire. Heck was licking his lips, his eyes glazed with simmering anger. The boy nodded to him, and Jimmie nodded back. That was all there was time for before the pack fell upon them, snarling, snapping.

Jimmie swung the flashlight and caught the one on the right hard on the side of the head. The little creature flew back several feet and dropped to the ground. It growled and sprang back up onto its feet, almost immediately, with inhuman speed and agility.

The one on the left Heck took. The Black-Eyed Kid launched himself at the biker from about ten feet away, making a sound like a scalded cat. To the creature's surprise, he was met in midair by the biker, who had also launched himself with impossible speed and distance, just as he had surprised Lovina by leaping out of the drain. The two crashed to the floor of the basin, and both found their feet almost at once. Heck crouched and quickly pivoted, using the knife to keep the creature at bay while it hissed and tried to get close enough to use its teeth. The thing fought more like an animal than like a human being.

The other four had veered off—two going to the left and two to the right of the vanguard. Lovina fired at the two scampering BEKs, who were almost on all fours as they crouched and ran. They were trying to drive a wedge between the lines of Heck and Jimmie and her and Turla.

Lovina exhaled the dregs of the fear, held her breath, and squeezed off two rounds. Behind her she heard Turla's gun bark as well. The Black-Eyed Kids moved at dizzying speeds, running up and launching off tree trunks like parkour runners, as if gravity didn't hold them. Her bullets struck one, and it fell, kicking, thrashing, and howling before it finally lay still. She missed the other, and it was on her, grabbing at her coat and opening its mouth full of death to sink its teeth into her throat. Lovina grabbed it by the throat and pushed it away with all her strength, but this thing, disguised in the body of a young boy, had the strength of a perp on bath salts. The mouth was moving closer, closer. An odd thought struck Lovina as she struggled with this thing for her life: Absolutely no odor came from the Black-Eyed Kid's mouth—no bad breath, nothing. Lovina brought the pistol up under its chin and fired. There was a flare of heat, a roar, and then the aural sensation of going underwater. Everything smelled of scorched gunpowder. There was a ringing in her ears and some nausea from the discharge, almost like being hit with a flashbang grenade. The Black-Eyed Kid was on the ground, mostly headless.

Lovina became aware that she didn't have a drop of blood on her. She should be bathed in blood and brains and bits of skull, but there was nothing. She looked over to where the other one she had shot had fallen. She was in time to see the body disappearing—evaporating into thick black smoke. She looked down at the headless one and saw the same phenomenon starting to occur. There was a groan behind her. Lovina spun to see Turla wrestling with the other two who had flanked him. His gun was still in his hand, smoking, but it looked as if he had been unable to hit the fast-moving creatures. One was wrapped around his gun arm, trying to pull it down and slowly succeeding. The other had him by his other arm and was getting ready to bite him. Lovina began to move to help the beleaguered ex-trooper, but she froze when she saw the face of the Black-Eyed Kid that was about to bite Turla. She almost vomited when the realization came to her. It was Shawn Ruth Thibodeaux.

"No, goddamn it!" Lovina shouted as she grabbed the little girl she had been searching for. She struggled to keep Shawn Ruth from sinking her shark teeth into Turla's forearm. Like the other Black-Eyed Kids, her strength was inhuman, and Lovina wrestled with all her training, all her might, to get her off Turla. The girl's eyes were dead space—hungry, oily nullity. Turla was trying with everything in him to get his gun arm free from the other one, whom Lovina now recognized from the long-studied case file as Shawn Ruth's friend Pierre Markham.

Jimmie's playmate had cleared the few feet he had been knocked back pretty fast. Jimmie clicked the flashlight beam to high power as the Black-Eyed Kid leaped on him like a squalling, rabid monkey. Jimmie caught the kid square in his weird eyes with the light, and it made the creature close its eyes and hiss. Jimmie used that instant to twist the creature into a wrestling hold he hadn't used since high school. They both went down, the Black-Eyed Kid on the bottom and Jimmie, and all his considerable weight, on top. At the moment of impact, Jimmie drove the flashlight against the thing's twisting, snapping head, with all his upper-body weight behind it. There was a sick crunching sound, and the little monster under him was still.

Jimmie groaned and struggled to his feet. He saw the lady cop and Turla locked in a struggle with two of the creatures. He looked to see how Heck was faring. The biker had slashed at the Black-Eyed Kid several times and seemed to have gotten a few bites on his forearm for the trouble. Ugly, black veins were radiating out from the bite wounds like webs. However, the creature was staggering from the knife wounds as well. Heck lowered his guard, rubbing at one of the wounds, and the

Black-Eyed Kid used the opening to lunge at his exposed throat. But Heck had been waiting for that. He high-kicked the thing hard in the chest. The Black-Eyed Kid went down, and Heck followed him, driving the knife deep into its small chest, with a snarl of his own. The creature struggled weakly for another moment, and Heck watched its face intently, eagerly, as it did; then, finally, it was still. When Jimmie glanced down at the one he had dispatched, its body had vanished.

There was another blast of gunfire. Turla had stopped struggling to keep his arm up and away from the Black-Eyed Kid. Instead, he shifted to the side as his arm went down and fired two rounds from the .380 into the monster's face. It fell back and down. However, the shift gave Shawn Ruth the opening she needed to bite Turla's other forearm deeply. Turla put the small pistol to her head, wincing in pain as he did. Lovina almost shouted for him to stop, but this was not the girl she had wanted to bring home to her mama and daddy—this was some thing, some force, walking around, using and profaning her skin. Turla fired one round, and the skull of Shawn Ruth Thibodeaux blew apart. Shawn staggered back, Turla's blood on her pale lips, and fell, beginning to churn black smoke as she vaporized. The smoke had no odor to it. Turla nursed his arm, obviously in great pain. Black, spidery lines began to radiate out from the blackening bite, crawling across his arm and hand.

"Everyone good?" Jimmie shouted, spinning slowly to circle the clearing, gasping for air. "We clear?"

"Clear," Heck said, slipping the knife away. There was no blood on the blade at all.

"Clear," Lovina called out, "but Turla's bit."

"Yeah," the ex-trooper said. "Little fucker. Hurts like shit."

"Tell me about it," Heck said.

Jimmie and Heck moved toward Turla and Lovina, then stopped. Black veins had begun to crawl up Turla's neck and to spread across his face.

"What?" Turla said. Black lines crossed his eyeballs and filled them completely with darkness for a moment, but then his normal eyes reasserted themselves. Turla gasped in pain and fell to the ground. Lovina caught him and eased him down. Jimmie knelt, joining her. Heck paused, hearing the wail of sirens off in the distance getting closer.

"Shit!" Heck said. "Guys, we got to move him. All that bang-bang got some attention! We got to roll."

Lovina checked Turla's pulse while the ex-trooper clenched his teeth in obvious agony. The black veins had covered the last unmarked skin. Lovina gave Jimmie a look he had seen far too many times on the battlefield, on the side of the Road. It told him all he needed to know.

"That bad, huh?" Turla said, wheezing a little. "Well . . . shit. At least we know what happens to the folks who let them in now, right?"

"Yeah," Jimmie said. "Guess so. I'm so sorry, Gil."

"Don't be," Turla said, coughing, then hacking. Lovina checked his pulse again. "I've been alone in that damn house dying for years anyway. This is how I wanted to go out. Thanks."

"Is there anyone we can contact for you, tell them?" Jimmie asked. There was the moan of another train's horn far down the tracks, just past the tree line.

"My wife passed away about four years ago," he said. "It was a mercy. She had been sick on and off for close to ten years." Turla shuddered. "Getting cold already. This crap works fast. Yeah, I guess you could let my kids know. I'd appreciate it, Jim."

Heck was standing behind Jimmie and Lovina now. He looked at his own arm. The bite marks were still there, but there were no black veins, no patterns.

"You make sure you tell them what happened. Tell them everything, Jim," Turla said. "Why I was here. About the Brethren. Why I wasn't home all those times, all those years. You tell them their daddy was out there fighting the monsters. Please, Jim, tell them."

"I will," Jimmie said. "I promise, Gil." Turla's breathing was coming quicker now, shallow panting. Lovina could feel his pulse skipping, growing fainter.

Turla looked at Lovina with eyes already beginning to see past this world. "You make sure when you tell my kids about all this it ain't no cold case." He tried to chuckle; it was a rasp. "You find whatever stole these poor kids' souls, destroyed them, used them. You stop it."

"Yes," Lovina said, taking his wrist. "We will."

Turla tried to smile. Each breath was a shallow hiss. "The wheel turns," he said, and died.

"He's gone," Lovina said, placing Turla's hand over his chest. His body was already beginning to smoke and dissolve, just as the children's bodies had.

"Damn it," Jimmie said as he stood.

"What was all that stuff he was talking about?" Lovina asked, rising. "'Brethren'? 'The wheel turns'? What is that?"

"Good luck getting a straight answer out of him, luv," Heck said.

Up the hill, blue lights could now be seen stabbing the darkness. The bursts and the static of police radios, shouting, and voices could be heard on the other side of the vacant lot. "We have got to go," Jimmie said, picking up Turla's gun—the only thing that remained of him. "Leave the drain open—they'll find Karen's body."

Jimmie paused at the edge of the drain, looking down into the darkness. He hated leaving her like this. He hated not being able to pull her up out of the horrible hole she had wedged herself into, to die, alone, in terror. He made a silent promise to the dead girl. He looked up and saw the lady cop staring at him.

"You are going to explain all this to me," Lovina said as they headed through the sparse woods in the direction of the train tracks. The train's horn bellowed again, much closer.

"Yeah," Jimmie said, "and you can explain why you're not running up there to join up with your brothers in blue and why the hell those things were gunning for you."

"Come on, come on, come on!" Heck shouted as he sprinted.

They reached the tracks. The engine's headlight was close, brilliant, like a nova. The rails were vibrating as the three ran across them. The horn on the train blasted again and again, a bellicose warning. They cleared the tracks just ahead of the thundering train—a wall of speed and mass between them, the cops, and the empty battlefield.

Walking the streets of downtown Atlanta, so full of life and energy, was like a dream to Mark Stolar after the past week. So many people, moving like guided missiles, to jobs or lunch, dentist appointments, or to meet friends and lovers. It was normal, petty, human, and after his time in Four Houses it was like gulping air after being beneath dark waters. It was April 27th, a Wednesday, around eleven-fifteen in the morning. If he were home, he'd be in his shorts watching Jerry Springer and eating Froot Loops. But all that changed yesterday, yesterday with Dewey, poor fucking Dewey. The small sliver of a flash drive in his pocket felt like a stone.

He hated doing this, doing the bidding of the creepy bastard that had murdered his best friend. He wanted to get him back, to kill that motherfucker. But life had already explained to Mark that that was all just movie bullshit. He wasn't a hero, he never had been. He was the sidekick, the occasional comedy relief. God's gofer.

Mark had met Dewey Rears in fifth grade while he was getting the shit beat out of him by two eighth graders who had called him "fag." Mark had made the mistake of flipping them off, instead of just taking it. He ran and reached the edge of the school's nature trails—the thick brush line that all the stoners hid in to have a smoke of one kind or another. His lungs burning, his legs rubbery with fear, he had fallen when the first one caught up and shoved him. They started kicking him, hard. His whole body felt like a bag of broken glass. He was crying, and that made them kick harder. He pissed himself, and that made them laugh and hoot and kick even harder. Then the kicking stopped, and there was a sound like a slab of hamburger meat hitting the floor. Mark forced open one of his swollen eyes, and there was Dewey, already towering a good foot over the other boys, driving his huge fist into another of Mark's attackers. He kicked the third one, and they scattered like cockroaches.

"You fuckin' fat-ass!" one of the attackers shouted as he ran away.

"Yeah, you come on back, shitheads!" Dewey whooped. "We'll do it again!" This big guy with a curly mullet, a "System of a Down" T-shirt, and kind eyes, reached down to help him up. "Won't we, man?" he said, grinning.

They had stayed best friends ever since. All through the bullshit of high school, all through Dewey's parents splitting up and Mark's mom passing away; through the nametag, hairnet jobs and the college promises and failures, through Dewey's weird-ass career as a writer, a Bigfoot chaser. They had stuck through all of it together. Dewey Rears was the closest thing Mark had to a brother. Had. Now Emile Chasseur, this psychopath who called himself the Pagan, the Master of the Hunt—whatever the fuck that was—had ripped Dewey's heart out, murdered him for some fucking insane horned-god-thing that couldn't, *couldn't really* exist, but that everyone had seen rising out of the trees, out of the woods, cloaked in sky and stars. Mark had seen it, and it made the insides of his brain itch. Just thinking of the Horned Man made him physically ill.

"I'm sorry, Dewey, man," Mark said. A woman in a suit, carrying a tote full of files, glanced at him over glasses attached to a bejeweled lanyard and walked faster away from him. "I fucked up, man. I should have done something, not just sat there shitting myself. Fuck, I'm sorry."

Mark wanted to cry. He felt the heat build in his eyes, but he fought it back. *Don't blink, don't blink.* Dewey was gone. All he could do now was try as hard as he could to make sure those other two kids, Cole and Lexi, didn't end up the same way. He had agreed to run this errand for Chasseur to keep the kids alive, yeah. How fucking noble of him. That was self-aggrandizing bullshit. That was what he told himself, what those kids might think. The truth was he was terrified of being dragged onto that rock and gutted like an animal, like Dewey, torn apart by those shadow dogs. He was frightened of the Master of the Hunt, and whatever the hell he served. He took this errand so that he could run, run, run, and never stop running. After he delivered the flash drive like a good little sniveling coward, he would run.

Chasseur wouldn't care. His bat-shit crazy plan would keep right on chugging, and Mark could hide and stay alive. That would be enough. And, truth be told, the only person he gave a shit about in this world was dead now. Fuck those kids. Fuck Chasseur's victims. It wasn't his fucking problem.

Mark entered the lobby of 191 Peachtree Tower. It was a massive, marble-floored rotunda, with huge globe chandeliers that looked like giant Christmas tree ornaments. There were large, live trees in huge planters. The planters doubled as leather-upholstered benches. For an instant, Mark swore he saw the Horned Man's endless, night-sky eyes peering out of the darkness behind the leaves. He looked away quickly, searching for some sign of banality to anchor him to this world, this reality.

He located the floor and suite number for the Intergalactic Planetary Radio Network on an illuminated computer terminal near the elevator annex. He took the elevator up with a muscular UPS delivery man—paragon of the brown cargo shorts—and two Asian businessmen, one in a cowboy hat with a strong Texan accent. He got off on the thirty-seventh floor, entered the glass-walled reception area of Intergalactic, and scratched his head as he waited for the attractive young woman behind the circular reception desk to acknowledge him. Mark looked like a homeless person, wearing the same clothes he had been abducted in, by the Black-Eyed Children, over a week ago. No shower, no shave, no deodorant. His hair was a greasy explosion. He had slept chained, suspended by his arms for days, and he had actually lost control of his bowels a little when he saw Dewey die. The Scodes had let him clean up a little, but he still stank of his own shit.

"May I help *you*?" the woman finally said when it was obvious that Mark wasn't going to just leave.

"Yeah," Marks said, smiling a yellow-and-brown-stained smile. "Um, I'm here to see Mr. Norse."

"Sir," the receptionist said, "if you're here about being abducted by aliens, or something like that, you need to call the tip line they talk about on the radio show, not—"

"No, no," Mark said. "I actually have an appointment with Mr. Norse, for real."

The receptionist gave him a look that Mark was sure she wore often—resting bitch face, the look of being a few seconds away from calling security. "Name?" she asked, almost accusingly.

"Mark," he said. "Mark Stolar. I'm here representing Dewey Rears."

The receptionist tapped the information into her keyboard and scanned the screen. She frowned, and then her demeanor underwent an amazing transformation. "Oh, Mr. Stolar. Mr. Norse will be with you in just a moment. Would you like a bottle of water or some coffee?"

"Yeah," Mark said. "Water would be great. Thanks." The receptionist delivered the water as if she were passing it to a leper and then made for the safe barrier of her desk. Mark chugged the water and tried to straighten his hair. After a few moments, a man walked out of the back corridor. He was of medium build, with black hair, dark, intelligent eyes, and a thick mustache under his prominent nose. He wore an off-the-rack houndstooth sports coat, a white broadcloth button-down, tan slacks, and worn but expensive leather loafers. Mark recognized the man from TV and stood to meet him.

"Mr. Stolar," the man said, shaking Mark's hand, "I'm George Norse. It's nice to meet you. Come on back to my office; we'll talk."

Norse's office was on the corner of the tower and gave an impressive view of the Atlanta skyline. One wall of the office was covered with awards, plaques, and photos of Norse with numerous celebrities.

"I'm a huge fan of your show," Mark said as Norse offered him a plush chair in front of his glass-topped desk. "I used to listen to you on the radio all night long when I was a kid. Your show scared the crap out of me, man."

Norse laughed and nodded toward another man, dressed in a very expensive suit. "Thank you, Mark. This is Brandon Sanjuro; he's IPRN's legal counsel." Sanjuro rose from his seat on the couch against the wall opposite the awards. He was Latino, with an expensive haircut and a well-trimmed goatee. He nodded to Mark but made no attempt to shake his hand before sitting again. Norse sat behind his desk and folded his hands in front of him. "So have you seen the show yet?"

"Oh yeah, me and Dewey never miss it," Mark said. "It's very cool. Dewey said you guys are number one in your time slot. Congrats."

Norse gave Sanjuro a nod and a slight smile. "Thanks, Mark. So Dewey said you had something for me, something for this weekend's show." Mark nodded as he reached into his pocket. He held up the small black plastic wedge of the drive.

"Listen, man," Mark said. "People have already died because of this guy. He's evil, and he's hooked up to something really, really old and powerful, man."

"I see," Norse said. His hands remained still and folded.

"I don't think you really do, Mr. Norse," Mark said. "Dewey said you guys were tight. You did a lot of work together a few years back?"

"Yes," Norse said. "Dewey's a damn good reporter. Fearless, professional, and thorough. That's why I offered him the money for the video. He's—"

"He's dead," Mark said, his voice cracking a little.

"Dead?" Norse looked at his attorney and back at Mark. "What happened?"

"This Pagan asshole killed him," Mark said. "Right in fucking front of me. He's going to kill a couple of kids he's holding if you don't run the video on the April 30th show."

"We need to notify the police," Norse said, "the FBI. Don't we, Brandon?"

Sanjuro shrugged. "Well, at this point we don't know if this is even authentic yet," the lawyer said. "It will take a few days to do all that, and we need to run it past the rest of legal to make sure we can run it without any liability on the part of the network. We can notify the authorities the afternoon before the broadcast if we have something here. It's too late for them to shut us down, and it covers the network's ass."

"Covers the network . . ." Mark said, looking back at Sanjuro, shaking his head. "Liability? Man, this guy's a fucking psychopath! He said if you get the cops involved he will slaughter a whole bunch of people on Saturday, and those two kids he's got will be the first to go! How's that for liability, man!"

Norse raised his hands. "Mark, look, I understand being upset, but we have to make sure we're not doing anything illegal here. Dewey was my friend, too, and I have to admit I'm a little wary of helping the lunatic that murdered him out by showing this video. We'll get the police involved quietly. Hopefully, this person claiming to be the Pagan will call in, as Dewey said he would, and the police can locate him."

"Okay," Mark said. "Sorry, sorry. I haven't slept for a week and . . . Dewey . . ."

"I understand," Norse said. "Dewey said this Pagan was connected to some supernatural power or force—is that true?"

Sanjuro snorted a little, but Norse quieted him with a simple raise of his palm.

Mark nodded.

"You look at this video, and then you tell me, man," he said, handing Norse the USB drive. Norse slid the thumb drive into his computer and moved his mouse about, clicking. After a moment, the office was filled with the sounds of a young girl screaming. Mark closed his eyes and rested his forehead on the edge of Norse's desk. His stomach clenched every time he heard the girl scream. He'd seen the video before—back when Dewey first encountered parts of it during his investigation of the Black-Eyed Children and the disappearing kids. He saw it for the first time in its entirety when Chasseur forced him to watch it on a battered old laptop, shortly after butchering Dewey. He had no desire to see it ever again.

"Jesus!" Norse muttered. Sanjuro moved behind the desk to watch as well. "The video time stamp on this is 1998. Is this for real?"

"The quality is shitty enough for 1998 phone-cams," Sanjuro said. "Very *Blair Witch*–looking." Mark looked up briefly to glare at the lawyer's bland face. Norse, at least, was clearly horrified by what he was watching. The girl was panting, running. The sounds of dogs howling pursued her as she staggered through the bright afternoon sunlight, deep in the maze of the woods.

"I . . . oh God," the girl shouted, her voice warbly, distorted. "Please, Jesus, please help me!"

"He uses dogs to chase them down?" Norse asked.

"Not, not real dogs," Mark said, wiping his eyes. "Shadows, living shadows."

"Shadow people!" Norse said. "They've been witnessed in haunted houses, on deserted roads, since the early 2000s."

"Well, these shadow people can shift into shadow dogs," Mark said. "He uses a pack of them to hunt."

"I don't know if anyone will ever see this," the girl said, sobbing. She had fallen and was panting. There was the sound of growling beasts all about her. "But I'm going to try to send it before he . . . before he gets me. He grabbed me at the gas station off I-81. He . . . Oh God . . . Mom, Dad, I love you. Jill—big sissy loves you. . . . Oh God, please, no, no!"

Mark knew this part of the recording, too. It was branded into the flesh of his brain. She was swinging the camera around. Catching part of her pursuer's jeans-covered leg, the bone-handled hunting knife clutched in his fist. A few of the shadowy, blurry figures of dogs. The quality was grainy, jerky.

"Why are you doing this?" the girl said. Her voice was bubbly, almost choking, from phlegm. Mark could almost see the snot running out of her red nose, mixing with the river of her tears, to mingle and drip down her chin. For an instant, he was lying near the nature trails again, his underwear wet, cooling on him. The smell of ammonia, of animal fear, the circle of bigger boys around him, kicking him. He wished he knew the name of the girl in the video.

"For him," the cold, monotone voice of the faceless hunter said on the video. Mark knew the voice—it was Chasseur. "For his glory, to grow his power in this world, so that he may be the strongest of the houses. To strengthen the hunt. Your sacrifice will feed him, like all those before you. Look upon him, now. Look. Truly see what has pursued you, has devoured you. . . . See."

Both Norse and the lawyer gasped audibly as they saw what the girl had swung her camera around to behold. Mark didn't want to see, didn't want to see it rise out of the woods, to plant one great, giant, cloven hoof onto the decaying toppled tree trunk, the dark hounds gathering around their creator. He didn't want to watch it turn a massive, antlered head, the face hidden by shadow and static, toward the girl and her camera. Mark put his head down and wished he'd wake from this nightmare.

"Oh, my God," Norse said. "What . . . what is that thing?"

Sanjuro had visibly paled and crossed himself. "*Santa Madre, nos salve*," he uttered. "This shit can't be real, George. It's got to be fake, it's got to be!"

The video ended abruptly, snapping to black. The office was silent for several moments.

"I want the ten grand to go to Dewey's mom," Mark said, finally. "And I want cash, at least a thousand, right now." He looked at Sanjuro. "Yeah, it's fucking real, man. That kid is dead, and my friend is dead. That fucking real enough for you? That enough liability for you? Nobody, no one, is gonna stop that thing, whatever the hell it is, and I am getting the fuck outta Dodge before it's in Bethlehem's zip code, okay?"

Norse closed his eyes and rubbed the bridge of his nose. He looked at Sanjuro. "Pay him out of petty cash," he said. "Give him five thousand." The lawyer blinked a few times, as if coming out of a trance. He nodded and exited the office. Norse stood as Mark did. "I'll make sure the check is mailed to Dewey's mom by the end of the day, Mark. I'm so sorry to hear about Dewey. Very sorry."

"Yeah, me, too," Mark said. "You take care, Mr. Norse. Be safe."

They shook hands. The lawyer paid him, and Mark shuffled out to the elevators. In a few moments, he was back on the streets of Atlanta. He had his credit card and a pocket full of cash. He knew where he had been ordered to go now, where he was supposed to be picked up by the fucking Scode brothers, but he was never going back to Four Houses, never. He saw a liquor store. He'd stop there and then find a hotel. That was enough thinking for one day. Mark Stolar vanished into the crowd, eager to be swallowed up among humanity. In the back of his mind, he could hear the hounds baying above the sounds of horns and car alarms.

. . .

George Norse sat at this desk, silent, his fingers steepled. There was no doubt that he was going to air this video on Saturday night. He was already visualizing the promotions and getting ready to call the network to make sure the commercial budget for the show was doubled. This was going to be huge, their best show ever. He was troubled, though, about allowing his program to be used as part of some madman's scheme. He would contact the FBI, and he would do all he could to locate this missing girl on the video. An odd thought struck him as he picked up the phone: Prophets came in all shapes and sizes. Maybe disheveled, smelly, fear-crazed Mark Stolar was the wisest man on the planet right now, to be running for cover ahead of whatever was coming.

"So," Lovina said, picking up another steak fry off the huge platter, swirling it in the gravy bowl, and taking a bite of it, "this ghost girl led you guys to her body hidden in the drainpipe? You know how crazy that sounds, right?"

"No, not exactly," Heck said. "Jimmie gave her a ride to her parents' house, she told him what happened to her, and then she vanished. He somehow or other got hooked up with Turla, and the three of us figured out where she had gone to hide from those Black-Eyed Kids that got her friends. And, yes, I am very aware that I sound like I need medication and a court-appointed guardian, telling that story."

"And you're his what again?" she asked, finishing her fry.

"Squire," Heck said, looking down at his burger and pushing his pickle spear around the plate. "Which, as far as I can tell, is King Arthur–speak for "butt monkey.""

Lovina laughed. Heck shrugged and flipped her off.

"You watch that, Red," Lovina said. "Or I'll kick your ass again."

Heck shook his head. "Whatever. You had some good moves," he said. "I got better."

"If I hadn't seen those things back there and saw two of my missing kids among them," Lovina said, pausing to take a long sip on the straw bobbing in her glass of Cherry Coke, "I'd think you and Aussapile were huffing diesel."

They had doubled back after the cops finished their job and found Karen's body. They recovered Jimmie's truck, Heck's bike, and Lovina's Charger and drove about twenty miles out of Granite City, finally pulling up at the Road Ranger truck stop just off Route 117 and I-64 to grab food and allow Jimmie to make a few phone calls.

"And these Black-Eyed Kids have been dogging you?" Heck said.

Lovina nodded. "Ever since I started looking into Dewey Rears's disappearance. What the hell are they?"

"Beats me," Heck said. "But I think fearless leader is getting that intel right now."

"From whom?" Lovina asked.

Heck shrugged. "I've been riding with him for a few days now, and I'm no closer to knowing who or what these Brethren are than when I started."

"Then why do you want to join them?" she asked, stealing one of Heck's onion rings.

"To save my family," Heck said, "my MC. Got no choice."

They ate quietly for a few moments. Lovina glanced over at Aussapile, who was still on the pay phone next to the trucker's library—spinner racks of paperbacks—stocked with Westerns that had names like *Longhorn* and *Lonestar* and action series with names like *The Destroyer* and *The Executioner*, and, of course, plenty of porn—*The Widow's Bed* and *Naughty Co-eds*, for example.

"How's your arm?" Lovina asked. Heck pushed up the sleeve of his black thermal T-shirt. The bite was still there, red and swollen, but the black veins were all gone.

"Good to go," he said, rubbing the wound, but he wondered again why he was still here and not dead like Gil Turla.

The connection on the pay phone was tinny, and it was hard to hear Layla's voice above the occasional electronic outbursts from the coin-pusher game near the entrance to the TRUCKERS ONLY shower and bunk rooms. There was also the music from the jukebox in the restaurant. Currently, it was "Six Days on the Road," by Dave Dudley. Jimmie jammed a finger in his ear and pushed the receiver closer to his other ear. Layla was telling him that Peyton's monosyllabic boyfriend was already history.

"So Christian is already past tense, huh?" Jimmie said, and smiled. "Good. How are you feeling, baby?"

"Well, the precious little angel has discovered he can use my bladder as a speed bag," Layla said. "I've been doing the hundred-meter pee dash for the last day or so. I think he's getting restless, Jimmie."

"You tell him to hold on, now," Jimmie said. He glanced over at the booth and saw Heck and the Louisiana cop, Lovina Marcou, laughing and talking. He glanced up at the clock; it was late, almost 3 A.M. "I'm sorry if I woke you up."

"I always keep the phone right here when you're on a run," Layla said. "Especially *those* kinds of runs. Are you okay, Jimmie? You sound tired."

"It's been a rough day," he said. "This thing I'm nosing around in—it may be bigger than I thought. . . . I'm okay, sweetheart, please don't worry."

"I do when I know you're holding something back on me," Layla said. Jimmie could see her on her side, in their bed. She'd be on the left side of the bed, even though she could roll over and have all of it to herself. It was force of habit. He slept on the right, near the door, even when she wasn't there, and she slept on her side, the left.

He wanted to talk to her—to tell her, that was why he had called her. After the shit they had just been through, after watching a good man die in a horrible way, he needed her, but it was cruel and selfish and unfair to lay all that on her when she was already fretting.

"It's . . . been a real bad day," he finally said. "I want to talk to you about it, but I'm gonna wait till I'm in that bed with you, okay?"

"Okay," Layla said. "You and Ale's stepson getting along? He showed up not too long after you rode out."

"Well enough," Jimmie said.

"Don't like the sound of that," Layla said. "He seemed like a sweet kid, Jimmie."

"Uh-huh," Jimmie said, glancing back at the table. "Sweet. That's the first word that leaps to mind for me, too."

Layla laughed. "Well, you boys behave, now."

"I always do," Jimmie said. "I love you, honey."

"I love you, too," she said. "Get some rest, baby. Talk tomorrow?"

"Yeah," Jimmie said. "You call me if there's anything happening with the baby, and you tell Peyton to stay close to home right now—"

"Jimmie . . ." Lyla said.

"Don't 'Jimmie' me," he said. "She needs to be close to help you and in case anything . . . happens."

"We still have about three weeks, honey," Layla said. "I'm okay, baby."

"Just be careful," he said. "Please."

"You, too," she said. "I love you."

"I love you, too," he said. He hung up the phone and wished for the millionth time today he was home with her. The juke had switched over to "Superstition," by Stevie Wonder. Jimmie punched a special code into the touch pad of the pay phone. You could enter this code into any public pay phone in the world and reach this line. He had memorized the code years ago but seldom had to use it. It rang once. There was no greeting, just a single beep.

"The wheel turns," Jimmie said. He knew that some machine, somewhere, was analyzing his voice and making sure it was him.

"Confirmed, Paladin," the voice said. It was female, and Jimmie was pretty sure it was a machine, too. "How may we assist you?"

"I need help with something I've never run into before," he said. "Black-Eyed Children. Can you get me a Builder, a research expert? I need one out in the field. We've already lost a Brother."

There was a pause, longer than normal in a human conversation. It reminded Jimmie of waiting for the ATM to spit out your money and receipt.

Finally, the voice replied. "We will connect you with a Builder who can help you, Paladin. They should make contact with you in the next seven days."

Jimmie had been expecting this, and he tried to contain his irritation. "No, no, no. Look, I know you guys don't get out much, but in the field things move a lot quicker than seven to ten business days, okay? I need help now. My team and I will be in Memphis, Tennessee, by 9 A.M. We'll be at a private club called TCB tonight. Have your expert there or I'll go find my own. The wheel turns." He slammed the phone down and walked back to the booth, shaking his head.

"You look pissed," Heck said.

"Yeah," Jimmie said. "I am. The damned Builders have no clue about fieldwork, none."

"What's a Builder?" Lovina asked. Jimmie slid into the booth beside her, his gut bumping against the table. He grunted a bit and adjusted himself to get comfortable. He took a sip of his coffee and found it cold. He motioned for the waitress with his cup.

"That's a long—"

"Don't say 'That's a long story,'" Heck said. "You've been telling me that for days now! Come on, tell me what the hell is really going on, Jimmie. Don't I have a right to know what weird shit I'm signing up for?"

Jimmie looked over at Lovina, then back at Heck. "Some things," he said, "can't be discussed with—"

"Listen," Lovina said. "I was ready to drag both your asses to jail. Now, I saw some very, to quote, 'weird shit,' back there, and I admit this case has been getting freakier and freakier as it's gone along. Now, you convince me that you're really the good guys and I'll share all the info I've got on my end of this case, and you share yours."

Jimmie frowned. The waitress came and refreshed his coffee. Everyone was quiet until she walked away.

"This secret is old," Jimmie said. "We each swear to defend it with our lives. My wife doesn't even know half the things I've run into out here on the Road. She sleeps better because of that. I can't just spill it to every person I come across, Investigator Marcou."

Lovina sighed and looked down at her glass of soda. "Nobody back home knows I'm here," she said. "I get caught, I'll lose my job, my shield. I'm here because . . . because a long time ago evil people took my sister off the street, just plucked her like a flower. No one saw anything, no one knew anything. Not too many people even gave a damn. They . . . did things to her, used her. Tortured her, raped her, sold her to other sick sons of bitches."

"Shit," Heck said. It was the quietest Jimmie had ever heard his voice, the gentlest.

"I'm so sorry, Lovina," Jimmie said.

"I found her," Lovina said. "I was a uniform cop, not too long back from Afghanistan. I almost lost my job—hell, I damn near lost my mind. Do you have any idea how guilty you feel sleeping when someone you love is out there, lost, in pain, and you have no idea how to reach them, where they are?

"I pushed as far as I could, and then some more. I made . . . bargains, promised to keep secrets, and I have kept them. I lost a lot of friends, made a lot of enemies; I turned over every rock until I got the truth. It turns out it was a whole damn secret club. There was an old police report—from over a century ago. It had been passed around from NOPD cop to cop like some kind of holy grail, or something. A New Orleans police inspector named John Raymond Legrasse led a raid out to the bayou in 1907. Fifty people rounded up, a few killed resisting—Cajuns, Acadians, Creoles, Poggie, swamp folk—all of them had been performing rites to . . . some . . . thing out in the bayou for as far back as people had lived out there. I found out they were still around, still trafficking in flesh, still sacrificing.

"Eventually, after months, they sacrificed her to their sick fucking god and left her in an abandoned building, figuring Hurricane Katrina would wash away all their sins."

"Did you catch them?" Jimmie asked. Lovina gave him a strange look. She looked down again, the way she had during her whole story.

"Yes," she said. "Every fucking one of them."

The jukebox was playing "The Grand Tour," by George Jones. Everyone was quiet for a moment, letting the chaotic sounds of the Road Ranger wash over them.

"When it was done," Lovina continued, "I couldn't be a cop in New Orleans anymore. I'm good at burning bridges. I was lucky enough to get my job with CID because of a very decent man, a good friend. He knows I have a thing for missing people, especially kids. He indulges me as much as he can, but I've stuck my neck out good and long on this one."

"So you're up here freelancing," Heck said. "Off the grid." Lovina nodded. "Cool," he added.

Lovina looked at Jimmie. "So if what you're telling me is true, Aussapile," she said, "then we're up here for the same thing—to find out who is hunting and hurting these children and stop them. I promise you, on my sister Delephine's grave, that's what I want, and I can, and will, keep your secrets. You can trust me, Jimmie."

Jimmie looked from Lovina to Heck, then nodded. There was a tiny gap of relative quiet in the Road Ranger. The jukebox clicked and began to play "Nights in White Satin," by the Moody Blues.

"Okay," Jimmie said. "You ain't gonna believe this, but have you two ever heard of the Poor Fellow Soldiers of Christ and the Temple of Solomon? They're also known as the Knights Templar." Jimmie paused as if for dramatic effect. Heck and Lovina looked at each other and then back at Jimmie.

"Sure," Lovina said. "Who hasn't? I watch the History Channel."

"Yeah," Heck said. "You talking like that Dan Brown–Da Vinci shit, right? I hate to break it to you, Jimmie, but Tom Hanks and his ponytail knows your secret, too."

"I knew this was going to be a pain in the ass," Jimmie said, rubbing his face. "A lot of the myths and the conspiracies about the Templars— that stuff was put out by the Benefactors as a smoke screen, a diversion from the truth."

"Does this have anything to do with that dude with the weird hair who talks about UFOs," Heck said, grinning, " 'Cause I freaking love him!"

"Look, do you want to hear this or not?" Jimmie said. Heck raised a hand and nodded, still smiling. "Do either of you smart-asses happen to know what the Knights Templar did, exactly?"

"Weren't they money lenders?" Lovina said. "They were, like, the first modern bankers, if I recall correctly. They invented checks."

Jimmie nodded.

"And they were into some freaky shit with Devil worship, too," Heck added. "The occult."

"Before all that," Jimmie said. "Before the power and the wealth and the mysticism, before they were feared and hated by the most powerful forces in the world, they were nine knights, too poor to afford their own horses. Nine knights drawn to a distant place to take up a quest. They were brought together to carry out the mission of protecting the pilgrims and the merchants who traveled the roads of the Holy Land from brigands and highwaymen who preyed on and slaughtered the helpless. The Knights Templar guarded the roads and defended all who traveled them.

"Now, they didn't stay poor for long, that's for damn sure. They became more powerful than any nation, any king. They possessed political, financial, and military power. They began to explore mystical powers from the dawn of humanity—some say from the time before humanity.

Eventually, they grew too big for their britches, and they were taken down by their enemies, hunted to extinction by King Philip IV and Pope Clement V in the early 1300s."

"Where did you learn all this shit?" Heck asked.

"The History Channel," Jimmie said with a smirk. "But, seriously, I learned it the same place I learned Latin, from my dad. He learned it from his dad, and so on back. We're taught the story, the language, the codes." He took a sip of coffee and then continued. "The Templars were powerful enough and had enough spies to know what was coming, though. They held a secret conclave on the eve of King Philip issuing warrants to arrest the order's leaders. The meeting was quite a barn-burner. Many groups within the order had different plans, different views, on how the Templars could survive. Finally, a plan was created—actually, more of a philosophy. It was decided that the goals of the order were more important than the order itself. The assembled agreed to hide the treasures of the order and bury and squirrel away as many of its political and occult secrets as possible. The Knights Templar did dissolve that night and was replaced by three new organizations, three philosophical orders, each committed to keeping the goals and the spirit of the Templars alive in their own fashion. They were the Builders, the Benefactors, and the Brethren—each is a spoke on the 'wheel.' Each group's leader agreed to aid one another and to work together to achieve their common goal."

"Which was?" Lovina asked.

"The protection and betterment of all mankind," Jimmie said.

"Seriously?" Heck said.

Jimmie gave him a stern look. "They had other options," he said. "They were powerful enough to assassinate Philip, to have the Pope 'fall ill.' They had the money and spies to rule the known world, and the occult power to rule beyond this world. They didn't do any of that, though. They opted to slip into the shadows and keep doing good works. I know it sounds hokey as hell these days, but it's true. They were, and still are, the good guys."

"Nothing personal, Jimmie," Heck said, "but I don't believe too much in good guys anymore. Not like that. Sorry, man."

"I understand," Jimmie said. "The world does its damnedest to make it hard to believe. But a few folks still do. Ale did, for whatever that's worth."

Heck looked back at his plate.

Jimmie continued, "After that night, they went their separate ways. A few Templars sacrificed themselves to arrest, torture, and death to save the majority, and to protect the treasures and secrets that remain hidden to this day. Each spoke of the wheel created subgroups, whole organizations, secret societies, that spun out from them, and still do even now. The Blue Jocks is a splinter group of the Brethren, Heck. Your granddad on your mom's side, Gordon, was a member of the Brethren. He founded the Jocks after he got home from 'Nam. Ale was one of the first members, and was president after Gordon. Ale was also initiated into the Brotherhood. Most of the secret societies, occult fringe groups, and such all trace back to one of the three spokes of the wheel."

"What's the difference between them?" Lovina asked, taking a sip of her Cherry Coke.

"The Benefactors focus on accumulating and shepherding political and monetary power. They control the media, too, pretty much," Jimmie said. "The Builders are linked back to the Scottish Masonic orders. They focus on the occult and the power of information. Their strength lies in the educational, occult, and religious institutions."

"And the Brethren?" Lovina said.

"We're the grunts," Jimmie said with a yellow smile. He reached into his jeans pocket to wrestle out his can of chaw. "Our order was founded on the original mission of the Templars—keep the roads safe and protect the innocent and the defenseless who travel them. We're the most important of the three spokes, the one that gets the least respect, and suffers the greatest losses."

"How you figure that you're the most important?" Lovina asked. "Those other guys deal in money and politics, knowledge, and magic powers. How does acting like a bunch of road warriors make you guys more important?"

Jimmie pinched a rich, dark wad of tobacco out of his burgundy Copenhagen can and tucked it into his cheek before answering. "A civilization is only as healthy as its roads," he said. "Merchants, politicians, scholars, pilgrims—they all need safe, consistent access from point A to point B to do what they do; otherwise, things start to fall apart. Do you have any idea how much the U.S. economy relies on goods moving across the nation by truck, airline, and train? That's all Brethren turf. Truckers, state troopers, outlaw bikers, mobile-home caravan cults, gypsy cabbies, airline crews, railroad men, sailors, teamsters—we have members and affiliate members everywhere, all of them sworn to protect the passages between. We've grown as the world has grown. We guard all routes of transport these days, not just physical paths—that includes the Internet, what they used to call the information super-highway, and telecommunication networks, too."

"So you guys are like the Illuminati?" Heck said. "You control everything?"

Jimmie laughed. "Nah, far from it. That Illuminati stuff is all tangled up with the Benefactors' business, not ours, as far as I can tell. Gives me a headache to try to figure it out. We Brethren are usually outmanned and outgunned. We're the last to know and the first to go."

"That sounds very, very familiar," Lovina said. "Like being back in the army again."

"Yep," Jimmie said. "Damn close to it." He raised his coffee cup, "Oorah!" he said.

Heck raised his glass of water. "Oorah," he echoed.

Lovina raised her soda glass. "Hooah!" she said. They clinked their glasses together.

"You a dogface?" Jimmie asked Lovina. She nodded, taking a sip of her soda.

"One Hundred and First Airborne," she said.

"No shit," Heck said. "You at Kandahar?" She nodded again.

"Oh yeah," she said.

"I heard tell from some old-timers that was some nasty shit," Heck said.

"They were right," she said, "and then some."

"So being in this Brotherhood means getting FUBARed on a regular basis?" Heck asked Jimmie. The jukebox had moved on from the Moody Blues to Carl Perkins's "Blue Suede Shoes."

"We look out for each other real good; it's only when you expect help from the other orders that things get fuzzy. Like tonight, I asked for some help from the Builders to figure out what these black-eyed things really are, and I got the runaround, but I laid the law down to them. We're soldiers, and the other orders may think we exist to fight and die so they don't have to, but we're damn good at what we do. They know how much they need us."

"Fight and die against what, exactly?" Lovina asked. Jimmie and Heck exchanged a glance. "What's with the look?"

"This part I can attest to," Heck said. "There's fucked-up things, monsters, that crawl in from somewhere else—lots of other places, it seems. I've seen some bizarre shit, all of it nasty and evil. They're drawn to the highways, the state and interstate roads. It also attracts scumbags—serial killers, lunatics, child abductors, road-ragers . . . no one knows why. My MC, the Blue Jocks, hunts those things, keeps them from hurting people."

"And the Brethren deal with them, too," Jimmie added. "It's one of our main duties. We call that world, the one living beside our normal world, 'the Road.' The Road seems to attract all kinds of monsters, human and otherwise."

"Like these Black-Eyed Kids," Lovina said.

"Yep," Jimmie said. "I'm afraid so. So now you both know what you're into. I aim to find who's responsible for taking these kids and turning them into monsters, and I'm going to shut them down. You in or out?"

"In," Heck said.

Both men looked to Lovina, who was trying to process what she'd just heard. The trucker's story was tabloid bullshit, conspiracy theories and fairy tales—not a shred of proof, and yet she believed Jimmie Aussapile. She remembered her conversation with Russ. There were things she had seen in her life, things that made perfect sense in the context of Jimmie's story. She thought of Shawn Ruth Thibodeaux, and then of Delphine.

"I'm in," she said.

"What do we do now?" Heck asked. "Wait for these Builder assholes to churn up some info?"

"To hell with waiting," Jimmie said. "I'll get my own damn answers. Kids, we're going to Memphis."

"What's in Memphis?" Lovina asked.

"The King," Jimmie said with a smile and a wink.

You ask the right people in Memphis where to go after dark, where the action is, they'll tell you some juke joint like Wild Bill's, or a club like Alfred's or Alchemy. If you ask the wrong people—the kind of folks you don't want to know in the cold light of day—they'll tell you there's only one place to hang your hat when the sun's been run out of town: the after-hours club called TCB. Jimmie knew how to find the place. They left his rig and Heck's motorcycle behind in a Walmart parking lot and took Lovina's Charger out to an old boat dock south of Mud Island River Park, on the slumbering Mississippi River. It was after eight, and the lights of the city were blurry smears, echoes of color, on the ancient black waters.

A group of partygoers were huddled near the dock. Most of them were in good spirits and had obviously already had a few drinks. A laughing young man, wearing a cowboy hat, several glow-stick neck-laces, and boots, offered Jimmie, Lovina, and Heck his flask. The cow-boy's eyes were bright and glassy from some type of chemical.

Heck grinned and took a swig from the flask. "Thanks, pardner," he said as the club-cowboy danced away, leaving his flask behind. Heck looked at Jimmie and said, "Shitty hat, good scotch." He took another sip.

"Remember, we're on the clock," Jimmie said. "Don't get too festive."

"Explain to me again where we're going?" Lovina said as they walked closer to the water.

"TCB," Jimmie said. "We're either meeting our contact from the Build-ers or I'm getting us answers through my own channels. Either way, we learn more of what we're up against and where we need to head next to shut them down."

Lovina's phone buzzed softly. It was a text from Russell Lime: "*Got some info on symbol in video. Possible lead on Mark Stolar, too. Will call soon. I hate texting, BTW. I hate BTW, by the way.*" Lovina smiled and slid the phone down into her pocket.

There was the hollow hoot of a boat horn and a forty-one-foot Stern cigarette boat glided toward the docks. A burly bearded man in a black shirt and jeans tied the lines to the dock while a slender black man in an impeccable Brioni suit, the pilot of the craft, greeted the line of partiers. Jimmie, Heck, and Lovina slipped into the line. Each party in line produced a necklace with a charm on it, and the pilot nodded and let them on the boat. There were couches set up along the bow and stern to accommodate them. When it was their turn, Jimmie fished a small gold chain with a charm out of his jeans pocket and presented it to the pilot. The thin man nodded, smiled slightly, and gestured them onto the boat.

"Let me see that," Lovina said. Jimmie handed her the necklace. The charm was a simple flat piece of metal with the letters "TCB" on it. The "C" on the charm was lower than the other two letters, and above it was a lightning bolt that looked like something straight out of a *Shazam!* comic book.

"That is some sad-ass-looking bling," she said, handing it back to him.

Heck took another drag off the flask and then passed it back over to the laughing cowboy. "You get that out of a vending machine somewhere?"

"Keys to the kingdom," Jimmie said with a laugh, and put the necklace away.

The passengers were all on board now. The pilot had to chase off a few folks who wanted to go but had no necklaces. The burly man in the T-shirt helped explain it to one drunk fella who tried to get on the boat. The drunk was politely but firmly deposited on the bank of the river, and a few moments later the lines were cast off. The boat rumbled out into the middle of the shadowy river, headed north.

The ride was short but very jovial, with the passengers drinking, laughing, and singing. The city began to give way to dark forests on either shore of the river, and the stars appeared, no longer hidden by light pollution. While dismissing offers of jugs of wine, joints, and key-chain grinders of cocaine, Jimmie returned to an earlier conversation with Lovina, who was peering out into the darkness.

"So Dewey Rears was looking into child disappearances and relating them to Black-Eyed Kid sightings?" Jimmie said.

"For almost eight years, until he disappeared," Lovina said. "Maybe abducted by these BEKs he was hunting."

"And you've got someone looking into the stuff that he had on his computer related to sightings?" Heck said, fishing out a cigarette and lighting up.

Lovina nodded. "There's a photo of my missing kids—Shawn Ruth and her friends—attacking your missing kids, Karen Collie and her friends," she said. "That picture has been making the rounds of various occult and supernatural websites for years now. I think Rears was close to uncovering the source of these BEKs and who's behind them. Rears had another photo in his files that he labeled 'Patient Zero.' Both our groups of missing kids had also seen that photo on occult websites. I think whoever started turning kids into these things abducted Rears and his friend Mark Stolar, maybe killed them."

"I've been fighting long-leggedy beasties since I was sixteen with the Jocks," Heck said. "These things feel . . . different, like something bigger is inside them, working through them. It's fucked up."

"There's something else," Lovina said. "Rears was mapping the missing kids and BEK sightings and linking them up to the interstate-highway system. There's a connection to this Road you guys were taking about."

There was music playing up ahead on the riverbank. Lights broke through the dense cover of the Barnishee Bayou. The boat slowed and turned toward a long dock with several other craft already moored to it. There was a long, tiered wooden staircase with multiple landings that ascended to a large, old, plantation-style mansion up on the hill at the edge of the bayou. The dock and the stairs were wrapped in small blue and white Christmas-tree-style lights. People were lounging on the landings, drinking, laughing, flirting, and chatting, while "Smokestack Lightnin'," by Howlin' Wolf, growled through the swamp and made the windows of the old mansion tremble. Everyone disembarked the boat, and staff on the dock once again examined the necklaces. Jimmie's charm passed inspection.

"Where did you get that thing?" Heck asked, smoke streaming out his nostrils, as they ascended the stairs with the other new arrivals.

"From the owner of this joint," Jimmie said. "We've helped each other out a few times over the years." They reached the top. The back porch of the mansion was wide and wrapped around the whole house. There were tables and a bar out here. A heavyset black man in a suit and a top hat opened the door to the interior for Lovina. Heck and Jimmie followed.

"And who would that be?" Heck asked.

Inside TCB, the walls sweated from the heat of hundreds of bodies and the cool breath of the swamp at night. The cigarette smoke swirled like hurricane fronts seen on radar—milky spiral galaxies, masking voices, promises, and lies. Howlin' Wolf faded away, to be replaced by "Dust My Broom," by Elmore James.

"Him," Jimmie said, pointing up to the balcony that overlooked the barroom floor. The man leaning against the rail, surveying his kingdom, had coal-black hair styled in a loose pompadour with sideburns. His eyes were as blue as a robin's egg and flashed even from across the room, cutting through the fog of smoke. He was handsome—a cross between an angel and a thug, with a sneer threatening at the edges of his full lips. He was slender, dressed in a partially zipped black leather jacket, with no shirt underneath, and tight black leather pants.

"Holy shit!" Heck said. "Is that?"

"It can't be," Lovina said. "It's got to be an impersonator." Then she added, "My goodness. Nice likeness, though."

"It's not an impersonator," Jimmie said, waving to the man, who appeared to be in his early thirties. The leather-garbed figure gestured for them to ascend the stairs with a thumbs-up and a wink. Jimmie gave the "okay" sign, and they began to slowly wrestle their way through the crowds toward the curving staircase. There were two such staircases on either side of the club's floor. Both rose to the man in black leather. "It's him."

"But . . . he's dead, man," Heck said.

"Yeah," Jimmie said. "He was for a spell. He got over it."

"Devil in Disguise" started to play. Jimmie was making good headway in the crowd. "Look, whatever you do, don't mention the dead thing, okay?" he said. "He's really touchy about that. I'll tell you later what the deal is, but just play along right now, okay? He calls himself Aaron now. Don't use his old name. He's got another nickname, too, in the occult underworld, but, for the love of baby Jesus, do not call him that to his face!"

"Call him what?" Lovina said. They had reached the stairs. Another security guy unhooked the velvet rope at the bottom of the stairwell and allowed them to pass after a thumbs-up from the man in the leather suit.

"Helvis," Jimmie said.

Another pair of suited attendants, obviously armed beneath their tailored jackets, opened another velvet rope and allowed the three to enter. The foyer at the top of the grand staircases had been roped off and turned into a private lounge with a long Chesterfield leather sofa and two antique high-backed wooden chairs that looked as if they came straight out of the Middle Ages. As they approached him, the black-leather-clad man who now called himself Aaron strode forward and offered a hand to Jimmie. Lovina noted that Aaron almost swaggered with power and confidence. It *was* him. She had watched enough of his movies with her pops to recognize the walk, but how could that possibly be?

"Jimmie Aussapile," Aaron said. "Gearjammin' knight of the ribbon! How are you, you old dog?"

Jimmie laughed and took the hand; it turned into a bear hug between the burly trucker and the black-clad, seemingly younger man.

"Keeping it between the lines and outta the ditches, A," he said. "This is Lovina Marcou and Heck Sinclair. They're friends of mine, working on something with me."

Aaron's eyebrow went up slightly, and the ghost of a sneer returned as he took Lovina's hand and kissed it. "Pleasure, darlin'," he said. The veteran detective couldn't help feeling her heart flutter and a flush of warmth on her face for a second. She suddenly understood all those women screaming and grabbing at this man in all the old black-and-white footage. The man had it, whatever the hell "it" was; he owned it.

Aaron turned his attention to Heck and narrowed his eyes. There was a flash of something there for a second—a glint of silver before the blue.

Heck took Aaron's hand and shook it firmly. "Pleasure," he said with a grin. "Huge fan."

Aaron looked to Jimmie for a second and found whatever validation he needed in the trucker's gaze.

"Thank you," Aaron said to Heck. "Thank you very much. Y'all have a seat. You hungry? Care for a drink?" He gestured for one of his attendants, a young man in a white silk shirt, to approach.

Aaron sat in one of the chairs. There was a stylized pentagram worked into the design on the chair's back. Jimmie took the chair beside him, and Heck and Lovina sat on the huge Chesterfield.

"I could use a scotch," Heck said. "Maybe a peanut-butter-and-nanner sandwich?" Jimmie frowned but said nothing.

"Water, please," Lovina said.

"I'm good, thanks," Jimmie said.

"Get me a rum and Pepsi and three bacon cheeseburgers," Aaron said. The attendant nodded and departed without a word. "So what you working on, Jim? How can I help you, after all you and the Brotherhood did for me?"

"Missing children," Jimmie said. "Being transformed into creatures, possibly a vessel for some other possessing force. It looks like it may be related to the Road, too. They're called Black-Eyed Kids. You hear anything about them from the left side of the street?"

Aaron's features lost their almost unconscious charm. He narrowed his eyes and the silver flash returned. "Children . . . sumbitches. Ought to be ashamed of themselves, if they could be. Me 'n the Memphis Mafia just cleaned out a nest of incubuses that were possessing priests in Chicago, molesting little kids. I've heard stories about these BEKs, but I figured it was all Internet bullshit." Aaron glanced up at Lovina and raised a hand. "Pardon my French, darlin'. The Internet is full of all kinds of lies and misinformation. Trust me, I know. I ain't never had any kind of relationship with Bigfoot. We're just good friends."

"These myths are real," Jimmie said. "We tangled with them just yesterday. Lost a brother in it."

The man in the white shirt returned with two lovely young women in long black evening gowns, slit to their shapely thighs. The man and the women unfolded and placed down simple TV dining trays that seemed somewhat out of place in the gritty opulence of the juke joint-mansion. The food and drinks were passed out. Heck downed half his scotch in a single gulp and started on the deep-fried, powdered-sugar-coated monstrosity in front of him with equal abandon.

The man in the white shirt leaned close to Aaron's ear. "A, got something that needs your attention," he said. Aaron stood.

"Y'all eat up, enjoy the music, and relax. You need anything, you tell Skeets, here," he said jerking a thumb at the attendant with the military crew cut and the machine gun under his coat. "I'll be back in a spell, and I'll see what I can dig up on these BEKs for you, Jim." Aaron and his man departed and headed down the stairs to the club floor below. Lightnin' Hopkins's "Bring Me My Shotgun" was playing below, above the river of the crowd's voice.

"Okay," Heck said, crumbs from his sandwich flying from his lips. "Trippin' my balls off during a night firefight in the Registan Desert is now officially the *second* most surreal experience in my life. Jimmie, what the fuck is going on here? What is his deal?"

"You all ain't going to believe this," Jimmie said. "His deal is that when he was alive and just hitting his stride, becoming the first great rock icon, his mother got sick, really sick. This was back in 1956. She was going to die, in days. He had heard enough tales from all the old blues-men he worked with; he went to the crossroads at midnight, and he made a deal with the man in the big black car."

"Okay," Lovina said. "I've heard that since I was a little girl—meet Papa Legba at the crossroads at midnight, just before dawn, bang on the shovel, name your price—all that jazz. You telling me it's true, that he sold his soul?"

"Crossroads are part of the Road," Jimmie said, "and sometimes they have power, act as places in between worlds. And powers and entries can gather there. In Aaron's case, it was real. He bought his mama a few more years, and he did all he could to spoil her and make her happy and comfortable. He never told her, told anyone, what he had given up for her, for love."

"So that's why he went downhill so hard," Heck said. "He knew where he was headed, knew there was no escape."

"Yep," Jimmie said. "It was pretty much a cloud over the rest of his life. He hid from it in drugs and food, bargained with it with all his gospel albums, raged against it in wrecked relationships and false friendships. Finally, he died, lost and alone; he fell into the pit."

"So what's he doing here, looking all fine and running a club, helping us?" Lovina asked. "Isn't he a demon? One of the bad guys?"

"He is a demon," Jimmie said. "He looks that way most of the time. If he gets pissed, he looks . . . different."

"Define 'different,'" Heck said, wiping the crumbs off his shirt and gesturing with his empty glass toward an attendant. Jimmie plucked the empty glass out of Heck's hand and shook his head to the attendant that another drink wouldn't be needed.

"Imagine him in his seventies, Vegas-sequined jumpsuit, but about nine feet tall and about nine hundred and fifty pounds, all firehouse red, bloated skin, and ram horns; able to rip the head off a grizzly bear and then probably eat it with a side of Memphis barbecue."

"Shit," Heck said.

"Let's keep him happy," Lovina added.

"I agree," Jimmie said. "Anyway, he became very popular in Hell—too popular. He was still a good ole Memphis Baptist boy at heart, and he actually tried to act like a missionary in the pit. He used the only thing he ever knew how to use to praise life and cast light in the heart of darkness: his voice. He actually had a following in Hell, and the management got afraid of him, so they shipped him back up here. He's been exiled from Hell, and due to his contract deal Heaven can't touch him. So he tries to help people not make the same mistakes he did. He's got a crew; he calls them his Memphis Mafia. They hunt demons, foil the plots of the Infernal Masters, and try to help regular folks who have gotten in too deep with the Devil or some other supernatural loan shark."

"Okay," Lovina said. "I'll buy all this, Jimmie, but I swear to God, if Slim Whitman turns out to be some kind of fucking yodeling vampire, or something, I'm out."

Aaron returned at that moment with his attendant and a woman. The woman was in her early thirties. She was short, only a few inches over five feet, with a rounded but slight figure and frame. Her skin was dark in color, as if, a few generations back, she was of Mediterranean or Middle Eastern ancestry. She had a mane of long, curly black hair that fell well below her shoulders. She wore glasses that covered wide, dark, and intelligent eyes, giving her a slightly owlish look. She wore no makeup or jewelry and didn't seem to want or need either. She was dressed in a pair of jeans, well-worn hiking boots, a gray sweater, and a hooded olive-drab parka jacket that fell to just above her knees. She had a large leather messenger bag slung over her shoulder and across her chest.

"This young lady was looking for y'all," Aaron said.

The woman held a hand out to Jimmie. "Mr. Aussapile," she said, "I'm Max Leher. I understand you need some consultation on a field case you're working on?" Leher offered her hand.

"First things first," Jimmie said, rising. "The wheel turns."

"The temple restored," Max said without missing a beat. "How can the Builders help the Brethren?"

"That's it?" Lovina said. "Anyone could know those passwords. For a secret society, you guys seem pretty lax about security."

"It's not just the words," Max said, turning to Lovina. They locked eyes for an instant longer than normal, and they both knew it and looked away. "Um, it's inflection, tonal range, breath control. To do it properly, it's almost impossible to deceive and hit the proper octave frequency. We call it 'speaking the soul.' Each order trains its members how to do it, to project the oaths the proper way to be recognized and to be able to recognize a true member. The Brethren train so they can even pick up tonal identifiers over CB-radio transmissions. It's not foolproof, but it's a lot more secure than it appears to the untrained eye."

"Lot like learning a birdcall," Jimmie said. "After a spell, you don't even think about it."

"Oh," Lovina said. "Okay. But you just told me all that, and I'm not a member of anything."

"Oh," Max said, turning red. She looked to Jimmie, who was smiling. "I . . . oh . . . that is to say . . . I'm . . . I didn't mean to . . ."

"This is Lovina Marcou," Jimmie said. "With the Louisiana State Police. She's working the same case as us and she's been a big help, and she can be trusted. This is Heck Sinclair—he's my squire."

"Sinclair?" Max said, looking at Heck and then back at Jimmie.

"What?" Heck said. "It's my mom's family name."

"William St. Clair, or Sinclair, if you prefer, was the third Earl of Orkney, Baron of Roslin, the first Earl of Caithness," Max said. As she spoke, she gathered verbal steam, her words always clear and precise but almost falling one on top of the next in her enthusiasm. "He built Rosslyn Chapel in Midlothian, Scotland, a location of great significance to Free Masonry, the Templar order, and the Builders. One of his descendants, another William Sinclair, was the first Grand Master of the Grand Lodge of Scotland. The Sinclair name is synonymous with Templar and Masonic royalty."

Heck grinned widely and looked at Jimmie, who appeared to have just swallowed a cup of thumbtacks. "Royalty," he said. "How about that!"

"Yeah, great," Jimmie said, shaking Max's hand. "Thanks for coming out so quick to help."

Aaron gestured to his people and more food, drinks, and chairs were brought out. There was a lull in the club's music, replaced by the murmur of the crowd. Jimmie offered Max his seat and took one of the new chairs. Heck began work on another scotch, and Lovina sipped her water.

"Coffee," Max said to one of the female attendants. "Lots of cream and sugar, please . . . or a Monster, or Red Bull, if you have them. Anything with caffeine would really be great. Thanks." She slipped a tablet out of the satchel she set beside her chair and turned it on. "I have to admit, I didn't know exactly what to think when I got the call to come out here. I've never done fieldwork, ever. The most action I ever see is trying not to get groped too many times on the DC Metro coming home from Georgetown."

Jimmie chuckled. "Well, they kind of threw you in the deep end of the pool, Doc."

"How did you know I was a doctor?" Max asked.

"Wild shot in the dark," he said. "So what can you tell us about Black-Eyed Kids?"

"They're contemporary urban myths," Max said. "A confabulation of the Internet."

"Peachy," Heck said, shaking his head. "Yeah, this was worth the wait, Jimmie."

"Doctor—Max," Lovina said, "we fought these creatures yesterday in Illinois. They killed one of Jimmie's Brethren. Several of them were formerly missing children. I can tell you, they are very, very real." Again, they shared a glance that hung in the air an instant too long.

Max shrugged and smiled. "I understand," she said, tapping the screen of her tablet. "But I searched the Builder database thoroughly on the way to you for any information on the phenomenon, and all I got back was online drivel. There are no documented cases of any Builder ever encountering a BEK. I'm sorry, I wish I could be more help to you than that."

"Any Builder?" Jimmie said. "You keep track of Brethren reports in that database of yours?"

"We do," Max said, eagerly taking the can of energy drink offered by an attendant. She eschewed the glass of ice and pulled the tab to open the can. "However, much of the information we gather from Brethren field encounters is, well, very hard to verify or quantify, to say the least. It's still recorded and maintained, but we can't put it all in the database, because a lot of it can't be confirmed as accurate data."

"You sayin' you don't trust us?" Jimmie said, his face darkening. "You think we're making this shit up?"

"No, no," Max said. "Of course not. It's just . . . look, I know vampires exist. I have the skull of one on my desk back in Georgetown. I know that in 1934 a salt golem was created in Poland that killed a number of Nazis operating covertly in that country. I know because we actually have film in the archives of the creature, as well as the journal of a survivor of the onslaught and several pounds of the actual enchanted salt—a preponderance of evidence that's been vetted, tested, and verified."

"Now all you need is for someone to create a pretzel golem," Heck said, "and you're set."

"We deal in what we know, what we can prove with one-hundred-percent accuracy," she said.

"Hell," Heck said. "Ain't a whole lot of that anywhere in the world, Doc."

"In the field, on the Road, we have to trust our gut," Jimmie said. "Sometimes that's all you have, Max."

Max sipped her drink. "I understand, Mr. Aussapile—"

"Jimmie," he said. "I really don't think you do understand, but I know it ain't your fault—it's just the way the Builders operate. I appreciate you coming out here, all the same."

"Well, I think I can still help," Max said. "I'm considered a bit of an iconoclast by my colleagues. One of my fields of research is crypto-zoology—"

"Icono-what? Crypto-what?" Heck interrupted.

"The study of hidden and unknown life-forms, Mr. Sinclair," Max said.

"Heck," Jimmie said, jerking a thumb in Heck's direction as he polished off another drink. "Call him Heck. Thinking of him as Mr. Sinclair makes my brain hurt."

"Even if I don't have these BEKs in my files," Max said, "I can help you figure them out—their patterns, their biology, their weaknesses, and their motives. I can help you track them." She looked from Jimmie to Heck and finally held Lovina's eyes again. "I'd really like to help, if I can."

"I ain't passing up any help at this point," Jimmie said. "But you do understand, Doc, things get pretty hairy out in the field. It's no damn intellectual exercise. I can't recall ever hearing of a Builder out on the Road before. I just don't want you getting hurt or anything."

"I'll be okay," Max said. "Besides, I'm engaged in doctoral work on sacred geometry and numerology at the Imperceptible Preceptory, and I have some data I need to collect to test a theory. This will be a great opportunity to do that."

Jimmie gave a slightly pained look. "Swell," he said before addressing their host. "Well, A, you got anything for me?"

Aaron smiled. "Well, I'm no doctor," he said. "But I got some pretty credible info on these BEKs from a bunch of folks in the occult underworld who ought to know the skinny."

"Spill," Jimmie said.

"Well," Aaron said, "they started showing up around the late nineties. They're linked to disappearances and abductions—mostly kids and teenagers, but some adults. They have to be invited into a personal space, like a car or a home, kind of like a vampire, but only if it's currently occupied. They have some degree of hypnotic ability, and they can induce an almost mindless fear in the right circumstances. When they get riled up, they become very angry and violent. They usually travel in pairs and seem to walk in unison, talk in unison—"

"A hive mind," Max offered. "A single, powerful consciousness operating through a series of drones. If I may, where did you get this data from?" she asked.

"Synn, from the Horror Show," Aaron said. "Joey Two-Shadows, the Antimatter Buddha, Laytham Ballard, and that tabby cat who's a telepathic exorcist—what's her name?"

"Jingles," both Jimmie and Heck replied.

"Jingles," Aaron said, snapping his fingers. "Right, right. Why can I never remember her name?"

"Forgive me," Max said, "but that's a pretty disreputable group of individuals in the occult underworld to trust for information."

"No offense taken, darlin'," Aaron said. "They are a pretty rangy-looking crew, to be sure, but they know what they're talking about."

"And when you're out on the Road," Jimmie added, "you can't always be picky about where your help comes from. From everything we've encountered so far, it sounds like the intel is solid."

"Does anyone have any idea who's behind this?" Lovina asked. "If it's some kind of powerful consciousness possessing children, then where does it come from? How do we find it and stop it?"

"I have it on the best authority that there's no infernal agency behind it," Aaron said. "Everyone who's had a run-in with BEKs has said the force animating them is old—older than Hell, older than people."

"Older than humanity is usually bad," Max said.

Jimmie nodded. "And tentacle-ly" he added. "I hate damn tentacles."

Lovina's phone hummed in her jacket pocket. She looked at the screen—it was Russ. "Excuse me," she said, as she stood and walked into the cool shadows away from the balcony. "You would not believe where I am or who I'm with," Lovina said into the phone.

"I'll call that and raise you the symbol on that BEK video you wanted me to track down," Russ said. "You know who the Pagan is, don't you?"

"That's like asking who's Jack the Ripper or Zodiac," Lovina said, taking a quick sip from her water bottle. "Serial killer, been hunting nationwide since the early fifties. Kills victims four times a year, sometimes multiple victims on the same night. He got his name because he kills on the seasonal equinoxes. The FBI figures him for a Pagan, or a Pagan wannabe. He's been on their most wanted list since the eighties, when they think he stopped killing. He's spawned copycats for decades."

"There's another reason they called him the Pagan," Russ said. "One the FBI kept secret, in case they ever did get a collar. There was a symbol carved onto the bodies of every victim, from the first, in 1956, onward. Care to guess what that symbol was?"

"You're kidding me," Lovina said, plugging a finger in her ear as the music started up in the club again. "That circle with the crescent moon over it that was on the video?"

"Bingo!" Russ said. "It's actually a Wiccan symbol for the Horned God—the masculine energy balanced by the feminine energy of the Triple Goddess."

"Triple Goddess?" Lovina said.

"The Mother, the Maiden, and the Crone," Russ said.

"You *have* been busy," she said. "Very Lilith Fair, Russ."

"This is really pretty fascinating stuff, *chère*," Russ said. "The worship of these anthropomorphized forces of nature dates back to the dawn of *Homo sapiens*."

Something was tumbling in Lovina's brain. Something in Russ's words—pieces shifting and moving—waiting for them to snap into place.

"So now we have a fifty-year run of occult serial murders tied in with these missing kids and the BEKs. It may be fascinating, Russ, but it doesn't put us any closer to a perp."

"Oh, ye of little faith," Russ said. "This will . . ."

. . .

"So this Dewey Rears was tracking BEK sightings and linking them to disappearances in a database," Max was saying to Jimmie and the others when Lovina stepped back into earshot.

"That's what Lovina told us," Jimmie said. "Even said he was linking it to the Road in some way or another."

Max's owlish eyes grew impossibly larger. "Really," she said. "I'd love to see his data."

"You can look it over on the way," Lovina said, handing Max a USB drive as she walked over to Jimmie. "My contact got a lead on Mark Stolar, the guy who was in Rears's apartment and went missing, too. He's turned up in Atlanta."

"Hot damn!" Jimmie said. "Good work. Okay, saddle up, everybody! Doc, you sure you're on board for this?"

Max was gathering up her satchel and replacing the tablet and other items she had scattered on her lap with one hand and chugging down the energy drink with the other. "Yes, please," she said, taking a breath between gulps. "I want to help, and it might prove my hypothesis as well!"

"Okay," Jimmie said, grabbing his coat.

"What do you know about Wicca, paganism?" Lovina asked Max. The Builder's notebooks and pens clattered on the floor as if she had been startled. "Specifically, the Triple Goddess and the Horned God." Max and Lovina knelt to gather the items off the floor.

Max kept her gaze fixed on the floor. "Um, quite a bit," she said softly. "I can tell you whatever you want on the way."

"You want me to call up a few of the Memphis Mafia? Shouldn't take more than a few hours. We could ride shotgun for you," Aaron said.

Jimmie shook his hand and slapped him on the shoulder. "Thanks, A, but we got to get on the road, ASAP. You've been a huge help, as always. I owe you another one, man."

"You don't owe me nothin', Jim," Aaron said, hugging the trucker and slapping his back. "You go take care of business, brother—TCB. Mafia's here if you need us."

"Goes both ways, A," Jimmie said.

Aaron snapped his fingers and gestured toward some of his attendants. A young woman with a silver tray walked among the group of travelers giving out gold necklaces like the one Jimmie and the other patrons at the boat dock had presented. Heck was given a "TCB" necklace, while Lovina and Max were given ones that said "TLC."

"You're a prince, man!" Heck said, tucking the necklace into his jeans pocket.

"Not exactly a prince," Aaron said. The club owner leaned back into Jimmie, as if hugging him again. "Jim, that kid, Heck, you know he's—"

"Yeah," Jimmie said, interrupting him. "I do, but he's also my squire."

"Just watch your backside, brother," Aaron said, stepping away. "Y'all come on back anytime," he said to the crew. "And good huntin'."

"Let's ride!" Jimmie said.

Mark's sleep was fitful, full of shadow hands grabbing him with fingers so cold they burned and palms, like cigarette smoke, clamping over his mouth and nose, smothering him. Sometime after sunlight began to burn at the edges of the hotel room's thick curtains, he awoke to the crash of the door flying open, the security chain raining down in tiny fragments. He froze, thinking they had found him; he would die now, like Dewey.

Strong warm hands grabbed him, and he felt a weight on his chest. He was pinned to the bed by a hefty-looking stranger, while a beautiful but stern-looking woman stood beside the bed aiming a gun at his face. "Mark Stolar," she said. "Don't move. You are under arrest in the kidnapping of Dewey Rears."

Mark couldn't help laughing, in spite of his terror. "You have got to be fucking kidding me, man!" he said. "You're busting me for Dewey? Of course you are."

The big burly guy on top of him, his knee planted on Mark's chest, didn't look anything like a cop, though he had a fancy pistol-grip shotgun resting against Mark's chest. He looked like a gear-jammer, a trucker. "Tell us what happened, then, Mark," the trucker said. "What happened to Dewey and you?"

Mark looked from one face to another. There were four people in his hotel room—the cop, the trucker, a woman with long curly black hair and glasses, who looked as if she should be on a college campus, and a biker, complete with his colors. Mark saw the patches on his back and the squat, ugly assault rifle he had slung over his shoulder, as the biker shut the door to the room. Mark suspected that he was the one who'd kicked it in.

"You wouldn't believe me if I told you," Mark said. "Who are you guys?" He looked at the lady cop. "Let me see some ID."

"Put the gun away, please, Lovina," Jimmie said, moving his shotgun away.

Lovina looked at him, frowning. "We don't know his part in all this yet, Jimmie," she said.

"My part?" Mark said. "My fucking part in all this is I got grabbed, tortured, got to watch my best friend murdered in front of me by some freak with a knife, and then forced to go do the bastard's dirty work. That's my part, Officer, and it's a bit-fucking-part, too."

Lovina slid the pistol back into her shoulder holster, under her leather jacket. "So Dewey's dead?" she asked. Mark nodded. Jimmie climbed off him and helped him sit up in the bed.

"Yeah," Mark said, not meeting anyone's gaze. "He's dead. And, in other news, the world just keeps on not giving a shit. How did you find me?"

"We tracked you by your credit card when you got this room," Lovina said.

"Stupid mistake," Mark said. "Another in a long line. Shit."

Lovina sat on the edge of the bed. Jimmie took a seat near the window, cradling his shotgun. He peeked out from the edge of the curtain to see if there was any response to the commotion. In this part of downtown Atlanta, you minded your own business; no one seemed even to have noticed their entrance. Max sat on the other, unoccupied bed in the room while Heck began to pour water into the small coffeemaker beside the sink. Through the walls, you could hear the muffled thudding of a boom box playing Wiz Khalifa's "Medicated" way too loudly, and outside the window was the moaning Doppler of the late-morning rush hour on the elevated I-20.

"Who took you two, Mark?" Lovina asked. "Who killed Dewey?"

"Like I said," he replied, rubbing his face. "You won't fucking believe me."

"Aw, we're a very understanding audience, man," Heck said, and tossed Mark the remains of his Lucky Strikes pack and his Zippo. "We just met Helvis. Try us."

Mark lit the cigarette with shaky hands and tossed them back to Heck. After a few long drags, like a drowning man gulping air, his hands were steady, and he looked up at his uninvited guests. The biker was pouring and passing out coffee in Styrofoam cups.

"Dewey was always looking into weird shit—loved it since we were kids. He was onto something he'd been researching for years. Said it had to do with these Black-Eyed Kids and with the fucking highway system. He said something about . . . what was it, it was a Chinese thing . . . long . . . something—"

"Wait, wait," Max said, almost spitting out her coffee. "Was it 'long xian,' by any chance?"

"Yeah," Mark said, nodding. "It was. He talked a lot of weird shit, and sometimes I just pretended to listen. Anyways, one night we were hanging out and there's a knock at the door—two kids in hoodies."

Lovina felt her stomach clench, filled with cold rocks. Her throat tightened.

Mark went on; his hand holding the cigarette was starting to tremble again. "I remember telling Dewey to shut the fucking door, but he wouldn't. It felt the way a nightmare feels," he said. "Awful shit is happening and you can't stop, even though you know you should. The kids said something, but I can't remember the words. I was so scared, so fucking afraid, and I couldn't run, couldn't move. It was like looking into a cobra's eyes. They came inside; Dewey let them in. The rest is like a dream that decays, fades, once you wake up from it. We walked outside, and he was there—at least, I think I remember him being there."

"Who?" Jimmie said. "Who was there, Mark?"

"The guy that killed Dewey, the motherfucker the fucking Scode brothers work for," Mark said, taking a last, long pull on the cigarette that was now mostly ash. Mark crushed it out on the nightstand next to him, beside the Gideon Bible and a forest of empty green beer bottles. "He rides an old black Harley, claims to be the Pagan—y'know, the serial killer." Jimmie and Lovina traded looks as Mark continued in a shivering voice. His eyes were wide with fear as the adrenaline flooded his blood and brain. "He sacrificed Dewey to some . . . there isn't a word, man. It . . . it was a god, some kind of god-thing."

"A god?" Heck said, glancing at Jimmie. "Fun."

"I don't know," Mark said. "I mean, I don't know what to call it. It was in our heads when we were out in the woods with it and the Pagan and the fucking Scode boys. . . . Its eyes were the holes in the clouds—the stars peeking through—and the forest was its . . . its body? Hands? Look, all I know is it made me feel like a fucking microbe, man, like the Devil had shit in my skull. It was so old and so . . . everywhere. And hungry, fuck it was hungry—ravenous! It wants to eat us, eat us all, chew us up—devour everyone, everywhere. Not anger, or hatred, just . . . beneath contempt. Food . . . all we are is food for it—prey—and it likes to play with its food."

"Old and hungry," Jimmie said, rubbing his face. The weight of the road and the hours and the stress settled over him. He shrugged it off as best he could. "Did the Pagan tell you what it was? Its name?"

"The Horned Man," Mark said, after staring and blinking for a moment. "He said he was sacrificing for the Horned Man. Chasseur, that fucker on the bike, said that the Horned Man had made him the Master of the Hunt, whatever the hell that is. He had dogs, lots of dogs, but they weren't dogs, they were shadows—shadow people . . . made out of shadows. . . . I know how fucking crazy this sounds, I do."

Max was furiously digging into her satchel. She pulled out her tablet and began to tap on the screen. Heck lit up his last cigarette, crumpled the empty pack, and tossed it in a corner. "Where were you when all this was going down, man?" Heck asked. "You said there was a forest—do you know where it was, where they took you and Dewey?"

"Some shithole of a town called Four Houses," Mark said. He was sweating, blinking. "I think it's in Kansas—that's what the kids told me."

"Kids?" Lovina said.

"Dewey said they teleported us, or some such bullshit. All I know is one minute we were outside Dewey's house and the next we were there. Like I said, it was like a bad dream. Maybe it was, maybe I just lost my fucking shit. . . . No, no, Dewey is dead—that's fucking real, that's true."

"What kids?" Lovina asked, leaning closer.

"Two college kids," Dewey said. They got stranded in Four Houses. I think the Pagan was going to sacrifice them, too. At least, that's what he told me to tell Norse yesterday."

There was a rumble in the parking lot below, the sound of a motorcycle gliding by, slowly.

"Norse?" Heck said. "Who the hell is Norse?"

"Karen Collie said something about Four Horses in her dream before she disappeared," Jimmie said. "Maybe she meant Four Houses."

"Can you tell us the kids' names?" Lovina said. "Where were they from, Mark? Are they still alive?"

"Did you have instructions to hook back up with the Pagan, Mark?" Jimmie asked. "How? Where?"

Mark covered his ears and leaned forward, his head on his knees. "Shut up, shut up and go away . . . all of you please just shut the fuck up and go away!"

"Hey!" Heck shouted out. The room stilled. "We all need to dial it down a notch, okay." Heck knelt beside Mark's bed, opposite Lovina and Jimmie. "Look, Mark, it's cool, man. We're cool. We're all a little jacked up, but we all want the same thing. I know you've been through some bad, bad shit, man. You saw your buddy slaughtered—I know how that feels. I know how it eats at you inside, like rats gnawing you. I know you want to wipe yourself out and never come back. I really do know, man. But we got a job to do, okay? You can help us get the bastards who got Dewey. But you have got to stay cool, okay? Do the job."

Mark nodded. His eyes were damp but dead. "Yeah, okay . . . okay, I'm cool," he said.

Heck looked from Lovina to Jimmy and then back to Mark. "Okay, who's Norse?"

"George Norse," Mark said. "Radio and TV guy. I was supposed to just deliver it and then call a number to be picked up. I ran. I got drunk, and I ran."

"What were you delivering?" Lovina asked.

Heck felt something, a flush or a warmth along his neck, then a shudder of cold, almost like the way he had felt in the desert when he got too much sun—freezing in the sunshine. He looked toward the door and didn't know why, but the part of him that never slept did.

"Guys . . ." he had time to say, his hand slipping to the handle of the

MP9, as he unslung it. Just the tone of his voice was enough for Jimmie and Lovina. Both began to raise their weapons, to stand.

The dark corners of the room moved, congealed into the form of dogs—a half dozen, silent, with eyes like greasy moonlight. The hotel room door splintered and broke from the force of the kick, wrenching itself off one of the hinges. The man behind the kick was dressed in black riding leathers, gloves, and boots. His narrow, plain face was impassive. His hair was slicked straight back in a style popular a century ago. He held a large bone-handled hunting knife. He stepped into the room.

"It's time" was all Mark said. He was looking at Heck when a shadow in the shape of a man freed itself from above the bed and sank its smoky fist into Mark's skull. Mark Stolar gave a deep groan as his eyeballs swelled, then sluiced out of his sockets, followed by a gush of blood and brains. He slumped and was quiet. The shadow removed its now ethereal hand from the dead man's skull and once more became one with the wall.

"No one escapes the hunt, Mr. Stolar," the Pagan said. "Ever." He turned from the corpse to regard the others. He opened his mouth to speak.

"Light him up!" Jimmie shouted, unloading the 12-gauge in a thunderous blast less than three feet from the man. Lovina fired on him with the .40 Glock, kneeling on one knee beside Jimmie, pumping round after round into the dark rider. Heck's machine gun clattered as he stood on the opposite side of the bed, hot brass hissing as it hit the cheap industrial carpet. Max, who had slid down between the other bed and the wall, her arm holding her tablet, popped back up to video the exchange. There was a sound like the world breaking: angry gunpowder bellows, the air scalded with the fury of bullets, then silence. The room smelled of warm brass and cordite. The gun-smoke fog drifted out the shattered door. The Pagan was unscathed; not even a bullet hole marked his leathers.

"Fuck us," Heck had time to mutter. In one, fluid movement, the Pagan backhanded Jimmie, the impact slamming him into his chair, breaking it, and then driving him into the corner by the air conditioner under the room's large curtained window. Aussapile gasped in pain as the force of the almost casual slap knocked his still smoking shotgun from his hands and shattered the plastic molding and the plasterboard of the room's wall. He slid to the floor. The Pagan continued, driving a low, clumsy kick toward Lovina. She blocked it expertly, but was startled when the sheer strength of the blow turned her block aside, like a child trying to slow down a rampaging bear. The power of the kick tossed her across the room, where she smashed into the heavy wooden dresser that the flat-screen TV was resting on. The dresser collapsed, and Lovina crumpled to the floor, buried under shattered wood and broken electronics. Heck stood between the two beds, between the Pagan and the still hiding Max. He lowered the MP9 but kept his eyes on the Pagan. Jimmie couldn't believe it: Heck was grinning.

"Now, as I was trying to say," the Pagan continued. "I have sensed your regard as you have hunted me. Though you are all mortal—made of soft skin, fragile glass bones, you fought well against the cubs I sent against you in Illinois. Only one of your number died, though I'm of a mind that it should have been two." The Pagan locked eyes with Heck. "Look at you."

"I am a sight," Heck growled. "That I am."

"The other animals are in pain, in fear, but you—you can't wait for the fight, can you?"

"I'm looking forward to kicking your ass, yeah," Heck said.

"Why were you not infected and overcome when you were bitten, as your ally was?" the Pagan asked.

"You drink the shit I've chugged at MC initiation parties, and I'm sure I can handle whatever venom was in the little love bites from your black-eyed boy band."

The Pagan cocked his head. It was an unnatural motion, like a machine trying to mimic human confusion. "You don't know what you are," he said. "You hear the song of oblivion screaming in you and hide from it, ignore it, try to silence it. You truly have no idea. How pathetic."

"Why don't you explain it to me, then," Heck said. Some of the sneering sarcasm faltered, and Lovina saw doubt and some fear creeping onto Heck's face, into his voice.

"You are a hunter of men, just as I am," the Pagan said. "A dragon walking among sheep. They are nothing but prey to you, as they are to me, to my master. You and I have more in common than you have with any of the simpering, bleating chattel."

Heck was silent, lost in the desert again, in the flames that talked. The Pagan's voice was there, in the fire. Jimmie struggled to reach the shotgun, and Lovina tried to rise from the debris.

"You have all witnessed the hunt," the Pagan said. "No one survives that." He raised a gloved hand, and the shadow hounds began to pad silently from the darkness. Max suddenly popped up from behind the other bed.

"Get down!" Jimmie shouted.

"*An fiach fiáin*," Max called out to the Pagan, in a quavering voice. Jimmie recognized the strange phrase. Karen Collie had said it to him when he picked her up, when she asked him to stop the monster that had devoured her and her friends. Max continued, "We honor the Divine Marriage, the Three Who Are One, the union of Cernunnos and Diana. Stay the Master of the Hunt's hand. We beg thee, and will offer the proper sacrifices."

"One of you actually knows the old ways," the Pagan said. "Very good, but far, far too late. The three who are one are gone—diminished by my master. Diana is dead. Only the Fury remains, only the Horned God. There is no place in this universe for mercy now." The Pagan looked at each of them. "Your hunt has ended," he said. He dropped his raised arm, and the shadow hounds surged forward as the Pagan turned his back and stepped through the doorway.

One of the beasts was on top of Lovina, even as she tried to get to her knees. The hound's mouth opened and a horrible keening spilled out across the room, as it began to close its massive maw on Lovina.

"No!" Max shouted. She held up a small cylinder, a laser pointer, and fired the red beam at the hound on Lovina. The creature's howl turned into a whine of pain as the beam cut through its inky hide and reduced the hound to a cloud of black smoke, much like what had happened to the slain BEKs they had faced in Illinois. Two more of the hounds were almost on Heck, and a third jumped the bed, over Mark's corpse, toward Jimmie. Another moved to maul Lovina, and the last knocked Max against the wall, pinning her behind the bed.

"The curtains, Jimmie, the curtains!" Max screamed as she tried to struggle with the shadow beast that was like fog to her touch but was more than capable of touching her, biting her. Heck snapped out of his daze and spun to meet the two hounds as they hurled toward him. Jimmie grabbed at the edge of the thick canvas curtain and pulled with all his might. The shadow hound was on top of him; its breath was dust and ice. He snarled into the beast's face and wrenched. The curtain popped, then tore free, and sunlight poured into the room. The pack howled in pain and rage—a sound that chewed on every nerve. The howl faded quickly, as each shadow dog became a plume of odorless black smoke, the sunlight knifing through the clouds, scattering them on the air.

"I take back everything bad I ever said about Builders," Jimmie said, struggling to rise, wincing with pain. "Thanks, Max."

Max smiled and scrambled to help Lovina to her feet. "You okay?" the professor asked.

"I'm alive, thanks to you," Lovina said with a groan. "How did you do that, the laser thing? How did you know that would hurt them?"

"I didn't," Max said. "It's a toy for my cat, Pyewacket. I had it in my bag, and I thought if they're cohesive darkness, then maybe cohesive light would . . . you know, affect them."

Lovina laughed. "Smart," she said. "And all that stuff you said to him?"

"If what he was saying is true," Max said, "then the universe is in terrible danger."

"The universe?" Lovina said.

Max nodded. "The whole universe."

Jimmie limped over to Heck. "You okay?" the trucker asked. Heck nodded. He pulled a sheet over Mark's face. A crowd of hotel guests were sheepishly beginning to peek inside the room. The gunshots had done the trick. Several had out cell phones to video or take pictures, and others were calling 911. There was a rumble of a motorcycle in the lot below.

"Yeah, sorry I flaked out," Heck said. "I let the asshole get to me."

"It's okay," Jimmie said. Aussapile looked at everyone. "Pedal to the metal, people—we're taking this son of a bitch down. No way in hell is he getting away."

SIXTEEN   "10-80"

The Pagan, the Master of the Hunt, drove his black 1945 Harley-Davidson WLA out of the parking lot of the motel and onto MLK Jr. Drive, headed east. Heck was the first out the shattered door of the late Mark Stolar's hotel room. He pushed past the crowd, jumped most of the first flight of steps, then flipped over the wrought-iron rail and landed, running, on the lot's asphalt. He had his helmet on by the time Jimmie, Lovina, and Max were crossing the lot to their vehicles.

"He's headed east on MLK!" Heck shouted as he slid the steel demon face over his own and kicked the T5 Blackie in the guts, bringing it to snarling life. He tore out of the lot after the Master of the Hunt.

"Ears on!" Jimmie shouted out to the biker as they reached his rig and Lovina's Charger. "Channel 23!" Sirens were filling the air. "You're with me, Doc," Jimmie said. "I need a consult." Max nodded and struggled into the passenger seat of the 18-wheeler as Jimmie climbed into the truck's cab. "You got that handset radio I gave you?" Jimmie asked Lovina as she slid behind the wheel of the Charger.

"Got it," she said. Jimmie gave her a thumbs-up and started up the truck.

Heck swung the turn out of the motel lot hard and fast. He heard horns bleat at him, blurs of motion at the edges of his periphery; he swerved to avoid a Volvo. There was a wall of flashing blue lights barreling down on the motel parking lot, westbound on MLK Jr. Drive.

"Shit!" he said, clicking on the radio on his belt. "Cops," he said into the mike. "All up your asses. I got 'em."

Heck swerved to a full stop on the street and sprayed the patrol cars with machine-gun fire, shooting out the light bars on the roofs of the cars. Squad cars swerved, braked, and crashed everywhere.

"What the hell are you doing?" Jimmie's voice boomed in Heck's ear.

"Being a good fucking team player!" Heck growled. He let the MP9 drop back to his side and flipped off the assembled horde of police cars. He spun out the back tire of the Blackie, streaming foul-smelling rubber smoke, and shot off the wrong way down his side of the street, headed west now. The police units that could still move chased after him, ignoring the 18-wheeler and the muscle car speeding in pursuit of the Master of the Hunt in the other direction.

Max clutched at her seat belt as Jimmie slid the lumbering rig through the jumble of late-morning rush-hour traffic, squeezing through gaps she didn't believe it was physically possible for Paladin's truck to move through.

"He's turning right onto Joe Lowery Boulevard," Jimmie said into his headset. "I think he's headed for the interstate." Jimmie keyed his mike to Channel 23 again. "Break 2-3, break 2-3, looking for any brothers out there, anyone. This is Paladin, and we sure could use some help right about now, c'mon?" There was no answer, only silence. "Damn it," Jimmie muttered, and swung the wheel to avoid a car and to slip through another impossible gap.

"I thought you Brethren were everywhere," Max said through gritted teeth.

"We are," Jimmie said. "Just not all at the same time." He glanced for an instant at Max, then back at the road. "What you said back there, in the hotel, about the universe being in trouble, what did you mean?"

"It's kind of complicated," Max said. "And—oh God, watch out!—shouldn't you focus on driving right now?"

"The Three Who Are One?" Jimmie said, ignoring her as he slid the rig between a minivan and a PT Cruiser. The Cruiser honked at him and the driver flipped him off. "That's a Wiccan reference, isn't it? I've dealt with enough good and bad witches over the years to know that much, at least. He said something about the three being dead—"

"Not dead," Max corrected, "diminished. I don't think they can actually die. If they did, that would be the end of everything."

"Okay, explain that," Jimmie said, stuffing some snuff into his cheek.

The Master's bike was a dark shape about half a mile ahead. Jimmie downshifted to allow the moving puzzle pieces of the other cars on the road to drift into a new pattern that, hopefully, would provide an opening.

"The three are the Maiden, the Mother, and the Crone," Max said. "Anthropomorphized representations of cosmic forces. It was a way for early man to grasp cosmology. Many cite the Triple Goddess as the creation of Robert Graves in the early to mid twentieth century. However, as early as the first century BCE—"

"Max!" Jimmie interrupted. "Not teaching a class here, chasing bad guys. What forces does the Triple Goddess represent?"

"Right, right, sorry," Max said. "The Maiden is the generative principles—new life, creation, renewal of a cycle, birth. The Mother is the balancing principle—stability, maturity, order, progress."

Jimmie swerved and the whole cab rocked. Max grabbed her seat belt again and gave a frightened little squeak. The truck broke free of the bottleneck in time to see the Pagan's bike ascending the 55A ramp. "He's on I-20 west," Jimmie said into his mike. "He's hauling ass."

"Jimmie!" Max shouted, her arms and feet locking in terror. Jimmie instantly realized that the truck in front of him had jammed on the brakes. He did the same, jerking the shotgun gearshift down. It was pure instinct; there wasn't time for anything else. The rig groaned and shrieked to a stop, with less than an inch between its grille and the rear bumper of the truck. Past the truck, Jimmie could see a line of traffic, all stopped.

"Damn it!" Jimmie said, slapping the wheel. "We're tied up. He's out of sight on I-20, copy?"

Lovina's Charger snarled past, gliding up the on-ramp's shoulder after the Master of the Hunt at eighty miles per hour. "I'm on him," she said over the radio.

Jimmie sighed and waited for the jam to clear. "What about the Crone?" he asked.

Max exhaled and rubbed her face. "Entropy," she said. "The end of the cycle—closure, death. The three represent the feminine aspects of creation—in eternal opposition, and complement, to the masculine aspects, represented by Cernunnos, one of the names of the Horned God.

Jimmie, if what the Pagan said is true, then the universe, at its most fundamental levels, is out of whack and is falling apart. We have to do something before it's too late."

"Right," Jimmie said. "Save the universe. Got it, but first we have to merge into the damned right lane."

Traffic on I-20 was light compared with the street, and Lovina's Dodge slid through it like a snake gliding on water. The hum of the engine was like being in love. She was going over a hundred now, and she saw the Pagan and his motorcycle ahead in the left lane, accelerating. She did the same.

When Lovina was in Afghanistan, she met a guy everyone called Benno—she honestly couldn't remember what his real name was. The reason Benno stuck in her head was that it was because of him that she loved so much weird-ass music. He'd play mix CDs all the damn time—back at base camp, on patrols whenever he could, and even a few times in the middle of a hot LZ, when he shouldn't. Benno's musical tastes were almost as wonky as the man himself, but some of them had rubbed off on Lovina, even back in the world. So now, far away from home, chasing a man she had just seen shrug off small-arms fire as if it were shower water, she had the Charger's speakers throbbing to a mix Benno had made for her when they were both headed home. Shriekback's "Running on the Rocks" flowed, morphed, into Billy Idol's "Rebel Yell," and it made Lovina will the muscle car faster, faster, closer to the Master of the Hunt.

The Pagan glanced back, and Lovina sensed his eyes on her, like a cancer creeping into her cells. He moved toward a cluster of traffic, sliding in and out between the cars, ignoring lanes and angry car horns. Lovina took to the shoulder of the highway again; the Charger shuddered and shimmied as she edged around the cluster of traffic. Gravel sprayed everywhere, and the motorists honked and flipped her off as she fishtailed the Dodge back onto the highway and around the island of cars and trucks. The Pagan did it again, threading between another mass of vehicles, ignoring the lanes and the inches that separated him from the other vehicles. The gap widened, and Lovina wished she had roller lights and a siren to get these people the hell out of her way. The Charger was a beast on the open road, and she knew she could run him to ground, but he was putting too many cars and trucks between them. She wrestled the Charger onto the edge of the road again, one of her tires almost dropping into a two-foot drainage ditch, but she jerked the wheel and managed to keep from wiping out. She was back on the road, but even more distance separated them now.

"I'm at Exit 53," she said. "He's about a mile ahead of me, and accelerating. He's going to be out of sight in a second."

"Stick with him, Lovina," Jimmie said over the CB. "We're on the interstate, and we're coming up fast."

"I'm trying to get up to him, but he's lane-splitting," she said. "He's driving like a maniac—no fear of crashing, none. Damn it! He just put another half mile and another group of cars between us. Hang on a second!"

Lovina began to try the shoulder trick again, feeling her tires scrambling for traction on the greasy loose gravel that littered the edge of the road. She whipped hard right to avoid an abandoned muffler on the shoulder and then turned hard to slip back onto the road. She succeeded, but fishtailed again and had to swerve and brake to avoid being T-boned by a silver Toyota.

"Lovina? What's happening?" Jimmie asked over the CB.

The Master of the Hunt was again in the middle of a group of cars, sliding between them. He edged closer to a compact smart car on his right, and Lovina saw him draw his nasty-looking hunting knife, its blade a glint in the late-morning sun. He brought his bike within inches of the driver's open window; his knife arm flashed inside the car for an instant, then withdrew, and the Pagan's motorcycle accelerated quickly away.

"Oh God, no!" Lovina shouted, downshifting and turning hard to avoid what she knew was coming. "Jimmie, he just killed someone!"

The compact veered over into the left lane. Lovina saw the driver slump like a rag doll, thrown by the inertia. The out-of-control car slid in front of a work truck. The two vehicles struck each other, the sound of metal screaming. Lovina saw the whole dance, of velocity and control, begin to fail as brake lights glared, and wheels were hastily jerked, all too late. She buried the gas pedal under her foot and weaved between the elements of the six-car pileup on instinct, slipping between the folding cages of shredding metal and the constellations of exploding glass. For an instant, the numbers on the various license plates of the crashing cars seemed hyperreal and in perfect, almost exaggerated focus. The numbers moved in front of her eyes and in her mind, unbidden, like a compulsion that could not be ignored. Her universe was the road in front of her, the Charger was her body, and she was nothing but engine and will. Then she was clear and she had no idea how she could possibly have done that. She was sweating and every muscle was tensed. She felt as if she had overslept and suddenly awakened.

The Master of the Hunt was almost out of sight, gliding through another set of cars and trucks, and then clear and open highway. He accelerated to, easily, a hundred and fifty miles an hour. Almost gone.

"I'm losing him, Jimmie!" she said. "I'm losing the son of a bitch."

There was a flash of black-and-silver on Lovina's right, something hurtling past at dizzying speed.

"I got him," a voice crackled over the CB. It was Heck. "Sorry I'm late."

Heck came up on the Pagan's right, slipping between the cars and trucks, using them as cover, drifting less than inches from paint and steel moving at a hundred and seventy-five miles an hour. The Master of the Hunt spotted him just as they both cleared the traffic. Heck veered hard left and was beside the Master of the Hunt, separated by a few feet. They were on open road now, passing Exit 52, headed toward I-285.

"Let's play, asshole," Heck muttered. He slipped his large combat knife out of the belt sheath with his left hand and twirled it, grinning behind his demon mask. The Pagan's reaction was hidden behind the black mirror of his helmet's visor, but he hefted his own bone-handled hunting knife and prepared to meet Heck's charge.

They were side by side, less than a foot apart, both traveling over two hundred miles an hour, both bikes shuddering with each flaw in the highway. The Huntsman flashed out with his blade, still wet with the dead driver's blood, toward Heck's throat. Heck parried it, and the two riders parted a few feet, only to swerve closer again for another pass. Heck slashed down, toward the madman's shoulder, and found the Pagan's blade blocking his own.

The two riders pushed against each other, then swerved hard apart to avoid a massive swarm of merging and jockeying vehicles that suddenly appeared on the highway as they reached the concrete octopus of the I-285 intersection. For several long seconds, both huntsman and outlaw biker did nothing but struggle to maintain speed and avoid crashes. A symphony of horns surrounded them. Heck struggled to maintain control; at this speed, every motion was exaggerated and any mistake was fatal. Then, as the traffic finally thinned, they were back together, grappling, blades flashing, sparking, with the force and speed of each strike. Their arms, their knives, moved almost as fast as their bikes were hurtling down the highway, blurring, showering sparks. Both bikes were pushing well past their limits, whining and shaking. Another flurry of strikes, each parried and returned, steel biting steel, again and again.

The Pagan lifted his leg off the peg, driving a powerful kick into Heck's side. Heck felt sharp pain blossom in his chest, and felt more than heard a sickening crunch as the steel-toed boot connected. Almost without thinking, he jabbed with his clenched knife hand, striking a jarring blow to the Huntsman's helmeted head. The black visor shattered, and he felt soft flesh and hard bone yield under his leather-gloved fist. Both bikes—both men, extensions of their machines—veered away and nearly wiped out from the force of their traded blows. Heck grabbed both handles, his knife still clutched. He glanced over at the Pagan. The killer's face was now partly exposed beneath the shattered visor, and Heck saw alien yellow-green eyes, almost glowing, full of hate, glaring at him. The Master of the Hunt's nose slowly reset itself, shifting back to its original shape, and the small cuts near his eyes sealed and vanished, like the bruises under his eyes. The Pagan pointed his knife at Heck, and Heck returned the salute with a wave, and the British two-finger salute that was the equivalent of a middle finger.

There was the bellow of a semi's horn, and both riders glanced back. Jimmie's rig and Lovina's Charger were coming up fast on the two riders.

Heck saw worry, maybe even fear, for just a second in the unearthly eyes, then the Master of the Hunt slipped his knife away and accelerated even more, his bike making a sick whine with the exertion. Heck holstered his blade and hunkered down on the pegs to push his own bike to its very last ounce of horsepower.

There were a couple of miles of clear highway ahead. The chase had already taken the hunted and the hunters out to where I-20 crosses the Chattahoochee River, near Six Flags. Heck was closing, less than half a mile between them, as the bikes crossed the river and continued heading west. Heck felt a strange sensation in his belly and spine, as he had just before the Huntsman kicked in Mark Stolar's hotel-room door—a feeling of fundamental wrongness, as if the air itself had become unbreathable, and gravity were cutting in and out. It was a quick sensation, in the blink of an eye, but Heck's instincts screamed, and he became very aware, very on edge. Something was wrong.

The road, the space in front of the Master of the Hunt, began to pucker, stretching inward toward an unseen point, as if the three-dimensional reality there were being sucked into a funnel, narrowed and compressed to a vanishing point. Even the sound, the howling tunnel of the road at two hundred-plus miles an hour, was distorting along with the space in front of the Pagan. Stolar had said something about "teleporting," and, as Heck watched the surreal landscape ahead of him, he suddenly recalled the dead man's words.

"No, no, no!" Heck shouted. "Fucking, no!"

The Pagan and his bike began to stretch, to elongate, as they were pulled into the narrowing, invisible vortex, as if the light painting them were being pulled into an impossibly small pinhole, along with the matter that composed the rider and his machine.

Heck bellowed in rage and tried to force his throttle farther forward, but it had nowhere else to go. "No, you don't, you son of a bitch!" he screamed. "You come back here!"

Lovina, Jimmie, and Max saw the phenomenon, too, as the killer began to vanish before their eyes.

"Aw, shit!" Jimmie said. "Not this. It figures."

Lovina had the same strange sensation come over her as when she had threaded the car crash—a sense of hyperawareness. She focused intently on the Pagan, on his bike. She was gaining, and she knew that she could overtake him, knew it. "You're not getting away," she said quietly as she focused on the Pagan. Her voice didn't sound right to her own ears. "Not from me." The cluster of highway signs off to the side of I-20, the metal tree of plaques, each bearing numbered routes and interstates, sprang into diamond-clear focus for her. Each number, each sequence of numbers, glowed in her perception and burned themselves into her brain. The Pagan was at the end of a shimmering, streaking tunnel—a shower of photons now. The world was gone, only the tunnel of light, only the Road, made up of iridescent fire, and the numbers—slithering, shifting, adding, multiplying, dividing in her mind, enveloping Lovina's thoughts, becoming Lovina's thoughts. Each number, each sequence softly clicking into inevitable place, into the only possible place it could go—pattern, motion, sequence, velocity . . . *click, click, click, click,* like tumblers.

Equation solved; solution found.

Heck slid to a stop on the highway, his bike skidding sideways as he did. The Master of the Hunt vanished into nothing, with a *whoosh* of air rushing to fill the vacuum. Lovina's Charger roared past Heck, and the biker watched in amazement as her car folded up, in defiance of space and dimension, as the Huntsman had, and then vanished with an identical gasp of air. Lovina was gone.

"What the hell just happened?" Heck shouted.

SEVENTEEN "10-44"

"Why?" Ava asked Agnes, almost pleading. "Why won't you help me get Cole and Lexi back?" They were in the backyard of Agnes's mansion, sitting in lawn chairs under a sun-faded tin awning. Agnes had made iced tea for the two of them. Across the yard were two graves: Julia's, covered in grass and wildflowers, and Alana's, only a day old. Ava's back still ached from digging her friend's resting place. The blisters on her hands from the shovel were still raw.

"My dear," Agnes said, "you simply don't understand the way things work here. It's not that easy." The old woman looked across the yard. A flock of Mississippi kites were splashing in Agnes's birdbath. She sipped her tea, the ice tinkling in the glass, and smiled slightly. "I'm glad Julia isn't alone out here anymore. She has someone to keep her company. That's lovely."

Ava stopped in mid-sip as she took her tea and looked at the smiling wisp of an old woman who had saved her life. This woman whom the hulking Scode brothers seemed to fear and cursed, whom the faceless woman behind the locked door—the one who had refused to let Ava and her friends in—had spoken of with reverence, as a protector. What had the woman and the Scodes called Agnes? The Crone?

"Look," Ava said, "I'm scared of that motorcycle guy, too—he grew fucking horns! I get it, but somebody has got to stop him. He's got to be behind the shadow people, too."

"Oh, yes, dear," Agnes said, still watching the birds. "They are the children of the entity he serves, parts of the entity he serves—I'm afraid I'm not completely sure how that all works myself."

"Well, what do you know?" Ava asked. "What is he? What do you mean 'he serves some entity'? *Entity?* What does that even mean?"

"As I said, it's not easy to understand," Agnes said. "Some of what I know is from the books in the basement of this house. Other pieces come from the original citizens of the Four Houses—families, like the Scodes, that he trapped here when he gained control over the town, and whom he won't allow to leave or release. He's trapped them here, poor souls, and a few of the old-timers recall when he was just an odd, quiet boy, before he became something other, and much less than human.

"And some of what I know . . . some of it is hard for me to disclose to you, my dear, for I fear you will doubt my sanity."

Ava laughed and shook her head. "Whatever," she said. "In this fucked-up burg, you seem like one of the sanest people here. Try me, Agnes."

"I dreamed of this place—this house, the house Dennis and I now live in—I dreamed about it many times as a young girl," Agnes said. "The dreams were different. Dennis was in many of them long before I ever met him. That was one of the ways I knew he was the one for me. There was a young girl, very sad, haunted, that I would dream of being here, being hunted by hounds. She always cut her own throat at the end, but we had many, many lovely talks. I always tried to stop her. She said she was going to get help for us. I saw knights in this house, oddly dressed, and they talked like Yanks, but their hearts were noble. They died in fire trying to defeat your motorcycle rider—he was the Black Knight. I didn't know his name then.

"This house was as much my home as the one I grew up in. The dreams about the basement were frightening, but when I found myself here the basement gave me the greatest comfort. It still does. This house has been calling to me, Ava, whispering things to me in dreams since I was nine years old. This is my house, my duty, and I'm not the first to own it."

Ava started to speak, but something behind Agnes's eyes cowed her. Her words had shifted something in Ava, but there were no words to go along with the feelings. The old woman set down her tea glass and dabbed her narrow lips with a paper napkin. "If you truly wish to know the enemy, his name was Emile Chasseur, and he was born here when

Four Houses was a trade camp—four wooden dwellings clustered together, like a fort, to provide protection against Native raids or attacks, a few small homesteads outlying the main trading post."

"Native raids?" Ava said. "A fort? When was all this?"

"A very long time ago, dear," Agnes said. "Emile Chasseur is old, much older than he appears."

"You saying he's a vampire or something?" Ava asked, leaning forward in her chair. "Or he's an agent of Satan?"

"I don't know exactly what he is," Agnes said. "I think he serves something that was the inspiration for the Western ideal of the Devil but is much older than Old Hob. When Chasseur was a boy, so the stories go, he was a quiet child; many thought him to be enfeebled of mind. He enjoyed his own company and the solitude of the woods. Then the animals began to die. They discovered the boy mutilating them and studying their insides, like an oracle, and drove him out of Four Houses. He retreated to his beloved woods and was thought to be dead. Emile Chasseur became a creature of myth, a bogeyman to make you walk a little faster as your path crossed the deep woods.

"Then one day—no one is sure of the exact date or even decade; it seems different depending on which citizen of Four Houses you ask—Chasseur returned to town. He burned down two of the finest homes here, damaged them terribly, and murdered the owners. The story says he tried to burn this house down, too, but he was driven away by the owner, who matched him in ferocity and will. She was a retired schoolteacher named Alma Kittridge. I found some of her journals in the basement.

"After that, Chasseur forced most of the townsfolk to serve him, almost worship him. Some families, like the Scodes, did so eagerly and came to hold power of their own, as his lapdogs. Others refused, rallying behind Miss Kittridge's example of defiance. Many of them ended up suffering a horrible price for standing up to Chasseur—a horrible price."

Agnes raised her glass again to drink, and Ava noticed that her hand was trembling slightly. For the first time since Ava met her, Agnes seemed just a frail old woman. It frightened her a little.

"I heard about Four Houses in history class back in high school," Ava said. "It was a trading post in Wyandotte County, in the early 1800s. It was near where Kansas City is now, they think—hundreds of miles from where we are. It was only around for a few years and then it was abandoned."

"Yes, dear," Agnes said.

"No one even knows exactly where it stood. It was nowhere near here, Agnes. It never became a town, it never had citizens or families, and it sure didn't last long enough to build grand houses like these. So where are we, really?"

Agnes stood with a bit of an effort. Ava jumped up to help her. "I think you need to see the basement, dear. Come along." They walked up the rear stoop and entered the house through the kitchen door. Like all the doors in Agnes's home, it was reinforced with thick wooden planks, nailed in place, and numerous locks and chains, all unlocked in the daytime and secured tight come sundown. Agnes placed the two glasses in the sink.

"Tell me, Ava dear," Agnes said as she rinsed the dishes. "Do you recall the home you lived in when you were a child? An infant?"

"Bits and pieces," Ava said. "We moved a lot when I was little. I can remember flashes of rooms. I think I remember walking down a long hall with burgundy industrial carpet, holding my arms out so the walls could catch me—I was really young and had just started walking, my mom said. I think my brother was trying to get me. We were playing and laughing. I remember the walls, the carpet, but no, not really anything else. I've seen pictures of the house, of the rooms, but that's pretty much it. Why?"

"I think Four Houses is like that," Agnes said. "A sliver of memory, something vaguely recalled from a dim past, but not too clearly. I think the history of the place, of the name, is that foggy remembrance, but it is more, much more, Ava. It has apparently always been very difficult to find this town, and it doesn't seem to exist on any map. You come to Four Houses because it invites you in, guides you to it. We are all part of some larger design, some half-dreamed life we awake from and forget. It would take a lifetime to understand this place, and maybe even a lifetime wouldn't be enough."

Agnes led her to a door that was just outside the kitchen. The door was on the back side of the main stairwell in the foyer, by the main en-trance. It was locked with a deadbolt. Agnes slipped the bolt and un-locked the door. It opened into yawning, cool darkness, as deep and impenetrable as the space between galaxies. She tugged on a thin cord hanging from an unseen ceiling. There was a click, and then washed-out yellow light from a feeble bulb showed a ceiling that angled down to a cobblestoned floor, dusted with dirt. Agnes clutched the old wooden rail and began to descend slowly. Ava followed, ready to intercede if the older woman lost her footing.

"For a long time after the fires, Chasseur ruled the town through fear and intimidation. Many families fled in the dead of night; others were blackmailed into staying. Back then, people could still come and go from Four Houses of their own will, but in the fifties something changed. I honestly don't know what, but Chasseur became much more power-ful, and he was able to seal the town, like a door that only he had the lock to."

"How could he do that?" Ava asked as she descended the stair behind the old woman. "How the hell could he still be creeping around since the 1800s?"

"He controls death here now," Agnes said. They had reached the basement. The old stone floor was uneven, and Ava saw their breaths drifting in the air, like silver gauze, in the dim light of the bare bulb. "He gifts those who serve him with eternal life while they are young and vital, to better act as his agents. I can only deduce that whatever entity, or force, grants him his immortality allows him to give a similar gift to others."

"This is crazy," Ava said, looking around the low-ceilinged room. "A psycho biker who's hundreds of years old? A town you can't find or leave?" There were huge, heavy wooden shelves against the walls. Several shelves held rows of canned and preserved fruits and jellies as well as vegetables. Other shelves held dark brown jugs with wide corks jammed into the stoppers. They looked like the moonshine jugs overall-wearing hillbillies in old cartoons would be clutching. Ava suspected that the jugs on the shelves contained some kind of high-octane rotgut. Other shelves held old books, scrapbooks, journals, boxes of letters, and even some very old, browned parchment rolled up like ancient scrolls.

There were old photographs of anonymous families in antique silver frames, golden pocket watches, tiny bronzed baby shoes, a sheet of glass with rows of four-leaf clovers sealed behind it, an old, yellowed-bone powder horn, and a heavy brass compass and nautical sextant were among the treasures adorning the wide shelves. There was a pair of old, comfortable chairs sitting by the shelves of books and artifacts. A shaded floor lamp huddled conspiratorially between them. A worktable was set up under the stairwell with a single bench. Ava saw molds and dyes and some kind of press. There were loose bullets of many different sizes on the table, manuals and textbooks and boxes and flasks of chemicals, and empty shell casings as well. Stacked neatly on one side of the worktable were full boxes of bullets, dozens of them. A hunting rifle, a shotgun, what appeared to be an old military-style rifle with a curved magazine, and several handguns were hanging on hooks on the pegboard wall behind the worktable.

"I saved the best for last," Agnes said. She walked toward the center of the room. There was a circular well, about four feet wide. Its base, made up of smooth rounded stones and crumbling mortar, stood about two and a half feet above the floor of the basement. A massive stone capstone sealed the well.

"What is this?" Ava asked as she and Agnes circled the well. There was a symbol carved deeply into the capstone; it was a circle with a crescent on either side. Both crescents faced away from the circle, points outward, the inner curve touching the edge of the circle.

"Watch this," Agnes said. There was a pair of small cracks in the capstone, and Agnes plucked away a small, V-shaped chunk of the heavy, crumbling rock that intersected the two cracks. As soon as she lifted it away, there was an audible hiss, like the air leaking from a tire, and then a *whoosh* as a shaft of blinding white light spilled from the small opening.

"Oh, my God!" Ava shouted above the roar of the perfect, brilliant, all-encompassing energy. "What's happening?"

Agnes's face was painted in the light, and she looked beautiful, Ava thought, and terrifying all at once. Agnes closed her eyes for a moment and sighed, a look of serenity on her face. She opened her eyes and carefully placed the V-shaped piece of rock back in its place in the well's cap. Instantly, the light vanished, and silence filled the cramped basement.

"That," Agnes said, "is power as old and terrible as what Chasseur traffics in. Couldn't you hear it singing?" Ava shook her head slowly, looking at Agnes and remembering how otherworldly, majestic, and terrible she had seemed only a few moments ago. "Perhaps it only sings for me," Agnes said, "to paraphrase the Eliot poem. Come along, dear. You need more tea, clearly."

Back upstairs and at the narrow kitchen table, Ava sipped more cold, sweet tea while Agnes brewed herself a proper hot cup.

"Just when I'm one hundred percent sure that none of this can get any weirder," Ava said.

Agnes poured the hot water into her cup and lowered the small silver tea infuser into the water as she sat in the chair across from Ava. "Are you familiar with the concept of sympathetic magic, dear?" Agnes asked.

Ava shook her head. "No," she said.

"It is the belief that by creating a proxy of a thing you can forge a link to the actual thing and have influence over it—like a voodoo doll, for example. I think this house, the other two houses that Chasseur burned down, represent proxies for . . . some . . . power. When Chasseur destroyed them, it decreased their influence and gave the power he serves greater influence."

Agnes removed the infuser, carefully added two lumps of sugar, and poured a stream of cream from a small porcelain pitcher. She stirred the ingredients with a thin silver spoon. "The town's name is Four Houses, dear," Agnes said. "Chasseur's is the fourth house."

"If you know all this—" Ava began.

"I know nothing," Agnes interrupted. "I suspect, I feel, I intuit, I deduce, but I don't know if any of what I just told you is true. It's simply what feels right, true, to me, Ava."

"Okay, it sounds like a pretty good guess to me," Ava said. "Why won't you help me get my friends away from the pervy fucking Scodes and this Chasseur asshole? I saw you the other night shooting those shadows. You are badass, Agnes! You used to be a spy. I can't do it by myself. I need your help. Please, Agnes!"

Agnes frowned and sipped her tea. "I used to work for Her Majesty's Government," she said, and then paused. "It still is *Her* Majesty's Government, correct? That big-eared ponce isn't in charge now, is he?"

Ava grinned. "No, no, he's not."

"Good," she said. "As I was saying, I did a job—at first it was during the war, and then later it was because I loved my work. I'm no—oh, what's his name, Sylvester Schwarzenegger? I'm an old lady."

"You saved me," Ava said. "I just want to help them."

"If he has them, I don't think you can, dear," Agnes said, looking down into her tea. "I'm sorry."

"Bullshit," Ava said, standing. "You're not sorry, you're scared. I don't get it. You weren't scared the other night when those things were coming out of the dark straight at you. You shot them as calm as if you were baking cookies. You're avoiding telling me why you won't help me, and you're ashamed of it, too. I can see—I'm not a fucking infant."

"At present, your language would tend to refute that statement," Agnes said, a cold, hard edge slipping into her voice as she looked up at Ava.

"Fine!" Ava said. I'll do it my fucking self! I'm going to go to those houses and see if you're right, see if there is some kind of power there; maybe it has the guts to help me save them." She grabbed her satchel off the back of the kitchen chair. "And, if not, then fuck it. I'm going to get Cole and Lexi, and if the Scodes or Chasseur or anyone else gets in my way I'm going to blow their sick, fucking heads off!" She removed the small gun Agnes had given her and examined it. "You want this back?" Agnes shook her head. Ava fumbled to open the cylinder. "And then I'm figuring out a way to get out of this fucking fishbowl of a town, since no one else here seems to give a fuck about being stuck here!" She examined the five rounds. Three of them had a red ring on them, and Ava recalled that Agnes had told her they were the fire-and-light-producing tracer bullets. She honestly had no idea what she was doing, but in the movies and on TV you always checked your gun like this before you went into the deep shit.

"Thanks for everything," Ava said.

"Don't," Agnes said. "This is not goodbye. I will expect you home before dark, young lady. Good luck, dear." Ava looked at her hard, the anger vibrating in her eyes, and Agnes had to look back at her tea.

Upstairs, Dennis was coughing, a dry, rasping sound. Agnes stood to attend to him. Ava strode out of the kitchen toward the front door. "Ava!" Agnes called after her, even as she was opening the front door. "Go to the house on this side of the road. Go there. I think you need to." The only response was the slam of the front door. "I'm sorry," Agnes said to the empty foyer as she began to ascend the stairs to see to Dennis and his unrelenting cough. "Damn it all to hell."

. . .

Ava headed north, up the two-lane. Her anger began to fade a little. Agnes was taking care of her very sick husband, and she didn't want to leave him. Ava had clung pretty tight to the old woman in the few days since Agnes had rescued her. Ava and her mother had a brittle relationship at best. They could talk about reality TV shows and singing-and-dancing celebrity shows. They could talk shoes and clothing. Beyond that, they hadn't had a meaningful conversation about anything real in more than ten years. They playacted in public and at family events to present the "perfect mother-daughter combo," but it was all hollow bullshit—an accessory for both of them to coordinate along with the event and the color of their eye shadow. In a few days' time, Agnes had given her more attention and seemed more interested in her—in *her*—than her mother ever had. Maybe this wasn't about Agnes being the one who was afraid.

"Shit," Ava muttered to herself.

A half mile up, on the other side of the road, Ava saw one of the dilapidated mansions. It sat back from the road and was surrounded by a moat of a yard, filled with overgrown grass and weeds. A chain-link fence bearing a large No Trespassing sign circled the front yard. A wide, long gravel drive stretched from a gate on the fence, next to the house, sloping down and ending at the edge of the two-lane. The house's façade was blackened from fire and festering with ragged holes from ages of neglect and decay.

Ava paused across the road and looked at the house. She imagined a well in the dark, silent basement—she could almost feel the cool stone, the crumbling mortar. Something chewed at her gut. It wasn't just Agnes's suggestion as Ava had walked out the door. In fact, Ava had planned to come to this house specifically because Agnes had suggested the other one farther up the road. But now her instincts, her gut, was telling her it wasn't for her—to move on, not to cross the road. Was it fear? What was happening in her? After a few moments of staring at the wooden corpse from across the road, Ava began walking again, headed toward the other house.

It took her another fifteen minutes of walking to reach the driveway of the other blackened, crumbling house. It was little more than a charred skeleton of rotting wood. Like the last time she had approached it, when she had been walking to Buddy's Roadhouse, Ava felt a pull to walk up the cobblestoned drive. Before, she had seen a man standing in the shadow of the tree line beyond the house, had felt eyes following her; this time she sensed no such presence, didn't see the man in the woods with the eyes that burned like cobalt. She reached the end of the drive at the top of the hill and cautiously crossed the main threshold, which no longer held a door. The sensation of remembrance, of homecoming and safety, filled her strongly, like the effects of a drug suddenly crashing down on you. The feelings had flirted with her when she last visited these ruins, but crossing the entry arch had somehow crystallized them in her.

The spring wind whipped and snapped off the hill, wandering brazenly through the collapsing walls and blackened timbers, making some loose tar paper and stripped Sheetrock covering shudder and snap. Ava found a room that may once have been a grand ballroom or dining hall. The wood floor was warped from rain and cold. Shafts of sun fell through the ragged roof, creating a silent forest of light and shadows. Ava walked slowly through the room, her hand in the pocket of her jean jacket, cradling the smooth metal of the gun, making sure each shadow was chained to an object. She turned a corner and found a cellar door resting at an angle on a single rusted hinge. She jerked on the handle of the door and the door made a sharp, snapping sound, tore free of the hinge, and crashed into a pile of rotten, splintered wood. Ava jumped back and nearly drew her gun. There was enough daylight for her to see the upper portion of the wooden stairs descending into pitch black. She wished she had a flashlight, but she didn't. She put her reading glasses in her satchel and pulled out a white Bic lighter. Ava snapped it on and cautiously took her first step on the creaky old stairs. The first one held her weight, and she carefully stepped onto the next one, the feeble flame of the lighter bouncing and shuddering with each step into the darkness.

"Hello?" Ava said, her voice cracking a little from fear as she took another step down. "Agnes sent me. She said you might be able to help me. . . . I feel stupid as fuck talking to an empty basement." She paused on the fourth step; there was a creaking sound below her. For a heart-stilling instant, she thought it was movement below in response to her calling out. She realized what it really was a second too late to do anything about it.

The lower half of the staircase to the basement disintegrated, cracking and splintering as it collapsed. Ava fell. She had time to squeak in fear and surprise before she hit the floor, hard. There was a hammer blow of pain and pressure on the back of her head and a brilliant nova of white light behind her eyes. The dark basement was nothing compared with the blackness inside her head as it swallowed her.

. . .

At some point, she became aware again, but she couldn't move. There was stuff on top of her, and she was cold and her head hurt. That was her last thought for a while, then she was back again. She focused on the white Bic lying in front of her face. She watched it for a time and then went away for a little while. She couldn't tell how long. She slowly began to try to get up. She pushed the boards and rotted wood off her. There was some light in the basement. It came from a few narrow, filthy windows high on the basement walls near the weed-choked lawn. Each window was only a few feet wide and long. They were covered in a greasy film of dust, grime, and cobwebs.

"Thanks for the help," she mumbled to the basement as she began to sit up. Nothing seemed broken, but plenty was sore and a few things stung, as if they had been cut or scratched. Her head hurt, but she didn't think it was serious. Alana could have told her, if Alana were still alive. She had dropped about five feet when the stairs caved in. She had gotten lucky; she laughed as the thought crossed her mind. She struggled to stand, groaning. The light outside was dimmer than it had been, even through the filth on the windows. It was late in the day, and the shadows were growing longer. Soon they would swallow the light. *I must have been out longer than I thought. Shit!*

The scent of wood smoke was strong, clawing at Ava's nose and throat. A rancid, sour smell, like greasy, rotten meat, was there, too. The smells mingled with the dust and the mold and made Ava feel as if she was coated by them.

There were shelves here, as in Agnes's basement, but these were overturned, and many had been devoured by fire, as had their contents. They were set up in rows, almost like a library or a pantry, and those that had fallen had knocked other shelves over as well, like dominoes. Ava moved between the maze of shelves and found a small cluster that hadn't fallen. She stepped between them and saw the well and the body.

The well looked exactly the same as the one in Agnes's basement, including the capstone with the symbol of a circle and two crescents. On top of the capstone was a skeleton, its back resting on top of the symbol, its yellowed skull, jaw agape, looking up at the rafters. Several ragged holes broke the pattern of the rib cage, and the sternum had been reduced to powder by the force of an impact. Old, dark stains had seeped into the capstone and the strange symbol that adorned it. Ava stepped closer, hesitant—half expecting the old bones to rise up, those hollow orbits, filled with shadow, to regard her as the figure climbed off the well and lurched toward her.

A flash of fading sunlight caught her eye, and she saw that the shelves had also hidden a basement door. The door was broken and had numerous holes in it, which were covered in scraps of patchwork wood. A few slivers of daylight were slicing through the cracks. Ava pushed against the door and felt it give a little and then hold. She could see the silver hasp of a padlock on the other side of the door through the small crack between the jamb and the door.

There was a creaking sound on the floorboards above her head—footsteps. For a second, Ava hoped it was Agnes, come to rescue her. Then she heard other footsteps follow; it was several people. She suddenly envisioned the Scode brothers finding her trapped in the basement, and dizzy panic vomited over her. The footsteps moved toward the open basement door and the demolished steps. She could hear shuffling and little sounds of movement now from the open doorway above. The pressure was building in her, a blind panic, like the night the shadow men killed Alana and Gerry—instinct kicking in, running like a terrified animal in the darkness. She moved to the basement door, picked up an old hammer handle off an intact shelf, and thought of desperately trying to pry the door open, to pop the lock's hasp, or to scream and tear at the old wood patches, to get out, get out!

Her fingers brushed the well's capstone—cool, ancient rock under her fingertips. A calm settled over her, water quenching the wildfire of fear and panic. She had felt this way the night she ran, the night she survived and met Agnes. The panic was pushed down, deep below, controlled. Ava knew—she knew, as she knew how to breathe—what she had to do to survive and to triumph. Some distant part of her, half remembered from a childhood dream, knew as well.

She took the hammer handle, chucked up on it like a baseball bat, and knelt low near the lip of the well. Her eyes locked with those of the skeleton on the well, and in that instant Ava felt a strange and unexplained kinship with the dead woman. She didn't even know how she knew, but she was certain this had been a woman.

There was the wooden moan of the damaged stairwell, and then the soft thud of feet hitting the basement floor—again, again, again. There were five of them. The daylight was bleeding out of the room, but there was still enough for Ava to make them out as she slipped her glasses back on.

They were children, all wearing baggy jeans, high-top sneakers, and hoodies, concealing their faces in shadow. They made Ava think of monks. There were two girls and three boys. The children weren't talking, but Ava thought she heard an odd sound passing among them—like dead winter leaves, blowing. Some hardwired instinct told her not to stand up or say hello. These weren't kids, not innocent children. They were ... wrong ... dangerous. She held the hammer handle tighter, her knuckles whitening.

One of the children was being held up by two of the others. He appeared to be in great discomfort, doubling over, wincing in pain, and making very human sounds of distress. That was when Ava saw their eyes, and she knew that her gut reaction had saved her life. Dark, lifeless pools of midnight peering out of innocent faces—reptile eyes, shark eyes. The child-creature screamed in pain, showing rows of needle teeth. It was a human voice, though, and deeper than Ava expected. All these kids looked to be in their early to mid teens. The one hurting seemed to be the oldest—maybe sixteen, seventeen. He screamed again and clutched his stomach with both hands, falling to his knees. The other children stepped back a few paces and formed a ring around him. The boy writhed and made a lot of noise. Whatever was happening to him, it was getting worse.

Ava's attention was locked on the spectacle happening in the last dingy motes of light her eyes could clutch. She felt a cool hand slip over her mouth and a presence slide up beside her. She screamed, but the hand was tight; it allowed for nothing to escape. She looked over and saw Agnes's disapproving scowl. The old woman's eyes demanded silence. Agnes nodded in the direction of the basement door, and Ava saw that it was partly open now, the outside lock gone.

The child howled again, and both women looked. He was on his hands and knees, convulsing. There was a sound like stitches being ripped from fabric, and the boy's body began to jerk. The back of the hoodie split cleanly and fell away. The boy's back was pale and waxy; his hair was the color of sand. There was another sick, tearing sound, like meat being pulled from a bone. A slit tore in the boy's back, along his spine. The boy stopped screaming; he crouched there, mindless, shuddering, mute. He seemed almost to sag. Inky, black fingers wriggled up out of the slit and clutched each side. They pulled, and the boy's body seemed to slip away as effortlessly as the fabric of his clothing. A featureless head appeared through the widening slit. The skin wrinkled and sloughed off, and a being made entirely of shadow crouched in the puddle of smoking, evaporating skin, born in the instant the sun died. The shadow person stood, and the four Black-Eyed Children bowed their heads.

Agnes grabbed Ava, pulling her up. The girl was shuddering in terror, and, truth be told, so was Agnes. They moved toward the door, only a few feet to go. All of Agnes's training was humming inside her. It had been a long time, but nothing helped you recall old skills like the chemical anthem of "fight or flight" thudding in your blood. Ava was moving, but shuffling—she was numb, clumsy with fear at what she had just seen. They were at the door, and Agnes was slowly, carefully opening it. There was a random sound, a small sound, but it was enough. The shadow person and the Black-Eyed Kids all turned and saw the two women in one horrible, frozen instant of a nightmare. Ava almost peed herself, but instead brandished the hammer handle. Agnes pushed her through the basement door as she raised her Mauser and began to fire at the hissing BEKs, who were already launching themselves toward her, bouncing off overturned shelves as they bounded forward.

"Run, dear," Agnes said calmly, as her bullets exploded in two of the small fanged creatures. They screamed and fell with ragged, burning holes in their chests. The newborn shadow person strode toward her silently. She could hear Ava running up the crumbling concrete steps outside the basement door. She closed the door and began to run back up the stairs, her legs already weak and trembling from the exertion; once, she could have run all night, but no more. Night had fallen, and they were very far from home. Far from Dennis, alone in his bed, helpless, dead if anything happened to her.

"Oh shit!" she heard Ava say behind her. "Shit!"

The shadow person slid through the narrow gap in the basement door. Agnes fired as she reached the top of the stairs. The shadow person hissed as the tracer bullets hit it and turned it to smoke. Agnes spun to see what had Ava so panicked, fearing that she already knew. She was right. The backyard of the manor was full of shadow people standing silent and still—dozens of them. More were dislodging themselves from the branches and trees of the forest that was encroaching on the edge of the manor grounds.

"Ava, dear, language," Agnes said, even as she did the math. She didn't have enough bullets, certainly not enough time to reload. "Run, run for the road, run for the house. Care for Dennis." Agnes started firing, dropping a shadow with each bullet, making each round count. Her breath was deep and even, and she controlled it as she squeezed each shot, just as old Wild Bill Donovan had taught her so long ago. She might be able to buy the girl time, time enough to live. Another shot, another shadow flaring, churning into smoke. She felt a hand on her shoulder. A hiss and a sulfur sting, like a match, bit her nose. Brilliant red light pushed back against the darkness.

"Bullshit!" Ava screamed, swinging the road flare that she had transferred from Alana's bloody bag to her own at the swarm of shadows closing in on them. The creatures backed away from the light, silently. "You can take care of Dennis. You run, old lady, run your ass off! Come on!"

Agnes couldn't help smiling. She ran, headed down the drive toward the road, firing behind her as she did. They stumbled, almost tripping and falling on the slippery cobblestones choked with weeds. If one got close to them or tried to flank them, Ava swatted at it with the flare. She hit several and saw them melt into black smoke. They reached the pavement of the two-lane and started to run. Agnes tried to reload as she bounced along the hard road, her knees and ankles screaming in painful protest. Her lungs were starting to burn. Ava, in her athletic shoes and with her youthful legs, could have been halfway up the road by now. She wasn't; she stayed right beside Agnes, dropping back to hold the line and give her a few extra feet to run. The young girl seemed angry, furious. The fear was gone, replaced now by something stronger.

"Come on, you bastards!" Ava screamed. "Come on! You're not getting anyone tonight. You hear me, you fuckers—no one!" Agnes fired the pistol again and again and destroyed a few more. She was almost out of bullets. They ran down the center of the two-lane, pursued by dozens of silent shadows, more spilling out from the darkness on either side of the road. It was like being chased by the night itself.

"I can't keep running," Agnes gasped, and fired again. Ava wondered how many of the castaway citizens of Four Houses were hearing the gunfire, the screams? How many were witnessing her and Agnes's last stand on the two-lane from the safety of their bright homes, behind curtains?

"Help!" Ava screamed. "Somebody help us, please!"

The night was silent.

Agnes fell. A slight gasp escaped her lips as she scraped her hands and knees on the asphalt. Ava knelt beside her, waving the flare as the shadow people swarmed toward them. Ava picked up the Mauser. She had never fired a gun in her life. Agnes gripped the young girl's arm with her bloody hand and squeezed gently. "It has been an honor," the old woman said. Ava nodded and stood beside the old woman, flare in one hand, pistol in the other. The shadows were legion.

There was a rumble, far off down the highway, echoing. Brilliant twin halogen stars of blue-white light came into view; it was headlights! The car was upon them in seconds—it must have been going over a hundred miles an hour. The high beams ripped through the army of shadow people, turning them to black steam and scattering the few that managed to avoid the accursed light. The car screeched to a stop only yards from Ava and Agnes, pinning them in the headlights. The engine rumbled like an angry steel god of thunder. The driver's door opened, and both women squinted to make out their rescuer past the wall of light.

"You two need a lift?" Lovina Marcou asked.

EIGHTEEN  **"10-20"**

Cecil Dann, FBI special agent in charge, stepped into an interrogation room in the Atlanta Police Department. Jimmie Aussapile was alone in the room, deprived of his baseball cap, his belt, and even his chaw. An empty Styrofoam cup sat in front of the trucker, and he was sitting back in his chair, napping. When the door opened, Jimmie yawned and sat up.

"Took your sweet time," Jimmie said.

Dann took the chair across from Jimmie and sat down. "You're lucky I came at all," he said. "You and your friends are in a hell of a lot of trouble—suspicion of murder, possibly kidnapping, firing on police officers, high-speed chases, reckless endangerment on the highway. You just bring a shit-storm around with you wherever you go, don't you, Aussapile?"

"How soon they forget," Jimmie said. "I handed you the Marquis a week ago, remember, Cecil? I'm trying to stop another one, and I need your help."

"It's not your job to stop them," Dann said. "Your job is to deliver produce, or batteries, or Tampax. Your job is to drive a truck. You're not a cop, Aussapile."

"We do what the cops can't do, what the FBI and the CIA and the NSA and everyone else who thinks they're such a BFD can't," Jimmie said.

"And again with the 'we,'" Dann said. "I'm tired of you jerking me around. Who is 'we'? Who hacks the Justice Department's systems and leaves no trace? Who can access my secure, encrypted phone? Who knows the things you people know? Who *are* you?"

"The good guys," Jimmie said. "And we need your help, because you're a good guy, too, Cecil. It's really that simple."

"Nothing is that simple," Dann said. "Anyone who thinks it is isn't just a fool but, in this kind of work, they're a dangerous fool. I'm done getting stuck with the check for you ass clowns." Dann stood and walked to the door.

"The Pagan," Jimmie said. Dann paused, his hand on the knob. He released it and turned.

"Ancient history," Dann said.

"You never caught him," Jimmie said. "He's still out there, making you guys look like ass clowns every time he kills another victim."

Dann sat down again. "The Pagan is dead or wearing a diaper somewhere in a nursing home. He's got fans who study the cases on the Investigation Discovery Channel and read the paperbacks, and a few of them are batshit enough to go copycat."

"He's one man," Jimmie said. "He doesn't age normally, and we were damn close to catching him. I need your help to stop him. Please."

The trucker and the federal agent stared at each other for a long time. Finally, Dann stood again and walked out the door. On the other side of the door was a door off from the hall. Dann knocked on it and stepped inside. The room smelled of cigarette smoke, had an old, worn couch and a few metal folding chairs. There was a desk, and above the desk was the two-way window on the other side of the mirror in Jimmie's interrogation room. A speaker hung on the wall above the window. A tall, muscular man with a shaved head and a goatee leaned against the table, his back to Jimmie. The lanyard around his neck held his Atlanta PD detective's badge and credentials identifying him as Captain Lewis Keegan. "Well, that was worth the plane trip down from DC, huh?" Keegan said to Dann, who smiled and shut the door. "I have to say, I'm surprised you came down at all, Agent Dann."

"Aussapile and I have a brief but colorful history," Dann said, nodding toward the trucker, who had gone back to sleep in his chair. "Have you got the phone call yet?"

"What phone call?" Keegan asked.

"The one from a superior, or someone way, way, way up the food chain that instructs you to drop the charges and let them go, no questions asked."

"You kidding me, right?" Keegan said, crossing his arms. "That punk Sinclair that's with Aussapile—he opened fire with a goddamned machine gun on a street full of Atlanta PD. Then wrecked about a half-dozen cars in a high-speed pursuit. There is no way in hell they're going anywhere but to arraignment and then, most likely, remanded until trial."

Dann sighed and sat down on the ratty couch. It was the source of the cigarette-smoke smell, and reeked vaguely of old farts. He imagined this was a crash room for detectives who couldn't head home yet because they were on a hot forty-eight-hour run to close a homicide, waiting to interrogate a suspect who was being processed downstairs, or waiting on the lab or the crime-scene guys for some tiny crumb that would allow them to close a case. This nasty couch was probably the next best thing to heaven if you were that beat. It was lumpy but soft. He groaned a little as he settled into it.

"When I met Jimmie Aussapile, I thought he was the Natchez Trace Parkway Killer. I was wrong. He helped the bureau and the Mississippi State Police close that case, though. I was going to hang him out to dry for being some kind of vigilante, but then I got the call, and I let him go. A few years later, I ran into him again, sitting in a holding cell after getting mixed up with a series of murders in New Mexico. Victims were being found off Route 375 in the Franklin Mountains State Park, mostly men. Aussapile said it wasn't a serial killer, at least not a mortal one. Said it was something called a Cegua, some kind of Mexican monster that ambushes travelers on lonely back roads—has the body of a woman and the head of a horse's skull."

Keegan laughed. "You're shitting me, right?"

Dann's face was placid. He gave a small smile, as if remembering a private joke, and shrugged. "I know, I know, but the murders stopped. The National Parks guys and the local PD were going to hoist Aussapile up by his balls—"

"But then they got this mythical phone call," Keegan interrupted, a grin on his broad face. "Maybe it was from some guy with the body of a dolphin and the face of a horse's ass." The detective laughed.

Dann mustered a chuckle. "I know how it sounds," he said. "But every time I hear the name Jimmie Aussapile a very weird murder case related to my task force gets closed shortly thereafter. And that makes it worth a trip out here."

There was a knock at the door. Another, younger detective in a sweat-stained button-down and shoulder holster poked his head inside the room. "Cap, you got a call on line three." The detective's head slid from view and the door shut. Keegan's face dropped, while Dann's remained as serene as the Buddha's.

Twenty minutes later, Dann walked back into the interrogation room. "You and your two friends are being cut loose," he said. "Your luck holds for another day, cowboy. You knew that was going to happen, so why did you really ask for me down here?"

"I was serious about the Pagan," Jimmie said. "I'm going to find him and bring him down. I need help. I need to know what you know about him."

"Why not just have your hacker buddies plunder our network again?" Dann asked as he sat down.

Jimmie shook his head. "Believe it or not, there are channels I have to go through, too," he said. "And, just like any other organization, we don't always play so nice with one another. That kind of hack requires more juice and more time than I got. That's why I asked you to come— because I know that, to you, saving lives is more than just an equation on some damned spreadsheet."

"Saving lives?" Cecil said, leaning forward. "Whose lives?"

"We got put onto the Pagan by that dead man you found in that hotel room—Mark Stolar," Jimmie said. "He was a kidnap victim from Louisiana, along with his journalist buddy, Dewey Rears. The Pagan killed Rears, sacrificed him. He still has two college students from Kansas, and he plans to kill them next. Not to mention a hell of a good state cop from Louisiana that's gone missing, too, chasing the son of a bitch."

"The Pagan has been sacrificing his victims since he first got on the bureau's radar in the fifties," Dann said. "Always near highways, always on traditional Wiccan holidays. He always leaves a mark carved on them somewhere, the same mark. That detail has been kept out of the press for over fifty years. We tried to keep the sacrificial angle out, too, but it got leaked in the late seventies."

"So no copycat would know about the symbol," Jimmie said, leaning across the table, his voice low, "but the symbol kept popping up, didn't it, Cecil? For over fifty years?"

Dann nodded. "Yes, it did. But the logical answer is the symbol got leaked. Damned if we've ever been able to confirm that, though. Cops hate weird shit, Jimmie. They like things that have boxes to check on a report form. The Pagan has been a boil on the butt of the bureau and a lot of other law-enforcement agencies for decades. It's high weirdness."

"Can you show me the symbol?" Jimmie asked. Dann sighed and slipped a small notebook and a pen from his jacket pocket. He drew the mark and slid it across to the trucker. It was circle with a crescent above it, barely touching the circle—points out. It was the same symbol Lovina had told him and Heck about on the road to Memphis—the same symbol found on the website where Karen Collie, Shawn Ruth Thibodeaux, and their friends had seen the video of the strange rite in the woods, the shadowy man with antlers.

"Our cryptography unit out at Langley," Dann said, "says that the symbol is pagan, that it represents—"

"The Horned Man," Jimmie interrupted.

"Yeah," Dann said, looking up from the piece of paper to the trucker's face. "The embodiment of the masculine aspects of nature. Yeah."

"Cecil, did the Pagan ever kill anyone in Kansas?" Jimmie asked. "Maybe in or near a place called Four Houses, Kansas?"

"Never heard of it," Dann said, as he tapped his smartphone and accessed the Justice Department's database. "Here we go . . . one victim authenticated—his first discovered, in fact. June May Hollinger, nineteen. Her remains were found by a highway-construction crew near Lebanon, Kansas, on May 3, 1957. Her body had been covered with soil, and the police were certain the killer expected her to be found, since the crews working on U.S. 281 were headed right to where the body was dumped. She was the first one to bear the Horned Man's mark. Historically and chronologically, the Pagan's first victim."

"And his only one in Kansas," Jimmie said. "Thank you, Cecil. I owe you big."

"You owe me an answer," Dann said, putting away his phone. "Why are you and this . . . whatever the hell it is you work for, contacting me? You know, sooner or later someone's going to insist that I bring you in, bring you down. And I'll have to, Jimmie, I'll have to."

"I understand," Jimmie said, standing. "Maybe that's when you'll get your answer. I need a few more things from you, Cecil, and I'm sorry to ask, but I got no one else."

Dann sighed. "Go ahead," he said.

"I need you to check out George Norse, the broadcaster," Jimmie said.

"You mean the guy who does *Paranormal America Live*—the TV show? My wife loves that shit," Dann said.

"Yeah," Jimmie said. "Mine, too. He's here in Atlanta. The Pagan made Stolar act as a courier for him before he killed him. Stolar gave Norse something from the Pagan, something the asshole wanted Norse to have. Can you find out what it was?"

"Sure," Dann said. "Done. Might even get the wife an autograph in the process."

"And if anything goes bad," Jimmie said, "I'd appreciate it if you could tell my wife and little girl—"

"Stop that, right now," Dann said. "You are staying alive until I get my answers, Aussapile, so shut your piehole. Now, get going."

. . .

Jimmie's truck sped down I-75, headed out of Atlanta. It was sixteen hours to Lebanon. Heck's motorcycle was strapped and chained to the back of the cab, and the biker and Max were riding along with him. Max was in the passenger seat, while Heck sat behind and between them on a foldable bench seat, eating a bag of chips. Skynyrd's "Simple Man" was playing softly on the cab's sound system.

"Jail was nothing like I expected it to be," Max said, almost cheerfully, as she typed on her tablet. "It was so . . . clean, and the officers were so . . . polite." Jimmie and Heck traded glances but said nothing. "Well, if the gang at the Wednesday Night Bookclub and Whovian Appreciation

Society could see me now—booked, fingerprinted! I'm an ex-con now, right? I've been on the inside."

"We're just lucky she didn't get a jailhouse tattoo," Heck said. "So, tell me where the hell we're going, and how does it help us find Lovina and the incredible disappearing dirtbag?"

"Max, did you find anything on Four Houses?" Jimmie asked.

"Nothing definite," the professor said, scanning the page on her tablet. "Some historical references, indicating a frontier trading post and fort, but, historically, it seems not to be anywhere near where we're going. It also says the place was abandoned after only a few years."

"So Karen Collie and Mark Stolar are both talking about a place that's not real," Jimmie said. "A place on no maps—that exists and doesn't exist. That sound familiar to you at all, Max?"

Max paled a little and looked up from the tablet. "Metropolis-Utopia," she said softly.

Jimmie nodded. "Yep," he said. "And that makes me think we're dealing with viamancy."

"Agreed," Max said, "which is fortuitous, because I've been developing some theories about that very subje—"

"Okay," Heck said, waving a hand and cutting Max off. "What the hell are you guys talking about? I can follow about every third word of this. Me caveman, okay? Does all this shit have to do with Lovina and Captain Puckernut vanishing into thin air?"

"Yes," Jimmie and Max said together.

"Good," Heck said. "Now, with very small words, spoken very slowly, talk to the caveman."

"The best we can figure," Jimmie said, "the Pagan used viamancy to cut out. Then it looks like Lovina used it, too, to follow him."

"Viamancy?" Heck asked crumpling his empty chip bag.

"Viamancy involves the bending of space and the altering of perception," Max said. "In relation to the Road."

"You probably heard it called 'road magic,' Heck," Jimmie said. "Folks who got the knack for it are usually called road witches."

"Oh yeah, shit, I heard of that," Heck said. "Witches supposed to be able to make a short ride go on forever, or you blink and you're there. Stretch a gallon of gas to cross a desert, or make a full tank go empty in the middle of nowhere. Hell, I heard a witch can make you fall asleep driving or keep you going longer than a bottle of yellow jackets."

Jimmie nodded, looking out into the sunset, the sky smeared with ocher, crimson, and saffron. "Some folks got the gift," he said. "They can listen to the Road and whisper back to it. I think Karen Collie had a touch of it. Apparently, Lovina does, too. But viamancy takes a toll on most who practice it. They go kind of crazy."

"Crazy?" Heck said.

"Most of them end up disappearing," Jimmie said. "One day they just . . . aren't there anymore."

"They end up in the city, the city of the viamancers," Max said. "The city that is everywhere and nowhere. According to the myths, it's the city you see whenever you're bending space—working road magic, if you will."

"The city of the mad," Jimmie said. "The city at the center of everything. Metropolis-Utopia."

"And you think this Four Houses is like this city of whack jobs," Heck said. "Not really there."

"Yeah," Jimmie said. "Unfortunately."

The road slid under them, and they glided through the early-evening traffic. They were all silent for a long time. They were nearing Nashville. Max was napping, and when Jimmie looked back Heck looked as if he'd conked out as well. Jimmie heard the opening to the Clapton song playing on his cell and tapped the answer button. It was Layla.

"Hi, baby," he said softly. "How is everybody?"

"We're okay," Layla said. "You sound worn out, baby. You headed to the job?"

"No, baby," Jimmie said with a sigh. "I'm still on that other thing."

"Oh," she said.

"What," Jimmie said. "What's going on, baby?"

"It's nothing, honey," Layla said. "How are you and Heck—"

"Layla, tell me," Jimmie said. There was a long pause on the line. The highway filled the emptiness with the noises of motion and velocity.

"We got a call from the mortgage folks," she said. "It's no big deal, baby. They do it all the time when we're a little late."

"Shit!" Jimmie said. "Shit, shit, shit! I forgot, baby—"

"It's okay, honey," Layla said. "It's not like you ain't got other things on your mind. I talked to them, and it's okay. We'll make do, baby. We always do, don't we?" He could hear her smile in her voice, but he could hear the thin quaver of stress there as well.

"I'm sorry, baby. I'll take care of it, I'll get it paid. I promise." In his mind, he was doing the math—he was already late to pick up the load, make the run, pay the mortgage. He also figured those college kids had maybe a day left to live, if they weren't already dead. Whatever this Pagan guy was up to had something to do with screwing up the universe—the whole damned universe. That all seemed abstract, vague, and pale compared with the mundane clarity of a collection call or a pink envelope in the mailbox labeled "URGENT NOTICE."

"The baby's squirming," she said. "He hears his daddy."

"Tell him I'm on my way and that I'm making sure he's got a house to come home to."

"He knows, baby," Layla said. "Please stay focused and stay alive, Jimmie. We can get through anything, as long as we're together, honey. I love you."

"I love you, too," he said. "I'm damned lucky to have a woman like you."

"Yes," she said, laughing, "you are. I'm proud of you, baby. Be careful. Bye."

"Bye, baby." Jimmie hung up the phone.

"Power bill or rent?" It was Heck's voice quiet behind him.

"Mortgage," Jimmie said.

"That sucks," he said. "You got a run to pay for it?"

"Yeah," Jimmie said. "But I'm about to fuck that up, running around chasing damned teleporting serial killers and Black-Eyed Kids."

"You could just say, 'Hell with it,'" Heck said. "Not your problem, man."

Jimmie glanced over his shoulder for a second. "It is my problem. I caught this, and it's mine to see through. And if you don't understand that, slick, then I'm going to tell you right now, you won't hack it with the Brethren."

"It more important than your kids, than your old lady?" Heck asked.

"No," Jimmie said. "Not exactly. Look, you were in the Corps, right?"

"Yeah," Heck said. For a horrible eternity of a second, the laughing fire was in Heck's mind, burning his screaming friends. It was what he always remembered first whenever he thought about being over there.

"We had a job to do," Jimmie said. "It was to protect our own, our families. We did it for them. This is like that, but even more so. How many lives has the Pagan ruined, ended? How many families has he destroyed? There are two kids out there right now, scared and wondering if they're ever going to see home again. What if it was my little girl? My son? I'm supposed to go home, plop my fat ass down on the couch? Drink a few beers, watch TV? Pagan's my responsibility now. I have to see this through."

"I was so focused on doing the job, getting it done, I missed Ale dying," Heck said. "I regret that. I fucking regret it a lot. He was the closest thing I ever got to a dad, and he's gone. There were things I wish I had said, had the chance to say, even if I punked out and didn't. Family's important, all I'm saying. It's the first duty."

Jimmie didn't say anything for a few miles. He seemed distracted, maybe even a little shaken. "The last time I talked to Ale he was damned proud of you," he finally said. "He understood. He may not have been your flesh-and-blood dad, but he damned well thought he was, Hector."

"Thanks," Heck said. He cleared his throat. "Okay, man. Well, I'm with you, come what may. You guys can crash at my house . . . well, my mom's house. But she won't mind, she digs on babies—unless, of course, they're me."

Jimmie laughed. "You might regret that invite."

Heck looked over at Max, curled up with her arms wrapped about her legs, her eyes closed. "She's turned out to be a damned sight tougher than she looks, hasn't she?"

"Yeah," Jimmie said. "Tough enough. Saved our asses back at that hotel."

"So where we headed, chief?" Heck asked. "Four Houses? The town that isn't a town?"

"Yep," Jimmie said. "If our professor's theory she keeps jawing about has any traction."

"It does," Max said, her eyes still closed. A grin slowly spread across her face, and she yawned. "I'm going to prove it, too. And you're welcome. I've never saved anyone's . . . um, ass, before. This has been a day of firsts."

"Playing possum? Jimmie asked.

Max smiled, rubbing her eyes. "Only for a little while," she said. "Didn't want to interfere with your male-bonding moment."

"Fess up?" Jimmie said. "What, exactly, have you been working on, Doc?"

Max sat up, crossed her legs, and hugged her knees. "We're going to get to Four Houses the same way Lovina and the Master of the Hunt did—by viamancy, by bending space."

"You're suddenly a road witch?" Jimmie said.

"No," Max said. "Viamancers tap into a system of power, and I think I've decoded that system—hacked it, if you will."

"The only people I've ever heard of doing road magic were road witches," Jimmie said.

"Well, have you ever wondered how they do what they do?" Max asked, as she slid her tablet out of her satchel. "I'm going to try to explain it," she said. "Please try to keep an open mind. My colleagues in the order have been less than unbiased about my research and my hypothesis. It's very disheartening to see scholars with such narrow minds."

"After the last few days, my mind is as open as a drunk's fly," Heck said, smiling. "Lay it on me, Doc."

"Go on, Max," Jimmie said. "How do the road witches do what they do?"

"Magic," Max began. "Real magic—not Penn and Teller stuff—"

"Actually," Jimmie said, interrupting, "I hear tell those fellas are the real deal. There was this deck of cards that stole souls over in Reno and—"

"Okay, okay," Max said. "How about the Chris Angel stuff, then?

Jimmie nodded, "Sounds about right—damned mind freak . . ."

"Anyway," Max continued, "real magic requires enormous amounts of energy, power. To bend space, in physics, requires the harnessing of suns—what they call total conversion power. In magic, it would require a harnessing of a significant amount of the earth's manasphere. Back in the hotel, Mark Stolar mentioned that his friend Dewey Rears had been looking into a connection between the U.S. highway system and *long xian—*"

"Max," Heck said, jamming a thumb toward his chest, "caveman, remember? Grunt."

"Right, right," Max said, nodding and waving her hand in front of her face, as if batting invisible cobwebs. "Grunt, of course. *Long xian* is Chinese for 'dragon lines,' or, as they're called in the West, 'ley lines'—powerful lines of magical energy that run through the earth—the lifeblood of the planet. The fact that Rears had connected ley-line energy to the highway system and to the Pagan's murders made a great deal of my theory fit, made it all click into place. The Federal-Aid Highway Act of 1956 was the genesis of the modern interstate-highway system. It spawned over forty-two thousand miles of highways and routes that completely cover America today.

"What I've been studying for several years now, and what the data Lovina gave me from Mr. Rears's computer seems to confirm," she said, holding up a small USB drive, "is that America's highways were planned and built to tap the energy of the earth's ley lines—its magical power—and redirect that almost limitless power the way dams control the flow of water."

"So the highways are magical rivers," Heck said, an evil light twinkling in his eyes. "Has anyone told the folks in Jersey yet, because I'm pretty sure they got screwed in this deal."

Max narrowed her eyes behind her glasses, "Open mind, caveman. You promised."

"Max," Jimmie said, rubbing his chin. "You have to admit that seems a little far-fetched. Don't you think someone would have made this connection before now? You Builders research everything, after all, and us Brethren are out here on the Road constantly." He downshifted the semi, gliding between traffic. "It just seems someone would have noticed."

"You actually just made part of my point for me, Jimmie," Max said. "I think everyone has noticed, but they just didn't see. You and the other Brethren are out here all the time—on the Road. You've all wondered, like everyone who has to deal with entities like the Master of the Hunt, for example, why—why does the highway attract these supernatural forces, these unstable and dangerous personalities? Why? The energies that the Road is conducting are the answer. They're drawn to it, like a light in the darkness, and the amount of the energies, the confluence of them, allows them to slip over into our world, close to the source, close to the Road."

"Son of a bitch," Heck said, looking to Jimmie. "That makes pretty good sense, Jimmie."

Jimmie nodded, "Yeah, it does—better than any of the other theories I've heard over the years, but forgive me if I withhold judgment, Doc."

"I've looked into the other theories that have popped up over the decades," Max added. She slid the USB drive stick into a port on her tablet. Her fingers were moving quickly over the screen. "Unlike my colleagues, I don't just dismiss a theory out of hand because I don't care for it."

"So your buddies got no love for this idea of yours?" Heck said.

Max nodded. "I researched the Builder archives and everything I could access from the other orders, and there's nothing. Not even a mention in passing. The Benefactors have the resources for a project like that but not the required occult architectural and geomancy know-how. The Builders have the knowledge but not the resources or the political pull. And, like I said, there is no mention of even a hint of any of this anywhere."

"I noticed you just skipped right on over the Brethren," Jimmie said. "Nobody knows the Road better than us."

Max looked up from her tablet. She had a distinct "deer in the headlights" look on her face. "Oh, oh, Jimmie—oh, no . . . I . . . didn't mean to offend the order. It's just that the Brethren . . . they just don't have that kind of, well, power."

"It's cool," Jimmie said with a thin smile. "We get that all the time. First to bleed, last to brief." Max looked back to her tablet sheepishly.

"Shit, it is like the military, isn't it?" Heck said

"Like I told you when we first met," she said, "I was very excited by the prospect of riding along with Brethren, because it gave me a chance to do more work on my research. Your order keeps so many secrets, Jimmie, from everyone."

"Gee, I wonder why?" Heck said. "Sounds like these other guys treat the Brotherhood like a bunch of garbagemen."

Max remained busily working on her tablet, her eyes down.

Jimmie laughed. "It's okay, squire," he said. "Let it go. Got to know your limitations. Well, for the record, I've never heard of any of this even as a wild truck-stop story. I don't think the Brethren are in on this conspiracy of yours, either, Max. You say Rears's research backs this up?"

"I've been trying to confirm the data Lovina got off his computer," Max said, swiping her screen with her finger. "Between running gun battles, attempts on our lives, car chases, and incarceration. It looks very promising, very promising. The majority of these Black-Eyed Kid sightings are near highways and routes that are part of the overall interstate system, part of the Road, and, interestingly enough, the Pagan's known murders also match up very well to being in the proximity of the highways."

"Lots of serial killers use the Road," Jimmie said. "Always have. Good dump sites, cuts between law-enforcement jurisdictions. That's why the killers formed the Zodiac Lodge, and the FBI set up the Highway Serial Killings Initiative—Cecil Dann's outfit."

"But the Pagan's murder sites aren't just on or near the Road," Max said, spinning the tablet around to show the two men. "They correspond exactly to the nexuses of ley lines. Those sites would have enormous supernatural power flowing through them."

"Great place for this Horned Man to do ritual sacrifices," Heck said. "Like the Masturbator of the Hunt is doing."

"Watch your mouth, squire!" Jimmie barked. "Lady present."

Heck balked, and Max smiled, looking down again. "Like the *Master* of the Hunt is doing," he corrected himself.

"You *are* twelve," Jimmie said to his squire.

Heck shrugged.

"Um, yes, yes," Max said. "Sacrifices to an entity would have enormous impact, spiritually, at those nexuses. He'd be strengthening the Horned Man, and he's apparently already weakened the Triple Goddess in some fashion. A very dangerous cosmological imbalance."

"You actually believe in all these gods, spirits, and stuff, Max?" Heck asked.

"From what I've studied," Max said, "I think the universe wears many masks for us, to help us keep from thinking we're in an empty, dark room, alone. We give those masks names and power, sometimes enough to take on a life of their own. The Wild Hunt is a very old power."

"I heard of the Wild Hunt growing up," Heck said. "I was raised by a bunch of mad Scot bikers. I know it's an old Celtic fairy tale; it's supposed to chase you, but that's about all I know."

"It's a myth from across Europe," Max said. "A spectral hunting party—huntsman and hounds. It's seen across the sky, or moving like phantoms through the forests and the roads. If you saw the Hunt, it was supposed to be a harbinger of some great disaster, either cultural or personal, for anyone seeing it."

"Sounds a little like the Black Dog," Jimmie said, eyes focused on the road, the night wrapping itself deeper around the highway, like a snake crushing and devouring its prey. "You ever hear of the Black Dog, either of you?"

Max and Heck shook their heads.

Jimmie downshifted and continued, "It's a trucker story. You're driving, usually when you're at the edge of what you can bear—tired, bone-tired. You see a huge dog, black as tar, glowing eyes, running beside your rig, keeping up with it, or it's in the road ahead of you, or on the side of the road, staring." He looked over to Max. "You see the Black Dog, it means death's courting you. Truckers who see it and keep on going, they don't keep going for long."

"Interesting, they both possess the same hound metaphor," Max said. "The same is true for the Wild Hunt. Those who saw it either disappeared or died."

"Like Karen Collie and her friends, or the kids Lovina was looking for," Jimmie said.

Max nodded.

"You think those kids saw the Wild Hunt?" Heck asked.

"They saw something," Jimmie said, "something on those Internet images Lovina chased down, something that came looking for them, and then they were gone—'gobbled up,' Karen said."

The cab was silent for many miles. They passed a wall of signs announcing routes and interstate numbers. They were coming up on I-64, and signs declared that St. Louis was ahead. Max silently mouthed the route and the interstate numbers and quickly made notes on her tablet.

"Assuming your theory is right, Max, and the Road is some kind of magic river," Jimmie said, "I want you to find out where in Kansas is the deepest pool—what did you call it, a nexus of magic?"

"I can do that," Max said. "Yes, of course."

"Good," Jimmie said. "Real good, Max. Let's go see what kind of road witch you are."

They drove on through the night. Jimmie kept his eyes locked on the road as his companions again slumbered, with the road rocking them gently. His mind was on Four Houses and overdue mortgages, the Master of the Hunt, and the baby kicking in Layla's belly. He thought of his daughter, of the kids her age who had been lost to and transformed by this force he hunted, and he focused on the two young people riding with him now—how young they both were and how much they truly didn't understand what they were driving into. Jimmie thought of his oath, and of Heck's words—"*You could just say, 'Hell with it.' Not your problem, man.*" He wished he could, he really, truly did—to have this pass over him, but it was way too late for that. Even though he didn't see it, hadn't seen it, Jimmie felt as if the Black Dog was watching him, staring with eyes full of warning and waiting death.

The Charger's headlights bounced as the muscle car drove up the bumpy, uneven stone drive of Agnes's home. The car came to a stop beside the porch, where Ava, Lexi, and Cole had made their last stand less than a week ago. The porch light was on. Lovina got out, and Ava slid out from the backseat behind her. The two younger women helped Agnes out of the passenger seat in the front. The older woman groaned as she stood and rested some of her weight on them.

"You okay?" Lovina asked, as she scanned the yard and down the drive to the main road for any more of the living darkness she had scattered when she drove into this odd little town huddled on the edge of an unnamed two-lane highway. The woman she had rescued from the shadow people told her that she was in Four Houses.

"I believe that I shall not endeavor to go for a jog again," Agnes said, groaning a little as she took the stairs. Ava helped her, while Lovina searched the night, Agnes's broom-handled Mauser in one hand and her own .40 Glock in the other.

"We may want to hurry a bit, if we can, Agnes," Lovina said. She paused behind the Dodge to unlock the trunk and get her night bag and her sack of weapons. She shouldered the bags, slammed the trunk, and picked up the Mauser again. Slowly backing up the stairs, Lovina heard Agnes fumbling with a ring of keys, then the thunk of the door locks and the front door swinging open.

"Dennis!" Agnes said. "Darling, what are you doing up?"

Lovina was on the porch now, and she glanced back from keeping watch to see a slender elderly man standing at the door. His legs were shaking. He was in pajamas and a robe. He held a large old revolver with a metal ring screwed into the base of the handle. His hands were trembling, barely holding it.

"Aggie, what are you doing out here," Dennis muttered. "What were you thinking, love? Get inside, get in, all of you. It's past curfew, and Paris is crawling with those damn Jerries. Come on!" Agnes held her husband and kissed him on the cheek. He slumped slightly against her.

"You take too many risks, my beautiful girl," Dennis muttered.

"Of course, my love, of course," she muttered into his ear. "I love you."

Lovina felt more than heard anything outside; she whipped her head around and saw a shadow person running toward the porch. "Shoot," Agnes shouted. "My gun, shoot, now!" Lovina didn't think, she reacted. The old Mauser cracked and a stream of red light hissed from the round and struck the shadow person. The creature flailed and then was devoured by the crimson light.

"Tracers," Lovina said, hurrying to the door. She handed Agnes her Mauser as they stepped inside. "Tracers kill them. Good to know."

The door was secured. Lovina looked around the sprawling but homey old house. Agnes helped Dennis back to his wheelchair and placed a blanket around him. She looked up the daunting spiral of a staircase and marveled at how he had managed to traverse it. She took the heavy breach revolver from his shaking hands and handed it to Ava. "How on earth did you find your old Webley, love?"

Dennis didn't reply, his eyes already drooping from all the exertion. Agnes turned to the two young women. "I'll put him to bed. Ava, please put on a pot and we'll have tea and talk. Now, Miss?"

"Marcou," Lovina said. "Please, just call me Lovina."

"Very well, Lovina. There is a guest room across from Ava's upstairs. You are welcome to it. She can show you where it is, and you're more than wel—"

There was a pounding at the door. All three women spun their guns in the direction of the sound, side by side, ready to fight.

"Agnes? Ava? It's Barb and Carl from Buddy's!" a woman's voice called. "Are you okay?"

"Oh, my soul," Agnes said, trying to hurry to the door and wincing in pain as she did. "Let them in, let them in!"

The door was hastily unlocked and thrown open. Carl and Barbara Kesner hurried inside, both brandishing flashlights. Their RV was parked beside the Charger. Barb hugged Agnes while Carl helped Lovina re-secure the door.

"We heard all the screaming down on the road," Carl said. "We came to help but were too late. We decided to come up and see if you two made it home. Then we saw that sweet car sitting out front and we figured we should see if you were all okay."

"We are, thanks to Lovina here," Agnes said.

"The car's mine," Lovina said, extending her hand to Carl, then Barb, to shake. "I'm Lovina Marcou. I'm a state cop from Louisiana."

Carl smiled and made an odd gesture, running his finger along the side of his face. He played it off as if he was scratching an itch, but he wasn't. The gesture seemed strangely deliberate and casual at the same time.

"Long way from home," Ava said. "How did you get here?"

"Chasing a killer," Lovina said. "Black leathers, old Harley. Kind of a Prince of Darkness thing going on?" Everyone looked to Agnes. "Obviously, I'm in the right place," Lovina said.

"You're chasing Emile Chasseur," Agnes said. "The Master of the Hunt."

Dennis moaned a little, and Agnes returned to his side. "All of you, please make yourselves at home. Carl, Barbara, please stay here tonight. We have the room. I'll tend to Dennis, and then we shall talk."

Agnes put Dennis to bed. Tea was made and served with various cakes and cookies. Ava filled a hot-water bottle and applied it to Agnes's aching hip, and everyone told their stories. The old grandfather clock in the parlor said it was well after two in the morning by the time Lovina finished with her tale of how she had come to Four Houses.

"You said this guy, Aussapile, you were working with was a trucker?" Carl said. "His name sounds familiar to me."

"Really?" Lovina said. "Well, you travel around long enough, you're bound to run into the same people, right? We all know how the wheel turns."

Barb and Carl smiled and nodded. "Absolutely," Barb said. "Small world, huh?"

"Minuscule," Carl said, grinning. His smile was as infectious as his wife's. "How can we help you, Officer? We've been waiting for a long time to have a shot at standing up to Chasseur. He's had this town in fear and under his control for a long time."

"Longer than you think," Agnes said. "I think we've been waiting for you, Lovina. I think the other house has been waiting for you, too."

"I don't understand," Lovina said. "But I know Jimmie, Heck, and Max will find a way to find me, and they will help. Apart from us, are there any other folks in town that could help?"

"Sure," Carl said. "Plenty, but the Scodes—the scumbags who are basically Chasseur's goons—they have everyone frightened."

"The good people here far outnumber the predators," Barb said. "But we're trapped here, and a lot of folks don't want to make their lives any harder than they have to be."

"How can he trap you here—how can this place even be?" Lovina asked as she sipped her tea.

"Chasseur's power has grown over time," Agnes said. "From what I've been able to research, he was able to seal Four Houses off completely, not just hide it, sometime in the fifties. It seems something happened to increase his power and, I assume, the power of the entity that he serves. For a long time he has threatened not to allow individuals or their loved ones to die while in Four Houses if they dared to defy him."

"Not die?" Lovina said.

Barb nodded. "Not die, just age and get sick, have their minds diminish and be in pain, but not die," Barb said. "He's terrified so many people with that."

"This place is already a prison," Carl said. "Watching that happen to your loved ones makes it hell."

Ava looked over at Agnes. The older woman caught her glance and smiled. It was a sad smile, a fragile, almost brittle smile. It came to Ava, in that moment, why Agnes had been so adamant about not going with her to the other house. Ava started to say something, her lips whispering, "I'm sorry," but Agnes only shook her head slightly and went back to focusing on the conversation.

"You make this Chasseur sound like some kind of god here," Lovina said.

"He is," Agnes said. "He's master of life and death here in Four Houses, and he loves that."

"We're going to have to rally people to help us," Lovina said. "If they want it to get better here, then they're going to have to step up and take a chance."

"Most folks in Four Houses don't have any weapons," Carl said. "The Scodes confiscate any they find or kill whoever has them, if they put up a fight, by siccing the shadows and the packs on them. It's a slaughter."

"Packs?" Lovina said. "You mean the Black-Eyed Children?"

"They're like larval forms of the shadow people," Ava said. "Agnes and I saw one of them . . . change. It was horrible."

"If the children bite you, unless you're pretty young, it kills you—pretty quick, too," Carl said. "If a child gets bit, it becomes one of them."

"Sadly, that's one of the few reasons Chasseur allows human beings to survive in Four Houses," Agnes said. "To breed children, so he can give them to the packs, to turn them into his shadow hounds."

"It was one of the signs of Chasseur's power growing," Barbara said. "The old-timers said there used not to be any shadow people or Black-Eyed Kids; they started showing up in town a few decades ago. He'd send them out into the world to do his dirty work, abduct more kids, make him a larger army."

"Jesus!" Ava said. "This is hell."

"I don't care for it," Lovina said, shaking her head, looking from one tired, scared, but determined, face to another. "No, not one damned bit, and it will not stand. Hell? I'm going to burn it. I'm going to burn it all down."

Agnes smiled. "The house has been waiting for you," she said.

. . .

It was cold in the garage. Lexi was chained to a group of large acetylene welding tanks in the corner, next to a stack of old tires. Her arms stretched behind her. Her head was fuzzy and thick. She couldn't remember how long it had been since she'd had water or food, and it was almost impossible to sleep with her arms in constant pain. She hadn't had her meds in a long time, either, and she was so far past panic now, she felt numb. It was getting hard to remember things, remember important stuff. How long had she been here? Days? Weeks? Time was a meaningless rubber band. She looked over at the still form of . . . Cole? Cole—yes, his name was Cole, and hers was . . . Lexi. Yes, she had that— hang on to that. They had beaten Cole at some point. It had been bad, and the old, mean one—Wald—had used a heavy black piece of exhaust hose to beat him so as to leave as few marks as possible. They had to be undamaged for their big day—when was it again? The day they were going to go meet the Horned Man in the woods. Was it . . . tomorrow? Yes, tomorrow night they would meet the Horned Man. *Shit, shit, girl, come on! You're going to die in the woods tomorrow night. Focus, damn it . . . come on.*

Lexi blinked a few times and used the pain in her arms and the cold biting her skin to shake off some of the haze she had been feeling for . . . how long? There were no clocks she could see in the garage bay of Scode's Garage. The bay doors were down, and she saw only darkness beyond the grimy windows.

"Cole," she hissed. "Cole, we have got to get out of here. Cole!"

Cole didn't stir. He didn't make a sound. The horrible thought that he was dead began to creep into her. She was alone, and Cole, beautiful funny, stupid, vain Cole, was dead now on the floor of a filthy garage in the middle of an unwaking nightmare.

He groaned and moved a little. Lexi almost shouted, but kept her silence. She looked in the direction of the open door of the glass-enclosed office adjacent to the garage bays. Toby was in there. She could hear the shitty old AM radio playing the same scratchy, hissing station they had played when the Scode boys first drove them into Four Houses. It was Gene Autry singing "You're the Only Star in My Blue Heaven." Wald had left on some errands. When he had left was impossible for Lexi to determine; it was taking a lot of effort to hold the buzzing in her mind at bay and not to space out or just start screaming until she passed out again. None of that would help them.

They hadn't bothered to tie Cole back up after the beating. Lexi was hoping he could crawl over to her and free her arms, then they could grab the tow truck and get the fuck out of this tumor of a town.

"Cole?" Lexi pleaded. Cole groaned again. "Please, come on, you have to get me loose, and I'll take care of you, get us out of here. Come on, Cole. Cole, wake the fuck up!"

He opened his eyes. He grunted and tried to drag himself toward her across the oil-stained, cracked cement. He made it a few feet. His eyes rolled back in his head, and he passed out again. Lexi almost cried, but her fear was stronger, and she knew that she couldn't waste time sobbing. *Think.*

Toby walked out of the office. He saw that Cole had moved a few feet and was shivering. He took an old, dirty plastic car tarp and pulled it over the boy like a blanket. He then walked to Lexi and knelt so that he was face-to-face with her. Toby's eyes never made it to her face; he was looking at her breasts, jutting out from the clothesline bonds that held her to the tanks. Toby's gaze filled her with dizzy fear and nausea. She had been several days without her meds, and the panic and all the other old ghosts were stirring in the folds of her brain; what he could do to her began to spool out like some awful movie in her mind. She fought with everything in her not to retreat into the fortress of screaming hysteria or catatonia.

"You okay?" Toby asked. "I can get you a blanket or something if you need it." He rubbed her shoulder with warm, calloused hands that lingered too long, and Lexi fought the urge to vomit. She tried to think, tried to think like Alana. Alana was the most together person she had ever known. Alana would have come and saved her and Cole if she hadn't died in that field. What would Alana do?

"T-Toby, I need to go to the bathroom," she said.

"I'll fetch the bucket," he said with a little too much enthusiasm. Lexi knew he had watched her before, as she had had to squat over the bucket to relieve herself, with him and Wald watching her with greasy eyes.

"Can't I go to the bathroom, please?" she asked. A plan was forming, even though she had no conscious awareness of it. Her instincts were babbling like water to her, giving her a tiny sliver of hope. "I'll keep the door open so you can watch me." She saw the calculations cross his bland, stupid face, and he actually looked around to make sure Wald, who whipped him on a regular basis, wasn't anywhere to be seen. It was so comical you could laugh, but Lexi didn't. She was in character now, looking only at Toby, not checking to see if Cole was even aware of what was going on. Her universe was Toby. *Focus on him, focus.*

"I'm not supposed to, but okay," Toby said. He began to untie her. "Wald would get really mad, but I'll do it for you."

She smiled. It took an effort, but she reminded herself that her life was on the line. "Thank you, Toby. You're sweet." She was loose, and she moaned in genuine relief as she let her arms drop. Toby never stopped looking at her chest and legs. She wrapped her arching arms around her chest, covering herself as best she could. For the millionth time, she wished she had her leather jacket from Gerry's car. She struggled to her feet, and Toby helped her up, taking the opportunity to grope her as much as he could. Lexi tried to ignore it. If this was what it took to get free, to help Cole, to live and get the fuck out of here, then she'd handle it. He led her to the single, dirty bathroom and threw open the door. The room smelled of stale piss. She knew Toby was watching everything she did, and she decided it was now or never. She slid her panties from under the black minidress, covered in metal buckles and rings, and down her legs past the torn black fishnets until they rested at her boots. If she got out of here alive, she swore to wear thick, warm, heavy pantyhose the rest of her life. Dressing like this was fun, and she did love her style, but she had been so cold in this outfit, and all she wanted now was to live and to be warm and safe. Granny panties and thick-ass pantyhose—hell, yeah.

She held her knees together as she perched on the cold toilet seat, sticky with old urine. *Obviously, you sick fuckers never had a lady tell you to lift the damn seat, did you?* She looked up at Toby, her dark eyes wide and focused on him with all her shivering will. "You are so sweet, Toby. Thank you. I don't know why Wald is always so mean to you."

Toby squatted in the doorway. Lexi was beginning to realize that Toby liked to be on the same level with whoever he was talking to; however, his eyes were fixated on her crumpled black-and-purple panties and her shivering legs up to the minidress. If he could rip it off her with his eyes, Lexi was sure he would.

"Wald's always been like that," Toby said. "When I was little, Father beat me in the head with an ax handle for breaking some green-apple preserves. Those were his favorite, and it was the last jar for winter. At least, that's what Wald told me. Mother had already displeased the Master and been fed to the pack. And by the time I was old enough to ask Father if the story was true, his mind had gone all soft and far away. What the Master does can keep your body alive, but your mind can still rot."

"God, that's horrible," Lexi said. She was sincere. "How old did Wald say you were when your dad hit you, Toby?"

"Wald said five, or six, maybe," Toby replied. "Anyway, that was when my head started feeling like something was broken in there, and it kept rattling around. Wald said that was why I was the town idiot and why he had to correct me the way Father did. All my brothers corrected me, too; Wald made sure they didn't do anything permanent, ever since Luther broke my leg that one time."

"Jesus!" Lexi said. "Where are all your brothers, Toby?"

"They got taken by the pack. Most of them became the first shadow people, but a few were too old to act as vessels for the Horned Man, and they just died."

"Just you and Wald left out of all your family?" Lexi asked. Toby nodded. "Why do you and Wald do it, Toby? Serve that psycho, and that creature in the woods?"

"We always have," Toby said. "Father did and his father before him and so on back. We've been doing it as a family for . . . two hundred years, I think Wald said once when he was drunk. Us Scodes been doing it since the Master was just a young man, since he came right out of the woods and took over the town. Wald and me, we've been serving him for, I reckon, about . . . a hundred and fifty years or so. Yeah, that sounds right."

There was a tea kettle in Lexi's brain, and it was screaming steam. This couldn't be real . . . this couldn't be happening. Living shadows weren't real, horned gods rising up out of the dark forest weren't real, and centuries-old madmen weren't real. Gerry was dead, Alana was dead. Ava was most likely dead. No, this *was* real, it was, and she was not in the hospital and not lost in her own mind. She looked past Toby to Cole on the floor, shivering, barely alive, and she felt her mind click back, snap into place. No, she was not going to let these freaks sacrifice them to their fucked-up god.

"The Master is old," Toby said, completely missing the look of horror that had crossed Lexi's face. "He's powerful, too. It has something to do with living in the old cabin in the woods. It's the Horned Man's house, and if he chooses you to live there he gives you powers—you know, like in a funny book. The Master's like a superhero, except he gets his powers from going out and sacrificing people to the Horned Man. He's really good at it. He's been doing it for a really long time."

"He's killing people, Toby," Lexi said. She tried to remember that she was talking to a psychotic child in a man's body—apparently, a one-hundred-and-fifty-year-old man's body. "Innocent people who didn't do anything to him or you. People with lives and families . . ."

"Shoot, if they're like my family they were probably happy to be crossing the Master's path," Toby said, smiling. " 'Sides, Lexi, Master says the highway always brings him to his sacrifices, like dowsing for water—they meet him halfway. He did something when they first started building all them big roads all over America; he dedicated a sacrifice out on U.S. 281, near here, to the Horned Man, and he said that made the power moving through the highway pour straight into the Horned Man's house. He got a lot stronger after that. See, Lexi, it's all part of nature's plan, just like what he's doing tomorrow night."

"Toby," Lexi said, leaning forward, "Toby, me and Cole, we haven't done anything to you. We just had our car break down. Please, Toby, you can let us go." Toby's eyes had shifted to her breasts as soon as she leaned toward him. "If . . . if you let us go, I'll be very grateful to you."

She saw a rusted tire iron leaning against a stack of tire rims a few feet to the left of the bathroom door. She stood and slid her panties up as she did, letting Toby get just enough of a flash of pale skin to make sure she had his attention—well, at least the part of him that seemed to do his thinking. "If you help us, Toby, let us go, you can . . . touch me."

She stepped out of the bathroom and sidestepped toward the crowbar, not looking at it but knowing where it rested. She was looking at Toby, focusing all her energy toward him. He was stronger, and she doubted that he felt pain as much as she did, but it was now or never.

"R-really?" Toby stammered. He actually licked his lips without even being aware that he had done so.

"You ever touched a girl before, Toby?" Lexi took another circular step toward the crowbar. Almost there.

"Not a live one," Toby said as innocently as he might talk about petting a puppy. "Wald lets me touch the ones the Master's given him—the 'scraps,' Wald calls them. After he's done with them, and slit their throats, I get them. Sometimes they're still twitching a little. I like it when they're still moving and warm. You're like that all the time, Lexi. That will be nice."

She couldn't take any more, not after that. She lunged for the crowbar with a shriek and grabbed it. It seemed weightless in that terrifying instant, when she was made of dizzy terror and adrenaline. Toby realized what was happening just as she swung with all her might and struck him on the shoulder. He howled and staggered back, knocking over a large metal tool chest on wheels. The crashing of the tools and the chest sounded like the end of the universe. Toby rubbed his shoulder and looked at Lexi with a mixture of betrayal and rage. She wanted to keep hitting him, but she knew that if she pressed it he would grab her. She moved carefully toward Cole, who was opening his eyes and trying to sit up, stirred by the crashing tools. He failed and slumped back to the floor.

"Cole, Cole, honey," Lexi said, kneeling beside him. "You got to get up now. We got to go, Cole. Come on, Cole, it's go time. Come on, I can't carry you."

Toby moved forward, and Lexi stood and swung the crowbar. "Back the fuck off!" she screamed. "I'll bash your fucking head in, finish what your scumbag dad started! I'll do it if I have to! Stay the fuck away from me!"

Toby nursed his shoulder and looked around the garage for a weapon of his own.

Cole made a groaning noise and tried again to get up. Lexi helped him. He leaned on her and tried to speak.

"Hurts all over," he said. "You okay, Lex?"

Her laugh was a little hysterical.

"You're kidding me, right? I'm saving you, superjock. How's that feel? You stay awake and keep walking, Cole. We're getting out of here." She looked around. She knew that there were cars outside. She moved with

Cole toward the pegboard by the office door. Dozens of key rings hung on small hooks there. She scanned them until she saw Gerry's keys. She grabbed them. Toby made another move toward her. She swung wildly, and Cole almost fell, but Toby flinched and stumbled back, still clutching his shoulder.

"I thought you were nice," Toby shouted, flecks of foam flying from his mouth. "You're just mean, like all the others!"

Lexi dragged Cole thorough the door to the office. The old AM radio was playing "Some Velvet Morning," by Nancy Sinatra and Lee Hazlewood, as they pushed through the office door out to the parking lot. It was chilly, and past the sodium-light terminator of the garage's lot light Lexi knew the shadow people waited. Gerry's SUV was parked in a corner of the lot and had obviously been fixed for some time. She leaned Cole against the car as she frantically struggled with the keys. She unlocked the Honda SUV, slid Cole across the backseat, and shut the door. She was climbing into the driver's seat when something whined and made the air hot near her cheek. Then, a second later, there was the crack of a gun. Toby was at the office door with Cole's small pistol in his hand. Bluish smoke rose up from it.

"Oh, shit!" She jumped into the car. Another crack, and a dull thud in the Honda's body. Gerry's car started smoothly, and she jammed it into gear, realizing that she was still clutching the crowbar. She tossed it on the seat next to her, the seat she had sat in and made fun of Gerry and made eyes at Cole from. Was that in a different age, a different life? *No time, no time!* The Honda lurched out of the parking lot, with Toby firing another round as it sped away. She nearly hit the Scodes' oncoming tow truck and the motorcycle it was following as she sped down the dark two-lane. Her whole body was shaking. She wanted to throw up, to scream, to pull off her flesh. She did none of it. She found a crumpled pack of American Spirit cigarettes in the compartment between the seats. They were Gerry's—fucking hipster, rest his soul. With trembling hands, Lexi lit a cigarette and took a deep drag. She felt her heart slowing to a gentle beat in her chest. It worked. She did it. They were free. She accelerated out of Four Houses and let a tiny bit of the tension bleed out of her body and mind.

The next hour was a nightmare—no, it was hell. They had all died on

281, in that crash. This was the Devil's playground, and he was laughing, braying like some animal. She looped along the two-lane, passing the same houses, the same trailers, the roadhouse, the burned-out houses, the fucking garage that she had just fled from over and over and over.

In the backseat, Cole murmured something she couldn't hear above the hum of the engine. She looked down at the gas gauge. She had less than half a tank of gas left. Something was itching in her memory—someplace someone had told them to go to where they would be safe, protected. It was the night Gerry and Alana had died. The night that Ava had run away and left them. She was probably dead, too, now. There was someplace where they could be safe. She fought to remember, but she had been so scared, hysterical, and sometimes she forgot things when she was like that. She passed the garage again and slowed slightly at what she saw. In the parking lot, under the twitchy, shivering lemon light of the lot, stood the Scodes, both of them being addressed by the motorcycle rider, the man named Chasseur—the servant of that unthinkable thing in the woods. All three of them turned to look at her as the Honda drifted by. Everything was in slow motion. Chasseur's eyes were midnight, and massive antlers grew from his head. He waved to her, slowly, deliberately, as she passed. Lexi jammed the accelerator to the floor and sped away. Panic had her. They had to escape, to get away. The house! The bitch who wouldn't let them in the first night had said head for the Crone's house. *The Crone's house!* She remembered. They had got separated from Ava trying to get there. She was close to it, to the driveway. She had noticed the porch light was on the last time she passed it. An RV and a car were parked up there, too. People were there, people and light.

Something was in the road. The headlights caught them. It was children, a line of children all holding hands, making a chain across the two-lane. All were wearing hoodies, and their heads were down, hiding their faces. Lexi slowed and then stopped when the kids didn't move. She was about to hit the horn to scatter them when their heads all came up simultaneously. Their eyes were as dark and empty as the Master of the Hunt's had been. Their skin was so pale as to have an almost milky opalescence in the headlights. Their eyes locked with

hers, and she felt herself putting the car into park without even knowing why. The children moved like a single organism to surround the
car. Two of them were at the driver's-side door, looking at Lexi, into
her, with eyes of fathomless void.

"Open the door," one of the children said softly, evenly. "Let us in."

"We need a ride home," the other one said. "Let us in. Open the door."
Their voices were like a warm narcotic syrup pouring over Lexi, into
her mind, filling the crevices. She saw her hand moving to hit the open
button for the doors. Part of her mind screamed, but she was still doing
it. She looked around the other windows; ghostly faces with eyes of
night were at each one, each staring at her and, seemingly, through her.
Tiny pale hands clawed at the glass, eager to get inside. Her hand was
almost to the button. She glanced at the cigarette in her other hand. She
fought with all her will to act. The smoldering cigarette pressed against
the smooth skin of her forearm. Lexi gasped. The nail of burning pain
cleared her head, and she jerked her hand away from the lock button.

The little creatures at her door, pretending to be human children,
hissed and showed mouths full of slender bone needles where normal
human teeth should be.

"Let us in," the children whispered. "Open the door. . . ." Lexi
heard the sound of the rear door unlocking with a thunk. She spun
around, reaching for the crowbar, only to see Cole, glassy-eyed and only
semi-aware, unlocking his door.

"No, no!" Lexi shouted, and tried to turn to pull the rear door closed,
but the children were already swarming into the SUV. She tried to fight,
swinging the crowbar as best she could as small, inhumanly strong
hands grabbed her and wrestled the weapon out of her hand. Her door
came open, and she fell on the cold, hard pavement of the road. She was
pinned, and she saw Cole's limp body being dropped beside her on the
road by the children. She wanted to curse, to spit, but small, viselike
hands and fingers held her and were stuffed into her mouth, rendering
her mute. She tried biting them, but the children didn't seem to register
the pain.

The headlights of the Scodes' old truck were blinding her. She looked
up to see Wald and Toby, then she saw the Master of the Hunt. Chasseur's
eyes were normal again, and he had no horns.

"She hurt me, Wald," Toby whined as he pointed at her. Lexi wished for an instant she had bashed his skull in with the crowbar. "And then she got away and—"

"Shut up," Wald said, looking with disgust at his brother, then looking at Chasseur with fear. "Master, I'm so sorry for Toby's incompetence. I had only stepped out for—"

"It is your incompetence as well, Walden," Chasseur said. "The boy is badly injured. Your zeal may lead to me not having the perfect final sacrifices tomorrow night on Beltane Eve."

"Sir, I made sure that there is not a mark on him." Wald's voice was picking up in pitch, and a little whine was creeping into it now, too.

"Shut your mouth," the Master of the Hunt said. "We have less than twenty-four hours until he and the girl must be sacrificed. I will not allow your ham-handed bumbling to interfere in the successful completion of all that I have toiled for."

Lexi was no longer struggling. She strained to hear what Chasseur was saying.

"Tell me your will, Master," Wald said. "I'll see to it personally."

"Gather our allies in the town. Arm them with the weapons you've confiscated over the years. The time has come to cleanse Four Houses of the infestation of the unbeliever. Tomorrow, you will lead our allies on a purge. They will slaughter every man, woman, and child in this town. In their bloodlust, I expect them to eventually turn upon themselves and kill each other. You shall clean up any stragglers who survive."

"Everyone?" Toby said. "But some people are nice and—" A single look from Chasseur was enough to silence him.

"The one that followed me back, the policewoman, she has power, power even she has no idea she possesses. She, the old bitch, and the whore she's taken under her wing could present problems for me and the plan. Kill them and the rest of the chattel before they manage to get the town organized against me. Kill all three women. Kill anyone else that gets in your way. Kill everyone, for his glory, and for mine."

"Yes, Master," Wald said, a slight gleam in his eye now. "Your will shall be done."

The Master of the Hunt looked at the Scode brothers and then at Lexi and Cole, lying on the ground. "Drug them, paint them, and keep them that way until it is time for them to be devoured by the Horned Man. If you fail in this, I will feed you both to the hounds a little piece at a time."

At the mention of drugs, Lexi began to struggle again, fiercely, but she couldn't get free, couldn't shake loose so many small, strong hands. The last thing she heard before she felt the silver sting of the needle, before the world became odd, and slow, and everything pointless, was the Master of the Hunt's voice.

"By this time tomorrow, on sacred Beltane, this entire planet shall become the Horned Man's prey," Chasseur said, "and the whole world will scream with one throat."

They were in Kansas. Jimmie's rig was rolling along on Route 36, headed toward a little town called Lebanon, near the Kansas-Nebraska border. Sam and Dave's "Hold On, I'm Comin'" was playing on the cab speakers, and the sky was so blue and clear it could break your heart.

"You have some of the weirdest musical tastes of any old white guy I know," Heck said, rubbing his eyes from the bench behind Jimmie's seat. "Didn't I hear Daft Punk a little while ago when I was sleeping?"

"You think he's bad," Max said from the passenger seat, tapping and swiping the screen of her tablet. She had a notebook open and propped against her knees, which were close to her chest. "Try riding with Lovina. Very odd music."

"Morning, sleepy head," Jimmie said. "Just in time for the party. And, for the record, you log as many miles as I have, and you get very open-minded about your music. It's a survival trait."

"Where are we, exactly?" Heck asked.

"Kansas," Jimmie said. "Close to the ground zero of mystical energy, if Max's theory is right."

"Max," Heck said absently. "That's short for Maxine, right?'

"Mackenzie, actually," Max said, not looking up from her tablet. "My grandfather was named Max, and we were pretty tight growing up. So he was Big Max, and I became Little Max. I liked it, and it stuck."

"Shouldn't you be Mac?" Heck said, grinning.

"Shouldn't you be Hector?" Max replied, again not looking up.

Hector scowled. "I need to get my boots on," he said with a snarl.

Max smiled. "Okay, Jimmie, up ahead you need to turn right onto Route 281," she said, examining her tablet map.

"Same 281 that the Pagan's first victim was discovered on in 1956," Jimmie said.

Max nodded.

"Okay, how does this work?" Jimmie said as they turned onto 281.

"We're very close to the geographic center of the conterminous United States," Max said.

"Is that the same exit as the worlds' largest rubber-band ball?" Heck asked, grinning once again. "And can we buy fireworks there?"

Max paused and looked up from her tablet to glare at him over her glasses. "It means that all that forty-two thousand miles of magic-charged highway converge here," she said. "This is the center of the magical circuit that is the U.S. interstate-highway system."

"So how do we get to Four Houses, Max?" Jimmie asked.

"I believe this occult-power system was designed to be tapped into and used," Max said, working furiously on her tablet. She seemed to locate what she wanted and nodded. "Viamancers simply do it by instinct and genetics. I think it's a by-product of so many people living and being in proximity to the source of all this magical power—children began to be born with the innate ability to tap into it, hence your 'road witches.'"

"Okay, but none of us are road witches, as we've already established," Heck said. "So what do we do, Doc?"

"The system used to number the routes and highways is part of a complex, evolving, and very esoteric system of sacred geometry and numerology," Max said. "All the occult secrets of the world, all the secret history of mankind, all the powers in the universe are hidden in the language of numbers."

"You mean the little road signs?" Heck said. "The interstate shields and the mile markers? All that stuff?"

Max nodded, pointing to a small mile-marker post as they passed. "Exactly," she said. "It's a formula for accessing and tapping the power of the earth's magic. In theory, it could allow a skilled practitioner of the mystic arts to perform all manner of impressive magical feats."

"Like hiding a whole town from being found," Jimmie said. "Or transporting us there?"

"Exactly!" Max said.

"So you're a skilled practitioner of the mystic arts?" Jimmie asked her.

"Um, no," Max said. "But I've read a great deal about it, and I'm sure I can—"

"Oh, shit," Heck said. "We're screwed."

"—activate the system and operate it to get us to Four Houses."

Jimmie sighed. "Okay, Max, do your voodoo." Max smiled at the trucker. Jimmie gave her a thumbs-up. "You got this, Max," he said. "Take us to Lovina."

Max took a deep breath and settled herself into a crossed-legged position in the passenger seat. She closed her eyes and took several minutes to control and focus her breathing. Jimmie shut off the music and turned down the CB. He slowed the truck, but Max shook her head, keeping her eyes closed. "Faster," she whispered. "Go faster." Jimmie accelerated down the desolate two-lane, barren empty fields on either side of them as they moved faster and faster. Max opened her eyes when he hit seventy. She began to recite strings of numbers, formulas, and equations, one smoothly sliding into the next. Solutions becoming new integers, streams of outcomes and possible outcomes, theorems, solidifying into something more.

The road in front of them began to waver, like the heat coming off a desert highway. They were at eighty now, and the sky was growing dark, filling with brooding clouds. There was a strange shift in pressure, which made all three feel as if their ears were going to pop. The semi was almost at ninety now.

"Damn," Heck whispered, tapping Jimmie on the shoulder and pointing out the driver's-side window. "Jimmie, what the fuck is that, man?" Far off in the field to the left of the truck was something massive and dark, squatting at the horizon. It was partially obscured by the wavering curtain of distortion and the looming storm clouds. A few stray droplets of rain began to pat softly on the windshield, as if they were driving into a summer thundershower.

"The city," Jimmie said. "We're crossing. You're doing it, Max."

"Hold the speed!" Max said, sounding as if she were dreaming with her eyes open. She recited more strings of numbers, and a thin black line of blood trailed down from her nostril and spread along her lips. "Hold the speed," she mumbled again, and then returned to her numeric incantation.

Heck looked over, and now the dark shape was closer. He could make out skyscrapers and spires, temple domes and Gothic cathedrals. "It's getting bigger, Jimmie," he said.

"Yeah," Jimmie said. "It does that. Pray we don't have to drive into it, or through it."

More blood was streaming out of Max's nose now, and she was convulsing a little, but she kept reciting the numbers and formulating complex concepts out of the basic building blocks. The raindrops hissed and steamed as they hit the hood and the windshield. Jimmie saw a massive green-and-white highway sign coming up on the right side of the road. It said METROPOLIS-UTOPIA 23 MILES.

"Why is it called that?" Heck asked, not taking his eyes off the city as it edged closer.

"Back when they were building the highway system," Jimmie said, "they put signs just like that up as place markers for real interstate signs. The stories say no one is sure if the city was always there and the Road just gave us access to it or if it was created along with the Road."

Heck tried to look away from the massive black tumor, the outline of architectural styles—lines and forms that didn't match and couldn't fully be processed by the human brain.

"Well . . . shit," Jimmie said, and glanced over to the left. The dark city took up most of the wasteland from floor to sky. The scene was much clearer now, and Jimmie recalled every detail from his nightmares after his last visit here. Heck made a noise, a catch in his throat, behind Jimmie. The trucker sincerely wished he could have prepared his squire for this, but he had no clue how one would do that. There weren't words.

Heck looked deeper into the city, and his mind tried to make some sense of it. All the buildings, all the bizarre hodgepodge of structures, were made of the twisted scraps and hulks of cars, trucks, semis and motorcycles. Some dark, shiny material held the millions of scraps of vehicle metal together like a glue. Whatever it was, the smooth organic nature of it—its sheen and its slightly viscous motility—made Heck think of a bug's carapace as it skittered across a dirty tiled floor.

There was a sound Heck could hear now that was growing louder above the semi's engine. It took him a moment to identify it—it was screaming, millions of voices screaming, howling, weeping, begging, singing, laughing. Millions of voices from every tower window, every roof, every parapet, every street. It was the sound of a million million lunatics, all looking straight at the tiny rig coming ever closer to their dark city.

Heck and Jimmie looked at Max. Her eyes were white orbs with tiny bloodshot cracks stretching across the surface. Black blood streamed down from her nose, and now from her tear ducts as well. She was still muttering formulas and hissing numbers. Heck grabbed an old flannel shirt and took off her glasses. He tried to wipe away the blood. "Jesus, this is killing her," he said.

The Road was burning at its edges with white fire. The simple lines of paint on Route 281 flared and sparked with blue-white current, and the light from the Road was now the only light, bathing the cab in a weird, refracted miasma, like lights underwater. The black thunderheads had blotted out the sky to the horizon; occasionally, chains of lightning bounced between the menacing mountains in the sky. There was a horrible crunching, rumbling sound all around the truck, like rocks being pulverized. Heck looked over at Jimmie. The trucker was focusing all his might on driving, staying inside the lines of the Road, staying on course. Jimmie was sweating, but his eyes were steely and calm. Past Jimmie, Heck saw through the driver's window something that froze the reason in him and let the fear run rampant for an instant. The city was there, moving, throwing rock and dirt aside as it plowed across the field, an unstoppable juggernaut of madness and movement. He could smell it now, as well as hear it: decades of human waste and garbage left unattended to fester and stink. The city smelled of death. From the vantage point they had now, Heck saw them, the viamancers, the road witches, the mad inhabitants of Metropolis-Utopia. They were little more than indistinct silhouettes, but he could feel all those eyes on him, burning him, like cigarettes and X-rays. He could see the wires of the city now—the countless bodies in various states of dress and decay, hanging across the skyline like a row of paper dolls. Some of them were missing limbs or heads; others were little more than skeletons held together by rotting tendons and cartilage.

"Fuck!" Heck said. It was like the war, every war—the madness, and the stench, and the bodies. It was like the place war retired to when it wasn't raging across the earth. It was a billboard for Hell. Every cell in Heck's body screamed to run, to get away. "Jimmie, man, punch it, come on, it's gaining on us."

"Got to hold the speed until she says otherwise," Jimmie said, as cool and calm as a fishing pond in winter. "Got to hold, squire."

Heck's heart thudded like a wild animal trying to get out of his chest. A wave of claustrophobic panic swept over him. He had to get out of this damn cab, get away from that fucking city, that thing. He looked out Max's window to see where he could bolt to and was horrified to see that the city was now on that side of the Road, too, ready to swallow them in its stinking, screaming maw.

"Turn, turn now, right!" Max screamed. "Now!" There had been no road to the right, but now there was one, a simple two-lane, its lines burning with cold fire. Jimmie turned hard onto the two-lane. There was a rumble of thunder and an audible *whoosh*, like the air outside the cab trying to regulate a difference in pressure. Then it was all gone. It was just a two-lane road, in the middle of quiet, normal farm country, with a blue sky and a cool, strong, wind—Kansas, Earth. From the position of the sun, it was early Saturday afternoon. The truck's clock said it was still late morning.

Jimmie slowed the rig and then stopped in the middle of the quiet road. He looked over at Max. Her eyes were normal again, but very bloodshot. Her hands were shaking, and she looked as if she might pass out. Jimmie handed her a jug of Gatorade, and she chugged it greedily.

"My glasses?" she asked quietly, wiping her mouth with her sleeve. Jimmie handed her another bottle. Heck presented the glasses to her, and Max put them on in between gulps. "We make it?" she asked.

Jimmie pointed in front of the rig. "That answer your question, Max the Great and Powerful?" he said, grinning. There was a simple wooden road sign on the side of the two-lane. It said WELCOME TO FOUR HOUSES.

"Hot damn!" Max said. Then she shook her head. "I think you two are rubbing off on me."

Jimmie stuffed a pinch of chaw into his cheek and laughed. "You should be so lucky. Here, drink some more. Working viamancy takes a hell of a lot out of you."

Max wiped some of the dried blood from the edges of her nostrils. "Clearly. I feel horrid."

"But you did it, Doc," Jimmie said. "Damn if you didn't. How did it feel?"

"Like I was losing control of my body, like a stroke, or maybe an epileptic seizure. It felt horrible, like a dream, like dying a little. I hope we don't need to do that again anytime soon."

"Nah, we're going to be here for a spell," Jimmie said. "We got work to do. You lay back on one of the bunks, Max. You did real good—now rest. I'll wake you when we're there."

Max, surprisingly, didn't put up a protest. She traded positions with Heck and disappeared behind the curtain that separated the living quarters of the cab from the driver compartment without a word.

"Tough enough," Heck said, looking back at the curtain.

"And then some," Jimmie said, smiling. "That she is."

Jimmie got out to stretch his legs and look around. It was a clear, perfect day. The cool of the morning was burning away and you could smell wildflowers and not a trace of exhaust. There was no traffic on the road, no sound of the freeway or any other man-made sound. Jimmie checked his cell and, just as he suspected, there was no service. He did notice that two texts had come through during the rough ride, most likely just before they crossed over.

Jimmie checked the numbers; the first was a Washington, DC, phone number. The text said, *"Mark Stolar gave George Norse a digital copy of a video from the Pagan. It involves a girl running in the woods being chased by the Pagan and apparently some hunting dogs. There is some Devil-looking thing with horns and goat legs too. Norse is cooperating. Gave us a copy of the video. He plans to run it tonight on his TV show. Spoke with DOJ and FCC about stopping him, but so far no word back. Good hunting. I refuse to say the stupid wheel thing.—Dann"*

The second text was much shorter: *"I love you. We love you. Be careful.—Layla"*

Heck returned from a piss break in the scrub that was on either side of the two-lane. Both men climbed back into the rig, and Jimmie started it up. He noticed that the odometer indicated that they had traveled only a few miles during the time Max performed the ritual, but his full tank of gas now read as three-fourths empty. He shook his head.

"Well," Jimmie said, rubbing his tired eyes. "Here we go—let's go find Lovina."

The rig lurched forward, and they cruised down the empty road headed for Four Houses.

"Hey, Jimmie?" Heck said.

"Yeah," Jimmie replied.

"That city . . . That fucked-up city back there . . . You drove *through* that before?"

"Yeah," Jimmie said. "I had to, for a friend."

"Fuck," Heck said. "Next time I give you any shit, feel free to smack the hell out of me,"

"Hmm," Jimmie said, spitting into a cup, "We'll see how long that lasts."

Usually in Four Houses, when you wake to pounding on the doors before dawn you pull the covers over your head and pray the locks hold. However, this time the booming voice of Wald Scode accompanied the pounding. "Get your lazy asses up! There is work to be about! He commands it!"

They gathered in the parking lot of Scode's Garage early Saturday morning. There were about seventy-five of them—all men. It was still dark when they began. Wald and Toby handed out hunting rifles, shotguns, and pistols and all the ammo that had been scrounged over the ages. Some weapons were old black powder muskets, and many were surplus military from World War II and Korea. When the guns were gone, they handed out machetes, axes, knives, pitchforks, baseball bats, and clubs. The sun was almost up when they were ready. The Master of the Hunt was not present, but everyone knew that Wald spoke with his voice. "Every home!" Wald shouted to the assembled army. "We kick in every door! Everyone, they all die! Spare no one! This is his will!"

"I'll go," one voice in the crowd called out. Albert Dalton was a regional salesman who had gotten stuck in Four Houses in 1993, ending his spree of serial rapes across the Midwest. "But I'll be damned if I'm messing with that old lady up on the hill!"

"Yeah," former police officer E. G. Wells shouted out. He fled his home and his job after allegations of corruption had ensured that he would see the inside of a prison; he'd ended up serving time in Four Houses instead. "That wrinkled old bitch has firepower up there! You want us to sweep and clear this town, fine, but no way in hell am I—"

"Wald shot him square in the face with a .44 snub-nosed revolver. Wells's wide face popped as the round entered between his eyes and exited, taking part of the skull with it. The dirty cop fell to the asphalt. No one moved to see if he was still breathing. The crowd just shuffled away from the corpse. Not their problem.

"Anyone else here care to blaspheme the word of the Master of the Hunt?" Wald shouted. "The old god's prophet? Anyone? You have guns, you could try to kill me. Well?" The crowd was silent. Wald nodded and put the ugly, squat little pistol back in the pocket of his windbreaker. "Good. Now go do his work, his will. Wipe Four Houses clean of the unfaithful, the unworthy, the weak. Go!"

They swarmed out of the lot just as the sun opened an accusatory fiery eye in the east, past the tree line.

The first few homes were easy pickings, didn't even need to fire a shot to take them. Like jackals, the mob decided to stick together to ensure their own safety. They smashed open a trailer door and dragged a family—mom, dad, and three children—out into the cold. They beat most of them to death. They took time to rape the mother and the oldest daughter, but Wald fired a round into the air and scattered the violators, like roaches when the lights come on. He executed the two sobbing women, each with a bullet to the head. "We ain't got no time for dallying around!" he shouted. "Just kill 'em, don't fuck 'em."

The mob complied, and several other families died. Short-lived screams smeared themselves across Four Houses along with the occasional shout or crack of gunfire. The mob grew more confident as they encountered little real resistance. Several times Wald thought he saw something—a movement in the morning mists, darting between the houses, the weed-filled lots, and the trailers. Each time it was gone before he could fully comprehend it. It troubled him, but there was work to be about.

By late morning, they had "cleared" about a half-dozen homes and murdered more than twenty-five people. The mob had begun to split into smaller clusters as the men grew arrogant and the lust for blood came on them. Then something changed. They started kicking in doors only to find the houses empty. It happened again and again. Then one of the clusters of the mob disappeared without a trace, without a sound.

More houses came up empty as they moved forward toward the main road and began to get closer to the center of town, near the Crone's mansion. Wald examined one abandoned trailer and found that blankets and preserved food had been hastily gathered. He began to get an uneasy feeling, but so far they had encountered no serious setbacks, other than the missing men, and they were most likely off somewhere doing things he had ordered them not to and getting drunk.

They moved past the Crone's place for the moment, focusing on the houses and trailers clustered between the far end of the junkyard and the burned-down old house across from the Stag's Rest Motel. Wald wanted to give his crew as many victories and as much opportunity as possible to get cocky before they took the Crone. There had been cars up at the old lady's house last night, but they were gone now.

A few more vacant homes past the middle of town, the crew sent to clear the Stag's Rest disappeared. When Wald and his men reached the motel, it was empty, with no sign of the family that ran it, the people who lived in the bungalows, or Wald's AWOL assassins, nothing. Wald began to grow very angry. He wished he hadn't exiled Toby to watch the two college brats. He needed his brother right now to suffer a good beating to help Wald focus. Where the hell was the majority of the town? Where the hell were his men?

It was past noon when Wald got his answer. Wald's army moved up the two-lane toward Buddy's Roadhouse and the houses and trailers clustered around and past it. As they approached Buddy's, they saw that the whole road was blocked by a group of cars, vans, and trucks. At the center of the barricade was the huge Winnebago belonging to the Kesners—the couple who had taken over Buddy's ages ago. There were men and boys mounting the barricade. Most of them had nothing more than knives or bats or, in a few cases, sticks. There were guns, but only a few. The watchmen were mounted in the bed of pickups and out the high side windows of the RV. Some were on the roofs of panel trucks. The barricade included earthen mounds and trenches dug on either side of the two-lane, apparently by a rusty old backhoe that Wald could glimpse behind the barriers. Hanging by clothesline from the barricade were the eight dead bodies of Wald's missing men. Each looked to have been shot.

"What is this shit?" Wald barked, as he walked to within a few yards of the barricade.

Near the front of the Winnebago, a window slid open and Carl Kesner stuck his head out. He waved to the assembled mob of killers and then produced a megaphone to speak to them. "Howdy!" Carl said, speaking cheerfully through the megaphone. "Hi, Wald! I'm sorry to inform you fellas that Buddy's has become a private drinking establishment and you must be a member to come in."

"Is that so?" Wald said, waving the pistol at Carl.

Carl kept smiling, and nodded.

From the window slightly behind him, Barb leaned out, also smiling. "Yes," she said. "It is, and I'm afraid we have a rather firm 'no A-holes' policy in place. So I'm afraid you and your goons are going to have to mosey on along."

"What are you and your wife going to do about it, bartender?" Wald said, leveling the gun at Barb now.

Carl kept the smile, but a dark fire was burning behind his kind eyes. "I'd have to use my magic megaphone ray gun," he said, his voice booming through the amplifier. He moved the bullhorn away from his lips. Wald's men were chuckling. Carl aimed the megaphone at one of the killers with a hunting rifle. "Pew, pew!" Carl said, and the gunman lurched and fell to the ground. Before any of the stunned killers could react, Carl aimed the megaphone at another of Wald's crew who was holding a double-barreled shotgun. "Pew, pew!" Carl said. The man's chest blew open and he fell dead. Carl spun the megaphone in Wald's direction, the smile slipping off his face. "Point a gun at my wife, you evil bastard. Pew, pew, motherfucker."

"Snipers!" Wald shouted, and ran for cover. His men followed his lead, and a few of them fell to gunfire as they retreated. A round kicked up dirt near Wald's foot as he ran. "Goddamned snipers." The assassins were pinned down on the sides of the two-lane. Several of Wald's people lay dead on the road from sniper fire, primarily the ones with guns. A cheer went up from the barricade as the killers retreated.

Up on the roof of Buddy's, Lovina scanned the road for any more targets through the scope on her AR-15 and saw only the bodies of the ones she and Agnes had already dropped. Lovina picked up the police walkie and clicked the talk button. "Agnes, looks like they're buttoned down."

There was a hiss over the radio, then Agnes replied on her own walkie that Lovina had provided. "Only for the moment, dear. I know Wald Scode, and he'll not back off this easy."

"We should have popped him first," Lovina said. "The rest would have scattered."

"They are driven by the fear of who they serve," Agnes replied, "and it isn't Wald. If we keep him alive, he can order them to retreat."

Lovina nodded. This old lady had her shit together, there was no doubt about that. Any senior citizen who had her own sniper rifle was all right in her book. Agnes was positioned up in the high grass of the hill that was part of the yard of the crumbling mansion—the house Ava had told them she and Agnes visited yesterday and nearly died escaping. As hurt and worn out as Agnes was, she managed to find a way to get in position unseen and take out half of the dead assassins on the road. Badass.

"Wald's rallying his people," Agnes said over the radio. "He's going to make an attempt to flank the barrier. See? He's got that party of men falling back to slip behind the Bohans' house."

"Barb? You copy that?" Lovina said.

Again, a hiss of static, and then Barb's voice. "We do," she said. "We'll try to get some of our guys over there to meet them, but Lovina, we don't have a lot of fighters over here. The only reason they didn't run when Wald's guys showed up is because of you and Agnes."

Lovina sighed. It was true—these were normal folks. Good people, to be sure, but frightened and not a lot of combat experience. "Just do the best you can, Barb. I'll try to cover your people as much as I can."

An hour passed. Lovina remembered this part really well. She had spent enough time in enough hot LZs in Afghanistan and New Orleans to know how to wait. Wald sent some of his men back down the road, running low and dispersing from her scope as they headed toward the burned house with the chain-link fence around it, a few miles down the two-lane. Lovina had an odd feeling of déjà vu as she looked through the scope in the direction of the old house. Agnes had said something last night about a house waiting for her. At the time, she had chalked it up to a woman who had been trapped in this little town for far too long. But now, thinking of that once fine old mansion, she felt some kind of vague association with it.

It was early afternoon now and starting to get warm. The group Wald had sent to flank had reached the point where they would need to break cover to come in around the barrier. They seemed to be waiting. Lovina suddenly noticed that more of Wald's crew had fallen back out of sight. Only a handful remained in cover on the ditches on the side of the road. Where the fuck was Wald? Lovina heard the chatter between Barb and Agnes over the radio.

"We've got a lot of folks here who need potty breaks," Barb said. "I'm going to start switching people off the line. Ava is taking the radio from me."

"Yes, dear," Agnes replied.

In the RV, Ava took the radio and peered out the small window. She was wearing a large leather gun belt with the huge old Webley revolver that belonged to Dennis in a holster. She watched the street and saw only a few sour faces peeking out of the ditches at her. One of the faces was Ricky, the nasty old creep who had accosted her on her first visit to Buddy's. Ava considered taking a shot at him but realized the futility of it. Barb and Carl were moving some sentries off the bus, and new volunteers were replacing those at the windows and on the roof, trading their few guns to the new watchmen. Ava frowned. Something was wrong.

About that time, Lovina's voice came over the radio. "Guys, something is up," she said. "Most of Wald's people have fallen back out of sight to the other side of the town. The ones here look like they're waiting for something. I don't like it."

The other side of town . . .

"Shit!" Ava shouted. "Hey okay! Everybody out of the RV, come on! Out, out, everyone!" Ava began ushering the whole watch crew out of Carl and Barb's Winnebago. Once out of the RV, she called out to the other spotters on the trucks and vans. "You guys get down, everyone in Buddy's now! Come on!"

"Ava, what the hell are you doing?" Carl asked.

"We've got to get everyone inside Buddy's right now with the children and the others, come on! We're about to get overrun!"

"What are you talking about?" Barb said.

"What's happening down there?" Lovina asked over the radio. "Why is everyone coming off the barricade?"

"Agnes?" Ava called into the radio. "Agnes, I'm coming to get you! We have to get inside!"

Barb grabbed Ava by the shoulders. "Ava, please, what is it?"

Ava held the mike button open on the radio so Lovina and Agnes could hear, too. "They fell back to the other side of town . . . the other side of the two-lane! What happens when you go far enough down the two-lane on either side?" She pointed east down the two-lane, behind them. "You end up on the other side of town!"

There was the sound of engines, many engines, down the road, behind the barricade, coming closer.

"Aw, shit!" Carl said. "Okay, everybody inside the roadhouse, now! Go, go, go!"

Ava handed the radio back to Barb and began to sprint across the road and up the hill toward the old mansion. "Agnes! Agnes!" she shouted as she struggled up the hill.

"Over here, dear!" A hand came up out of the tall grass. "I seem to be having a spot of trouble standing up." A bullet whined near them both and knocked up a clump of dirt. One of Wald's men in the ditches had taken a shot when he saw Ava running up the hill. Ava drew the heavy old revolver and returned fire as she reached Agnes's sniper nest. The kick of the gun nearly dropped her on her ass, but Ava managed to stay upright. She doubted that she'd hit the guy, but all of Wald's men ducked after the shot. She offered a hand to Agnes, and the former OSS agent took it and pulled herself to her feet.

"Very embarrassing," Agnes said, hefting her rifle, sack, and radio. "Old Wild Bill Donovan would be very disappointed in his girl."

"Well, I'm not," Ava said. "Screw Wild Bill, whoever he is. We've got to go, Agnes!"

"Too late, I fear, dear," Agnes said. "Look."

Coming into view down the eastern side of the two-lane was a caravan of vehicles, roaring toward Buddy's and the blockade. There was an old eighties Ford pickup with a nasty-looking snowplow attached to the front of it. A half-dozen armed men were crouched in the truck bed of the Ford. Running slightly behind the Ford was a seventies-model Chevy truck with another complement of men in the bed. Bringing up the rear was the Scodes' ancient tow truck, with more men huddled in the back on either side of the tow winch.

"Damn it!" Ava looked around frantically. The ruins of the house behind them called to her again. Agnes looked at her and then nodded. "Tell Barb and Lovina we're going to hole up in here," Ava said as they headed for the house's entrance. Bullets again began to hiss past their heads.

Below, Wald's men in the ditch opened fire while the group that had been waiting to try to flank the barricade made their move. Some of the volunteers sent over to counter the killers died as they retreated before the advance.

"Damn it!" Lovina shouted, and flipped the selector on her AR-15 over to full auto. She stood at the edge of Buddy's roof and sprayed death down on those of Wald's men who had broken through the lines. Several of them screamed, fell, and died, but others fired up at Lovina and forced her to fall back. She climbed off the roof on the other side of Buddy's and tried to provide covering fire for the stragglers out front. Many volunteers fell to shots from the advancing trucks. Wald's men in the trenches moved past the barricades, overrunning them.

Lovina was the last one into Buddy's as the men from the trucks disembarked right in front of the roadhouse, guns barking as their feet hit the ground. Lovina rolled one of her few precious flash-bang grenades into their midst. The grenade exploded in a blast of blinding light and deafening sound, giving her time to fall back and for Barb and Carl to secure the main door to Buddy's behind her.

"That went south fast," Lovina said, checking her magazine and then slapping it back into the rifle. "How many we lose out there?"

"Eight, ten?" Carl said. "Too damn many. Would have been more if not for Ava."

Lovina looked around the roadhouse. Every window was boarded up, with at least one citizen with some kind of firearm manning it. The children, the elderly, and all the other noncombatants were on the stage side of the roadhouse, huddled at the picnic tables, looking frightened and confused. There were over fifty of them, who had been saved in advance of the purge. There was the low murmur of tense conversation punctuated by the squalls of children and infants. Jesus, infants!

Lovina laid the rifle on the bar, walked over to one of the walls, and leaned against it. She rubbed her face and tried to think of a way out of this. "Agnes and Ava?" Lovina asked Barb without turning from the wall.

"Holed up at the old mansion up on the hill," Barb said. "I just radioed them and they're okay."

"You guys carry Dixie Beer?" Lovina asked, her face still to the wall.

"What?" Carl said. "Um, no."

"It's okay," Lovina said. "Just wishful thinking."

There was a squawk of static on the walkies, and then Wald's voice. "Hello in there? You hearing me?"

Lovina sighed and turned; she picked up her walkie and keyed the mike. "Yes, we hear you," she said.

"Who the fuck is this?" Wald asked. She could almost see him holding the CB mike, standing at the door of his tow truck.

"I'm the person on the roof who should have blown your big old potato head clean off the minute I saw you," she said. "What do you want?"

"You must be that bitch that followed the Master in," Wald said. "He said you might be trouble. I think he gave you too much credit. I want you to bring everyone outside, right now. No weapons, hands on heads."

"Why?" Lovina asked. "So you can execute us, like those other poor souls you killed this morning?"

"Yes," Wald said. "But we'll kill you all clean—a bullet in the skull. You wait a few more hours and then the shadows will creep in, and the packs of Black-Eyed Children. They'll kill you all much more painfully, with much more terror for all those stupid cattle in there. Those babies you have in there, those children . . . every single one of them will be bitten, infected, and turned—their sweet little souls eaten like cotton candy and made to become shells for the Horned Man. You want that?"

"Why?" Lovina said, resting her head on the wall now, closing her eyes. Her voice was low but strong. "Why children, you sick fucker? Why do the adults who get bitten die?"

There was a pause for a moment, then Wald's voice replied, "I asked the Master once," he said. "He told me that only youth still had souls pure and intact enough for the shadows to suckle, to feed on, and grow strong—to incubate. By the time you're our age, your soul is shot—tattered, torn—but you already knew that—I can tell by the sound of your voice, by the way you killed those men." There was another pause on the radio, and then Wald's voice returned. "So what do you say, whore? Come on out and everyone gets a quick death, even the kiddies."

Lovina opened her eyes and stood. "How about if I walk through that door and kill as many of you as I can, taking extra-special care to shoot your ugly ass first, bitch."

"I don't think so," Wald replied. "I guess we do this the hard way. I set fire to the old gin joint and then you and the lot burn to death in there, or you run out and we cut you down. Either one is fine by me."

Barb and Carl looked at each other. Barb ran to the bar sink and grabbed a wash bucket. She turned the faucet and only a thin trickle of water came out "They shut off the water," she said. Carl looked at Lovina, and she looked down at the radio in her hand.

"What do we do?" Carl asked.

Lovina switched the channel selector on the radio to Channel 23. "Break, break, 2-3," she said. "This is Lovina Marcou, I'm a Louisiana State Police officer, and if anyone can hear me, I need assistance, repeat, 10-78—officer requesting assistance." She closed her eyes as she spoke. She had been here so many times in her life. Outside, she could hear Wald's killers busying themselves with jerricans of gasoline. How many times do you get to sidestep death in a single lifetime? She thought of the children, the babies laughing, playing, shouting, crying, cooing on the other side of the room, unaware of what was happening, what was about to happen, and she did something she seldom did anymore: she prayed. To what or to whom she was praying, she had no idea. "Please, if anyone can hear me, please respond," Lovina continued. "We have civilians, about seventy-five, including children and infants, in a roadhouse in Four Houses. We are surrounded by armed hostiles. Please 10-78, 10-78. If anyone can hear me, we need help." Lovina opened her eyes. She looked over at Carl and Barb; the couple were holding hands and looking at each other. Lovina could smell the gas now; soon the enemy would begin splashing it on everything. She had one last prayer in her. "The wheel turns," she said into the walkie. "The wheel turns." She set the radio down and took up her rifle. She would open the door and charge and take as many of the bastards with her as she could. Suddenly, Barb and Carl were beside her. Carl had an old 12-gauge shotgun, Barb a .357 pistol.

"What . . . ? What are you—" Lovina asked.

"The wheel turns," Barb said.

Carl nodded, and jacked a shell into the chamber. "The wheel turns," he said. "We're with you."

The walkie crackled on the bar counter. "Break 2-3, break 2-3," a booming voice said. "You hang in there, Lovina. You've got help coming. The wheel turns, darlin'!" Outside, there was the bellicose blast of a semi's air horn, coming from down the two-lane. There were shouts of confusion and orders barked, then a horrendous crash. There were screams of evil men dying, the ugly burp of automatic weapons fire.

"Jimmie?" Lovina said, grinning from ear to ear. "Everyone stay low!" she shouted. "Barb, Carl, cover me and protect the civilians. Get on the horn to Agnes and Ava! See if they can lay down a little cover fire, too."

The door to Buddy's slammed open, and Lovina came out firing. What she saw made her heart leap in her chest. Jimmie Aussapile's rig had rammed the lead truck, flipped it, and demolished it. The mangled bodies of Wald's killers were scattered everywhere. Heck Sinclair, his face hidden by his Oni demon mask and helmet, was outside the truck, standing on the step used to climb up into the cab; one hand was holding on to the large grab handle, and with the other hand he was spraying bullets into Wald's people with his MP9. Jimmie backed the rig up, freeing it from the tangled mess that had been the Ford, and, with another blast of the horn, rammed the old Chevy, sending it flipping over and crushing several of the gunmen in the process. Heck laughed maniacally and blasted another group of the fleeing killers. Several of them fell and were still.

Lovina sprinted out and opened fire on a group of Wald's men who were using the mangled Ford's hulk for cover. They screamed and fell. A few dived for cover and ran. She saw Wald's tow truck driving away down the eastbound side of the two-lane, the way it had come not too long ago. She had raised her rifle and sighted the fleeing truck in her scope when she heard the heavy click of a shotgun chambering just behind her ear. She froze. There was the distant crack of a rifle, and she heard a thud behind her. She turned to see one of Wald's assassins, dead, with a neat hole in his forehead. She looked up the hill toward the old mansion and saw Agnes lowering her rifle and giving her the "V for victory" sign. She looked back up the two-lane, but Wald's truck was out of sight.

Jimmie had backed up the rig and was shutting it down. Once the semi's engine was still, it was very quiet on the road. Heck hopped down off the stoop and ran over to Lovina. They both laughed and fist-bumped. "What took you so damn long," she said, with a smile, and hugged the biker.

"We literally just got here," Heck said. "Heard your SOS and hauled ass."

Barb and Carl walked out the door of the roadhouse, followed by the citizens inside Buddy's, who began to stream out, shouting and cheering, as they realized the fight was won. Jimmie and Max made their way through the crowd of thankful citizens toward Lovina and Heck.

"Well," Jimmie said with a smile, "going to need a little paint and body work, I reckon."

Lovina hugged him tight. "Thank you," she said. "I knew you'd come."

"Hey," Jimmie said, "out on the road we look out for each other, look out for our own."

Lovina hugged him again and then turned and hugged Max. The professor stiffened at the contact for a second and then melted into it, almost collapsing in Lovina's arms.

"You got Max to thank for getting us here," Heck said.

Lovina pulled away from Max enough to look into her big, dark eyes, hidden behind the glasses. She had very beautiful eyes—almost innocent, actually. "You keep saving my life," Lovina said. "Thank you."

Max looked down, "Uh, you don't have to, um—that is, uh . . . Thanks . . . you're welcome," she said. Lovina looked past Max and saw Ava helping Agnes down the drive of the old mansion, back toward the roadhouse. Both women were smiling and talking.

"First round's on the house," Carl called out to much renewed cheering.

It was well after three in the afternoon, and Buddy's hadn't been so rowdy, so alive, in decades, perhaps longer. The joint was filled with the sounds of laughter, toasts, and cheers. Those who had fallen had been gathered, their bodies safe and at rest; their families, if they had any, were enveloped in love and care by the whole town. A few noble souls volunteered to man the barricades, armed with a duffel-bag cache of weapons Heck had obtained from the Blue Jocks' Kansas City chapter on the way up from Georgia. However, the general consensus was that the majority of the Master of the Hunt's servants had been killed, and the few surviving stragglers posed little threat.

For most townsfolk, today was a huge victory, a change in the way things had been in the town for centuries. But for the occupants of one of the picnic tables near the back of the stage area, the mood was slightly muted.

Jimmie, Lovina, Heck, Max, and Ava devoured all the food brought out from the kitchen to their table by Barb and Carl, with very little talking and lots of eating. Enough time was afforded between gulps, chomps, and furious chewing to make introductions and for everyone to compare notes on how they had come to Four Houses. Lovina and Jimmie, especially, were happy to learn that Ava was one of the missing children they had been looking for.

Agnes joined them after feeding Dennis, who was bundled up on a cot with the other civilians, and making sure that he was resting comfortably. "Oh, very nice to see I was afforded a few scraps," she said, smiling and plucking a chicken leg out of Heck's hand before he could take his first bite.

"Don't get between me and my chow, old lady," Heck said. "We'll tussle."

"You'll lose," Agnes said, taking a bite. "Food's always better after a battle. Sex, too."

Jimmie's horrified face came up out of his plate. Max, Ava, and Lovina laughed, and Heck hugged Agnes and leaned in close to take a bite of her chicken leg.

"Aw, a lassie after my own heart," Heck said. "Care for a quick snog, you fiery vixen?"

"Away with you, child," Agnes said, taking a bite of the leg now herself. "I am a married woman, you crass highway brigand. Now, if I'd met you in, say, 1942, you might have stood a chance. I always had a thing for Scots. Don't tell Dennis."

"Nae a whisper," Heck said, affecting his best Scottish brogue.

Having cleared the meager remains of the platters of fried chicken, biscuits, baked beans, mashed potatoes, and collard greens from the table, the Kesners joined them.

"That was as good a meal as I can recall ever having at a roadhouse, folks," Jimmie said, burping slightly. "Thank you."

"Aw, thanks," Barb said. "You guys deserve it."

"Everyone is celebrating," Carl said. "I don't have the heart to tell them that in about four hours we have another fight on our hands when the monsters come out after dark."

"I think we can help with that, somewhat," Max said. "A little secret weapon in the truck."

"Chasseur is up to something," Agnes said, dabbing her lips with a napkin. "He picked today, after all this time, to finally wipe out everyone in the town. No, something's about to happen—an endgame, I'd wager. And I believe that it's predicated on Ava's, and now Lovina's, arrival in Four Houses."

"What's so special about me?" Lovina asked.

"You both threaten his superiority here," she said. "The house with the chain-link fence called to you. It needs you to heal it, the same way the house on the hill needs Ava. The houses have been waiting for someone to come to undo what the Master of the Hunt did so long ago."

"The wells," Ava said. "The wells in the basements. Chasseur sealed them in some kind of ritual sacrifice when he burned the houses and murdered the old occupants."

"Yes, dear," Agnes said. "Correct."

"Are there CliffsNotes for this?" Heck said. "Because I'm lost here."

Max gasped and jumped to her feet. "Yes, yes, of course, yes!"

"Oh, that explains it," Heck said. "Thanks for clearing that up for me, Doc."

Max shook her head, and her great mane of dark hair flew back and forth. "Four Houses! Of course, Four Houses . . . One, two, three, and then the fourth, three plus one . . . in opposition—the many versus singular . . . Yes! The tetragrammaton—the four-letter name of God! Don't you see?"

Jimmie frowned. Heck grinned and looked to Lovina, who seemed confused as well.

"Um, Dr. Leher," Carl said. "I'm afraid I don't . . ."

Max was pacing around the table now, with the fervor of a child playing musical chairs, waiting for the music to stop. She pointed to Ava. "Maiden," she said, then she pointed to Lovina. "Mother."

"I beg your pardon," Lovina said, raising an eyebrow.

Max went on, pointing to Agnes. "Crone," she said.

Agnes nodded. "Yes," she said. "You're getting it, Professor."

"Wait, that's the Triple Goddess thing you were talking about," Jimmie said. "You said that had something to do with the universe being all messed up."

Max eagerly pointed to Jimmie, then to her own nose, nodding. "Exactly, yes, yes!" Max said. "Four is a powerful number in numerology. It is a number of renewal, of clearing a system—of rebooting it, if you will! If this town and those dwellings are, in fact, conduits for primal powers, then Chasseur has unbalanced everything by tampering here!"

"Hold it," Lovina said. "Are you trying to say that those old, burned-down houses are linked to the fundamental forces of the universe, and to me, Ava, and Agnes? Seriously?"

Max sat down as abruptly as she had stood. She grabbed a biscuit from the napkin in front of her and began to pull the bread apart layer by layer. "The universe operates on multiple levels, multiple scales," she said, holding up part of the biscuit and then popping it into her mouth. She kept talking around the food. "All at the same time. Like the old saying 'as above so below.' At some point in time, this space became a place of power; it attracted individuals that the power could work through, that mirrored its purpose, like water seeking the cracks in stone."

"So there's some kind of cosmic war taking place in this little town in Kansas?" Heck said. "If this is, like, fundamental forces of nature, how can teeny, tiny little human beings upset shit so badly? How would the universe not have been screwed up a long time ago if it was that easy?"

"In the truck headed here," Max said, "we reasoned that the Master of the Hunt had sacrificed one of his first victims on the highway near here, tapping into the Road and all that ley-line energy it was channeling. If he dedicated that to his patron, to the Horned Man, then all that additional power would have tipped the balance even further and upset the interaction between the forces more. The Horned Man is ascendant; the Triple Goddess is diminished."

"It's not a war, Heck," Agnes said. "Nature is not good or evil. We put those names on it. These powers simply are, like water or wind. The Horned Man is part of the natural cycle. He has his place in the making and unmaking of things. His image, that of Cernunnos, was taken by the early Christians to embody their concept of evil—Lucifer—but that is simply us, putting faces on what we can't fully understand. We dress these powers up in human forms, attribute to them human motives. We can no more comprehend them than bacteria can comprehend us. Chasseur is insane, and he's tapped into true power. The Horned Man is the essence of predation, of negation, the mercilessness, the rutting of life, of nature."

"Sounds like a perfect fit for a serial killer," Heck said.

"He's a narcissistic fiend," Agnes said. "Chasseur has no clue, and less care, what he's wrecking."

"What, exactly, is he wrecking?" Ava asked. "The world, the planets, the galaxies—they're all still spinning along okay, it seems. He's been at this for decades."

"You tell me," Max said. "The forces of creation, moderation, and stability have been lessened on every level from the quantum to the macro, and the fury of nature—the unchecked, uncaring, unreasoning force that seeks dominance over all systems, over all life—is riding high. Sound familiar to you?"

"Point taken," Ava said. "It does seem like the world has gotten crueler, nature more brutal. But if Chasseur already did all this and things are already screwed up, all out of balance, then what's he doing now?"

"He sent Mark Stolar," Jimmie said, "to give to George Norse, the paranormal-TV-show guy, a video of him hunting a girl in the woods back in the nineties to air on his show tonight. Cecil Dann messaged me that the video had the shadow hounds in it and, apparently, a glimpse of the Horned Man, too."

"Like in the Internet videos Shawn Ruth and Karen Collie and their friends saw," Lovina said.

"Sounds like it," Jimmie said, sipping his iced tea. "I think it might be the whole video that the kids had seen parts of on various paranormal websites." Again, Jimmie had a weird feeling something was very important, and he wished he could reach out and grab whatever it was. That video . . . something he had heard recently . . . something about watching, looking . . . seeing? Seeing, yes.

He looked to Max. "Max, you said people who saw the Wild Hunt . . . bad things happened to them, right?"

"Yes," Max said. "It was bad luck to see the Hunt. Those who did see it disappeared, or—"

"Or died," Heck said, the realization coming to him, too.

"Oh, no," Lovina said. "No, no . . . that video . . . Norse's show. Millions of people, all over the world watch that show. . . ."

"And will see that video," Jimmie said. "They'll see the Wild Hunt."

"Yes," Agnes said. "And the Hunt will come for them, claim them—every single last one of them, men, women, and children. Especially the children. That's his endgame."

"Aw, shit!" Heck said, rising, even as his voice did. "No fucking way, no! That son of a bitch! I'll suck his fucking eyes out! We've got to call Dann, have him stop that fucking video!"

"Mind your language, squire," Jimmie said. "Got children in here. Don't need to get them all riled up. We can't call Cecil or anyone else; I wish we could. Remember where we are? This place don't exist."

"Tonight's April 30th," Max said. "Beltane. As the Pagan, Chasseur always murdered, always sacrificed, on Wiccan holy days, like tonight. He's about to perform the largest sacrificial rite in human history. That much energy, that much death, focused in his belief," Max said. "It sends everything crashing down."

"Define 'everything,' " Ava said.

"Imagine the universe tearing itself apart," Max said. "The imbalance would become too great for the system to right itself: the serpent eating its own tail, devouring itself—the death throes of creation."

"We've got to stop him," Barb said. "There's no one else, and no more time."

"What's the plan, chief?" Heck asked Jimmie.

Jimmie rubbed his face. Everyone at the table was looking at him, waiting for what came out of his mouth next. It occurred to him that he had been up for almost three days straight now. His mortgage was past due, his ribs and his back ached from the beating he took in the Atlanta hotel room. He was going to miss his window to pick up the load that his family desperately needed him to deliver. And the universe was teetering on the brink of collapse. He sighed. It all seemed too big, too much. He thought of Layla and the kids, and he pushed the exhaustion, the doubt, and the fear away.

"I ain't got one, yet," Jimmie said. "But I'm damn sure we can improvise."

They walked out of Buddy's just before 7 P.M. The final brilliant struggle of sunlight was above the line of the horizon, and the sky had deepened to a gunmetal blue. The light was dying, and soon the shadows would come to feed upon it.

Everyone had wanted to get moving sooner—they had less than an hour before Norse's show went on the air, in the network studio in New York. However, there were parts of the plan that had to be hashed out, and the protection of the innocents remaining at Buddy's had to be organized.

Heck, Jimmie, Ava, Lovina, Max, Barb, Agnes, and Carl stood outside the roadhouse. Each was carrying weapons and bags of gear, and each was lost in thought. They all looked up at the darkening sky. "Everyone good?" Jimmie asked the group. "Everybody knows what they have to do, know our timetable?" The party nodded, gave a thumbs-up, or muttered in the affirmative.

"I know we're all scared," Jimmie said. "This all seems so damn big, so important, and we're all so . . . not. I want you to think of someone on the other side of the world, someone you love or care for, someone who might be watching that show tonight. Think of them and do what you need to do. That's all I got for you. Let's move like we got a purpose, people."

The party scattered.

Heck walked over to Jimmie. "I ain't scared," he said, lighting up a Lucky Strike. "I'm looking forward to it."

"Yeah," Jimmie said. "I kind of thought you might be. That's why I'm sending you to do the job. You have the best chance of pulling it off, and you'll have the best time doing it."

"When you met me, you got pissed because I cut loose, all Ted Nugent *Double Live Gonzo*, in that restaurant full of psychos, remember?" Heck said.

"Yeah, I do," Jimmie said, as he slid some chaw into his cheek. "Right now, I need you to go a little *Double Live Gonzo* on these sumbitches."

"I can do that," Heck said. "I'm real good at it. Second nature."

The men nodded to each other and then went their separate ways. Jimmie paused and turned. "Just bring your ass back," he said. "I ain't done squiring you yet." The biker raised a hand as he walked toward his motorcycle, now sitting beside Jimmie's battered semi. "I'll bring it back, boss," Heck said without turning around. "My ass is my best feature."

. . .

Lovina was huddled with Ava and Agnes near the semi, going over a few final details. Max hovered near the circle of the three, silently. Lovina sensed her and turned to look at her. She walked over to her. "You okay?" Lovina asked.

Max nodded, her lips pursed. "I am," she said. "I . . . wanted to . . . wish you good luck."

"You did?" Lovina's eyes were bright as she spoke, stepping a little closer to Max, who for all the world reminded her of a deer—skittish, gentle, almost too gentle for this world. "You stay close to Jimmie; he'll look after you. And don't get hurt. I hear you nearly died getting here. I don't want you doing that again, you hear me?"

"I do," Max said. "I don't want you getting hurt, either."

"I promise I won't, if you do the same," Lovina said.

Max laughed. "Deal," she said, and extended her hand. "Shake on it." The handshake held; neither wanted to break it, the sensation of warm skin on warm skin, the power that moved from their fingertips to their arms and passed between them in their eyes. Max's red lips parted in a nearly audible gasp. Lovina's eyes held Max's, almost losing herself in them. Max felt as if her body were made of helium, and her stomach made of lead.

"Gotta go now," Max said. "Um, world to save, and um, things."

Lovina nodded, and the sphinxlike smile returned to her lips.

"Me, too," she said. "I'll see you on the other side of this. Remember your promise."

They walked away from each other. Neither looked back out of fear, a fear very different from any that could be summoned by serial killers, murderous shadows, or horned gods.

. . .

"Well," Ava said to Agnes, "I guess this is it." Ava looked up the high hill and the winding stone drive to the old burned husk of a house that called to her. "I shouldn't be the one here," she said. "It should have been Alana. I'm . . . I'm not a good person, Agnes. I'm not even sure, most times, what kind of person I really am. I react—I don't think, I'm selfish, and superficial. I'm not the person for this. The person for this died in that field the first night we came here."

Agnes took her by the shoulders. "Dear, none of us knows who we are and what we can do until the world forces us to. You've shown me all I need to know about you. If you can't trust yourself, then please, trust me. You will do well, Ava. Very well. Goodbye for now, dear, and thank you for all you've already done." The two women parted, Agnes toward Jimmie's rig. Ava remained, alone now in the gathering dusk. She sighed, wiped her eyes, gathered her pack, and began walking toward the Maiden's house up on the hill.

"We'll hold down the fort," Carl said to Jimmie as the trucker helped Agnes up into the cab of his idling rig. "We're all as ready as we can be. Those shadow bastards and BEKs won't know what hit them."

"Good luck, guys!" Barb called out, as they drove away. "Go kick their butts!"

In the rig, Jimmie set the clock on his mounted laptop to give him a countdown till showtime. The clock said 7:21:00. Jimmie hit the start button, and the countdown began. He pushed Play on the digital player. Neil Young's "Rockin' in the Free world" tore its way out of the cab's speaker. Jimmie looked back at his own eyes in the reflection of the driver's-side window—gut check. Less than forty minutes to save the world, to save Layla, and Peyton, and his baby—to save his world. He jammed the rig into gear, felt it snarl.

"Let's roll," he said.

TWENTY-THREE "10-10"

Scode's Garage was lit up, as always, in the darkness of Four Houses, a Judas beacon, a false promise of aid and comfort in the night. Wald was sitting outside in his chair, beside the door to the office. He cradled a shotgun and was sipping a grape Nehi. The old, hissing AM radio in the office was playing Johnny Cash's "Ring of Fire." Today's sweep had been a disaster because of the old witch, because of the one that had followed the Master back to Four Houses, and because of that damned truck driver. The Master would make them all pay tonight. Let them live another night—if they survived the shadows and the packs, tomorrow would find them in a world where everywhere was like Four Houses.

He took another sip of his soda, a simple pleasure, and relaxed, closing his eyes like a snake sunning itself on a rock. There was a crash and a clatter, and Wald felt the sour wad of acid in his belly hiss. He opened his eyes and looked toward the source of his irritation. Toby was in the garage bay. He was pushing trash from the floor of the garage outside through the open bay doors and had accidentally knocked over a metal toolbox. He wore a gun belt with an old revolver and a knife on it. He had a hunting rifle slung over his shoulder.

"Hey, Wald," Toby said, "are you still mad at me?"

"Shut up," Wald said, and took another swallow from the narrow glass bottle of soda.

The heavy bass purr of a motorcycle engine could be heard heading west, toward the station. Toby stopped pushing the broom and looked in the direction of the lone headlight stabbing the darkness. "Is that the Master?" he asked.

Wald slowly lowered his Nehi as the light grew brighter and the engine louder. He leaned forward in his chair. "No," he said, hesitantly, at first. "No, it isn't!" Wald stood, his Nehi bottle crashing as he leveled the shotgun.

Heck's bike tore into the parking lot of the garage like wrath itself, his metal Oni face mask reflecting the harsh light of the lot in its demonic grin. He fired on the gas pumps with his MP9, spraying a rain of tracer rounds at them. The pumps exploded in a column of brilliant flame, climbing high into the night sky. Wald fired as he flew backward from the blast. The glass walls of the garage office buckled and shattered in the wake of the fireball. Sizzling drops of gasoline rained down across the lot, hitting cars and the roof of Scode's Garage.

Toby unslung his rifle and ran out to find his brother in the hellish tableau. "Wald! Wald!" he screamed as he swept the rifle before him. He saw a figure walking toward him through the smoke and the fiery rain. It was Heck, walking slowly toward him, machine gun pointed toward the ground, his leering mask hiding his eyes in the wells of jumping shadows caused by the fire.

"The kids," Heck said, his voice muffled by the steel and the cackle of the fires. "The college kids, where are they, asshole?"

Toby raised the rifle to his shoulder to fire. It was an awkward motion. Heck's machine gun came up smooth, fluid, like breathing. Toby closed his eyes in anticipation of the bullets ripping through him. There was a roar, and for a moment Toby thought the gas pumps were exploding again. He opened his eyes to see the man in the demon mask lying on the ground, his gun a few feet from him.

Wald stepped into view, his shotgun still smoking. He looked at Toby and shook his head. "Goddamned useless," he muttered.

Toby smiled. "Thanks for saving me, Wald!"

"Shit!" Wald said as he kicked Heck's still form with his work boot. The biker groaned a little but didn't move. "I didn't give a shit about saving your miserable ass. You gave me a chance to drop him, dead bang. Fucking scooter trash, wreck my livelihood, will you?" Wald kicked Heck in the side, hard. Heck groaned a little more. "Looks like his leathers, helmet, and mask stopped most of the shot, but not all. He's alive. He's gonna wish he wasn't."

The fire was still raging, but the rain of gas seemed to have stopped. Wald kicked Heck again and then grabbed him by one of his ankles. "Make yourself useful, moron," he said to Toby. "Grab the other one. We're going to drag him inside."

"What you going to do to him, Wald?" Toby said as he grabbed Heck's other ankle and they began to drag the biker across the asphalt toward the garage bays.

"Get me the blowtorch and I'll show you," Wald said.

. . .

Lovina walked toward the Mother's house a few miles down the road from Buddy's—the burned house, the one with the chain-link fence and the NO TRESPASSING sign. It was dark when she reached the fence. A few stars were beginning to show themselves in the dark, cool night. Lovina grabbed the bar of the fence and swung herself over. She landed low and looked up into the growling maw of a shadow hound.

"Beat it," Lovina said as she fired the tiny laser pointer in her hand at the hound's face. The shadow howled, smoked, and staggered away before melting into the night. Lovina stood and moved across the lawn toward the front door. "I hope you little suckers don't leave shadow poop all over the lawn," she muttered.

She found the front door locked and knelt, slipping out her picks. A sense of déjà vu settled over her. This had all started with her picking Dewey Rears's apartment door. Was that a week ago? Seemed like aeons had passed. The lock was old and stiff, but it clicked. Lovina felt the tumblers give and the front door clicked open, a little too loudly for her taste. She slipped inside and clicked on her Maglite flashlight. The house smelled of smoke, burned plastic, and a faint, sweet-stale hint of something else—something that had gone bad. She closed the door and locked it, in the hope of not having uninvited guests to the party. The place had the feel of a seventies house, despite the much older façade. The carpet in the entry hall was pale blue industrial. Dark stains, drag marks, ran from the door into the dark. She moved along the hall carefully, quietly, each step measured, her breathing even, flashlight in one hand, her Glock in the other. She held them together, the way she had learned as a cop, sweeping each area to make sure it was empty before moving along.

She scanned the stairwell to the second floor on her left with the light and the pistol—clear. She moved past the stairs. Two doorways—one to the right into a den, most likely, and one ahead into what was almost certainly a kitchen. She swept the gun and the light into the den, putting her back to the hallway wall, so that the kitchen doorway was on her left.

The halo of light from the flashlight swept the room. The carpeted floor of the den was covered with huddled Black-Eyed Kids, apparently slumbering. There were dozens of them, lying on top of one another, as if they had simply fallen there. More were crowded, sitting in a row, on the tacky plastic-covered old sofa, their hoodie-covered heads bowed like monks in prayer.

Her breathing caught a little and she quickly swept the kitchen door. More BEKs, at least a dozen more, slumbering everywhere—on the kitchen counters, on the floor, like a nest of rats.

Lovina used the wall at her back as a guide to slide farther, hoping she would find the basement door just around the corner. She holstered her Glock and reached back, slowly, carefully with her hand, half expecting to feel vise-strong hands grab her wrist and then the agonizing bite. She felt a cool, smooth doorknob. It turned easily. She swept the flashlight back into the den. In the pale wash of the light, the BEKs on the couch all raised their heads as one and regarded her with Stygian eyes.

"Shit!" Lovina had time to say as she went for her slung AR-15. In the bouncing circle of light, the universe had become a jerky, time-stop movement—angry, screeching, pale cherubic faces with maws of razor-sharp fangs, all moving at blinding, strobe-light speed, all launching straight toward her.

■ ■ ■

As night fell, the celebration at Buddy's quieted. The realization of what would likely be coming for them made everyone still and awkward with fear. They had defied the Master of the Hunt, and now his inhuman servants would come to do what his human hounds could not.

Those who could fight got ready to, armed with the gear that the trucker, Aussapile, and his allies had brought into Four Houses. Those who could not prepared to run ammo, treat the injured, or comfort and calm the infirm and the children.

"Where did my blasted pistol get to?" Dennis Cottington asked Barb as she pulled his blankets up closer to his chin. "I do believe that I gave it to that girl Julia," he said.

Barb nodded and smiled her "everything is going to be okay" smile. "We'll find it," she said. "You rest, Dennis. I have to go, but I'll be back to check on you."

"Tell Aggie I love her, and I'm sorry I got shot and can't help her," Dennis said, his eyes slightly damp, the tears hovering at the borders. "Not that she needs my help. Tell my beautiful girl to give the Jerries what for, for me, yes?"

Barb laughed and put something in Dennis's hand. "You see any Nazis you shoot them, okay?"

"Very good, Brigadier," Dennis said, and saluted her.

There were about forty men and women ready to defend the roadhouse. Barb joined them, next to Carl. "Everyone is tucked in and has defenders," she said. "We moved all the emergency lights and generators in there in case they decide to cut the power. How we've had power at all in this town all these years, anyway, is a mystery to me."

"Good," Carl said, and kissed her. "Okay, everyone. We've planned this out and we know what to do when that plan goes to hell, right?" The assembled group muttered agreement, nodded.

Steve Franco, the retired schoolteacher who had been stranded in Four Houses with his wife and kids for a little over a year, spoke up. "Carl, you think these things will really work?" he asked. "If not, this is going to be . . . well, a massacre." He lowered his voice at the last, glancing in the direction of his boys. His wife, Ann, stood beside him, ready to fight.

Carl nodded. "You're right, but from what we've found out today there's a massacre coming all across the world in less than an hour. There are good people out there right now trying to stop it, maybe dying to stop it. Here, right now, this is our battle in that war. We're going to keep our people alive and safe, and we're going to destroy as many of the enemy as we can. This is our only chance of doing that, Steve, the only chance we've had in a long time. I say it's worth the risk."

The temperature inside the bar dropped. Something in the silence of the vacant corners shifted, flowed. The shadow people began to appear everywhere, dozens of them, dozens upon dozens, stretching out of each sliver of darkness, grasping toward the terrified living, huddling against the light.

"This is it!" Carl shouted. "Keep them away from the kids and the seniors!" He turned to Barb and saw all he needed to see in her eyes. They kissed. It was just like the first kiss. Carl turned, holding his wife's hand, as Barb moved to cover his back. "Make the bastards pay for every one of us!"

The shadows fell, enough to devour even the memory of light.

. . .

Agent Cecil Dann felt the interminable discomfort of not having a plan, not having an idea how to solve the puzzle—hell, of not having all the pieces he needed to know what the damn puzzle even looked like. This was how he felt every damn time he heard the name Jimmie Aussapile. He checked his phone for the millionth time. No call back from the Justice Department's attorney. No call back from Aussapile or any of his freaky friends, no one hijacking his cell phone, nothing. He paced back and forth in the greenroom—the guest lounge in the studio of George Norse's TV show, "Paranormal America Live." The studio audience was being warmed up by a series of video interviews Norse had done previously on the show and on his international radio program. Dann could watch all that on one of the large monitors in the lounge. On another monitor, he saw the promo for the show for the third time in the past hour. The network was pushing this broadcast and promoting the hell out of the fact that an infamous serial killer had made contact with the show.

Dann checked his phone again. He was hoping the Department of Justice's lawyer would give him the go-ahead to pull the plug on the show and confiscate the original tape, but Norse's network attorneys had been screaming about First Amendment rights, and the weasel from Justice was ducking for cover. He wished he knew exactly what was going on, but his gut told him it was a bad idea to do what a murdering psychopath wanted you to do, and this was exactly what the Pagan wanted to happen.

Dann looked at the clock on the wall: nineteen minutes until air time. "Typical," he said. "The one time I want you to butt in you're nowhere to be seen."

. . .

Ava dropped down into the basement of the house of the Maiden. She swept the flashlight around. The basement was empty—no monsters waiting to gobble her up, no BEK chrysalises or bloodthirsty shadows. The door that she and Agnes had escaped through swayed open in the night breeze. She had taken her time approaching the mansion, waiting until the attack on Buddy's had begun, then moving painfully slow, inches at a time, through the high grass. A pack of Black-Eyed Children had waited languidly near the entrance to the Maiden's home.

With only a few minutes remaining until eight, the pack had suddenly frozen for a moment and then sprinted off in the direction of the house of the Mother. It looked as if Lovina was in and keeping them busy, just as they had planned. That was good. Ava was no badass, like the Louisiana cop or even Agnes. She was a college student and a coward, she knew, regardless of Dennis's gun on her hip. Once the BEKs were gone, Ava moved quickly inside and made her way to the basement.

She moved to the capstone of the well. She carefully removed the skeleton. Some of the bones clattered, falling apart as she lifted them. She shuddered and laid the other bones down as gingerly as she could. "Sorry," she whispered. She took out the small pry bar and looked around the stone for a weak point to begin. She found as good a spot as any and began to work on the crumbling stone. After a few moments, a small chunk cracked and came loose. Ava pulled it free and tossed it aside. A shaft of painfully white light hissed from the opening, like what Agnes had shown Ava in her basement. Ava reached toward the light and felt a force pushing her hand away. A crashing flood of images and memories swarmed her mind. Other voices, other lives. She looked at the bones on the floor and knew her name. Ava struggled to pry more of the stone loose, and more light erupted. The whole basement began to fill with the harsh light. The pre-set alarm on Ava's cell phone began to chirp. It was the end of the countdown; they were out of time. The TV show was starting. Ava thought of her dad, her brother, even of her aloof mom watching, being devoured by some faceless, timeless thing.

A group of shadow people appeared at the open basement door, trying to slide inside. The light obliterated them. A swarm of BEKs dropped into the basement from the ruined stairs, and the light reduced them to smoke instantly. Ava kept tearing the stone away, prying it loose and smashing more, frantically, as the creatures continued to try to reach her. Each crumbling bit of stone freed more and more light.

She began to feel the presence behind the memories and the images; it was relentless, swelling up in her head like a cluster migraine. The pressure made her feel as if her skull was going to crack and fall apart like the crumbling capstone. As the pressure behind her eyes grew stronger, Ava had an awful thought: The force at the bottom of her well was powerful, primal, and it would stop at nothing to be free. She struck the capstone again, and another chunk of the stone shattered and fell away, devoured by the light. What if, she thought through the storm of alien memories and squeezing pain, the inhuman forces that they were trying to free tonight were no better, no less ruthless or relentless or destructive, than the Horned Man? Her hands were smashing stone of their own accord now. The light was pouring forth, shining through every window, every crack and crevice in the old house, filling the night with its awful, remorseless beauty, and filling Ava with the ghosts of other lives, an unrelenting fear, and an alien purpose.

. . .

The semi pulled up in front of Agnes's house, the house of the Crone. Off to the left, there was a rumble and a brilliant rising ball of orange fire and trailing black smoke.

"That would be Heck," Jimmie said, jabbing a thumb in the direction of the explosion. "Subtle, our kilted ninja." Jimmie helped Agnes down out of the cab. He noted that the countdown clock in the truck said time was almost up—it was fifteen minutes until eight o'clock.

Jimmie helped Max down next. The professor had her face in her tablet and was working furiously, even as she climbed down. "Jimmie, I'm not sure I can do this," she said, shaking her head at the numbers.

"Viamancy works off motion and spatial formulas, and the power coming off the Road. I don't have any of that here. I don't know if we can get a message out to Agent Dann. I'm sorry."

They were walking up the stairs to the porch. Jimmie had his shotgun and was sweeping the darkness. The porch light they had left on seemed feeble, but he was thankful for any cover from the shadow people he knew were out there. "You're sorry for not pulling another miracle out of your hat, Max? It's okay. We'll figure something out. Always another option, always a way out."

Max looked at him strangely.

"What?" he said, as Agnes opened the front door.

"When you say all that, it sounds plausible," Max said. "Like we actually have a chance."

"We do," Jimmie said. "I've been in a lot worse scrapes than this, and I'm still standing. You just got to stay positive."

Agnes gasped as the front door swung open; a pair of BEKs snarled and launched themselves at the old woman, tackling her before she even had a chance to draw her Mauser. Jimmie fired the shotgun through the open door, scattering part of the horde of ink-eyed, fanged children that were hurtling toward them. He chambered another round and fired again, as more of the fast-moving little monsters filled the breach he had just made. He glanced down for a second at Agnes. She was wrestling the two children with great ferocity, more than Jimmie would have figured her capable of. One of the children tried to bite her left arm, but Agnes pushed the frightfully strong creature away. That left an opening for the other BEK, who sank its razor-sharp teeth into her right hand. Agnes moaned a little and dropped her Mauser in pain from the savage bite. Black tendrils began to creep across her hand, radiating from the bite.

"No!" Jimmie screamed, and lowered the shotgun against the BEK's head. The gun's blast was thunder; the BEK's head exploded in a bloody smoking mass. Several BEKs from the swarm in the hallway used the momentary distraction to pounce on the trucker, and now Jimmie had three of the strong, fast-moving creatures on him, their teeth snapping like piranha.

"Jimmie!" Max shouted behind him, as he struggled to keep the teeth at bay. He looked back to see Max backing away from the stairs. The night was roiling with shadow people. They were on the truck, all over the yard, everywhere—hundreds of them. The slight sound they gave made Jimmie think of a swarm of bats, their leathery wings whispering as one. Agitated, the shadow people were throwing themselves against the flickering porch light, smoking and unraveling in a mad effort to reach their human prey, slowly forcing themselves farther up the stairs, farther into the painful but dying light.

Jimmie struggled to bring the shotgun up, but small, too-strong hands were pinning his arms. Teeth clattered very near his ear, the sound of snapping bone.

The porch light made a sizzling sound and began to fade, then it came back up, but the shadows were closer now to Max, who was fumbling with her satchel. The light faded again, worse this time and a second longer. The shadow people were closer.

Jimmie thought of Layla and of Peyton, of his unborn child. The weight of failing them was greater than the monsters pinning him to the porch, preparing to tear into his flesh.

The light failed.

The shadow people were the night—they were everywhere, slipping through every narrow crack in Buddy's, surging toward the helpless, fragile humans who huddled together in fear and a primal instinct to cling to one another when death was nigh.

"Light 'em up!" Carl shouted, as he, Barb, and the other defenders brandished the small souvenir laser-pointer key chains that Jimmie and the others had delivered that afternoon. The red beams sliced through the shadows like knives and made the creatures melt into odorless smoke in their wake.

A shadow's long, slender fingers had begun to slide toward the face of a screaming, terrified six-year-old when it was struck by a crimson beam. The shadow flailed, as if in silent pain, and boiled away into smoke. Dennis Cottington, sitting up in his cot, nodded and gave the confused child a "V for Victory" sign with the hand not holding the laser pointer. The child smiled at the old man.

"Bloody Jerries," Dennis said.

"Now, Christina!" Barb shouted to Christina Moric, one of the defenders behind the bar. Christina flipped a switch on an independent power supply running to multiple power cables, and the whole interior of Buddy's was illuminated with powerful carbon arc light from a series of tripod-mounted klieg lights—the lights used in television and film production—another part of the arsenal Aussapile and his allies had brought with them. The lights made the interior of Buddy's as bright as daylight. The shadows began to come apart, smoking, almost diluting, like too little ink in too much water. In a matter of several chaotic, terrifying moments, it was over. Barb looked around the roadhouse. It was still, and no shadow remained. She looked over at Carl and smiled. His eyes narrowed, waiting for the next wave of monsters, but it didn't come. They hugged each other and listened to the tiny scary noises the thwarted shadows made, out in the night. They worried for Aussapile and the others, out there with no daylight to protect them.

. . .

Heck opened his eyes. He hurt. His side throbbed, as though someone had driven a few cigarettes into his flesh with a sledgehammer. He took a breath and felt the sharp stab of a broken rib. He'd wiped out enough times on a bike to know how that felt. He tasted some dried blood on his lips and realized that his face mask was gone. A shitty AM radio somewhere was playing Hank Williams's "Lost Highway" through a curtain of static rain. His wrists were wrapped in nylon clothesline, and he was hanging a few inches off the ground; the line binding his wrists was cradled in a mechanical winch hook. Wald and Toby Scode were in front of him. Toby was preparing a battered acetylene tank and a torch rig, while Wald watched Heck with his arms crossed and a shit-eating grin on his craggy face.

"I wouldn't smile too much with a mug like that, man," Heck croaked. "Someone might mistake it for your bum and try to wipe it." Wald's smile fell, and he drove a powerful right hook into Heck's face. There was a flash of white light behind Heck's eyes and then numbness. He was pretty sure Wald had broken his nose, also not a new experience for Heck. "Oh, oh, wait," Heck said, sucking a glob of blood up out of his crushed sinuses. The pain that caused chased the numbness away and confirmed the status of his nose. He spit the blood on Wald's work shirt. "Have we started? Okay, the safe word is . . . umm . . ." Heck looked the Scodes up and down. "Inbred?" Wald punched him again. "You sure got a purty mouth? Banjo music? Children of the Corn? Any of these working for you two scholars?"

"Give me the damn blowtorch," Wald said to Toby. "We'll see how glib this little punk is when his skin is melting off his skull like butter." The torch hissed like a cobra; a tongue of blue fire moved closer to Heck's face. Wald's eyes were glassy with rage and anticipation as the flame came closer to Heck's skin. "You're a pretty boy," Wald said. "Let's see how smart-ass you are when no one will look at you without gagging."

The blowtorch's searing flame traced a line from Heck's cheek across his broken nose and then to his other cheek. Heck jerked wildly as fire hot enough to melt steel caressed his skin. He jerked and then got very still, almost stuporous.

"Stupid bastard's already gone into shock," Wald said. "No damn fun at all." He moved the torch up to Heck's forehead, leaning in to admire his disfiguring work. Wald frowned. He moved the torch away from Heck's face and ran a finger over the blackened trail the flame had made. Under the soot was healthy skin, unmarred by the torch's heat. "What is this shit?" Wald snarled in disbelief.

Heck's eyes popped open, and he grinned the way a wolf shows his fangs to his prey. "Black magic, baby," he said. "I'm too fucking pretty to die." Heck swung both booted feet upward and drove them into Wald's abdomen, hard. Wald groaned in pain and flew backward, the torch flying backward and catching Toby in the chest. Toby screamed as skin began to blacken and crisp. His shirt caught fire. Heck used the momentum of the kick to swing back on the winch chain and wrap his legs around Toby's neck. He slipped his bound wrists off the hook and twisted as he fell to the ground. Toby's neck twisted under the torque of Heck's weight falling. There was a dry, snapping sound, and Toby's burning body hit the concrete floor of the bay and lay still. Heck tumbled and came up in a crouch, his hands still tied.

"Toby!" Wald screamed, charging toward Heck with a tire iron. "You killed my brother, you freak!" Wald swung downward with the iron. Heck raised his arms and snagged it between the coiled rope that tied him. He felt the throb of the impact deep in his wrists, but the rope caught on the edge of the tool and held long enough for him to lunge up from the floor and head-butt Wald squarely in the face. Wald fell back, blood pouring from his own broken nose. Heck stood, the fallen blowtorch in his hand. He turned it inward, the flame raking across his hand and wrist, leaving a blackened line in its wake, but no pain, no injury. The torch cut through the ropes, and they fell away. Heck looked at the torch and his hands with a mix of amusement and bewilderment before checking on Wald.

Wald was beside Toby's burning body. Tears, snot, and blood covered his face. "I'm going to kill you," he said, his voice distorted by mucus and crushed cartilage. He stood, wincing in pain but defiant. He raised the tire iron.

There was a drumming in Heck's ears, the rush of blood like massive, beating wings. A cold cruelty settled over him, slithered through him—an intrinsic knowledge of himself, like the certainty of fact. It was not an entirely alien sensation; he'd felt it in the war, in many firefights, and one horrible time, long ago, when he was young. Each time he'd felt it, it startled him, frightened him deep, deep down, below the black ice that hid his fears, his regrets. *This is me, as much as any other part— maybe even more so than the other parts. This is who I am.*

"No," Heck said in a voice that didn't sound entirely like his own. "No, I'm going to take that iron away from you, then I'm going to burn you with this torch in all the ways you were going to hurt me, and eventually you will beg me to stop. I won't."

Wald paused. His raised arm, with his makeshift weapon, trembled.

Heck continued, stepping closer, the blue flame illuminating his face, filling it with sinister shadows. He ran the torch's flame over his arms, his palm. "Then I'll ask you where those two kids you're holding are, and you'll tell me," he said. "You'll try to hold out, try to be tough, but eventually you'll tell me where they are. And I still won't stop. You're going to die in pain, fear, and regret, just like your brother, cooking away over there."

Wald looked back at his brother's still burning body. "Go to hell!" he growled, and charged at Heck, who stood, smiling, his arms raised and open, as if he were awaiting an embrace.

Heck laughed. The sound bubbled up out of him, unbidden, like a death rattle—bone raking over slate. It frightened Wald, like ice water in his guts. It frightened Heck even more.

. . .

Lovina fell down the basement stairs backward with three hissing, snarling BEKs at her throat, her AR-15 spraying fire and lead at the rest of the descending swarm as she fell. She caught herself at the base of the stairwell, grabbing hold of the railing and swinging herself wildly to one side. She smashed into an old water heater and felt a sharp stab of pain as a jagged metal part of the old tank stabbed her in the lower back.

The sudden swing helped her ditch the three BEKs. They flew to her right, and Lovina fanned the assault rifle in their direction. All three were torn to pieces by streaking tracer rounds, their burning bodies dropping near the foot of the stairwell.

The victory lasted less than a second. Lovina stepped to the mouth of the stairwell and fired upward into the mass of oil-eyed children raining down the stairs toward her, howling like rabid animals. She could feel the clip emptying as the blurring, darting small forms fell and fell and fell. Her hands moved to free a fresh clip, but her gut told her she wouldn't have time to reload. She could smell the hot brass as spent cartridges sailed from the gun past her face. More screaming faces, illuminated in gunfire, more fangs. The flash of the muzzle and the hiss of the tracers as they ignited. Tiny pale hands reaching for her, grasping toward her. Another few seconds at the most . . . three, two, one . . . out.

The AR-15 fell silent, but so did the stairwell. The shot BEKs were all evaporating into smoke before her eyes. Lovina cleared the empty magazine, slapped a fresh one in, and slid back the bolt to chamber a fresh round in the space of a single breath. She looked down to see one of the creatures, its childlike face marred by the unnaturally wide open mouth, its fangs inches from her ankle. The face melted into black smoke, like the ones they had killed with Turla in Carbon City, as she watched.

Lovina had a choice and no time to reason it through. She bounded up the stairs, through the swirling smoke of the decaying bodies, and slammed the basement door shut. She slid the small brass deadbolt into place, sealing the door. None of the bodies on the stairs had grabbed or bitten her; no tangle of strong hands had reached out from the darkness past the doorway.

Lovina gave herself a three-second vacation to catch her breath. Her gamble to risk the stairs and to shut and lock the door had paid off. She reached to the small of her back and winced. Her hand returned covered in blood. She wiped it off on her pants until her hand was dry and then headed back down the stairs. The pounding began on the basement door before she reached the bottom of the stairs. There were snarls and shrieks from the other side of the door—sounds like the ones cats make in the dead of night.

She found the well and its capstone in the northwest corner of the basement, covered with an old canvas painter's tarp. Lovina pulled the tarp off. The former inhabitant of the house, who had been sacrificed atop the well, scattered across the floor in a hollow, clattering rain of old, dry bones. Lovina cursed under her breath as she unslung her pack. The almost mechanical pounding on the thin door grew stronger, more insistent. She didn't have much time. She slung the rifle, took the small pry bar, and began to work on the edges of the capstone. The rock cracked and crumbled as she pried the heavy stone up off the lip of the well. Streams of brilliant light, like that Agnes and Ava had spoken of, poured out of every opening Lovina had broken open. Her cell phone began to chime as eight o'clock struck, but Lovina could hardly hear the alarm above the roar of the light that was filling the basement, flooding her mind. She saw vaguely through the glare of the light that the BEKs had knocked down the door and were pouring down the stairs. The light, the terrible presence within the light, tore the things that had once been children apart effortlessly.

Lovina focused on the broken capstone. She grabbed the edge of the heavy ancient stone, her fingers gripping the rock, the tendons in her forearms straining as she lifted with all her might; the light filled every cell of her body with a power and an awareness old as the stars in the cold heavens. Lovina roared as the hundreds of pounds of stone cracked, rumbled, and fell as the capstone flipped free of the well, and all the radiance—long imprisoned—fountained out. The light was everywhere, was everything, and Lovina was lost in the whiteout. The force was rushing up the stairs, filling the ground floor of the old house and spilling out every window, every crack between the bricks and wood, hurling upward, defiant, into the endless night.

. . .

The porch light failed just as Max pulled a bulky cylinder out of her bag. It took both hands for her to heft it. She flipped the switch on it as she shouted, "Eyes!"

The HellFighter spotlight fired a three-thousand lumen, xenon-fueled beam of pure white light that illuminated the porch as if it were day. The shadows grabbing at the fringes of Max's clothing, all the shadows that had vaulted onto the porch in the second of darkness, turned to smoke. The BEKs wrestling with Jimmie clutched their eyes and screamed like wounded animals; the light didn't destroy them the way it did the shadows, but it definitely hurt them. Jimmie, squinting against the light, kicked and punched them off him. Kneeling with the shotgun, he fired again and again, and the howling BEKs fell and were silent. Jimmie struggled to stand. Max's spotlight was a military-grade gadget that was designed to be mounted on vehicles in combat or on .50 machine guns. Jimmie recalled having something similar on the Abrams tanks he had crewed during Desert Storm. Cecil Dann had looked confused when Jimmie asked him to use his law-enforcement credentials to secure the HellFighter for them, but he was damn glad he had asked for it now. If he'd had more time in Atlanta, he could have had a few of the spotlights mounted on the truck, but they had been racing a clock. The porch was clear of shadows, and the BEKs still in the house had slunk back down the hall, confused and blinded by the HellFighter for the moment. Jimmie reloaded the shotgun as he knelt by Agnes. Black veins were creeping up her hand and moving toward her arm.

"Can you move?" Jimmie asked, looking at the old woman and then glancing back down the hall at all the hateful pale faces snarling at them, lined up between them and the basement.

"Yes," Agnes said. "I can." She struggled to her feet with Jimmie's help. She picked up her Mauser and inspected it to make sure it was ready to fire, returning it to her uninjured hand. "The little blighters' bite packs quite a punch." She staggered a bit, and Jimmie righted her. Max had joined them, still carrying the spotlight. There was a beeping sound, the 8:05 alarm Jimmie had set on his phone.

"Damn it," Jimmie said. "Okay, straight to the basement. We have no more time. Kill whatever gets in the way. We don't stop, y'all clear on that, we don't stop."

"Yes," Max said, nodding, blinking in fear.

"Yes, dear boy," Agnes said, a pained smile on her face. "Let's kick their asses, shall we?"

Jimmie had to smile in spite of himself. "Yes, ma'am, let's. Max, keep that light on them. Let's go!"

The three plunged into the house of the Crone, into the wall of monsters before them, hoping that they weren't already too late to stop the force that lived behind those soulless eyes.

. . .

"Good evening," George Norse said to the television camera's Cyclopean red light and to the twenty million viewers on the other side of the camera, "and welcome to *Paranormal America Live*. I'm your host, George Norse. Tonight, a ruthless psychopathic murderer who has stalked the highways and byways of America for over sixty years breaks his silence as we uncover shocking found footage that will show you that the so-called Pagan is linked to supernatural phenomena."

In the control booth, Cecil Dann watched the monitors, his arms crossed, looking dour. Most shows would have milked this footage thing and shown it in the last few minutes of the program; however, the show's director, Jonah Gage, who was giving orders to the studio's floor crew through a headset, had told Dann they were going to lead with the Pagan video. "Audiences these days don't possess the attention span necessary to wait forty minutes to see it," Gage said during a pre-show conference with Norse and Dann. "They will already have flipped channels if we wait that long."

"These are the folks who elect politicians for us?" Dann had said. "Fantastic."

"And the killer himself has let us know he's watching tonight," Norse said to the camera. "Who knows, maybe he'll call in on *Paranormal America Live!*" The show's credits began to roll on the control-room monitors and on millions of TV screens. The studio audience cheered. The red light on the camera went off. As the credits faded to black, the first round of commercials began on the monitors, and the in-studio audience murmured excitedly.

"We're clear," the floor manager called out. "Back in five."

Norse walked over to his assistant and took a headset she was holding. He placed the earpiece and the mike near his face without messing up his makeup and hair. "Jonah, let me talk to Agent Dann," George said.

A deep voice responded through the headset a second later. "Mr. Norse, it's Cecil Dann."

"Agent Dann," Norse said, "I just wanted you to know we have a special phone bank set up; in case the Pagan calls in, we can trace his call."

Up in the booth, Dann shook his head, even though Norse couldn't see him do it from the stage below. "Mr. Norse, the bureau is ready to trace any calls coming in on any line you have. He won't be stupid enough to make that mistake, though. He'll know we're doing that."

"I'm just trying to help," Norse said as the floor manager gestured that he had less than two minutes to get back to his mark for the camera. Norse, still holding the headset to his ear, nodded and gave a thumbs-up.

"Mr. Norse, I appreciate that," Dann replied into his own headset. "You seem like a genuinely decent fella, but showing this video is dangerous. We have no idea what the Pagan will do."

"We don't know what he'll do if we don't show it," Norse said. "His courier said he would kill two college kids if we didn't. Look, the point is pretty academic now, right? I just wanted you to know that I'll do whatever I can to help you guys catch him."

Dann sighed. "Okay, Mr. Norse, thanks for your cooperation."

He handed the headset back to Gage, who had begun giving orders to the cameramen and the floor manager even as the final seconds of the current commercial counted down.

This was wrong, Dann knew. He could feel it in his bones, but without the DOJ giving him clearance to pull the plug, what the hell was he supposed to do? The audience was applauding again as the program come back from the break. Norse turned to address the crowd and another camera.

"This week, we received a digital video file from a source claiming to be the infamous serial killer the Pagan," Norse said, "who has been active across the United States since the 1950s. The video shows the horrifying last moments of a young girl's life as she is stalked and slain by this brutal killer. However, the video also clearly shows the presence of some kind of supernatural entity—perhaps a demonic force—that is also present in the girl's final, tortured seconds of life. We're going to show you this video now. We warn you—the content is violent and disturbing, and parental discretion is strongly advised."

With those magic words, Dann, sitting in the control room, knew that millions of younger viewers, watching alone, just scooted closer to the screen. He hoped his wife, Jenna, wasn't watching, but she might be. He had told her what was going on when he called her earlier from the hotel.

The video began. Norse's people had "sweetened it up," in the parlance of the biz. It was cleaner, the audio clearer. Dann closed his eyes and swallowed. It was still hard for him to watch it, still hard to believe that the thing visible in the last few seconds of the video wasn't some computer-generated special effect. It had to be—no matter what some crazy truck driver said. Dann kept telling himself that, but he also earnestly wished, prayed, that the crazy trucker would call him and tell him it was all going to be okay. The video played on. The girl's screams ran along the electron highway, racing across the land.

▪ ▪ ▪

The darkness above the earth spun mutely with cold indifference. The stars, the moon, the seasons, the great endless hall of time itself—all tumblers, turning, locking into place.

In a New Orleans hospital, Russell Lime sat beside the bed of his beloved bride—her name was Treasure. She slept, and he held her hand. On the hospital television, he watched the video play out on *Paranormal America Live*. He wondered if Lovina Marcou was okay. It had been a few days since they had spoken. Thoughts of Lovina always led Russell to thoughts of her father, his old friend. He squeezed Treasure's hand tighter, and, even in drugged sleep, she squeezed back.

There was a knock at the door. It was slow, almost mechanical, but insistent and strong. Russ expected a nurse or a doctor to open the door a second later, but that didn't happen. The knock repeated, again. Again.

"That's damn odd," Russ said, slowly rising from the chair by Treasure's bed and moving to open the door.

▪ ▪ ▪

In Leesburg, Virginia, just outside Washington, DC, Jenna Dann, dressed in her pajamas and a robe, rose from the couch where she had been watching the video play out on that paranormal show Cecil was investigating. She wondered who could be knocking on her door at this hour, and why they weren't using the doorbell? It was most likely someone from Cecil's work looking for him, some new crisis that couldn't wait. It was part of the price you paid for being a cop's wife. Jenna walked toward her front door.

. . .

In his beer-bottle-littered living room in Harnett County, North Carolina, Jethro, Heck's best friend in the world, cussed as he heard slow, steady, insistent pounding at the door.

"Fucking coming!" Roadkill said, getting to his feet. His long possum's tail was hanging out the top of his sagging jeans. He lost control of his shape sometimes when he got good and shit-faced. He moved toward the door, to see who the fuck had interrupted watching that hardcore serial-killer video on TV. This had better be good.

. . .

Down the road from Jethro, in Lenore, a universe away from Jimmie, Layla struggled to stand, but Peyton beat her to it, jumping up quickly. "I got it, Mom," Peyton said, waving the pizza money. "Tell me what I miss on the video!"

"Okay, baby," Layla said, settling back into the cushions of the couch with an audible *"Whoosh"* and holding her pregnant belly. "Look before you open the door! And make sure they got the anchovies on my side of the pie."

"I know, I know," Peyton said. "That baby has gross cravings, Mom!" She paused. "Mom, it's not the pizza guy; it's two little kids."

Layla frowned. She began to rise again, turning sideways to get herself off the couch. "Kids? See what they want, baby. I'll be right there."

Peyton reached for the doorknob.

. . .

Across the East Coast, at millions of doors, there was knocking—insistent, relentless knocking. Strong, small, pale hands knocking. Soulless eyes, filled with the will of an old, bloody, hungry god, waited for the doors to open, waited for those who had seen the Wild Hunt to offer themselves, waited for the sacrifices to begin. In the void, beyond the corpses of light in the sky, beyond the tiny island we call reason, something older than names licked its chops in anticipation.

Lexi's head was full of angry bees. It was the bitter broth the Scodes had forced her and Cole to drink when they took them out to the woods earlier. Her thoughts were like water; she tried to hold on to one but it would slip away, splash into a million droplets of disjointed words and images. She looked up and saw the dark edges of high trees at the periphery of her vision, like jagged teeth trying to eat the sky full of stars. The rock was sharp and cold beneath her bare flesh. She suddenly realized that she was on the sacrifice stone, where Dewey Rears had been murdered, and that she was nude, then the thought slipped away, fell, and splashed—*drip, drip, drip.*

Cole was beside her, staring, trying to form words. Tears ran from his glassy eyes down the side of his head and fell onto the cold, uncaring stone. He was painted, as she was, in thick pastes of blue and white. The paint had been drawn in spiral circles all over their bodies and faces. Lexi reached out to him; he was so beautiful, and so sad. She tried to use her words, but they were lost in the hum of her brain, the crunching sound of the gears of the universe. She loved him; she had loved him for a very long time, and only now, when the world was running like chalk drawings washing away in the rain, could she feel it, know it. She took his hand, and he held hers tightly.

Lexi looked up and saw him standing above them, the Master of the Hunt, the bright waning half-moon crescent behind him. The blade was in his hand, the same bone-handled knife he had killed Rears with on this very spot. He had a bowl in his other hand. It was very old, and stained brown.

"You two have a great privilege," Chasseur said to Lexi and Cole as he knelt to carefully place the bowl in a cradle of stone. His leathers creaked. "Your blood shall be the first the Horned God drinks upon his full manifestation into this world. Your young, vital life force, your lust for life, for each other, shall slake his thirst after his long journey along the road between worlds to here—his new kingdom."

Two large columns of brilliant white light sliced the darkness. They came from the direction of Four Houses. Chasseur looked up, and Lexi saw worry cloud his face for a moment, even if she could not hold on to the comprehension of it. The Master of the Hunt waited, and after a moment the cruel razor cut of a smile returned to his pale, bland face. "Only two," he said to Lexi and Cole as he stood. "It would seem my pack was too much for them. They were worthy prey, but such is the fate of mortals who would oppose a god."

Chasseur raised the blade above Lexi; it flashed in the moonlight. *"Is sine de gods, tugaimid ar dhuit,"* he intoned. *"Devour na saol, céim idir an saol mar a osclaíonn an imbhalla agus ar an mbealach soiléir. Tar Pan! Tar Amun! Tar Ammon! Tar Cernunnos! Osclaíonn an doras agus muid a thabhairt faoi shaoirse tú an fuil, dí agus siúl saol seo!"*

The Master of the Hunt looked into Lexi's, then Cole's, eyes. Lexi's mind cleared for a moment as the horror overcame the drugs. She saw, felt, the death of all things in Chasseur's eyes. She saw him with great horns branching out of his temples, reaching skyward, to gore the moon itself. The knife began to fall. Lexi squeezed Cole's hand, and he hers—a final, frail human act of love, so small in the face of such a rapacious universe.

. . .

Jimmie was almost out of shells for the shotgun. He swung the gun like a club and knocked two more of the clawing BEKs away from him as he held the doorway, while Max helped Agnes to descend into the basement. Mercifully, there were no BEKs or shadow people down there—Max theorized that they would instinctively avoid proximity to the well and the light within that could so easily annihilate them.

Agnes was not looking good; the black veins were creeping up her neck now, and she gasped audibly in pain. Max helped her off the last step, and the two women moved toward the crumbling well cover. There were two loud booms as Jimmie discharged the shotgun again with a few of his remaining precious shells.

"We good?" Jimmie yelled.

"Yes!" Max called back. Agnes rested against the lip of the capstone while Max set down the heavy spotlight and rummaged in her pack for the pry bar. Max checked her phone—it was well after eight.

Jimmie kicked one of the hissing child-things back and slammed the door to the basement. There was no lock on his side. He held the knob and braced himself with the railing as the door was jerked by powerful hands on the other side. "I can't hold them but a few minutes!" he called down. Pounding started on the door, and a thin seam of a crack began to appear in the wood.

Max began to take the small bar and work on the capstone of the well, but a frail, black-veined hand took the bar from her. "This is my work to do, dear," Agnes rasped. "It has to be." Agnes took the bar and began to strike the crumbling edges of the stone, near the spot where the loose chunk she had shown Ava was. Rock chips flew. A finger of light lanced out from the disintegrating stone, and it seemed to invigorate Agnes. She struck again and again, with more strength than her age and condition should allow. She looked up at Max, the black veins crawling up her face toward her eyes now. "Go help Jimmie, dear," she said to the younger woman. "I can manage."

Max ran up the stairs to stand beside Jimmie as he struggled to keep the door closed. "Shells in my jacket pocket," he said. Max took the shotgun and rummaged in his pocket. She retrieved two shells.

"The last," she said, and began to slide them into the feed.

"How's she doing?" he asked.

Max shook her head. "This is bad, isn't it, Jimmie?" she asked. "Like, 'we're not going to make it' bad, right?" Jimmie braced his shoulder against the convulsing door. Max helped him as best she could, leaning against the door with her slight frame.

"We're not dead yet," he said through gritted teeth. "Still liking field-work?"

Max gave him an odd smile; her eyes lightened. "Yes," she said. "Yes, I am. Thank you. It's been an honor and a privilege."

"You stow that down with the ship crap," Jimmie said. "I got a family to get home to and a load to pick up and deliver. Ain't got no time for dying."

Max snapped her fingers and cradled the shotgun as she reached into Jimmie's inside jacket pocket. Downstairs, there was a loud *whoosh,* and the chamber began to fill with light.

"What you doing?" Jimmie asked. Max pulled out his cell phone and began to tap and search on it.

"I think I know a way you can reach Agent Dann," she said, "but it has to be right now. When that energy is released from the wells, I think it punches a hole in the reality of this place for an instant. That hole should allow a signal to pass over to the next adjacent dimension—our earth. The principle is similar to what Chasseur's trying to do with the Horned Man."

The door bucked hard, and the crack in the wood widened. Dozens of tiny, pale fingers appeared at the edges of the door, prying it open. "His number's in there," Jimmie shouted. He grabbed the shotgun from Max, jammed the barrel through the widening opening, and fired. The small hands slid out of sight. One round left. "Do it, do it!"

"It won't be a long message," Max said. "What do I say?"

Jimmie told her. Max quickly typed in the message, ready to send it. The light was getting brighter, filling the stairwell, starting to white out everything. Sound accompanied the light—it was like a hurricane now. The door was splintering. "Get downstairs!" Jimmie shouted. Max ran down to Agnes and the light, and Jimmie followed. The door crashed open as he jumped down to the bottom stairs. He fired behind him without looking back and heard the screams of the things that pretended to be children.

Max and Jimmie saw Agnes vaguely in the geyser of light from the well. She struck the final piece of the capstone, and it fell into the roaring nimbus of pallid fire, along with the pry bar. Agnes's skin was smoking, the radiance engulfing the darkness twisting inside her. The well was open. Agnes climbed onto the low lip of it, her features almost obscured by the long-imprisoned power.

"Tell Dennis I love him," she shouted above the howling gale. "And tell Ava . . . well done." She fell into the heart of the Crone's fury and was gone. The BEKs that had dared to rush down the stairs to press their assault ceased to be in the face of the merciless radiance. The monsters upstairs had a few seconds longer before they suffered the same fate. The light tore free of the house and arched skyward, to join the other two beacons in the night.

"Agnes!" Jimmie screamed, but his voice was nothing, drowned out in the maelstrom. Max hit Send on Jimmie's phone as everything was washed away, consumed by white.

. . .

The battered old tow truck screamed, tires smoking, out of the parking lot of the blazing inferno that was Scode's Garage. Heck turned a hard left down the two-lane and kept accelerating. The cab of the truck reeked of gasoline, and he could hear the jerricans full of gas rattling against the acetylene tanks in the bed of the truck. He fumbled in his jacket with his free hand as he stared coolly out into the night, the raging fire in his rearview, his headlights grasping at the white lines of the road. He had clicked on the old radio in the truck, and through the ghostly AM static he heard Molly Hatchet's "Flirtin' with Disaster." He found his crumpled pack of Lucky Strikes and removed the only cigarette not destroyed by his tumble with the late Scode brothers. He stuck the cigarette in the corner of his mouth and looked at the mangled package. Heck laughed— it was a cold, sharp thing. Two absurdities amused him immensely in the moment. One was the Lucky Strike slogan on the package: *"It's Toasted."* The other was that he realized he didn't have a light. He laughed again at this as he swung the truck right onto the access road next to the small shrine and sacrifices left for the Horned Man. The truck bounced down the rutted gravel road.

He rubbed his soot-covered face again, the one that had been kissed by a 5,700-degree-Fahrenheit-blowtorch flame. He glanced down at his arm that had been viciously bitten by a Black-Eyed Kid. He had survived the corrupting bite when it killed Gil Turla within minutes. He pushed in the small plug of a cigarette lighter on the dashboard of the old truck. He recalled what the burning, laughing thing had told him after it killed all his friends, deep in the Afghan desert. It had tried to burn him, too, before he destroyed it. He remembered what Chasseur had said to him in the hotel room in Atlanta and how it had made him feel. A dark, hungry hole at the center of him told him that what the Master of the Hunt had said about him was true, all true. A snake made of ice writhed in Heck's guts. He didn't feel like himself, yet he had never felt more like himself. Nothing seemed to matter except the velocity, the diamond-edged oblivion he hurtled toward, and the growling hunger in him to rip everything apart. He stomped on the small pedal on the floorboard, and the high beams of the truck snapped on. The dark forest gave way to a clearing and a field. An old cabin squatted in the field: the house of the Horned Man.

The lighter popped out of the dash. Heck grinned; there was no joy in it. He glanced down to the empty gas can beside him. His clothes, the whole truck—inside and out—was soaked in fuel. He took the lighter plug and lit his cigarette with the cherry-red end of the plug as he drove off the road and straight toward the old house. "It's toasted, mother-fucker," he said as he dropped the lighter into his own lap and felt the gasoline catch. The cabin was engulfed in flames and laughter.

. . .

The video was reaching the part where the girl had fallen and was say-ing her goodbyes to her family, to her sister. It made Dann ill in the core of him. There was a buzz in his pocket from his cell. He read the message sent from Aussapile. It said, *"Stop it, Cecil, now."*

"You need to turn that off . . . now," Dann said to John Gage, the director. Dann put his phone away. Gage snorted.

"Yeah, I know; it's pretty awful," Gage replied, "That poor . . ."

"No, I'm ordering you to turn it off right now, on my authority," Dann said. Gage spun in his chair.

"Agent Dann, I can't do that. It's only got fifty-three seconds left, any-way. We're live right now. You need to talk to the legal department about this. I'm sorry, but—"

"No, I'm sorry," Cecil said as he drew his sidearm, a Springfield 1911A1, and pointed it at Gage's suddenly pale face. "I don't have time to explain. Stop the video, right now." Gage spun in his chair and punched a series of buttons on the panel in front of him. The images on the monitor vanished, replaced by black. The clock counting down to the end of the video was blinking, stopped at 39 seconds.

"Tell George we're back to him in three seconds," Gage shouted into his mike. The control room erupted into chaos as techs and staff hustled to adapt and manage the sudden crisis. "Tell him the Feds shut us down and we're going to commercial in ten."

Norse suddenly appeared on the monitors. He looked a little surprised, but only a little. "Ladies and gentlemen, agents of the federal government just shut us down from showing you the truth of this astonishing video. What is the government hiding from you, and why?"

"Oh, he's good," Dann said to Gage as he holstered his gun. Gage smiled and nodded, pushing buttons and preparing for the commercial break.

"Yeah," Gage said. "The best. You might have just pushed up our ratings for the whole season."

On the monitors, Norse went on, "We'll discuss why our government is hiding the occult connection to the Pagan murders with our panel of experts when *Paranormal America Live* continues—unless they shut us down, too! Stay with us."

The audience erupted in thunderous applause, and Norse, seeing that the camera's red light was out, gave a big grin and a thumbs-up to the monitors.

Dann shook his head. "Sorry about the gun," he said to Gage.

"Meh," the director said with a shrug. "You work in network TV long enough, some meshuggener's gonna point a gun at you."

Across America, the knocking stopped. Doors were opened or peeked through, and, where only a moment ago there had been small hooded figures, waiting, now there was only the night.

. . .

The Master of the Hunt's knife descended toward Lexi's chest just as there was a roll of thunder across the black velvet sky and a third beam of white light rose out of and above Four Houses. Chasseur stopped in mid-strike.

"No," he growled. "No! The door is closing! Those bitches have ruined everything I've worked for, for centuries!" He noticed a bouncing, fluttering ball of yellow-and-orange fire moving quickly through the field on the other side of the dense curtain of forest. He couldn't make out what it was. A huge explosion tore through the forest. A massive plume of fire soared into the air, and Chasseur knew . . . he felt it: the house of the Horned Man was burning.

"No!" he screamed. He jumped off the rock and sprinted toward the fire and the massive cloud of black smoke rising above the tree line. "I'll flay them all!" The Master of the Hunt sprinted into the night and was gone, leaving his two sacrifices on the cold rocks.

Lexi rolled over and pulled at Cole. The drugs were making everything fuzzy and hard to hang on to, but the explosion had helped. "Cole, Cole, we have got to get up!" she said. The boy clutched her hand, refusing to let go, and together they climbed to their feet. They stood naked on the stones and watched as the huge fireball burned and continued to send jets of fire and debris skyward.

Chasseur cleared the tree line and saw the house of the Horned Man engulfed in flames. He ran closer, his face swollen and twisted in rage, ruddy in the light from the inferno.

Heck coughed a few times and opened his eyes. He was alive, barely. Apparently, he was good with fire, but explosive concussion, being thrown through the air, and debris raining down on him all still hurt like a son of a bitch. Between this and getting shot by Scode earlier, he was in pretty bad shape. His clothes had been on fire, but the concussive force of the blast and rolling to a stop in the field had put them out. He was covered in soot, ash, and badly burned and tattered clothing. He groaned as he struggled to his feet. When he saw Chasseur's house burning, he laughed and whooped, letting out a rebel yell.

"Fuck, yeah!" Heck shouted. Then he saw Chasseur walking across the field, a silhouette against the fire. "Hey! Sorry about the truck, asshole. You insured?"

"I tried to tell you what you were," the Master of the Hunt said, his voice cold slate above the roar of the fire. "You have no idea what you've just done, how much you and your foolish friends have undone." Chasseur raised the knife.

"Not a clue," Heck said. "I find mindless violence loses its charm when I actually know what's going on." He slid his knife free of his belt sheath. The sheath fell apart and dropped to the ground, but the blade was in good shape.

"I'm going to skin you," Chasseur said, spinning and tossing his own knife between his hands. Only twenty feet separated the two men now. "I'm going to put your head up on the sacrificial rocks and let the birds pick it clean."

"I'm just going to fucking kill you," Heck said. Ten feet now between them, and they were circling each other. Behind them, the house burned. "Nothing special, nothing fancy—just like you. You got jerked around by some big cosmic hoo-ha and you think that makes you important? Any asshole can kill people. Here, let me show you."

Heck launched himself at Chasseur, tackling the Master of the Hunt. The two men rolled around in the high grass, grappling.

"Why don't you sic your shadow puppies on me?" Heck said, driving his fist into Chasseur's face. The killer rolled with the punch and disengaged from Heck, coming up in a crouch, slashing out with his knife. The blade cut across Heck's stomach, leaving a trail of dark blood, but it didn't cut deep. Heck punched Chasseur in the face again and connected solidly. The Master of the Hunt stumbled backward, almost falling. "Oh yeah, I guess it's not as easy to call them up now, is it?" Heck said, pressing his advantage. The two men's blades flashed and sparked as they lunged and swung, blocked and parried. "Same with those things you made from innocent kids, huh? All those little tricks aren't working right now, are they?"

Chasseur's knife darted out toward Heck's chest. Heck tried to move, but he was too hurt, too slow, and the blade sank deep into his stomach; he gasped at the sharp, bright pain in his guts. He grabbed Chasseur's hair and swept his own blade across the serial killer's throat. A spray of blood covered Heck's face. They staggered away from each other, both bleeding out.

"You bleed easier now, too," Heck said, and coughed up some blood. Chasseur held his throat as blood gushed from his neck. "Just regular folks, right?"

"I'll live along enough to kill you," Chasseur gurgled. He charged Heck, swinging the knife wildly. Heck parried as best he could and tried to move out of the way, but he suffered another cut, this one deep to his biceps; part of his arm burned and another part went numb. He countered with a shallow cut to Chasseur's shoulder and another punch, this time to his cut throat. Heck roared and hit the killer again, and again, driving him back.

Heck briefly blacked out from the pain, the lost blood. He swam back to awareness and found him and Chasseur staggering in a clinch. He could feel the heat from the blaze clawing at his face, the acrid smoke burning his lungs. Heck didn't know where his knife was, and he was gripping Chasseur's wrist, keeping the bone-handled blade from slipping into his gut again. He head-butted Chasseur. They both stumbled back to the very edge of the fire. Heck thought he heard voices shouting, calling to him, but his awareness was locked onto the killer's bloody face.

"What you are . . . will devour you," Chasseur spat through a throat full of blood. "Just . . . remember that. I wish I could watch it happen, watch you fall, watch you destroy everything and everyone you love, and laugh as you do it."

"Bullshit," Heck muttered. "I'll never be like you, you mass-murdering psychopath." Heck struck him again, slapped the blade from his hand and sent it flying. The universe was only Chasseur, only hurting him, making him shut up, forever. Heck heard a hissing, felt heat, but no pain from it.

"You'll . . . be . . . worse," Chasseur croaked. "Tell me, noble hero, how did you find me? Find the children? You got my loyal hound, Walden, to . . . tell you. He . . . would never betray me, his master, never betray . . . the Horned Man . . . he worshipped." Blood was pouring from Chasseur's mouth as well as from his throat now. His eyes, usually dead and dark, were bulging as he fought for the air for every word. "So . . . tell me, tell the evil psychopath, what noble means did you use . . . to find me?"

Heck remembered the blowtorch in his hand, the cool indifference, almost a controlled anger, with which he had used it on Wald until the old bastard gave him what he wanted. But he hadn't stopped there; he had kept going, enjoying the pain and degradation he was inflicting. The cold rage roaring in his mind, at the center of him. Wald died begging, unable to cry because his tear ducts had been seared. He kept torturing the body even after Wald's diseased soul had been pulled down into Hell.

There was hot ash blowing around them as Heck grabbed Chasseur by the shoulder and drove a combination of punches into the killer. Chasseur tried to block them as best he could, but the fury of the punches drove both men back farther and farther. There was a rumbling, like a furnace. Heck was locked into looking at the killer's eyes. Off at a great distance, somewhere away from the furnace, voices shouted his name, pleading. But now there was only the man in front of him that he was going to kill and the fury of the flames.

The Master of the Hunt tried to smile as best he could with the muscles in his throat severed. "I . . . see," he rasped as he struck at Heck again with a feeble combination of blows. "You do recall it . . . good. You always will."

"Fuck you!" Heck screamed. He mustered the last shreds of his strength to strike Chasseur again and again, punch after punch. His awareness winked out and then back again, in a jerky, non-linear continuity. His knuckles were raw; his wrists ached as he drove punch after punch into that evil, broken, smiling face. All around them were glowing cinders floating in the smoke-smeared air like fireflies that stung his lungs and skin but left no mark, no harm. They were deep into the fire now—it was all around them. The heart of the blaze, the roaring skeleton of the house, was close. Each punch, each stumbling clinch, brought it closer. Heck felt the flames, but his eyes were only for Chasseur.

"You think . . . killing me is the end?" The Master of the Hunt said as the maelstrom of Hell fell down upon them. They were both on fire, and the whole world around them was crackling flame and the snap and groan of the house of the Horned Man dying. There was no clear sky, only smoke; no cool grass, only hot ash. "You . . . are the greatest of predators, my brother," Chasseur said, his voice dry gravel. "I was initiated . . . into this life, but you . . . you have it . . . in your very blood and bones."

"Shut up!" Heck screamed. They fell among the ashes. Heck straddled Chasseur, punching him again and again and again as they burned, as the house burned, as the world burned. The thudding in his ears returned, like great leathery wings flapping in time to each punch, each broken bone in his hands, as he struck the Master of the Hunt again and again. Chasseur no longer moved; his skull was on fire, but Heck continued to strike him, hearing his very blood hiss, devoured by the fire. Some distant corner of his mind thought this was not the sacrifice of blood and fire that Chasseur had planned on tonight. Heck laughed at this. He couldn't stop laughing as he beat the serial killer called the Pagan to death with his bare hands in the collapsing frame of the Horned Man's home. Heck's tears evaporated from the fire that covered him. He *was* the burning, laughing thing in the desert now. That thought made him laugh and weep uncontrollably. It was his last thought before he slid off Chasseur's blackening body and fell into blissful, cool darkness.

Jimmie stood as close to the burning house as he could. Max, Lovina, and the others from the town, from Buddy's, were shouting, trying to figure out how to get into the blaze to go after Heck.

"I can't believe that crazy SOB just fought his way into that!" Lovina shouted over the blaze. "He's dead!"

"No!" Jimmie shouted. He grabbed a couple of plastic jugs of water that he and Max had fetched from the semi, which was idling in the field, near the access road. Jimmie poured them over an insulated fire blanket. He wrapped the blanket over himself as best he could.

"You're not seriously going to try to go in there, are you?" Max asked as Jimmie adjusted the blanket.

"He's my squire, my best friend's son. He's saved my life," Jimmie said to the professor. "He's my friend, and I don't leave friends behind." Jimmie sprinted to the edge of the fire; building speed, he closed his eyes and dived past the threshold of fire, vanishing from view in the smoke and flame.

"What do we do?" Max asked Lovina, who sighed and shook her head. A minute passed, then two. Lovina was pacing, looking for anything she could use to make a run into the flames. She was considering driving Jimmie's rig in when a smoldering, stumbling figure appeared at the edge of the fire, carrying a still, smoking form. Jimmie staggered out, flames licking at the blanket covering him. He dropped Heck's limp, blackened body as gently as he could in the grass, staggered a few more feet, and then fell, coughing and rolling, to extinguish the flames.

Jimmie heard shouting across the field and knew help was coming.

The night air was cool, the stars were beautiful, and he was struck by how breathtaking this world truly was. He looked over to Heck, covered head to toe in black smudge and, he assumed, burns. His body was so still and had felt strangely cool to the touch when Jimmie found him beside Chasseur's flaming corpse. Heck suddenly convulsed and coughed, and Jimmie smiled. Jimmie struggled to sit up. His hands were hot and hurt and were kind of numb. He recalled shock from his time in the Gulf, and knew that his hands had some burns and his arms and shins, too, but the fact that he could feel it made him think they weren't too bad.

Sitting in the field, he looked across it to the dark woods. Then he saw it. It was close to the edge of the woods, vaguely visible in the jumping, frenetic light of the house fire. A dark man wrapped in shadows, with massive antlers, like the branches in the trees, spreading from his head, stared at Jimmie, at the cool, beautiful world, with burning, hungry eyes—predator's eyes. The shadowy pack of hounds around him—eyes like moonlight, stared, too, silent and ready to heed their master's command.

"Go on now," Jimmie muttered through dry lips and a raw, soot-caked throat. He matched death's gaze and did not blink this time. "Git."

The Horned Man and his hounds retreated into the deep shadows of the ancient woods and were gone.

There was no body to lay to rest, so Ava had constructed a little shrine of smooth stones to act as a marker for Agnes's grave. She placed the stones between Alana and Julia, near the wildflowers Agnes loved so much. Ava thought she would have liked that. She stood before the stones. It was a real spring day; the sun was warm and birds sang. She wanted to cry, but something held her from it, some knowledge that Agnes would not have wanted it.

Dennis sat in his wheelchair. He held a photograph of himself and his young bride, and he struggled to remain in the now, but Ava knew that he was already slipping across time again to a place where he and Agnes were together, would always be together.

Ava turned to look at the crowd that had come for the impromptu memorial. Folks like Barb and Carl, who had known Agnes for decades, and strangers who had become friends in the heat of battle: the trucker, Jimmie Aussapile, his arms and hands bandaged from the fire, and his companions, Max, Lovina, and Heck. Heck was also covered in bandages, and only recently up from his bed. Even Lexi and Cole, recovering from their own hellish ordeals, had come, for her more than for a woman they had never even met.

"I have no idea what to say," Ava said, pushing her glasses back up on the bridge of her nose. "Thank you. Thank you for coming. Agnes was the most amazing person I've ever met. She saved my life, saved the lives of everyone here. She taught me what I could do; she believed in me even when I didn't. And she died as she lived—with courage, determination, and the knowledge that some things in this world are worth

fighting for, worth dying for. I'm a better person for having had the privilege of knowing her. The world owes her a debt that it will never know,
never be able to repay."

Ava looked up at the turret of the house that overlooked the backyard and the garden. Something had drawn her attention to the open
window there for just a second. She thought she saw a figure standing
there—a slender woman in white lace, pale, like old porcelain. But whatever it was she thought she'd seen past the fluttering transparent white
curtains was gone now. She glanced at Dennis and saw the tears streaming down his cheeks. He began to sob.

"Thank you again for being here," she said. "I wish I had more to say."

...

The service was breaking up. Ava had wheeled Dennis inside and was
caring for him. There was talk of gathering at Buddy's for food. Jimmie
walked up and shook Carl's hand and hugged Barb.

"Whatever Chasseur did to the town, it's gone, too," Carl said. "People
can come and go again. It's pretty great."

"I guess you two will be headed on down the road, then," Jimmie
said. Barb and Carl looked at each other, and Barb smiled. "I think
we're going to stay, at least for a while," she said. "There are good
people here, and more of them are staying than leaving. It's nice to
have a choice now, though. Thank you, Jimmie."

"Don't thank me," Jimmie said, smiling. "No way we could have
pulled this off without you two. Thank you. The wheel turns."

"The wheel turns," they both said. "If you ever want a cup of coffee
or a plate of grub on the house, you come see us, Jimmie," Barb said, and
hugged him again.

Inside the house, Ava walked down the stairs from Dennis's room to
find Lexi and Cole waiting for her, holding hands.

"This place is yours now, huh?" Lexi said. "Pretty cool. Very Addams
Family."

"Actually, mine's down the road a ways," Ava said. "It needs some
work, but I have time."

"You staying?" Cole asked her. "You sure?"

"Yeah," Ava said, nodding. "I'm supposed to be here. I need to build that house back up, take care of it. I'll take care of this one, too, until a proper owner comes along, and look after Dennis—Agnes would have wanted that."

"You want us to tell your folks anything?" Cole asked. "Still no cell service out here. I doubt GPS works, either."

"It doesn't," Ava said. "The houses like their privacy. I'll get out to see Mom and Dad soon. Just tell them I'm okay . . . and I'm happy." She nodded toward Lexi's and Cole's hands. "I'm happy for you guys, too. Truly."

"You're not mad?" Lexi said. "You know, Ava, you used to be . . . um—"

"A bitch?" Ava said. "Yeah, I still am." They all laughed, for what it was worth. "This place shows you what you are, what you can be. I see it in you two as well. Listen to it, believe it. Take good care of each other."

Lexi hugged her, then Cole. Then they were gone. Ava stood in the foyer, the ticking of the grandfather clock the only sound. The spring sun came in through the open door that only a few days ago had been barred and locked. She had stumbled through that door terrified and helpless before the powers of darkness and fear. The sun warmed her face, caressed her cheek like a gentle hand. Ava embraced it and smiled all the way down to her core.

. . .

Good-byes were said in the parking lot of Buddy's Roadhouse following another amazing meal. Jimmie was happy to see a station wagon with Nebraska tags, towing a pop-up camper, roll down the two-lane. Not too far behind was a Kansas state trooper looking very confused that he had never noticed this little town in his jurisdiction before.

"We're going to miss you guys," Barb said.

"Hell, with that cooking, you won't be missing me for long," Jimmie said. "I'll be back through, promise. And if y'all have any trouble you send me the word, and me and the other Brethren will come running."

"You know," Ava said, as she shook Lovina's hand, "you could stay. The Mother's house likes you; you could claim it, repair it. And I sure could use the help."

Lovina smiled broadly. "You're doing great," she said. "Agnes would be proud of you. But I don't think I'm quite ready to settle down just yet. Besides, my name doesn't start with an 'A'"

Ava laughed. "Okay," she said. "But don't be a stranger."

"It's nice to know I have a retirement option," Lovina said. "Don't worry, I'm sure we'll be back. Take care, Ava."

The crowd drifted back inside the roadhouse. The jukebox was blaring "All my Rowdy Friends are Coming Over Tonight," by Hank Williams, Jr. The music muted as the door banged shut. Finally, it was down to the four of them—Lovina, Max, Heck, and Jimmie.

"This has been a hell of a run," Lovina said, shaking Jimmie's hand. Jimmie pulled her to him and they hugged.

"Thank you, Lovina," Jimmie said. "I'd be honored to ride shotgun with you anytime. You're one of us now—you know that, right? You need anything, you call me."

Lovina nodded. "Goes both ways, Jimmie," she said. "Now, get on home to that baby quick—and let me know the exact weight. Heck, Max, and I got a bet going."

Jimmie laughed.

Lovina hugged Heck tight. He grunted a little bit in pain. "Sissy-ass marine," she said, smiling.

"Take care, New Orleans," Heck said.

Lovina walked to the door of her Charger and opened it. She looked back at Max, who had been standing very still and quiet. "You need a ride to DC, right?" Lovina asked.

Max's face spread into a wide smile. "Yes, yes, I do, actually," she said.

"Never seen DC," Lovina said. "And I want to know more about this 'road magic.' Come on, I'll give you a ride."

Max squeaked a little and hugged Jimmie tight. "Thank you for all this, Jimmie," she said. "It's been amazing. I never dreamed . . ."

"What I said to Lovina goes for you, too, Max," Jimmie said, hugging the small woman tightly. "You can ride with me any day. You're one of us now; you earned it. Don't ever forget that. Be safe."

Max climbed into the black Charger. "We saved the universe," she said brightly. "Any chance we could get Krystal burgers?" The door shut, and Jimmie couldn't hear Lovina's reply. Lovina turned the ignition, and the Charger rumbled to life. Lovina nodded slowly to Heck and Jimmie through her open window. They nodded back, slowly—the knowing badass nod. All three laughed at the realization. The car glided out of the lot, spitting a few gravels as it went, and shot down the two-lane. In less than a minute, they were out of sight.

"You good to ride that thing home?" Jimmie asked Heck as he slowly climbed onto his T5 Blackie.

"I still got arms and legs, so yeah," Heck said. "I'm cool."

"You're damn lucky you didn't get burned to a crispy critter in that fire," Jimmie said. "Don't push that luck, Heck."

"Yeah," Heck said with a dry chuckle. "Lucky. I'm good, Jimmie, promise."

"You did good. Ale would have been proud of you. I'm proud of you."

"So, we square on the whole squire thing?" Heck asked. "So I can get home and get on with dealing with Cherokee Mike?"

"Go home," Jimmie said. "You're not a Brother yet, but you're on your way. You are definitely on your way, squire."

They fist-bumped and then hugged. Heck climbed onto the bike. He slid his helmet on and paused to look at the dented, blackened Oni mask for a moment.

"Hey, you okay?" Jimmie asked. "Whatever you need, I'm here for you, okay. Anytime."

Heck smiled; it was a ghostly thing.

"You're not alone," Jimmie said. The words seemed to strike Heck like a physical blow. He looked up at Jimmie with lost, pleading eyes for just a second—eyes full of pain and fear, and something Jimmie couldn't quite comprehend.

Heck beat it all back down again. He grinned, nodded. "I know," he said. "I know, and I'm thankful, Jimmie, more than you can know." Heck started the bike with a kick, wincing in pain for a second. He looked back at Jimmie. "'A civilization lives or dies based on the safety of its roads.'"

"What?" Jimmie said.

"*A cultu vivit, nec moritur a viis suis salutem*," Heck said. "That Latin phrase, my first homework. It says something kind of like that, yeah?"

"Yeah," Jimmie said, a smile growing on his face. "Something like that. You got it right, Heck."

"Nice to get something right for a change," the biker said. He slid the steel demon mask over his face. "Keep it between the lines, Jimmie." He roared off without a backward glance.

Jimmie was alone in the parking lot; a warm breeze kissed him as if to say, 'Thank you.' He sighed and walked to the semi. He climbed in and checked the clock on his laptop in the cab. No way in hell he'd make it in time to pick up his load in Arizona—no way. He slid some chaw into his cheek, adjusted his cap and headset, and started the rig. The big engine bellowed like a bull. He snapped on his music; it was Tom Cochrane singing "Life Is a Highway." He rested his hand on the shotgun gearshift, slid the truck into gear, and slowly rolled out of the parking lot.

He would make it, make his run—he'd get his load, get his paycheck. He had a mortgage to pay, diapers to buy, college to plan. His family was alive, the world was alive. It was seventeen hours to Arizona; he'd make it there in ten. There was always a way.

He accelerated along the two-lane and saw a young girl, a hitchhiker in a white sundress and a jean jacket, on the side of the road ahead. She was smiling in the warm afternoon sunlight. She raised her pale hand to wave; then she was gone in the wake of diesel and dust.

Jimmie grinned and shifted gears. The song of the highway, the hum of the engine, took him, carried him. The promise of the road stretched out before him. "Break 2-3, break, 2-3," he said into his mike. "This is Paladin. I'm 10-24 and clear, c'mon."

And the wheels turned, on and on.

"What the hell were you thinking, Cecil?" Deputy Director Guy Revees asked Cecil Dann. Reeves had a properly intimidating desk for a man in his position, a vast moat of mirror-polished mahogany. The window behind him gave a great view of downtown DC. Dann was sitting on the side of the desk where you were supposed to be impressed or terrified or both.

"I was thinking about saving lives, Guy," Dann said calmly. Two years ago, Jenna had had a very deadly, very close call with ovarian cancer. Since then, there were very few things in this world that Cecil Dann allowed to rile him too much. Losing his job wasn't even on the radar.

"Have you actually read this shit?" Reeves asked, holding up a report encased in a shiny plastic protector.

"Yeah," Dann said. "I wrote it. It's all true, Guy."

"Immortal serial killers, Black-Eyed Kids who are the husks of missing children, vigilante truckers, and my favorite part—where you screw the pooch and shut down a high-rated, nationally viewed, live fucking TV show to save the world from some imaginary fucking asshole with antlers—who the fuck *is* he? Mr. Moose?

"Look, Cecil, we've been friends since Quantico. I buried this report, but if word of all this happy horseshit gets out . . . do you have any idea what they will do to you, to your career?"

"It's all true," Dann said. "It's crazy as shit, and I know that, but it's also the truth. It's also a fact that my unit has taken down two of our most wanted highway killers in the last week—the Marquis and the Pagan. Even if you don't believe the report, believe the results."

"Results?" Reeves reached into his desk and pulled out a bottle of multicolored antacid tablets, dumping a handful of them into his palm. He began to pop them into his mouth like M&Ms as he continued talking. "There is no body. You said your contacts told you this Emile Chasseur died in a fire, so we have absolutely nothing to prove a damn—"

Dann interrupted him by dropping a thick plastic evidence bag onto the desk with a resounding thump. Inside it was an old, brown-stained bone-handled hunting knife.

Dann stood. "This is Emile Chasseur's hunting knife," he said, picking up his trench coat from the chair beside him. He retrieved a thick bound report and dropped it on the desk with another loud thump. "He used it in all his murders over the years. These are the forensic reports; I had them double-checked and verified by two different federal labs. The knife matches the wound patterns on the victims we could recover that information from—it's the knife that killed the Pagan's victims. It has some DNA from several of them tucked away under the hilt wrappings and the interior surfaces of the blade construction."

Cecil was walking to the door now, slipping on his coat to prepare for the warm spring rain outside. "And the recovered prints off the knife, while they don't have a match in our computer system to a known individual, they are a perfect match for partials found at several of the Pagan's crime scenes. Oh, and the estimated age of the blade is about two hundred years. That enough proof for you, Guy?"

Reeves looked down at the knife and the report, then back up at Dann. He nodded mutely.

"Good," Dann said. "I'm taking the Pagan off the HSKI most wanted list and calling the case closed. We got the son of a bitch. I like these little talks, Guy. I'll be in my office if you need to send the men in the white coats over. My love to Paula." He shut the deputy director's door and walked down the hall. "Mr. Moose, my ass," he said to no one in particular.

. . .

Dr. Max Leher paced back and forth by the window to her Georgetown University office. She glanced back at her old friend and colleague Dr. Norman Pillar as he sat on the leather couch by her office door silently reading her findings. Pillar was a member of the Builders, too, and had been Max's mentor in the organization after her grandfather died.

"Well?" Max asked, almost humming with anticipation. Pillar set the document in his lap and sighed. "Max, that's the fourth time you've done that in the last twenty minutes! You drink too many of those damn energy drinks! This is a lot of data to take in."

Max crossed the room and knelt down so that her eyes could meet Pillar's. "But do you think I'm right? Do you find the data convincing?"

"The whole United States interstate highway system is an enormous occult circuit designed to capture and direct ley-line energy?" Pillar said. "It's a hell of an accomplishment in occult engineering, I'll say that! Rivals Stonehenge, the Serpent Mound, and the Sphinx. Do you have any idea who would build this, Max, or why—to what end?"

Max shook her head vigorously. "No, no, not a clue—that's for later! Right now I'm just asking you if you think it's ready for me to present to the chairs of the Imperceptible Preceptory?"

Pillar stroked his full white beard. When she was little, Max had always thought Norman looked like a skinny Santa Claus. "You'd be putting your academic reputation in the order on the line, Max." He sighed again. "May I take this and read over it? I can give you my informed opinion in a few days."

"Yes, of course!" Max said. "Thank you, Norman. Thank you for having an open mind, at least."

"I'm just glad you survived your adventure with those unwashed gearjammers. Who was the idiot that thought it was a good idea to send you out with a bunch of Brethren mouth-breathers?"

"I don't know, exactly," Max said. "And you stop that. I wouldn't be alive, or have made this discovery, without those people. They're my friends, and they do very difficult, dirty work."

"Sounds like you've gone native," Norman said, and laughed. "Still, I'm glad you're home, where you belong."

He hugged her and departed. Alone in her office, Max sat behind her desk and spun the chair around. She was excited, elated, and nervous as hell. She also felt restless. She patted the vampire skull she used as a paperweight. "What do you think, Yorick? I think we convinced him."

Max looked over to one of the myriad overflowing bookcases in her cluttered office. On it was the HellFighter spotlight, her TLC necklace, a toy from a Krystal-burger kids' meal, and two photos she had taken with her phone and had printed out and framed. One was of her with Jimmie, Heck, Agnes, Ava, Barb and Carl Kesner, and Lovina—taken at Buddy's during the meal in celebration of defeating Wald's men. The other was of her and Lovina smiling, so near each other that both could fit in the picture—taken on the road back to DC.

Max tried to pull her eyes off the picture of Lovina. It had been almost a month since they had spoken. She thought of calling her, then felt silly and strange, and very, very shy about it. She wondered if Lovina thought of her at all.

There was a tiny jingle of a bell, followed by a small meep from a black cat. A jet-black Bombay pounced from a shelf to land in Max's arms. She laughed and cuddled the now purring cat, stroking him.

"All right, Pyewacket," she said. "Enough pining for today. Let's get back to work . . . right after I love on you for the next twenty minutes."

The cat's only response was to purr louder.

. . .

On a park bench on the Georgetown campus, Norman Pillar flipped through the thesis that Max Leher had given him. He had a cell phone to his ear. "She knows," Pillar said to the person on the other end of the phone. "She's sussed out the general details of the highway project. I'm holding her findings in my hand right now."

"Any way to bury it?" the man's voice on the other end of the phone asked. His voice was oil and silk.

"No," Pillar said. "She shared the findings with some Brethren, and she's determined to bring it to the attention of the Builder council."

"We could eliminate the Brethren easily enough," the voice said. "And Dr. Leher herself. Then destroy all her data before this spreads any further."

Pillar rubbed his face. "I'm not going to kill her," he said. "Christ, she's practically my daughter. Look, she is as pure an academic as you will ever find. She has no interest in the who or the why of the Road's creation. She just wants to prove it exists, prove her hypothesis."

There was a long pause on the line. "If she becomes interested in the who and the why, we will all need to deal with this, especially if the Brethren get wind of it. Your people have as much to lose here as we do, and, if it is needed, Dr. Pillar, you *will* kill her. Do you understand?"

"Yes," Pillar said, lowering his head. Then he added, "The temple restored."

The voice on the other end replied with "The invisible hand," and hung up.

. . .

"The good news is I'm not firing you," Leo Roselle said from across the Formica table at the diner down the street from his office. He sipped his coffee and then dabbed his lips with a silk handkerchief that matched his rose-colored bow tie. He was in his white linen suit and looked as if he had just had it pressed, even though he was coming off a forty-eight-hour shift.

Lovina sat across from him, sipped her iced tea, and waited for the "but."

"I'd end up getting poor old Russell Lime in hot water, too, if all this came out, and I'm not going to do that, especially with Treasure being in the state she's in right now," Roselle said.

"Look, Leo," Lovina said, "Russell didn't do anything—"

"Hogwash," Roselle said. "But it's very decent of you to try to cover for him. Okay, here's how it goes. You are off Major Crimes, off investigative detail, as of right now."

"Leo, what the hell am I supposed to—" Lovina said, her voice rising.

Roselle calmly kept talking. "The Center for Missing and Exploited Children has been reaching out to law-enforcement agencies," he said, "looking for law-enforcement personnel who can act in the capacity as a liaison and case analyst between their agency and the center." Lovina sat back in her chair. Roselle sipped his coffee for a moment. "Yeah," he said. "I thought that might shut you up. You've got the job. You still work for me. Any more of this nonsense, any more freelancing without bringing me into the loop, and I will fire you. We clear, Investigator Marcou?"

Lovina's smile was radiant and wide. "Yes, sir," she said. "Thanks, Leo."

"Don't thank me," he said. "It's going to be lots of long hours, lots of dirty work, sad, sick stories, ice-cold cases, and, most likely, lots of missing people you never, ever find. Lots of stories with no ending. Don't thank me for that, Lovina." Roselle looked even more hangdog than usual as he spoke, sad, almost weary. "In a way, I'm letting your devil run loose. I hope I don't end up regretting it."

"You won't," Lovina said.

Roselle stood up and examined the check. He fished a shiny silver money clip out of his pocket and pulled a few bills from it. "Good," he said. "Take the next few days off. You start Monday." Roselle dropped the money on the table. "Oh, and one more thing," he said.

"Yes?" Lovina said.

"The wheel turns," Roselle said, and touched her gently on the shoulder. He walked out of the diner, not looking back to see Lovina's expression.

. . .

"It's a boy!" Jimmie said into his cell phone. "Ten pounds four ounces!"

"Damn, Jimmie—that's great, man!" Heck said on the other side of the call. "Congratulations! Max won the bet, but that's okay. I'll win on the next kid."

"Bite your tongue, boy," Jimmie said, smiling ear to ear. "No way in hell we're going through all this again."

"That's what they all say," Heck said. "Hey, how did things turn out with that run? You guys going to be okay?"

"Turned out the dock foreman was one of us," Jimmie said, laughing. "He smoothed it all over. Made the run, barely on time, and got paid, so now we're back to being about a paycheck away from homeless."

"That's awesome, Jimmie," Heck said. "Just keep on keeping on, man. All we can do."

"Today, I'm too damn tired and too damn happy to let it stick," Jimmie said. "I want you to come on down next week. We'll cook out and you can meet the family proper, and we'll talk about the next part of your squire training. You okay, kid?"

"Right as rain, Obi-Wan," Heck said. "Congrats again, Jimmie. Tell

Layla and the fam I said 'good job,' but work on the whole birth-weight thing. Lovina and I owe the doc two cases of energy drinks now.'"

Jimmie laughed. "Okay, squire, I got to go. My folks just went in the room. See you next week. Take care, Heck."

The call ended, and Heck placed the phone on the bar next to him. There were a dozen empty shot glasses in front of him and two empty pitchers. George Thorogood was playing on the jukebox of the honky-tonk. "Set me up again, Ray," he said to the bartender, and lit a fresh Lucky Strike.

He took the Zippo, the flame still flickering, and held it over his arm, held it there until he should be in excruciating pain and suffering a serious burn. He snapped the lighter's lid down, killing the flame, and looked at his arm. It was fine—not a mark, no pain. No pain—that was funny. He took a drag on the cigarette and then tossed back the shot Ray had just delivered. No pain.

In a few more rounds, he'd get up and talk some shit to the rednecks at the pool table who'd been talking shit about his MC cut since he got here. He'd start the fight and finish it in a cell. He'd sleep then, finally, when the monster in him had been allowed to run for a spell and then was, appropriately, locked up in a cage. Just another Friday night.

He glanced over to the cell phone. An odd thought crossed his fuzzy brain: *What would Jimmie Aussapile say about all that?* Heck laughed a little bit at that, but the thought stuck with him. *A squire, someday a knight—Jesus Christ, what a joke that was.* He picked up another shot and examined the dark amber whiskey, sloshed it about a bit in the glass. The beast growled to get on with it.

He set the full glass back down on the bar and picked up the cell. He fumbled as he searched his contacts and hit the call button. After a moment, the call was answered.

"Roadkill," Heck said, "Sup, man? Hey, you up for hanging with me? Yeah, I am a bit pissed . . . come on, you in or not? Yeah, I'm paying, don't I always?" Heck laughed at the answer Jethro gave him. "Okay, I'm at the Last Chance, down on Route 321. Okay, cool, man. See you in a bit. Hey, Roadkill. Thanks, man."

Heck put the phone away and listened to the music from the jukebox, not to the beast howling and shaking to free itself from his rib cage—someday, but not tonight. He listened to George Thorogood's gravel growl, smoked his Lucky, and waited for his friend.

. . .

Jimmie stepped back into the hospital room, slipping his cell phone away. His mom and dad were sitting on one side of Layla's bed; Peyton was on the other. Jimmie took a seat between his wife and his daughter and took Layla's hand. "How you feeling, baby?" he asked.

"Like I never want to have sex ever, ever again," Layla said, leaning toward Jimmie. He leaned over and they kissed. "But I'm sure I'll get over that."

"Do they have those little throw-up things in here?" Peyton asked. "The ones that look like giant condoms? Because I need one right now. Parent sex—gross!"

"Don't knock it," Jimmie's mom, Ella, said.

"Mom!" Jimmie said. Everyone laughed.

"Grandparent sex," Peyton said. "Even grosser."

The nurse came in with the baby, tightly wrapped in a white hospital blanket. "Someone wanted to come say hello," she said. She carefully placed the baby in Layla's arms. Everyone huddled close to see.

"You were that little once," Jimmie's dad, Don, said to Peyton. "And just as purty."

The baby boy squirmed a little in Layla's arms. His face was red and blotchy, and his eyes were puffy and shut.

"He's beautiful," Layla said, then looked over to Jimmie. "Oh, I'm sorry. I mean handsome."

"You mean beautiful," Jimmie said, his eyes getting wet. "And he is, he is beautiful—just like his mama."

"And I bet he'll be brave, and true, just like his old man," Layla said softly, touching Jimmie's cheek.

"Y'all still calling him Jesse Junior?" Ella asked.

"You know, Don is a fine name, too," Don said, smiling. "Very dignified."

"Jesse James Aussapile, Jr.," Layla said. "That's his name. Better luck next baby, Grandpa."

They laughed and there was talking, but Jimmie barely heard it. Looking into the face of his baby boy, Jimmie saw all the promise in this world, all the futures and the dreams that we fight through the darkness and the despair to reach. He wanted to give his son a world without monsters, without villains—a world of light, and truth, justice, and mercy, especially mercy.

The tears came, and Jimmie barely noticed them. His whole world was here, in this room. It was a small world, especially in the grand scale of things, compared to gods and galaxies, magic roads and secret societies. But everything counted, and maybe, just maybe, it all counted square, equal, in the end.

Jimmie Junior opened his eyes and looked into the battered face of his father, and there was a wisdom there in the baby's eyes that is lost to us as we grow.

"Hi, buddy," Jimmie said, tears wet on his cheeks.

It was a small world, but it was worth fighting for.

ACKNOWLEDGMENTS

Thanks to The League of Extraordinary Beta Readers and Editors—Susan Lystlund, Faye Newsham, and David Lystlund. These good folks slogged through the mess of my manuscript and made it so much better, and tighter. I am, as always, in your debt.

To Barb and Carl Kesner. Yes, they are real people and they are awesome.

To the incredible people at Tor that, as always, provided amazing support and expertise—Patty Garcia, Desirae Friesen, Christopher Morgan, Diana Pho, and my superb editor, Greg Cox. I am reminded of how fortunate I am to work with consummate professionals, who also happen to be such wonderful, kind, and generous people.

Thank you to my agent, Lucienne Diver, and all the family at the Knight Agency. Lucienne saw the potential in Jimmie Aussapile when she was reading *Nightwise*, and this book is a direct result of her talent, encouragement, and belief in me.

To my beautiful, brilliant, and kind children—Jon, Emily, and Stephanie—who have all passed through fire and darkness in their own ways, and come out the other side stronger. I am so proud of each of you. You all have made me feel so loved and I am so very thankful for you. I love you.

None of my books would ever have been written if not for the love, dedication, and support of my mother, Mabel T. Belcher. She passed away during the work on this book and I am so very, very thankful that I was fortunate enough to have this strong, determined, and compassionate woman as my mom. I love you, Mama.

Turn the page for a sneak peek at
the next novel of the Six-Gun Tarot

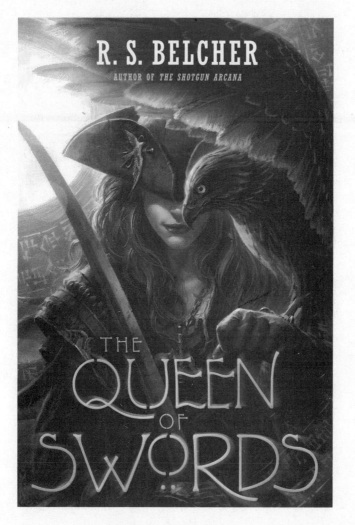

Available June 2017

ONE

The Devil (Reversed)

Port Royal
Isle of Jamaica
June 11, 1721

She swore an oath that the child would be born in freedom. The baby's first breath would not be in the stinking air of the Marshalsea Prison, even if it took her last breath to see to it. The English guard had been true to his bargain, and that made it worth the pain. His price for the secret of escape, for looking the other way, was the gold in her mouth. She had ripped the back tooth out with her bare hands. After months of starvation, and, before that, a bout of scurvy on Jack's ship, it was easy, and that pain was nothing compared to the contractions.

The trapdoor was where the guard had said it would be. It led to a small tunnel—a simple storm drain, designed to slow the overflow of seawater if yet another hurricane hit the island. She crawled through the damp darkness, unable to drag herself on her belly anymore with the baby, so she did it on her side, pausing every few feet in the pitch blackness to gasp in pain and curl up as best she could as another contraction wracked her body. They were coming closer together, but her water had not yet broken.

After what seemed an eternity, she caught sight of moonlight beyond the grate at the end of the drain. She heard the sweetest sound she had ever known, the crash of the waves, the hiss of the sea foam. The ocean did what it always did; it promised freedom.

The storm drain's grate was loose in the crumbling mortar channel just as she had been told. If she were her old self, she could have kicked it free easily, but starvation, illness, and the child in her belly had all conspired to sap her strength. She gripped the bars and pushed, then pulled, with all her might. She was so damned weak, now. It made her angry.

As she gritted her teeth and struggled with the bars between her and the welcoming sea, that snotty bastard, Willie Goode, forced his way into her mind. He had thought he could have her, right there in that alleyway in Charleston. He was sixteen and she was twelve. He outweighed her by a good fifty pounds, the slobbering, full-gorged lout. He had pinned her and began to pull at her skirts. The pressure of him on her, the sour smell of his breath, her heart like a hare, thudding, kicking in her chest. He was so strong, so insistent, like his pego poking her stomach. She remembered London, what had happened there, and bit off Willie's ear. When he screamed and rose up she drove her knee into his bollocks and was satisfied when she felt a pop. It took two grown men to pull her off the sobbing little git.

She wouldn't let the bastards win then, and she had no intention of doing it now. With a final grunt and gasp, she tore the bars free. They fell with a dull thud to the ground, and her arms loose, like rubber, fell with them. Her water broke then and she knew she didn't have much time.

The pain was intensifying. She crawled out of the pipe and let the cool, damp air of the beach caress her like a lover. It took great effort, but she stood, resting her hands on her knees for support. A contraction knifed through her, taking her breath away, but she refused to fall. She staggered across the wet, packed sand toward the tumbling waves. She stood at the edge of what the sea had claimed for itself, the rushing foam tickling her dirty, scabbed feet. She looked up at the moon, as swollen as her own belly. She smiled at the pockmarked orb burning silently with ghost light, its scars and wounds making it even more beautiful. "Good to see you too, luv. Been too long," she whispered.

The water covered her feet now and grabbed greedily at her ankles as it sped past her. Tide was coming in, the sea's way of telling any sailor worth his salt it was time to move on. The pain came up sharp and sudden; it made her feel as if she had to void herself. She breathed through it. The wind and the surf were her midwives. She gulped in air when the birth pain passed. She tasted blood in her mouth where once there had been gold.

She wandered farther out into the water, up to her waist. For a moment she thought of the nasty saw-toothed sharks—the wee ones—that prowled the shallows, eager for a tasty leg to claim. But after the night she had endured to be here, she knew she could wrestle any fucking shark and win, probably claim a bite out of it too, she was so hungry.

The pain came again, like her insides knotting and trying to spill out of her hat. She gave a little shriek but muffled herself; the water lapping against her belly was helping. She began to time her breaths to the rhythm of the tide. She had once acted as midwife, along with Mary, to a hostage off a Dutch sloop. Neither of them knew a fucking thing about delivering a kid, but Calico Jack figured since they were both women it was instinctual or some such shit. She recalled that breathing through the pains seemed to help, and pushing—pushing was good—but Mary had argued with her that the girl had to wait to push. "Wait for fucking what?" she had said, "A goddamned invitation?" In the end it hadn't mattered whether she pushed or not. The baby came on its own. It lived a few breaths longer than its mother.

There was a shiver down her spine as the pain stabbed her again, and then again, coming closer and stronger with each passing moment. The urge to push was maddening. The waves smashed against her and still she stood her ground; the cold water splashed across her face, the sea pulled at her trying to draw her deeper into its embrace, and still she stood.

She raised her head to scream; she forced her eyes wide open, looking up at the mute moon and the uncaring stars. In this moment she was the universe—her, a petty thief, a liar, pirate, adulteress, murderess. In this final effort of breath, she was a goddess, the creator, and all the cogs spun in the heavens just for her.

The baby arrived beneath the dark churning waters of Mother Ocean, and she did not fall; even as her knees buckled and her legs became like seaweed, she remained on her feet. The child arrived swimming, vibrant and hale. She gathered the infant up in her arms. As it broke the surface, the child snorted the saltwater from its tiny nose and let loose a scream, an angry howl of protest at life itself. She laughed as the baby spit, and cried.

"Ah, marriage music," she chuckled. "You go right ahead and get it out, wee one. This may be your first, but it sure as hell won't be your last cry."

She held the child up to examine and tisked when she saw the tiny penis. "So, it's a boy, you are then. Well, lucky you, lad! This chamber pot just got a little rosier for you with that twig between your nethers." She laughed and pulled the baby to her bosom, spinning and trying to dance in the waves. She was dizzy and weak but she also felt high, like she had been smoking the poppy. She hummed a tune from her child-hood in Cork, "Molly Brannigan."

The baby screamed then slowly calmed himself. "I know," she said, "as a singer, I'm a bloody fantastic dancer." He nuzzled into her small breasts and she helped him find a nipple. The child drank eagerly and she could feel him sigh and relax in contentment. "Not much of a meal, I'm afraid, wee lord," she said. "My milk's gone dry from my stay in the governor's digs, but take what you can."

She looked at the tiny squirming thing in her arms and for a long moment she considered forcing it back under the dark waters until it was still. It had no life worth living at her breast, that was sure and true. She thought back to all that had come before this in her life, and how often she had prayed to never have been, yet here she was. She recalled hearing Mary's screams a few cells down from her only a month ago, as her own baby arrived. After a time there was only the baby's screams and Mary was silent. Eventually guards came and took the child and Mary's body away.

She and Mary had both pled their bellies after the trial when they had been captured along with the other survivors of Calico Jack's crew. But Mary had found her way to hell anyway, and she knew it likely that if she tried to flee with a baby at her hip, she would soon be at Mary's side again. So all reason, all her instincts, told her to drown the child and be on her way.

She glanced up at the moon again. The heavens were no help at all, as silent in their regard as they were beautiful. She sighed and looked down to the face of the baby boy. "You have any notions on this?" she asked. He grunted and released his first shit, dropping it in the ocean. "I couldn't agree more, lad," she said with a smile. "How could I drown anyone who already has such a perfect understanding of how all this works?"

She bit the birthing cord free as she walked slowly back to shore, the taste of the infant's blood mixing with her own, and the brine of the sea, in her mouth. She spat and tied the cord off with a reef knot, muttering as she did, "Right over left, left over right, make a knot both tidy and tight. There, you go—your first sailor lesson, my wee lord."

She was exhausted, cold, and starving. She needed to tend to those things and she needed to be off this accursed crown-kissing island by dawn. She tore at her filthy gown and used the fabric to clean and swaddle the baby. Off to her left, down the cove, she could see the silhouette of town against the brilliant moonlight. There she would find roast pig, and bread and cheese and bitter grog and wine, sweet, sweet wine, and a proper bathtub, and loot, and sails to take her away from here. But first she would need to find steel, and with it gold, to make all the other things possible. She hefted her son, headed toward the sounds and smells of the port and plotted her first crime with her boy as an accomplice.

It was the devil's hour when she entered the common room of the Witches' Wrath. The Wrath was built on top of the corpses of the taverns Port Royal had once had in the golden days before piracy was outlawed on this island, and before the great earthquake had destroyed most of the city. The righteous claimed the quake was the anger of God Almighty, sweeping away the pirate nation and all their blood money had created. She knew well enough, though, that God annihilated saint as easily as sinner and didn't give a fuck where the tithe came from.

The stink of the place—pungent human smells, the fetor of old ale, all poorly hidden behind the sickly sweet vapors of burning clove—was familiar to her. To her surprise, she found she had missed it, missed the parrots squawking as they drank their fill of ale from discarded flagons, missed the chattering of the monkeys and the booming laughter of the sailors, the tittering of the wenches. A good tavern was all of life on display, a sweating, mumbling, drinking, fighting, fucking museum.

She had acquired clothing—warm breeches, decent, if somewhat-too-large boots, a tunic and a vest. Her greasy red hair fell well below her shoulders. She wore a cocked hat she had crimped off the same fine fellow who had donated the rest of her clothes—he wouldn't be needing them anymore. She wore the tricorne low, to allow the shadows to hide part of her face, but she made no attempts to pass for a man at present. Her sleeping son was strapped to her chest in a sling she had fashioned from her prison gown. She carried the dead man's steel, a heavy and well-worn machete, in one hand, and rested the palm of her other hand on the butt of the pistol hanging from the wide sash wrapped about her waist. There was a subtle change in the current of conversation when she entered. Eyes flicked to rest upon her, sizing her up as victim, weak and ready to be culled, or as one of the hunters. When she felt the attention, sensed the menace, she smiled a little. She was home.

"Port," she said in the cant, the secret language of the old pirates. She dropped a few Spanish reales on the bar. The tavern keep frowned; then his face lit with surprise, and she knew he had recognized her. He slid the bottle to her. The tavern keep smiled. She saw most of his teeth were black or absent. He deftly pocketed the coins.

"Glad ta see you avoided gitting noozed," the keep replied in the cant. "Din't think they could git a rope about that pretty neck, Lady Calico. Too many brains in that skull of yours for the rope to fit about it. Sorry ta hear about your man's demise."

She took a long draw off the port. It was the sweetest thing she could recall after a year of stale water and maggoty bread. She wiped her mouth with the back of her hand. "Shit," she said. "I told Jack I was sorry to see him in the gallows with his lads, but if he'd fought like a man, he wouldn't have had to hang like a dog." The tavern keep had a laugh like a cannon going off. "Herodotus Markham? Where is he?" she asked. The tavern keep nodded toward the rear room. An old man with a mane of gray hair, and a tattered red velvet coat, sat on a bench, smoking a pipe.

"Makes his way here every few nights," the keep said. "He's dying, but it's a slow kind o' dying. Still the smartest man I ever knew—not that all skull music will keep him breathing one more day."

She slid more silver to him, "for your service, and your silence." The keep nodded and the coins vanished. She took the bottle and headed for the back of the tavern. A dirty hand shot out of the darkness as she walked past a table of men, grabbing her. "How much you selling the brat for, luv?" Her blade was at the man's throat before the utterance had finished leaving his lips.

"A damn sight more than I wager you're willing to pay," she said. The hand slipped back into the smoky darkness.

"I told you it was *her,* ya tosspot!" she heard one of the other sailors hiss as she walked on. "Yer damn lucky she didn't lop your sugar stick off."

Herodotus Markham looked as he had when she had last seen him just before she, Jack, and Mary had stolen the *William.* He resembled an old country squire—a gentleman of means who perhaps had fallen on hard times, or maybe had been laid upon by ruffians. His white wig was in disarray, with faded ribbons of red still grasping on for dear life to the tail of it. His velvet coat was a deep burgundy marred by stains, faded by the sun and the salt of the sea. The coat had burnt patches and every cuff and collar was frayed. His face sagged like a half-empty sack of potatoes. His florid complexion was a combination of old rouge and too much drink. The only part of him that wasn't sad was the wicked steel glint in his dark eyes. It was the last place anyone would care to look and the only place that told you this broken-down old man was still very dangerous.

Markham's face lit up when he saw her. "*Rough with black winds and storms,*" he recited, "*unwanted shall admire.*"

"Always charm with you, Dot," she said, sitting down next to the old man. He hugged her and she returned it. Markham gasped as the baby made a cooing sound from his hammock across her chest.

"A babe!" he exclaimed and she couldn't help but laugh at his surprise and delight. "Oh my sweet girl! Is it Jack's?"

"That's the prevailing theory," she said, adjusting the infant in his snug hammock. "Best I can figure he would have been conceived just before we took off with the *William,* or maybe on her."

"If it was on ship that makes him a true son of a gun," Markham said, "a sailor born, just like his mother."

"I wasn't conceived on a ship," she said, taking a long pull off the bottle of port, "more likely the scullery maid's closet. Da gave Ma the goat's jig in between her changing linens, sometimes during."

Markham puffed his long churchwarden pipe and shook his head. "No," he said, a wreath of tobacco smoke preceding his words, "if ever I met someone born to the tides, it was you, Annie. You're more a sea dog than old Calico Jack, Charlie Vane, or any of their ilk."

She laughed. "One big difference," she said, "I'm still breathing." Dot nodded.

"It's the end of the golden age of the freebooters, lass," he said. "The world will be less legendary, less wild, without them. We're replacing pirates with politicians."

"I always found pirates to be a damn sight more honest," she said. "They tell you up front what they're going steal from you."

The old man chuckled. It turned into a dry, booming cough. "Come to say goodbye have you, girl?" She knelt and took the old man's hands in her own.

"Yes, I have to be gone by first light. I need one last favor from you, Dot," she said. "That chest Jack left with you before we took the *William*, do you recall it?" Dot nodded.

"Aye," he said. "The queer one, painted up with all those strange marks on it. Oh, yes, I recall it well. Sometimes . . . sometimes at night, I think I hear . . . singing coming out of it."

"Singing?"

"A strange language, one I've never heard," he said. "It sounds like a lot of voices, like women."

"I need it," she said.

"Of course, love, but are you sure? There's something damned in that box—it's the devil singing," Dot said. "It makes me dream of some steaming, scorching place—of unforgiving heat, of a city made out of . . . dead things. I think I dreamt of Hell."

"That box is this baby's birthright and the final share due me from Jack," she said. "It will lead me to a big enough score to lay down my sword. Can you fetch it for me, Dot?"

"Of course. Meet you here before dawn?" he asked. She stood, and helped the old man to his feet as she did.

"No," she said. "The north docks, near Fort James and the custom houses."

"Done," he said and headed for the door without another word. She got the impression Herodotus was glad to be ridding himself of the box and wanted to waste no time doing so.

She sat back on the bench and took another long sip on the bottle of port. The box was not natural—she knew that—had known it since she and Jack had taken it from the cargo hold of that merchantman headed back to England from Africa. One of Jack's crew, a Spaniard named Thiago, had jumped from the crow's nest onto the deck below, screaming of a city of monsters that was eating the dreams out of his skull. He screamed a name as he took his fatal plunge—"Carcosa."

Both she and Jack had awoken from dreams of the necropolis squatting still and silent in the middle of some verdant, primal place. When they made it to port, they had consulted the smartest man either of them knew—Herodotus. He had no wisdom for them, but promised to keep the box safe.

She never told Jack but she, alone, had a final dream of the bone city. In it she stood in a sun-baked courtyard, vast like an arena. The floor of the place glittered with rubies, millions of them. She stood before a shining statue of a woman, flaring with the light of the bloated red sun. The statue was at the center of the arena, and was made of gold and ivory, diamonds and other precious stones, a king's fortune a hundred times over, or a queen's.

She was going to find that city and claim its treasures and its secrets, and she knew, she knew the first step on that path was the box, and then to head for Africa, from which it hailed. Now sitting alone in the noise and life of the Witches' Wrath, she recalled the eyes of the statue in her dream. They were terrible, the immortal gaze of a goddess—regarding her, judging her with eyes darker than a murderer's soul, burning red at their core, hotter than any earthly forge.

She rubbed her eyes, and pushed the memory out of her mind. She realized then how much she wanted a pipe and some good tobacco.

"Now," she said to the baby slumbering at her breast, "what do I do with you, you little snapper?" She noticed a man sitting alone at a table writing with an inkwell and pen in a ledger, occasionally popping his head up to look about, or to drink from his tankard. He was a slender man, his hair and beard the color of wheat. She rose, and moved towards him.

"Nate?" she said. "Nate Mist? I'll be a fussock, it is you!" The man turned, frowning at first, but then broke into a wide smile once he recognized her.

"I heard your neck got stretched, Annie," Mist said. She raised the port in salute and Mist raised his tankard.

"Haven't found a rope clever enough." she said. "I'm surprised to see you here. I heard you were back in England—a writer they said."

"Publisher," Mist replied. "Oh, and down here I'm going by Charles Johnson these days—Captain Charles Johnson. Ran into a spot of trouble back home. Thought I'd travel a bit and see if I could finish my research on the history of pirates I'm writing."

"Well, 'Captain,'" she said laughing and taking another drink, "I'm a walking, talking expert on that lot."

"That you are," Mist said. He flipped to a fresh page in his ledger and dipped his pen in the inkwell. "Let me ask you about . . ."

"You'll make a pretty bob off me and all my dead mates, won't you, Nate?" Mist began to answer, but she waved her free hand to dismiss his reply as she sat at his table. "I'll give it all to you, mate—you were always a good lad back then—always an honest sea dog. I'll tell you the tale of the last days of Calico Jack and his crew. How old Eddie Teach supped with the devil and stole some of his cursed gold for himself. I'll tell you the story of how we came across this great metal vessel the size of a hundred galleons! How it traveled under the waves and was captained by a mad genius."

Mist leaned forward, frantically scribbling in his ledger.

"I'll tell you the time I was stricken by the black mark—the one all pirates fear," she went on, knowing she had Mist now, her eyes locked with his, her voice weaving her stories tight about him, "and how I had to filch wine from Neptune himself to dodge that curse. You want to know about the island where immortal cannibal children are led by a ten-thousand-year-old boy who has no shadow? I'll give all the secrets of the pirates and the worlds they've been brave enough to sail through to you and you alone—enough for a hundred books—but first I want you to swear an oath to me, and do me a service, Nate. I want you to swear it on that god of yours that keeps getting you in so much trouble back home."

"What's the favor, Anne?" Mist asked.

She set the bottle on the table and slid her arms around and under the baby. "This," she said. "Take him to my Da in Charles Town, Oyster Point."

"Carolina? The colonies?" Mist said. "I was thinking of sailing north in a few days. Why don't you just go yourself?"

"I have something to tend to first," she said. "You tell my father to keep him safe and I'll be along once I'm finished." She placed a bag of coins before Mist on the table. "For him and for you. Do you swear you'll keep him safe and deliver him to my kin?"

Mist looked at the baby's face, then to hers. "I swear it," he said. They spit in their palms and shook to seal the oath. "Now," she said, "let me start by telling you about the Secret Sea . . ."

Night was unraveling in the East; threads of pink, orange, and indigo frayed where the sky met sea. Herodotus hobbled along with the small chest. Sailors, eagerly preparing to leave with the morning tide, darted past the old man. There were shouts, curses, songs, and orders in a dozen languages, all along the crowded row of docks and piers. Herodotus turned to look about and found himself facing a slender sailor, a man, his face shadowed with dirt that hinted at a beard. His long red hair was tied in a ponytail, the rest under a cocked hat. He wore a vest and tunic, a heavy blade and pistol held fast by a sash around his waist, breeches and boots. A ditty bag was hung over the man's shoulder. The sailor smiled and Dot suddenly recognized her.

"You're damned good at that, lass," he said, keeping his voice low. She laughed and even that had a rough, male sound to it.

"Lots of practice." She nodded to the box. "Thanks, Dot." He handed her the oddly painted wooden cask and she held it with both hands. "My ship is off in a few moments."

"You be careful with that twice-damned thing," Herodotus said. "Where's the boy?"

"Safe and on his way to my family in the colonies. Here," she said, handing him a purse full of coins. She had managed to increase her dwindling stolen stakes with a few games of bones on the docks while waiting for Dot. "There's a ship leaving later today for the Carolina colony," she said. "You remember Nate Mist? He's a passenger aboard, and I've secured you passage as well. Nate has my boy, taking him to my Da. I'd consider it a kindness if you'd accompany them and see to my boy until I return."

"Nate's a good man," Markham said, nodding. He took the purse. "Very well, perhaps the change in climate will be good for what ails me."

"Thank you," she said. "And don't worry. I'm taking this thing home, scoring one last haul of loot, and then I'm quits with this freebooter life."

Herodotus laughed until he began coughing again. "I'll believe that when I bloody see it," he said. "You're born to this, Annie, moon and tide, steel and gold."

"Well, I'm retiring to be a proper lady," she said with a grin. "One of goddamned means, to boot. Goodbye, Dot. Take good care of yourself and my lad." They shook hands and she began to head for the gangplank of one of the ships.

"And good luck to you too, Lady . . ." Herodotus paused. "Anne, what the hell do I call you, now? Lady Rackham? Cormac? What?"

She turned and gave the old pirate sage a wink. "I always liked my married name," she said, "liked it better than I liked the fucking marriage. I'll stick with that one, I think."

"Fair enough," Herodotus said. "Then good luck to you, Lady Bonny."

TWO

The Queen of Swords

Northern Utah
December 5th, 1870
(*one hundred and forty-nine years later*)

The train rumbled through the badlands, the ancient, snow-silvered mountains indifferent to its blustering advance. The Transcontinental Railroad was the great artery, the road connecting civilization to the wilderness, to the frontier.

With the planting of a single golden spike, a flurry of speeches, pomp and circumstance, the track had been made whole, and the gateway to the mythical West swung open. Alter Cline, sitting in the mostly empty passenger car, foresaw the railroad's recent completion as a harbinger of death for that very myth.

Cline was twenty-four. His black hair fell to his shoulders in ringlets, parted on the side. He sported thick, stylish sideburns. Alter possessed a wiry, slender build with long legs. He stood a hair over six feet. His brown eyes were expressive and intelligent, and currently they fixed on the striking woman sitting near the center of the passenger car.

The woman was traveling unchaperoned, which was queer. She was quite unaware of his notice, Alter was certain. Her hair was auburn, shot through with red-gold and silver strands. It was long, but she wore it up, away from her face, in a tight bun. Her skin was pale, her wrists small and delicate. Her figure was slight, and her overall appearance not the sort that would capture a man's second glance in a crowd or busy street. However, there was something—something that hid in this woman beneath her surface appearance. Alter enjoyed the mystery, the parlor game of guessing who she was, why she was here, where she had come from.

The mental exercise helped Cline take his mind off his unease that this untamed place, this magnificent frontier, was living on borrowed time. He was happy to be headed back to New York, but there was a freedom, a spirit, awake in these wild lands, something that slept in a lot of people back East. He'd miss that rawness, that primal feeling once he was home—not that there weren't a few neighborhoods in New York City that he was sure the toughest cow-puncher or gunslinger would find daunting.

It troubled him to think that when this frontier was gone, perhaps that raw part of the human spirit would die with it. However, what he had witnessed out on the plains suggested that the same old human stains—greed, cruelty, callous indifference—traveled hand in hand with our primal selves wherever, whenever, we go. It gave him grim reassurance that mankind was far from domesticated just yet. It made Cline wonder, too, that perhaps "civilized" people didn't respect the freedom and the splendor out here enough to deserve it, or keep it.

He had been sent out by his editor to cover the brisk expansion in the business of buffalo skinning, as a perfect example of man's knack for destroying wonder. It wasn't truly buffaloes that blackened the plains in their vast numbers, that made the ground shudder like thunder in their passing, but bison. Not that those killing them in the hundreds of thousands and leaving their skinned corpses to rot on the plains, leaving sun-bleached mountains of wide, horned skulls, cared a damn about the semantics of what they were killing.

Alter had ridden out with a skinning crew for several weeks, chronicling their lives and gory, lonely work. He had lived and worked as one of them, though they joked he had no stomach for it. The demands for the hides back East were bringing more and more men, mostly restless young soldiers from the war, out to the frontier.

Alter understood that gnawing restlessness all too well, an unseen wound of the war. It was like a metal spring—humming, made of bright, warm brass—wound too tight inside you. He had felt it after the war. Sitting in one place too long would wind the spring tighter, make it snap from the tension. A soft bed, a quiet meal, silence in the darkness, could fill him with a tension that he could not voice or explain to anyone who had not seen the elephant, and men did not speak of such things to one another in polite conversation. Men didn't speak of it at all, if they could.

The pressure, the restlessness, was one of the reasons, perhaps the primary reason Alter had taken the position offered to him by *The Herald*. It afforded him the opportunity to travel—movement, the hint of action—those things seemed to unwind the bright coil within him. His parents, who had objected to him joining the Union Army, objected to him working for the newspaper, too. They thought it unseemly, cheap, and far beneath him. He didn't care; he loved it.

Alter had used the trip west for the buffalo piece as an excuse to work on a second story, one he thought even more indicative of the dark side of the great frontier. Chinese railroad workers for Union Pacific were making thirty-two dollars a month in wages compared to the fifty-two dollars their white peers earned, and this was causing a row among those whites seeking work, and a growing anti-Chinese sentiment that the immigrants were unfairly competing for jobs. Alter had seen this less as an insidious plot by immigrants and more of an underhanded act by the Rail Barons to exploit cheap labor from an alien people far from home and with no protection or advocates.

He hoped he could convince his editors to run both stories; however, *The Herald* had a reputation for leaning a bit to the nativist ideology of the Know Nothing party. Still, he was bringing back an adventure tale of roughing it on the incomprehensibly vast plains. He had even sketched a few decent drawings of the mighty bison to include in the tale. The public back home was eager for any stories of the Wild West. Alter thought he had a chance of getting the labor story out, before things got truly ugly for the Chinese, by piggybacking it on a ripping yarn about cowboys.

Alter opened his copy of *Around the Moon* and tried to read again, but his attention kept drifting back to the woman. There was . . . something, something about her—about her bearing—that fascinated him. Whatever it was, it made it very hard for Cline to focus on Monsieur Verne's prose. He used his skills as an investigator and professional observer to remain unobtrusive, and the lady's continued lack of notice seemed to indicate he was doing a fine job.

———

A few aisles away, the object of Alter Cline's attentions watched the Utah mountains drift past her window. Maude Stapleton felt the young man's eyes moving over her. He was trying very hard to be discreet, behind his book, and to untrained eyes he was doing a fine job, but there were few upon the Earth with senses as keen as Maude's.

Maude's mind drifted to Constance, her daughter, and to Maude's father, Martin, and all that lay ahead of her. That made her think of Mutt, of Golgotha, and what she was leaving behind. She was pulled from her thoughts by the young man's eyes, as insistent to her as if he had tapped her on the shoulder and cleared his throat.

The attention was pleasant and, if she had allowed it, her blood would act of its own accord and produce a physiologic reaction, and she would blush. Maude decided it was best not to encourage the stranger, so she didn't blush. She had only allowed herself that freedom, that dizzy abandonment—out of control of her body and emotions—with one living man, and this train was taking her farther and farther away from him, possibly forever.

Maude did not consider herself a woman who attracted notice; in fact, she had been taught how to blend in, not even becoming a memory in the mind of others. However, the young man seemed rather focused in his attention on her. Her features might be called plain, handsome, or mannish by some men. Maude could give less than a damn what "some men" thought.

Beside herself and her admirer, a Chinese family—a husband, wife, and their two small children—were the only occupants of the passenger car. When Maude had boarded the train at Hazen, the closest train station to Golgotha, the conductor, a corpulent man, sweating in his heavy, dark-blue coat with fancy brass buttons, had tried to roust the Chinese from the car.

"Don't you worry your pretty little head, Miss," the conductor said, brandishing a wooden truncheon at the obviously terrified family. "I'll chase these coolies straight back to the nigger car. They won't give you a lick of trouble."

The father stood, about to interpose himself between this ugly little man and his family. Maude caught his eye and silently entreated him for patience. She turned to the conductor.

"I'm sure that will not be necessary," she said as she shifted her body language and vocal tone with the conductor, locking eyes with the odious creature. "You are a kind man, a merciful man, someone of great power and responsibilities. I can see that in your manner and bearing, sir. Obviously, such a menial chore is far beyond a man of your importance, isn't it?"

"Er, I mean to say . . . yes?" the conductor muttered. He found himself absently nodding with each subtle movement of this woman's head, her hands. Maude's voice was gently playing upon his nerves like she might pluck the strings of a harp.

"In fact, don't you think it's best they stay here with me, where they won't distress the other passengers?" In the end, the man had thought it his own idea, which was precisely what Maude had intended.

"Thank you," the father had said, in English, as the conductor lumbered away, very pleased with himself. "We are returning to New York to work in my uncle's business. My job on the railroad is complete. I did not know we were not allowed . . ."

"It's a foolish rule, created by foolish people," Maude replied in one of the Yue dialects of Chinese that Gran had taught her. "He won't trouble you again. I hope you and your family enjoy your trip." One of the children, the little boy, looked at her in amazement, having never heard the language of his parents coming out of a white person's mouth before. Maude smiled. The little boy waved and Maude waved back. The boy hid his face in his mother's leg and giggled.

The young man watching her had come aboard at one of the stations sometime later and begun his furtive surveillance of Maude. In her own assessment of the young man, she noted that his clothing was of good quality. They spoke of some means but were not the clothes of the idle wealthy. He was obviously a working man in a field that left his hands smooth, but he had done a spot of rough work recently, and he had the blisters to show for it. She also saw in him the bearing of a man trained for war, but now looser, mostly relaxed or forgotten. He still carried the stress of combat in his lower spine, and that would catch up to him one day. He was handsome, though, she had to admit.

Gran entered Maude's mind unbidden, swaggering, as she usually did. Maude knew what Gran would say about her admirer, if she were still alive. She'd cackle like one of Macbeth's witches and say something like, "*Go on, lass, have a go at 'im! Get all hot cockles with the pretty boy. Life is too damn short for mooning about and playing it safe. Nobody gets out of this world alive, 'cept for me, of course!*"

The ghost she had summoned made her smile, and the young man almost dropped his book in response to it. Maude nearly laughed, but she lowered her eyes and held her composure.

The car's rear door opened with a bang, and a group of men entered the compartment. There were seven of them. They were dirty with trail dust, and they reeked of the sweat of their horses and their own bodies, of leather and gun oil. All of them were armed—six-guns and knives; some carried rifles and shotguns, too. They slowly advanced down the car's center aisle. The leader, a burly man with a thick red beard and hooded eyes full of coiled violence, nodded to two of his men. They responded by dropping back from the pack and lingering near the rear door. The menace from them radiated like heat.

Maude silently prepared herself for what she knew was coming, had to come. She adjusted her posture subtly from one of avoiding notice to that intended to attract the eye, drawing the crew's attention towards her and away from the immigrant family and the young man.

She altered her breathing, preparing for a fight with a fast-fast rhythm of breath—drawing on her abdominal muscles—just as she had been taught. She had practiced different styles of breathing for different purposes over many years and under a harsh teacher. Again she heard Gran's cackle, saw the old woman beside the ocean with her wadaiko—her Japanese drum—on her lap, calling the tunes Maude's muscles and lungs learned to obey.

"*There is no learning before you learn to breathe proper, girl,*" Gran had told her. "*Technique's called by many names in many lands. The Japanese call it Ibuki, and it's the first step in making you truly free. The air in your lungs is the fuel.*"

Her blood was filled with oxygen now. Maude was ready. The menacing men were armed and, now, so was she.

"Excuse me," the young man said, standing before her. "If I am not being too bold, may I join you?" He was pretty, to be sure. He was also the master of the worst possible timing imaginable.

"Of course," Maude said, directing him to a seat with a nod, "please."

"I'm not normally in the habit of being so forward," Alter said as he sat, "but I was concerned." He leaned closer and lowered his voice. "Those b'hoys coming in the car look like trouble, and a lady like yourself traveling alone . . ."

"That's very kind of you, Mr. . . . ."

"Cline," he said, "Alter Cline."

The men walked past Maude and Alter. She saw their brutal intent radiating from the tension in how they moved, ready for trouble, to explode, with every step. Cline was turning to face them—the worst possible thing he could do. The men each gave her a rapacious glance as they passed and then saw the grim look on Alter's face. One of the men stopped before Cline and began to say something, his hand dropping to his six-gun. Maude placed a hand lightly on Cline's shoulder and Alter suddenly shifted back toward her, a surprised look on his face. For such a slip of a woman, she seemed quite strong.

"If you want to stay alive, Mr. Cline, be still," she said, whispering. Cline began to open his mouth. "And quiet," she added.

"Leave the little dude be," one of the gunmen muttered to his kinsmen whom Alter had riled. "We're on a schedule. 'Sides Nick and Jed will see to 'em. Shake a leg."

The group of armed men opened the car's front door. They stepped through, man by man. The leader looked back at the two men waiting in Maude's car. He nodded to them and stepped through the door, shutting it behind him.

"Damn it," Maude muttered. Only Cline heard her. The younger of the two gunmen, close to Cline's age and with a lump of tobacco in his cheek, walked toward Maude and Cline. He paused, rested his hand on his holstered gun and looked Maude over like he was examining horseflesh to purchase.

"Well ain't you a little stick of an adventuress," the boy said, laughing. The man by the rear door laughed too and turned toward the Chinese family. Maude's face remained emotionless.

"She's gotta be a whore, if'n she's ridin' in a car with these here yeller niggers, Nick," the gunman, obviously Jed, said. He cradled a Winchester rifle as he looked at the husband and his family.

Nick grinned. His teeth were brown and stained. He looked over to Cline, who was reddening in response to the coarse words. "I hope you didn't pay this scrawny little thing too much for her to upend her legs, boy. Or maybe you're her pimp?"

"You filthy . . ." Cline growled. The reporter began to rise, his fists clenched. Nick drew his six-gun—a fluid motion as natural to the man as breathing. Nick cocked the pistol aimed at the young man's face. Alter Cline was a dead man.

Alter and Nick were scarcely able to fully comprehend what happened next. The muscles in Nick's arm, wrist, and hand fluttered in response to the command of his brain to pull the trigger, the quicksilver language of nerves and electrical impulses. Maude's eyes registered the movements; her body responded faster than thought allowed. Maude's arm flashed out and clutched Nick's wrist with a grip like iron. Her other hand chopped at his arm precisely above the elbow. Nick's gun arm folded, the gun turned upward toward his face as he pulled the trigger. The sound of the .44 was a hammer shattering the world. Alter jumped back, his eyes squeezing shut, anticipating a spray of hot blood. It didn't come. Nick crumpled to the floor. As he fell, Maude caught his still-smoking revolver. She flipped the gun in midair, clutching it by the hot barrel. She turned, using the strength of her pivoting hips as she hurled the gun at Jed like a tomahawk. Jed, just beginning to realize what was happening, raised his weapon. Nate's six-gun caught him square in the face. There was a gush of blood from his shattered nose, and he collapsed in a heap against the train car's rear door.

"How . . . how did you . . . do that?" Alter asked, looking down at Nick's motionless form. "Is he . . ."

"Dead?" Maude stepped out into the aisle over Nick's body. "No. The bullet grazed his chin, just knocked him out. The other one is alive too." She knelt by Nick, tore a strip from her dress, and began to bind his hands behind his back. Alter looked out the window, so as to not gawk at the flash of Maude's exposed leg. Nick groaned.

"Oh," Alter said. "I've never seen anyone move that fast before. How . . ."

"We really don't have time for that," Maude said, moving down the aisle toward the other gunman and the Chinese family. "If it makes you feel better, you can consider it a lucky accident—an hysterical woman's thrashing about that had a fortuitous outcome."

"I will do no such thing," Alter said. He knelt by Nick and examined the odd-looking but sturdy knot Maude had used to bind him. He did not recognize its make. "You are in complete control of your faculties, madame, and furthermore, your quick action saved my life. Thank you."

Maude paused in tying the other outlaw up to look back at Alter. She looked mildly surprised and smiled. "You're . . . quite welcome."

"That smile," Alter said, standing and adjusting his puff tie. "I imagine it gets you in a lot of trouble."

"Apparently so," Maude said as she stood. She handed Nick and Jed's bloody revolvers to the immigrant father. She said something to him in Chinese that Alter didn't understand. The father nodded, replied in his native tongue and took the guns. Maude knelt to retrieve the rifle. She spoke quietly to the little boy and ruffled his hair. His expression changed from fear to a smile. Maude stood and tossed the Winchester across the car to Alter. He caught it, and cocked the lever, chambering a round.

"You were in the army, and you know your way around a rifle, better than most," Maude said. She was putting on Jed's coat now and was tying his kerchief around her neck loosely. She walked past Cline headed toward the door the rest of the outlaw crew had passed through.

"Yes," Alter said. "But how on earth could you possibly know that? Wait, I know, 'no time.'"

"You're a quick study, good," Maude said.

She paused by the door and tore her dress in the front and back, giving herself enough freedom to run. Alter instinctively looked away again at the pale, bare skin. She tied the loose pieces of the brown dress together at each ankle—it now looked like she was wearing baggy ripped trousers. "Alter, I need you to backtrack, check the cars behind ours. See if they left any more men behind. If they did, I need you to deal with them, understand? Can you do that?"

"Yes," Alter said, looking back at the rear door. "Where are you going?"

Maude slid the kerchief over her mouth and nose and tightened it. She picked up Nick's floppy-brimmed felt hat from the floor and stuffed it on her head. Something in her posture, her way of walking, changed, and for an instant, Alter thought he was looking at a completely different person. "I'm going forward to do the same. Disarm these two completely before you head back."

"I thought you already did," he said.

"Nick has a knife in his left boot. This one has a parlor gun tucked in his vest pocket," she said. Even her voice sounded different now, deeper—more like a man's. "Be careful."

"How do you know th—" Alter began. The car's front door banged shut behind Maude. "The people you meet on the train, eh?" Alter said to the bewildered family as he pulled the blade from Nick's boot.

Outside the passenger car the winter wind was bitter as the train sped along at over forty miles an hour. Maude directed the blood within her body, willing it to act against the decrees of biology. Her skin warmed. The condensation of her breath that had trailed away from her mouth in silvered streams vanished.

She crossed the narrow gap between the train cars, hearing the coupler, which held the cars together, clatter beneath her. The window on the door to the next car was painted in frost, so she crouched by the door and placed her palms against it.

The vibrations of the train car, the rattling, shaking song of the distant engine, became part of her. She closed her eyes and breathed through the filter of the outlaw's filthy bandanna. Her senses began to reorder themselves—some growing still and silent, others opening wider . . . wider. She felt the pulse of the train, the hum of motion and vibration, the rhythm and pattern, and then she began to assign each pattern a distinctive identity.

One of the many games Gran had played with her when she was a young girl had involved three hard, thick, identical wooden boxes. She had to tell which box held the hornet's nest by touch alone, by letting her hands drink in the vibrations and motion. Then she was to open the two boxes that didn't hold the hornets. She had been stung so many times learning the game, but like all of Gran's games, it served a purpose. Now, Maude was thankful for the painful lesson. "*Good!*" Gran had said, clapping, when Maude had mastered the game, "*Now, girl, tell me exactly how many hornets are in that nest . . .*"

The vibrations that were counter to the heartbeat of the train were people—one was five feet north of her, on the other side of the door, the other twenty feet farther away—two more gunmen, pacing. The other counter vibrations were lesser and ordered in their locations—seated passengers, about fifteen. She could afford no mistakes in this or people would die.

The outlaw by her door was facing away from her now. She had felt the wobble in his vibration, the subtle shift of his weight as he turned to face his comrade and the passengers. She stayed low and leaned in as she swung the door open violently. Maude's leg shot out like a snake striking and swept both the outlaw's legs. The gunman fell hard on his face. Maude was up and moving, a blur. As she stepped over the fallen man, she drove a well-placed heel into a cluster of nerves at the base of his spine. The man moaned in pain but then was abruptly silent—he'd be powerless to move for at least thirty minutes.

His companion was twenty feet away and less than a second from firing his pistol at Maude's heart. The passengers were screaming and shouting, just beginning to comprehend the stimuli their brains were receiving. Maude launched herself off the paralyzed man, using his body like a ramp.

Her eyes read the language of the gunman's muscles as the pistol barked. In midair she twisted, tumbled, changing her trajectory using the canvas support straps mounted vertically above the seats along the length of the car. Angry, buzzing heat fluttered past her cheek as she came down feet-first on the outlaw's chest. Her legs folded and she followed him to the floor. With a single strike from the heel of her palm, she knocked him out.

"Thank the Almighty for you, stranger!" one of the passengers said as Maude stood.

"I've never seen a body move like that, fella," another man said, starting to rise. "You with the carnival or circus or something?"

Maude moved quickly past them toward the next door. Four down, three to go. She pointed toward the forward car door. "The other men who went this way," she asked, her voice still disguised as a man's. "Did they say anything, anything at all?

"They said something about the mail car and then coming back to fleece us," a woman said, her children clinging to her. "The Lord be with you, brave sir."

"Disarm these men," Maude said. "Bind them. Stay here until you hear something from the conductor or the engineer. Any of the others come back, shoot them."

"Don't you need a gun?" one of the men called out, picking up one of the outlaw's pistols.

"What for?" Maude asked. She was through the next door and gone.

Connolly "Big Tooth" McGrath held the shotgun to the head of the postal clerk in the mail car. The boy had wet himself when they had shot through the door and now was on his hands and knees, shaking like a sick dog. "I know you got the damn key to the lockbox," McGrath told the clerk. He gestured with the still-hot scattergun toward the mostly headless body of the other clerk that lay beside the locked and chained heavy metal chest. "He thought he'd play at hero, too, and you see what that got him."

"They didn't give me a key in case something like this happened," the clerk screamed, his face looking down at the blood-soaked floor. "I'm no hero!"

McGrath stroked at his heavy red beard and sniffed the air, catching the stench of gun smoke and piss. Even with the cold December air whistling through the car, it still reeked of fear. "Clearly," he said. "Well, then," McGrath said, addressing his two men—one gathering up the canvas sacks of postage, the other standing watch by the now-destroyed rear door. "I guess we blast the chains off the chest and carry it off, then. That means we don't need you, hero, so say so-long to your hat rest."

McGrath glanced up at his men. The one by the door had vanished. There was a rapidly diminishing scream, then a sound like meat hitting the tracks at forty miles an hour. The scream stopped.

"What the hell?" McGrath snapped his head toward his other conspirator. The outlaw's motionless body was slumped on a mattress of scattered mail sacks. A masked man stood beside the body, a postage envelope in the stranger's hand. "Who the fuck are you?" McGrath asked.

"Postmaster General," Maude said in her counterfeit male voice. "You're in a great deal of trouble."

"I don't care if you're General fuckin' Forrest!" McGrath shouted. "You picked the wrong desperado to mess with, stranger." He brought up the shotgun, leveling it at the masked man. Maude flicked her wrist, and the letter flew across the room accompanied by a snapping sound. McGrath felt a sharp sting at his wrist, and his trigger finger no longer worked. He strained, but the finger drooped in the trigger guard. He struggled to shift the gun to his other hand, now seeing a slender line of his blood trailing from the wrist of his gun hand. He never had a chance to complete the task before Maude crossed the room, grabbed the shotgun barrel, and jerked downward on it. The butt of the gun caught McGrath in the face, and he collapsed in a heap.

"There any more?" Maude asked the terrified clerk.

"N . . . no," The clerk said. "Whoever you are, thank you. I was sure I was dead, like . . . like Henry over there."

"He'll never shoot anyone with that hand ever again," Maude said, picking up the letter from the floor and dropping it back into the pile of mail.

"Are you a passenger?" the clerk asked. There was no reply. The masked stranger was gone.

The train halted on the tracks near Promontory. The robbers were bound and gathered together by the train's crew, then forced into one of the passenger cars and guarded at gunpoint. The passengers were all taken off the train while it was searched to make sure no additional members of McGrath's crew had escaped notice. Alter, rifle still in hand, was talking with the conductor and the engineer.

"We were damned lucky you were on the train, Mr. Cline," the engineer, a balding man in greasy coveralls, said. "You have any clue who that masked fella was? He seems to have vanished just as quickly as he showed up."

"And we didn't even get a chance to thank him," the burly conductor, still managing to sweat in the numbing cold, added.

Cline glanced over his shoulder toward the throng of passengers milling about, cussing and complaining about the cold. He spotted Maude standing in the cluster of Negro and Chinese passengers. She had removed Jed's coat and wrapped it around the two shivering Chinese kids. Somehow, she had managed to replace her skirt with an undamaged one, and she looked like she was shivering, just like the other passengers, but Cline noted no line of visible breath trailing from her lips. Maude's eyes found Cline's, and she nodded to him. He nodded back, and that hint of a smile returned to her face. Cline looked back to the engineer and conductor.

"Not even a notion, I'm afraid, gentlemen," Cline said. "I suppose I'll chalk it up to another mystery of the West."

"At least you'll get a hell of a story out of it," The conductor said. Cline looked back toward Maude. She had vanished.

"Yes," Cline said, "that I shall."

ABOUT THE AUTHOR

R. S. BELCHER is the acclaimed author of *The Six-Gun Tarot, The Shotgun Arcana,* and *Nightwise.* He is a former newspaper and magazine editor, and lives in Salem, Virginia.